CONGO SQUARE

Hammond

NEW ORLEANS

HOUMA

Tremé Street

Henriette Delille Street

Esplanade Avenue

Governor Nicholls Street

Barracks Street

Louis Armstrong Park

North Rampart Street

Ursulines Avenue

Royal Street

St. Philip Street

Laffite Avenue

Dumaine Street

Decatur Street

St. Louis Street

Orleans Street

St. Peter Street

Chartres Street

The French Market

Basin Street

THE FRENCH QUARTER

Toulouse Street

Jackson Square

THE MISSISSIPPI RIVER

Burgundy Street

Bourbon Street

Dauphine Street

Conti Street

Bienville Street

Canal Street

Iberville Street

North Front Street

Common Street

NEW ORLEANS

D0529512

PRAISE FOR THE MARVELLERS

A *NEW YORK TIMES* AND INDIE BESTSELLER

★"An enthralling fantasy adventure full of bravery, love, and humor."

—*Kirkus Reviews*, **starred review**

★"[A]n intersectionally inclusive, fantastical adventure."

—*Publishers Weekly*, **starred review**

★"An exemplary example of diversity with a Black girl . . . This fun, immersive tale is a must-purchase."

—*School Library Journal*, **starred review**

"You can stop looking at admissions brochures for all those other schools of magic. The Arcanum Training Institute for Marvelous and Uncanny Endeavors is definitely where you want to apply."

—**RICK RIORDAN**, #1 *New York Times*–bestselling author

"With fantastical twists at every turn, Clayton has created a world that readers won't want to leave. *The Marvellers* is magical!"

—**ANGIE THOMAS**, #1 *New York Times*–bestselling author of *The Hate U Give* and *Concrete Rose*

"A 'Marvellerous' middle grade debut! Delightful, charming, exceptionally clever, and filled with suspense and humor."

—**LISA McMANN**, *New York Times*–bestselling author of The Forgotten Five series

"Never in all my years of reading have I encountered a book that so seamlessly weaves together mind-bending marvels, cultural relevance, and powerful historical themes."

—**NIC STONE**, #1 *New York Times*–bestselling author of *Dear Martin*

"An expertly crafted amalgamation of rich, cultural representation wrapped up in a magic school adventure . . . sure to be a well-loved favorite."

—**J. ELLE**, *New York Times*–bestselling author of *Wings of Ebony*

"*The Marvellers* illuminates stellar storytelling through the lens of a Black girl learning to embrace the full potential of her magic."

—**KAREN STRONG**, author of *Just South of Home* and *Eden's Everdark*

"A new classic. Clayton creates a luminous world where everyone can find themselves within the halls of the Arcanum Training Institute."

—**ZORAIDA CÓRDOVA**, award-winning author of *Labyrinth Lost* and *The Way to Rio Luna*

"The fantasy adventure the world needs . . . the kind of thorny, exciting, and magical story that I've needed my whole life."

—**MARK OSHIRO**, author of *The Insiders*

ALSO BY
DHONIELLE CLAYTON

The Marvellers: Book 1

Tiny Pretty Things

Shiny Broken Pieces

The Rumor Game

The Belles

The Everlasting Rose

The Beauty Trials

Shattered Midnight

Blackout

Whiteout

AS A CONTRIBUTOR

Meet Cute

The Radical Element: 12 Stories of Daredevils, Debutantes, and Other Dauntless Girls

Unbroken: 13 Stories Starring Disabled Teens

Black Enough: Stories of Being Young and Black in America

Vampires Never Get Old

THE MEMORY THIEVES

A CONJUROR NOVEL

DHONIELLE CLAYTON

HENRY HOLT AND COMPANY
NEW YORK

For Zoraida Córdova, my partner in crime,
and Ace in all things mischief.

Henry Holt and Company, *Publishers since 1866*
Henry Holt® is a registered trademark of Macmillan Publishing Group, LLC
120 Broadway, New York, NY 10271 • mackids.com

Text copyright © 2023 by Dhonielle Clayton.
Illustrations copyright © 2022 by Khadijah Khatib. Map copyright © 2023 by
ChickenLittle, Dhonielle Inc. All rights reserved.

Our books may be purchased in bulk for promotional, educational, or business use.
Please contact your local bookseller or the Macmillan Corporate and
Premium Sales Department at (800) 221-7945 ext. 5442 or
by email at MacmillanSpecialMarkets@macmillan.com.

Library of Congress Cataloging-in-Publication Data
Names: Clayton, Dhonielle, author.
Title: The memory thieves / Dhonielle Clayton.
Description: First edition. | New York : Henry Holt Books for Young Readers, 2023. |
Series: The Conjureverse; Book 2 | Audience: Ages 8–12. | Audience: Grades 4–6. |
Summary: In her second year at Arcanum Training Institute, Ella grapples with fame,
unearths a perilous school secret, and faces a mysterious magical illness outbreak,
prompting her, alongside Brigit and Jason, to clear her name, while working tirelessly to
safeguard the Marvellian realm from impending chaos.
Identifiers: LCCN 2023017472 | ISBN 9781250174970 (hardcover)
Subjects: CYAC: Fantasy. | Diseases—Fiction. | Magic—Fiction. | Schools—Fiction. |
African Americans—Fiction. | LCGFT: Fantasy fiction. | Novels.
Classification: LCC PZ7.1.C594725 Me 2023 | DDC [Fic]—dc23
LC record available at https://lccn.loc.gov/2023017472

First edition, 2023
Edited by Brian Geffen and Margeaux Weston
Book design by Samira Iravani
Production editing by Lelia Mander
Copyediting by Jackie Dever
Proofreading by Diane Joao
Printed in the United States by Lakeside Book Company, Inc., Melrose Park, Illinois

ISBN 978-1-250-17497-0
1 3 5 7 9 10 8 6 4 2

THE PARAGONS

PARAGON OF TOUCH

"The hand has no fear!"

The brave

PARAGON OF VISION

"The eyes are wise!"

The sage

PARAGON OF SPIRIT

"The heart beats true!"

The intuitive

PARAGON OF SOUND

"The ears listen well!"

The patient

PARAGON OF TASTE

"The tongue tells truth!"

The honest

THE ARCANUM TRAINING INSTITUTE FOR MARVELOUS AND UNCANNY ENDEAVORS

— LOWER SCHOOL —

Good Day, Good Wishes, and Greetings of
the Most Marvelous Kind,

We are thrilled to welcome you back to the Arcanum Training Institute for Marvelous and Uncanny Endeavors for your second level of Marvellian training.

Last year, you discovered the marvel inside you and demonstrated what it took to return to our illustrious school for another year. Be sure to complete your summer assignment before the start of term. A slip from Sakamoto's Stapier Showroom will be required for full credit and enrollment in Intermediate Marvel Light Channeling. Enclosed please find your Level Two timetables, dormitory, roommate assignment, and supply list.

The Institute is located above the Norwegian Sea this year. Bundle up! Snow has already started to fall. See the attached coordinates. Sky-ferries will leave the Vellian Port hourly on September 12 as well as from all Marvellian cities. Please arrive before 6:00 p.m. GMT.

All the light to you and yours! Good marvelling!

Laura Ruby
Executive Assistant to Headmarveller MacDonald and
Headmarveller Rivera of the Lower School

P.S.: You definitely don't want to share this letter with Fewels. Not after you've made it this far. You know what will happen. Do I have to remind you? P.P.S.: We've included more coupons this year to encourage the patronage of our favored Marvellian shops.

THE ARCANUM TRAINING INSTITUTE FOR MARVELOUS AND UNCANNY ENDEAVORS

— LOWER SCHOOL HANDBOOK —

LEVEL TWO TRAINEE TIMETABLE
SECOND YEAR TRAINING SESSIONS
Name: *Ella Durand*
Roommate: *Brigit Ebsen*
Dormitory: *Azure Dragon of the East*

CORE REQUIREMENTS:

History of Marvels and Marvellers from the Eastern and Southeastern Hemisphere	Dr. Julie Dao
Intermediate Marvel Light Channeling	Dr. Liya Yohannes
Marvellian Theory— the Right Path	Dr. Benjamin Mackenzie
Conjure II	Madame Sera Baptiste
Global Incants: Form and Function	Dr. Noah Goldblum
Marvellian-Adjacent Beings: Creature Study	Dr. E-Jun Choi
Global Elementals— Fire and Earth	Dr. Michael Huang

PARAGON REQUIREMENTS:

Future Forecasting II— Divining the Future Around the World	Dr. Nour Al Sayed

EXTRACURRICULAR ACTIVITIES:

Kitchen Marvels from All Over the World	Location: Paragon of Taste Kitchens, Adviser: Chef Oshiro
Marvellian Monsters	Location: Arcanum Menagerie, Adviser: Dr. Adam Silvera

PART I

NEW HORIZONS

CHAPTER ONE
THE VELLIAN PORT

Nosy.

That was another word besides *marvelous* that Ella would use to describe Marvellers. As her family (and their conjure companions) entered the Vellian Port and prepared to catch a sky-ferry to Celestian City to buy school supplies, people couldn't keep their eyes off them. Some tentatively waved. Others whispered their thanks and congratulations. A few smirked . . . and many (more than Ella wanted to admit) scowled at her.

Ella was famous *again*, and this time not for being the first Conjure student to successfully enroll and complete her first year of study at the Arcanum Training Institute for Marvelous and Uncanny Endeavors, the great magic school in the sky, but rather for saving their world from a power-hungry villain named Gia Trivelino and her marvel-stealing elixir.

But the attention made Mama squirm and Papa chuckle. All summer the family had chased away Marvellian newsies from lurking around the house or aggravating Gran in the conjure pharmacy, looking for exclusive stories about that fateful night three months ago. Ella's face had been projected from every Marvellian news-box—and even the Conjure papers from New York to Colón to Paramaribo reported what had happened in the skies.

Ella felt a little nervous about it all, but she didn't want to let on and have Mama even more scared or have her make good on her threat to keep Ella home and re-enroll her at Madame Collette's Conjure École. She thought if she was brave enough, it might encourage more Conjure students to enroll in the Arcanum, and maybe she'd end up with even more friends this year.

Even now, she grinned at onlookers, and each time she glanced up at the Vellian Port's beautiful domed ceiling, it was filled with flickering heliograms of her face beside the most wanted criminal in the world—Gia Trivelino—and all her various disguises.

Headlines filled the ceiling:

GET TO KNOW THE CONJURE GIRL
WHO OUSTED THE ACE OF ANARCHY

ON THE RUN—NOTORIOUS CRIMINAL SPOTTED
LEAVING A FAE TEAHOUSE IN ASTRADAM

ELECTION SEASON TO FOCUS ON THE TWO C'S—
CRIME AND CONJURORS!

"A star's blessing to you," a nearby man whispered to her as they went through the entryway. "Stopped that thorn in our side."

Ella flashed him a short-lived smile because as soon as they walked into the atrium, a squat woman glared in her family's direction. "Newsies lie. Feels like a Conjure agenda. You all trying to take over the skies, if you ask me. Hmph!"

"How'd you do it?" A willowy man squinted down at her. "What's your Conjure secret?"

Mama pulled Ella close. Her voice drifted through Ella's thoughts: *Eyes ahead, keep walking. All of this can turn on a dime.*

Ella didn't have time to worry anyway. She twirled around and around, gawking at the amazing sights, her floating juju-trunk spinning with her, trying desperately to keep up. Massive windows gave a view of gigantic sky-ferries arriving and departing from long, gilded docks. Thick Cloud Nests played peek-a-boo with the morning sun; buttery rays bathed the whole hub in golden tones. Sometimes she couldn't even imagine that they were floating above the Indian Ocean right this very minute. The walls cycled through vibrant colors as constellation maps chased each other, and the stars arranged and rearranged their names and configurations in hundreds of languages.

They passed a massive tower, one of the Cardinals. Ella gazed up, admiring how it soared into the high ceiling and looked identical to the one in the Institute's courtyard. Small children threw bronze sonnes into the shallow fountain pool ringing it.

Ella took a step closer, moving away from the nosy people staring at her, and read the placard:

THE VELLIAN CARDINAL

THIS TOWER REPRESENTS THE PRINCIPLE OF ORDER IN OUR GREAT MARVELLIAN WORLD.

Only by the one sacrificing for the many will our synchronized rhythm allow us all to survive far above.

A deep squeeze pulled at her heart, the crossing tug she'd always felt when she went with Papa into the Underworld. The same thing happened last year when she'd visited the Arcanum

Cardinal with Masterji Thakur too, and she hadn't found any satisfactory explanation for it yet.

"Do you feel that?" She turned to her parents, but they were too busy fussing about this trip to hear.

Ella slipped out of earshot before this disagreement about Mama hating to shop in Marvellian cities turned into their never-ending argument about whether Conjure folk should even continue traveling in and out of the Marvellian world given the dangers and the history of Conjurors going missing in the skies. Ella hoped they wouldn't discuss the sad story about Aunt Celeste, Mama's twin, and her disappearance again. Every time it was mentioned, Mama stiffened and frowned, and Ella didn't want her to have to relive painful memories from when she was around Ella's age. It'd been over twenty years, but the wound remained fresh.

Ella wanted this to be a happy day for everyone. She didn't want to be any more nervous than she already was with everyone staring at her. She was headed into her second year at the Arcanum, and she had big plans. There was a lot to do once she was back . . . things to investigate about the building, things to ask her mentor Masterji Thakur. She tossed a conjure coin into the Vellian Cardinal fountain and made a wish that everything would go perfectly, extraordinarily, in fact, and that this year at the Arcanum would be even better than the last.

The water turned black and thick as tar. A foul smell made her frown.

"Oh no!" Ella looked up, finding a girl about her age staring back. She clutched a vial and continued to empty its contents into the fountain. Two dark braids framed her sullen face, and her hazel eyes almost burned into Ella. "What did you do?"

A coldness dropped into Ella's stomach. What was this girl's problem? Why would she do that to the water? Ella repeated her question, but the girl didn't answer; instead she scampered away.

Weird, Ella thought, watching her disappear into the crowds.

"Let's go, baby girl," Mama snapped, and Gumbo, her conjure companion, slapped his tail, making Ella jump.

"Sorry, Mama," Ella called out, taking one last look at the Cardinal and pressing a hand to her chest.

The crossing tug eased. As she looked back at the Cardinal, she couldn't decipher what about it could even possibly be conjure related. Maybe her conjure was getting adjusted to her being back in the skies—and she would definitely *not* be telling Mama that and giving her an excuse to re-enroll her in Madame Collette's Conjure École.

Ella darted under a schedule board that stretched high overhead detailing dozens of the sky-ferry destinations. Glittering archways led to various platforms, ticket booths, and decadent waiting rooms she wished she had time to visit.

"This way, baby." Papa put a hand on Ella's shoulder, redirecting her. "We need to exchange money. I don't have enough gold stellas for shopping." He pulled out his wallet, thumbing through pitch-black conjure dollars, then whispered, "It's so silly that they prefer such heavy coin."

"But Sebastien, the refinement of it all. They must feel the weight of bloated, old-fashioned purses and hoard the coins in their overflowing safes." Mama mocked a typical stuffy Marvellian accent. "Easier to show off."

Ella rolled her eyes and wished Mama would give this community a little bit more of a chance, but she knew right now was probably not the time for this request.

They entered an open hall, passing under the archway labeled

CURRENCY EXCHANGE, and joined a short line of other Conjure folk who nodded in their direction. A sign above toggled through the current exchange rates, numbered tiles flipping over every few minutes to showcase the latest and most accurate amount:

MARVELLIAN STELLAS +1	CONJURE DOLLARS $1.82
MARVELLIAN STELLAS +1	FEWEL MONEY $1.36

Ella watched Papa and Mama exchange their conjure dollars for small satchels of golden stellas and silver lunari. Winnie begged until the clerk slipped her a bronze sonne. She held it up, admiring how the coin changed colors as she squeezed it, the beautiful patina almost rainbowlike.

An announcement echoed: "The eleven a.m. sky-ferry to the coliseum will depart from platform three. Marvel Combat ticket holders, be sure to have your passes ready when boarding."

Ella's heart jumped with excitement. This year at the Arcanum, she'd get to learn more about the Marvellian sport, perfect using a stapier, and even try out for the Paragon of Vision Combat team at the end of the year. She couldn't wait.

"Over here!" Mama led the way back into the main hall and headed for the immigration area.

Well-dressed Marvellians stood in neat lines, some clutching briefcases and marvel-valises, others toting shopping trollies, as they inched their way toward official-looking people perched in glass boxes. Their Paragon pins proudly decorated their lapels, and Ella couldn't stop touching hers; she was slightly afraid it'd eventually stop its charming wiggle.

Every night before bed, she blinked back at the winking eye and slipped it under her pillow. She was now a Marveller, a Paragon of Vision with a cartomanic marvel at that, but also a Conjuror. She couldn't wait to study the similarities and differences between using conjure cards and Marvellian tarot to tell fortunes. The thrill of it had been a steady rolling bubble inside her for months.

She could be both, despite Mama's worries. And it'd all be fine. She'd prove it.

"Ugh! I don't want to wait in line. Why can't we just go back to the Stardust Pier?" Winnie tugged at Papa's coattails, but he was too busy examining their Marvellian visas.

"It's only for Level Ones. I'm a Level Two now, remember?" Those words felt great on Ella's tongue since she'd almost been kicked out because of Siobhan O'Malley's pesky night pixies. Mama still couldn't understand why she'd wanted to return to the Arcanum for a second year after all that drama.

But Ella had also had the best time of her life with her new friends Brigit and Jason. She couldn't wait to see them after what felt like forever. They'd sent starposts back and forth for months, but Ella had so many things stored up to tell them in person, confidential things. *Secrets* she'd been keeping all summer.

Masterji Thakur had given her a set of closely guarded Arcanum blueprints—blueprints that showed that Conjure folk had been involved in the history of the Arcanum Training Institute long before Ella walked through the school's gates. An item that could change everything.

"Be safe." Ella gazed up to find Mrs. Landry, the sweet old lady who owned Paulette's Praline Palace in the Conjure Quarter back home. She reminded Ella of Gran, the deep brown of her skin almost an identical shade but covered with makeup to hide her conjure marks.

Mama held the woman's hand. "You too, ma'am. I wish your grandson had escorted you all the way up here. Don't like you being alone."

Mrs. Landry blew Mama a kiss. "I'll fare. Don't you worry, sugar. Took a small cooking job to help with three grandchildren heading to university. Plus, this old girl's got some fight in her."

"Wouldn't dare cross you any day of the week." Mama winked at her.

"Conjure is good," Mrs. Landry said with a hum.

"All the time," Mama replied with the usual phrase.

Papa tapped Ella's shoulder. "Almost our turn." He handed her a small black passport. The cover showed a skull holding conjure-roses and diamonds; the United Conjure Congress symbol and the American Congregation flower emblem. The ink pulsed beneath her fingertips as she touched the words NEW ORLEANS DELEGATION.

Ella spotted several other Conjure folk probably headed to shop or work. They clutched various Conjure passports. Similar black leather casings flashed symbols of various global Conjure congregations: their skulls, diamonds, and signature flowers.

Ella remembered the big family trip they took to Bahia, Brazil, for the United Conjure Congress convention two years ago. She'd loved seeing the entrance to their part of the Underworld, those bright yellow doors. One day she wanted to see them all, the various communities, and their entryways into the Land of the Dead.

Mama tapped Ella on the shoulder. "Pay attention, please. Open to the last page and prepare to show the Port officer. No talking, no games, no funny business." Mama's brow furrowed, and Ella sensed her mother *still* didn't want her attending the

Institute or traveling in and out of Marvellian cities, no matter how many times she'd pretended to be okay about it in the weeks leading up.

They took a step forward. Ella opened her Conjure passport. A heliogram of her face illuminated and stared back at her alongside all her details.

Name: *Ella Charlotte Baptiste Durand*
Age: *12*
Birthday: *June 26*
Birthplace: *Rose Hill, Mississippi*
Residence: *New Orleans, Louisiana, USA*
Nationality: *American*
Classification: *Conjuror*

Papa removed his top hat as he approached the port officer. His conjure companion, Greno, leaped from his head to his shoulder and ribbited. Mama swept Ella, Winnie, and Gumbo forward along with Ella's juju-trunk.

Stay silent. Mama's whispered warning fluttered into Ella's thoughts, and presumably Winnie's, because they both nodded in her direction.

Papa smiled. "Good morning."

"Papers," the man spat; his white cheeks flamed red at the sight of them. "Visas for all creatures moving in and out of Marvellian cities."

Mama sucked her teeth. Gumbo slapped his thick tail against the floor. People in nearby lines jumped and whispered about the scandalous sight of an alligator being in the Vellian Port.

Ella thumbed through the pages to the final one; a celestial blue sticker illuminated beneath her fingers as the visa revealed itself.

"What is the nature of your business here?" the man asked.

Papa cleared his throat. "We plan to go shopping and have lunch before—"

"Where is your final destination?" he snapped.

A jolt shot up Ella's spine. Why was he being so rude? Didn't he recognize her and her family? Not that she was "feeling herself," as Gran would say, but a heliogram of her face filled the Vellian Port dome this very minute. Surely, he knew who she was. That "Conjure Whiz Kid," as the *Star Weekly* reported.

"We're headed to the Arcanum Training Institute. Dropping off my brilliant daughter." He grinned back at Ella, and it made her all warm inside. There was nothing like Papa's smile. "You might've heard of her, the one and only Ella Durand." He pointed up at the projection high above.

The man didn't blink.

Ella waved. Mama sighed.

"How long is your visit?"

"A few hours, and then we will gladly leave," Mama interjected, arms crossed.

Ella gulped, hoping Mama would remain calm. She spotted coppers posted all throughout. The last thing she needed was Mama hot-grease mad so far from home.

Papa flashed Mama an exasperated look.

"Any stopovers before going to the Arcanum?"

"Celestian City," Papa added.

"Our crown jewel of the skies is closed to entry due to tsunami winds over Polynesia. No sky-ferries can land."

"Then Betelmore." Papa slipped Mama's hand into his.

"Betelmore's Cloud Nests are being reset, so there will be a bit of a delay. Ninety minutes behind schedule. Astradam is the only open city currently. It's over the Aegean Sea. The next sky-ferry leaves in eighteen minutes."

Ella's stomach dropped. Astradam was the only city Mama *really* didn't want to go to. She hated all Marvellian cities to be sure, but this one especially. It was where Aunt Celeste had gone missing.

Papa and Ella made eye contact with Mama, waiting for her to nod. They needed her blessing. Ella heard Mama take a deep breath. Maybe this would be worse than a bad day . . . maybe it'd be a terrible one instead. Maybe she shouldn't have pushed so hard for a shopping trip and ordered her supplies from the Arcanum store instead. Maybe it was a fool's errand to think Mama would ever be okay in the Marvellian world.

Mama sucked her teeth, then nodded.

"We'll wait for Betelmore to reopen," Papa replied as he handed the family's passports through the metal slot.

The man stamped each one, then returned them.

A tiny disappointment bubbled up in Ella's chest. She'd wanted to explore one of the other great flying cities. Plus, the last time Ella had been in Betelmore, she'd come face-to-face with Gia Trivelino. Her evil cackle rang in Ella's ears all summer. She wondered if it would haunt her forever.

✦ ▪ ✦ ▪ ✦

"LET'S GO, GIRLS!" MAMA BARRELED FORWARD WITH GUMBO lumbering behind her.

The family shuffled through the immigration gate and into a showroom of wonders. A gigantic open store spread out before them, each section dazzling with goods and stuffed with crowds of eager shoppers.

Ella didn't know where to begin. The shopping galleries sparkled. Tables overflowed with all sorts of sweets: Marveller-bars, chocolate and caramel Paragon coins, ginger stars, milk dragon eggs, cinnamon starbread and tornado tea with hiccupping honey, and even an edible version of the Marvellian Assembly House with its thick columns and glass dome. Shelves held souvenir stapiers and stellacity spheres, heliogram postcards with amazing projections, maps of the three cities, scarves and flags boasting famous Marvel Combat teams, and more.

Vendors stood at various carts shouting about their delicious delights:

"*Bodacious bocadillos to go. Best sandwiches in the skies!*"

"*Pocket-sized pot pies for your flights—they'll give you no trouble in transit!*"

"*Bursting boba tea is the best—will bedazzle your tongue!*"

At the gallery's center sat a display with a banner stretched over it: THE TRICENTENNIAL—THREE HUNDRED YEARS OF MARVELLIAN INNOVATION AND INDUSTRY.

Charts triumphantly displayed years of Marvellian history and boasted about the society's accomplishments. A news-box reel projected construction footage of the three flying cities and the Arcanum Training Institute: early Marvellians from all over the world working together to live in the sky.

Ella's heart flipped as she stepped closer and closer. Would there be a mention of Conjure folk? But to her disappointment, the Marvellian history exhibit said nothing about Conjurors, instead detailing the very first Gatherfeast and emphasizing the artifacts preserved from it. One unrecognizable object caught her eye. She read the label: UNKNOWN, CIRCA 250 YEARS AGO.

Ella pressed her face to the glass. "What are you?" she whispered at it, almost expecting an answer. The object began to glow like a buried star with small wisps of light pushing through tiny crevices. The crossing tug vibrated inside her again, strong and piercing. The sensation made her wish she could clean the item and have a better look. Her fingers tingled with an overwhelming itch to touch it. Why was she so drawn to it?

Ella turned to call out for Papa—maybe he knew why she felt this way. Maybe it was just her conjure and nerves mingling with her curiosity.

But Mama waved for Ella to return, and she scampered away reluctantly. "Stay close, please."

"Can you come look at—"

"Not right now," Mama replied.

Winnie tugged at Papa's coattails in full hyper mode. "Can I get a fizzlet? No, actually, I want a Marveller-bar. Wait, both, please, and there's shortbread stapiers! I want those too. And, and, and the boba bursts like little bombs. I need the biggest tea they have!"

Ella tried to get her parents over to the exhibit but had no luck. Winnie's tantrum grew bigger and bigger.

"Relax, Winnie!" Ella took her little sister's hand. "Let's go look around."

Papa winked at her. "Thanks for the rescue, baby girl. I'm grabbing tickets for Betelmore."

"Don't you get out of my sight line, you hear?" Mama warned, trailing them.

Winnie yanked Ella left and held up shining mooncakes. Ella shaded her eyes from the brightness.

"Put that back. It's overpriced here, and we're already going shopping today." Mama plucked them from Winnie's little hands, prompting more upset and tears and lots of curious stares from onlookers. Ella bit her bottom lip, frustration raging inside her. She slipped away, weaving through the crowds. People pressed heliogram posters and watched candidates talking about their campaigns in the upcoming Marvellian election. She went to look at postcards to get a break from it all.

Today felt like nothing was going according to plan. She'd written out every detail in her notebook, picked out her parents' outfits (Winnie's too), and carried a voyage root in her pocket for safe travels from Gran. But there'd already been so many hiccups. She'd wanted her return to the Arcanum Training Institute for Marvelous and Uncanny Endeavors to get off to the perfect start. Just like last year.

"Ella!" Her name echoed through the gallery like a firework.

She whipped around, coming face-to-face with Jason.

A rescue.

The Marveller Weekly

FIND OUT MORE ABOUT THE CONJURE KID WHO SUPPOSEDLY SAVED THE WORLD!

PROFILE: ELLA DURAND

AGE: 12*

Ella Durand saved the Marvellian World . . . supposedly. That's what everyone would have you believe in order to further the Conjure agenda. She is the firstborn daughter of well-known Conjurors Aubrielle Baptiste and Sebastien Durand. Her mother's family runs the Conjure Rose, the oldest and most famous conjure pharmacy in the world, rumored to have been visited by notorious Marveller criminals. Her father is a prominent conjure-politician, the Grand Walker of the Land of the Dead, and the most powerful man in their society aside from the head of the United Conjure Congress. She has a younger sister named Winifred. Her uppity, rich family has not one but two homes—a mansion in the Conjure Quarter of New Orleans and the Durand farmhouse in Rose Hill, Mississippi. During our profile research, several suspicious reports about the family have surfaced. Told to us by their neighbors in the country and speaking on the condition of anonymity, one said that if any family member walked on their land, the cows would start giving blood instead of milk and their chickens would lay empty eggs. Another witness claimed the trees on their property would turn away from the road, cowering with fear. Make no mistake, this kid comes from two of the most powerful Conjure bloodlines in the world, and she shouldn't be so easily welcomed. Beware!

*Since many Conjurors have been known to extend their lifespans, one can't be sure if she's actually, in fact, a child.

CHAPTER TWO
REUNITED!

W hat are you doing here?" Ella hugged Jason so tight he coughed. She didn't realize how much she'd missed him until right this very moment. They'd sent each other weekly starposts, but nothing could replace getting to see each other. She wanted to hear all about his adventures in the field with his dad: the chimeras he worked with in the Greek Isles and the adze that followed him home after their research trip to Southeastern Ghana. A story was always better told in person. Plus, if anyone could turn this day around, it'd be him.

"School shopping, like you, I'm guessing," he said.

Once she'd finally freed him from her grip, she combed over every inch of him. He was a little taller than her now, and his locs had grown longer. But his big, toothy grin remained the same.

"Missed you too." He yanked one of her long twists. "My dad's already in Betelmore with Beatrice, Allen, and Grace. Wes went with his friends to get stuff for the upper school. He hates shopping with the family. I got stuck helping Mom with the little terrors." He pointed at two toddlers, twins, doing laps around his very beautiful and very tired mother. She was in the midst of wrestling a wiggly baby back into her chest carrier. "But they're not *too* too bad. That's Priscilla, and that's Harold. And the littlest one putting up a fight is Caroline, but we call her Cookie."

The baby cooed, and out popped a small tortoise nestled beside her. Ella squealed at the sight of its smiling, reptilian face.

Mrs. Eugene laughed. "Oh, don't mind old Hare. He usually stays out of sight, and I probably should've left him home, but he always acts like he's little Cookie's companion and not mine. Won't leave her side. Old guy has favorites, it seems." Her smile felt like a million stellaric bulbs blazing at once, and now Ella knew where Jason got his grin from. She had tons of hair, thick and dark, twisted into the most ornate and beautiful updo, and she wore long sleeves and a bulky dress despite the mid-September heat, making Ella wonder if she was hiding her conjure marks like Mrs. Landry.

The last time she'd seen Mrs. Eugene, they were all hustling out of the Conjure Quarter when the Cards of Deadly Fate had been breached, back when she'd first discovered Jason had Conjure ancestry and hid it from her. Ella had so many questions (and tried her best not to cast judgment on why someone would want to hide themselves away). All she could hear in her head was Mama grumbling about how *Conjure folk who abandon their people have sunken minds*. But after meeting Mrs. Eugene, Ella felt like there was much more to the story.

Jason nuzzled Hare's pointy nose. "Ella, this is my mom," he said sheepishly. "Mom, this is Ella."

"Ah, I was wondering when I'd finally get to lay my eyes on *the* Ella Durand. The girl that my son—and the whole world—keeps talking about. The one that kept my starpost box overflowing with mail." Mrs. Eugene grinned at Ella.

A wave of embarrassment consumed Jason's face. "Mom! Ugh!"

"Nice to meet you too, Mrs. Eugene. I'm sorry about the mail," Ella replied, then glanced up as Mama, Papa, and Winnie made their way over. When Mrs. Eugene spotted Mama, she bristled.

Papa removed his top hat and nodded at Mrs. Eugene. "Conjure is good."

Mrs. Eugene nodded, but *didn't* respond with the customary Conjuror response, *All the time*.

Ella cringed.

Mama pursed her lips. "Nice to see you again, Barbara."

"And you too, Aubrielle," Mrs. Eugene replied before turning to catch one of the toddlers mid-tumble.

Boarding announcements called for passengers headed for Betelmore. Papa scooped up the other toddler twin, throwing him over his shoulder like a tiny sack of rice. Big laughs and happy squeals echoed all around.

"Thank you, Sebastien. Thought I might never make it onto a sky-ferry with these two turkeys." Mrs. Eugene wiped her brow.

Winnie took Priscilla's hand, and they all made their way to Betelmore Hall and platform four to catch their sky-ferry. Ella couldn't stop stealing glances over her shoulder as her parents and Mrs. Eugene made small talk.

Ella wondered if Mrs. Eugene would ever be open about being a Conjuror, and if Mama would ever give her a full chance if not.

They shuffled onto the sky-ferry, inching down the long aisle. Marvellians looked up from news-box projections or their books to watch them. Ella spotted other Arcanum students, most likely also headed to shop like them. Many gawked at Gumbo (which wasn't surprising because a chubby alligator on a sky-ferry was a sight to behold). A few of them waved, several shouted hello, and others avoided eye contact at the urging of their parents.

Ella leaned forward, cupping her hand to Jason's ear. "I have a weird question. A nosy one," she whispered.

His eyes opened wide. "What?"

They crept along the aisle and Ella made sure to lower her voice even more. "I didn't think your mama would have a conjure companion."

"Well, she's a Conjuror, and all of them have one, right?"

Of course, Ella thought, feeling slightly embarrassed. She'd never met a Conjuror who didn't have a companion. *Even if she hides it, she's still one.*

"Do your siblings? Will you too?"

"Most of them do, but it's a fifty-fifty chance. My dad is jealous one won't show up for him. He still looks out the window every birthday, waiting, even though he's not a Conjuror."

"I've never seen Wes with a companion before," Ella recalled. Maybe Jason's older brother didn't have one? Unless he'd hidden it in his dorm room or something? But a Conjuror couldn't go very long without being close to their companion. It would make them sick.

"Wes has a black racer snake named Tank. He's usually coiled around his arm, hiding in his sleeve, or asleep in his mantle hood. He doesn't let anyone see him. Even uses veiling spells to make sure of it. Allen didn't get one. Claims he didn't want one. Bea has her bumblebee, Sting. He's always asleep on her hair comb. If Grace gets one, the family's got a bet that it'll be a bat because she stays up all night."

There was so much she knew about Jason's family and so much she didn't know. Up until meeting him, she didn't even know if Marvellers and Conjure folk felt comfortable making families with one another and how their gifts might change as a result. And now she'd learned that a companion wasn't a guarantee for blended families. She had so much to learn.

"We were told to hide them. Pass them off as Marvellian pets," he admitted as they tumbled into window seats while Winnie argued about having to sit across the aisle next to Mama and the twin toddlers.

"Thanks for telling me," she whispered.

His eyes grew big and filled with worries. "I don't want you to feel weird about . . . you know . . . because I should've told you last year . . . and . . ."

Ella flashed him her biggest, brightest smile to keep his anxiety from snowballing. "It's okay. I know now, and it makes you even more of my best friend."

He smiled back at her.

Speakers crackled overhead: "Passengers, please find your seats, secure your seat belts, and prepare for takeoff. We will be airborne in five minutes."

Ella and Jason grinned at each other. She reached for a Betelmore guide from the booth's side pocket, spreading it between her and Jason. She pressed all the heliograms, watching snippets of the current shows playing in the entertainment district, and advertisements for the latest stapiers—the Sabrewhizz 2.0 and the Dueluxe 4. The tiny projections made her fingers glow bright and her stomach flutter with excitement.

After the sky-ferry took off, servers snaked through the aisles offering fizzlets and ginger stars. Ella and Jason guzzled their drinks, stuffed their cheeks full of those sweet cookies, and burped until they laughed despite the sharp stares from both their mothers.

"I'll get an extra one for Brigit. She loves these." Ella slipped a ginger star into her satchel. "The only Marvellian food she doesn't complain about."

"You heard from her?" Jason asked while crunching on another cookie. "She didn't answer my last starpost. It's been, like, two weeks."

"Same. Not since August. She went to Arcanum camp after summer school. But I know she'll be there tonight. We're rooming together again." Ella grinned to herself, thinking about last school year and how Brigit had made her very own parachute and tried to run away from the Arcanum. Ella felt confident Brigit was over that feeling, but she did wonder how she'd deal with the secret about her mom being Gia Trivelino. "I need to show you both"—she looked left and right, then leaned forward to whisper—"the you-know-what I told you about." She'd been writing to him in code all summer about the blueprints and the things she and Reagan had discovered at the Griotary. "I tried to ask my parents about it too. But they acted like they didn't know what I was talking about."

"Did you show them?" he asked.

She shook her head. "I was too scared they'd take them. But remember what Masterji Thakur said at my discipline hearing— about the Conjure architect? They don't remember that."

"At all?" Jason's mouth dropped open.

"Every time I bring it up, my mama just gets mad and doesn't want to discuss it. Thinks I'm making things up." Ella felt like it was the biggest puzzle in need of solving. This kind of information could change everything.

"Maybe they—?"

"Hey, Ella! Hey, Jason!"

Their classmates Anh and Luz stood in the aisle. Anh's black hair had grown long, and Luz's curls sprang all over her head. Ella asked about their summers and listened as they dove into fun tales of camp and trips to the Fewel cities of Ho Chi Minh City, Vietnam, and Rio de Janeiro, Brazil. She felt like her break was boring in comparison.

"Can you tell us about Gia?" Luz's bright eyes grew to the size of stella coins.

"What was she like?" Anh whispered. "Everyone wants to know."

A jolt shot up Ella's spine. She shared a tense look with Jason. Brigit's secret stretched between them.

"Evil," Jason replied with a shudder.

"And was there really a leviathan there?" Luz added. "It was all over the *Marvellian Times* newsreels."

"I saw it in the *Celestian Chronicle*." Anh pulled out a copy of *Mr. Jay's Pocket Guide for Leviathans*. "And I got obsessed with them. They're very sensitive creatures, you know?"

Jason sat up straight, grinning at Anh's pocket guide.

"His name was Poco." Ella had worried about him after everything that happened, and she watched the Marvellian newsbox reports too, combing for information on Gia's hideaway, the Commedia Close, for mentions of him. But she hadn't seen anything.

"I heard—" Luz began.

The loudspeaker crackled: "Docking in ten minutes. In

preparation for landing and disembarkation, please return to your seats, fasten your seat belts, and stow any items you've taken out."

Ella and Jason waved bye as Anh and Luz scuttled back to their seats. Three adults passed by, staring down at them with curious eyes.

"Is it weird?" Jason asked.

"What?"

"Being famous."

"I'm not really *famous* famous," she replied. "Not really."

"You kind of are."

Ella guessed he was kind of right, and she figured she didn't have to hide her fears from him. She sneaked a glance at Mama before answering and watched as Mama mopped her sweaty brow with a handkerchief.

Ella hated seeing her so stressed and nervous. Mama had never been anything but an immovable oak to her: roots firmly planted in the ground, able to weather any storm and handle any trouble.

"I don't like it," she whispered, to make sure Mama couldn't hear her.

"Look!" Winnie screamed, to the whole sky-ferry's chagrin. "We're here! We're here!"

Outside the window, the Cloud Nests parted and the great city of Betelmore shone like a stella coin. Glowing billboards projected heliogram snippets of plays and concerts and advertisements, the bright stellaric bulbs lighting up the skies. Soaring air-trollies sailed along glittering ropes headed in a million directions. Streets boasted starfruit trees and window boxes spilling over with moonflowers. Ella's stomach lifted with excitement. Now that she was seeing Betelmore in the daylight, it felt brand-new, even though she'd been once before.

The sky-ferry landed on the dock without a whisper. Everyone lined up to file out. As they stepped outside into the warm September day, Mama put one hand on Ella's shoulder and the other on Winnie's.

A voice flitted through her thoughts: *Listen up, my baby girls. While we're in this godforsaken city, you mind every instruction. Stay close. We are very far from home. I want no mess, you hear?*

"Yes, ma'am," Ella and Winnie replied in unison.

Papa winked at them as Mama walked forward. Ella noticed tiny quivers in Mama's usually steady hands.

Ella took her palm. "We'll be fine."

"Of course we will," Mama replied. "Because both of my girls will listen, and we'll move quick as crickets to get what we need and get gone from here."

Ella plastered on her best fake smile and nodded. She'd do whatever it took to make sure the rest of the day went on without a single problem.

CHAPTER THREE

STAPIERS ON THE HIGH STREET

Mrs. Eugene and Jason led the way from the dock through the Betelmore sky-ferry station and suggested they hire a car together. They piled into a beautiful eight-seater that stretched around them like a velvet pillow. Stellaric lamps made the interior glow, catching every gold accent and plush cushion. Gumbo stretched out on the floor and the twins played with his tail.

The cab whizzed down various streets until arriving in the shopping district. The driver dropped them at the top of the high street.

Betelmore looked completely different in the daytime, and it made Ella wish she had a time marvel to slow the clock down and be able to investigate every single thing: eat in each restaurant, press her face against every shop window, then slip inside and wander every aisle and study all the peculiar Marvellers headed this way and that.

There were shops selling stationery and styluses, shops selling mantles, windows boasting Paragon paraphernalia and the latest in Marvellian fashion, sidewalk displays of floating marvel-valises and gorgeous news-boxes with state-of-the-art reels for every major paper outlet. Everything and anything needed for marvelling sat on display.

A sugary breeze escaped Jackson's Lolli & Pops as the revolving door turned, kids tumbling out with chocolate mustaches and pockets full of sweets.

"Wow!" Winnie's mouth hung open, and Mama quickly touched her chin to close it.

"You'll catch flies," she said. "It's no different than our very own Conjure Quarter. Don't get too excited."

But it was different. Back home, they had to deal with Fewels, so all Conjure stores had to have proper veils and protections to keep them safe and undetected in case one might wander in and become too curious. Here, nothing needed to be hidden. Marvellers didn't need to look left or right before ducking into a shop or restaurant. No one had to find the golden filigree seeping through city sidewalks or the Conjure emblem above a doorway to know if it was safe. Everything felt loud and enchanting here.

They turned a corner.

A *Marvellian Times* newsstand swallowed part of the sidewalk. Shelves boasted shiny news-boxes and baskets of reels with today's morning and midday reports.

"Sign up for the *Marvellian Times*. All new subscriptions come with a state-of-the-art news-box for free," a newsie hollered. "Your number one election news source! Most up-to-date info on most wanted criminal the Ace of Anarchy's whereabouts. See it here first."

"Look! Gia's got a new face now!" Someone motioned at one of the projections.

A bright word crawl announced a Gia Trivelino sighting

earlier on Betelmore's low street, and then another supposedly in the entertainment district at a matinee. Her grinning face flickered under the word WANTED.

The sight of her sent chills over Ella's skin. Whispers exploded through the growing crowd. Onlookers found Ella. Panic hit her.

"That's the girl who stopped her." A newsie pointed at her, while another one rushed forward with a camera. "Can we get a quote for the evening editions? Or your autograph?"

They swarmed Ella, shouting their questions:

"What was the Ace of Anarchy really like?"
"Seen the other Aces? Are they out of hiding?"
"Do you know what she's doing with those marvels she stole?"

Ella didn't know what to say or do. Their interest in her felt like a stellacity current surging through her veins.

Jason turned into a statue beside her. Anxiety radiated off him like heat.

Mama flinched. "No, no, no. Get away from my child." She swatted at them with her purse. Gumbo hissed, bared his sharp teeth, and thrashed his tail. People screamed and leaped out of the way. The commotion drew nearby coppers, who tromped over, ready to act.

Papa raised his hands in the air. "Enough!" His glare froze them in place.

Ella saw each newsie's and copper's neck stiffen. She knew they wanted to look away but couldn't because Papa had the kind of conjure gifts that demanded obedience.

"We're here to shop. Please respect our privacy at this time." He ushered Mama, Ella, and Winnie down the block right behind

Mrs. Eugene, the toddler twins, and Jason. The newsies and coppers didn't move until the entire group slipped out of sight.

Ella and Jason exchanged terrified glances. Ella's heart thudded. She could even feel Mama's worries like a tiny earthquake.

"Everyone's all right, yes?" Mrs. Eugene placed a warm hand on Ella's cheek. Ella's nerves quieted a little. "This way. Let's reset ourselves, shall we?" Mrs. Eugene winked at Ella, then corralled everyone toward a nook of sweet shops.

Sweat poured down Mama's face, and she struggled to wipe it away.

"Should we sit, Mama? Are you sick?" Ella asked.

Papa swept his arm around Mama's waist. "Let's stay out here for some fresh air, Aubrielle, while everyone gets a treat."

"I can't leave my babies in—"

"I'll be right here keeping watch." Mrs. Eugene stepped forward with Winnie, Harold, and Priscilla in tow. "Won't let them out of my sight. I promise. We'll pop into this sweet ice store and won't move until you're ready to join us." Little Cookie cooed from her carrier as if trying to lift Mama's spirits.

Mama and Mrs. Eugene exchanged a long, tense glance. Ella felt like her heart paused midbeat waiting for Mama to respond. She spotted the clench in Mama's jaw and felt the distrust. She wondered what history lay between them.

"Just for a minute. We'll be right back." Papa tipped his top hat and led Mama and Gumbo a little way down the block. Ella kept her eyes fixed on her parents, watching how Mama looked like a rag doll in Papa's grip.

"Is she okay?" Jason asked.

"Nervous." Ella nibbled her bottom lip, the worries piling up. A hot wave of guilt rippled through Ella because she'd desperately wanted to shop, and now this had happened. "She had a sister, a twin, who went missing in Astradam when they were kids. She's hated Marvellian cities ever since."

"The Lost Folk," Mrs. Eugene added. "So many have been swallowed in the skies and never found."

Ella wanted to ask Mrs. Eugene more questions . . . like why she wasn't afraid and if this was the reason why she hid her Conjure roots, but she knew Mama wouldn't want her asking such nosy questions and accidentally offending Mrs. Eugene.

"But all who are lost aren't gone forever," Mrs. Eugene said.

Ella started to ask her what that meant, but a voice cut through the noise of the busy street.

"You miss me?"

Ella and Jason spun around, finding Brigit, her blond hair swept into a long braid and her nose streaked with a sunburn. She clutched her knitting needles. The trio tackled each other. So many questions flew around that no one could get a word in.

"Take a breath, everyone!"

Ella looked up to find a woman she'd never seen before. She was beautiful and round, with dark hair pinned up like a swirled ice cream cone. Her white cheeks held a rosy flush much like Brigit's.

"This is Ms. Mead, my guardian," Brigit announced.

The woman smiled down at them. "Hello, best friends of my Brigit," she said, her voice deep and warm.

Feste poked his head out of Brigit's satchel to say hello. Ella and Jason hugged him too before he nestled back inside and out of sight.

As they barreled into Hiraya's Halo-Halo Haven, Ella, Jason, and Brigit dove into what they had done over the summer (even though they'd sent each other dozens of weekly starposts).

They piled their small mountains of ice with sweet red and white beans, jackfruit, ube ice cream, and coconut, then drenched the treats with evaporated milk.

Brigit read the wall sign aloud: "'Must eat halo-halo within twenty minutes; otherwise, the ice will be up to its own devices. You have been warned. We cannot be held responsible. Happy eating!'"

Ella didn't have to be told twice as she dug her spoon into the mix.

Brigit grumbled, fighting the tiny snowball of coconut and ice cream already forming in her bowl, ready to attack her.

Mama entered the shop with Papa, and Ella noticed she looked a little better. A wave of relief rushed through Ella, and she thought maybe today would turn out okay after all. Mama winked at Ella before helping Mrs. Eugene wrangle the little kids into a nearby booth.

Jason took out his supply list. "You ready for the stapier test?"

"For what?" Brigit asked.

"The Level Two channeling test. You've got to prove you can channel your light to get your stapier for class," Jason said. "They sent home a letter about it."

Ella had done her summer homework, practicing channeling her marvel light into her stellacity sphere until it was a perfect ball of twilight. She didn't want to be one of the only students to show up to Intermediate Marvel Light Channeling and not be able to join.

"I had to do that every day during summer school; I guess I still know how." Brigit rolled her eyes, then cupped her hands and grimaced. A tiny ball of sputtering light appeared in her palms.

Not long ago, Brigit had lost that light. Ella blinked away the memory of Brigit drinking the Ace of Anarchy's evil elixir and almost losing her timesight marvel, this gorgeous light.

Ella grinned; a swell of pride filled her. They were both ready.

✦ ✳ ✦ ✳ ✦

THE AFTERNOON WENT BY IN A BLINK NOW THAT THEY WERE ALL together. Ella and Brigit got their fortune journals and prophecy pens from Fanny's Fortune Fortress while Jason got his tuning forks and kindred-gloves from Samuelsson's Sound Stockpile. They each got fitted for their new Level Two mantles, and even Mama remarked how the orange color of it complemented her complexion.

They stocked up on the books they needed for the year from Cárdenas' Coliseo de Libros. They traded theories about what the Arcanum Training Institute might look like this year. They procured their set of fire jars and vivariums from Woodfolk's Wonderous Wares and incant logs from Idahosa's Incant Island Market before heading to their final destination.

The last store stretched high above them, four, maybe five stories of stapiers. Silver letters skated across the window: SAKAMOTO'S STAPIER SHOWROOM. A massive stellacity sphere consumed the central window—golden rings spun around an electrified blue core.

Ella gazed up, trying to take it all in, and realized the entire stellacity sphere was bigger than her very tall and very broad Papa. Two smaller windows held the latest stapier models, the Sabrewhizz 3.0 dueling the SpeedFoil 3.5, the brightness of the blades almost blinding.

The doors stretched open as they entered, the space overflowing with Level Two Arcanum students, some in their new orange mantles already, theorizing and taking bets on what their channellors would turn out to be.

Glass display boxes advertised the store's stapier inventory, ready to be purchased. There were Fleetblade models known for their speed and Dueluxes known for their strategy. There were Poweredges known for their strength and Flexiswords known for their versatility. Ella had forgotten which ones Level Twos were allowed to buy. Some of their long blades glowed in stellacity blues or golden yellows, all depending on their make and model. Their handles showcased different gripping mechanisms and boasted clever abilities.

Store clerks doled out instructions to the excited crowd. "Line up! Line up! Any Level Twos in here for your universal channellor, get a ticket, and then see Mr. Khorram in the back for your test."

As Ella followed Jason through the crowds, she watched him salivate over the displays, eyes big and expectant.

"Look," he said to her, "the new SpeedFoil is the best stapier ever, supposedly—"

"Don't even think about it," Mrs. Eugene called out. "You know what the instructions are—Sabrewhizzes, 1.5 edition only. Now, have a look while I grab tickets for each one of you."

Ella nodded, then searched for her parents. While Papa wrangled Winnie and tried to keep the twins from riding Gumbo, Mama stood in the corner, arms crossed, biting her bottom lip. Ella flooded with guilt again. She'd thought Mama had gotten better earlier, but maybe she'd spoken too soon. But the other part of her was overwhelmed with excitement as Jason droned on and on about how the Fleetblades had special handles for left-handed people like him.

"Numbers 230 to 240, please line up," a store clerk announced.

Brigit raced back down the aisle with Ms. Mead. "That's us!"

Ella, Jason, and Brigit joined the line. Papa tipped his hat at her while holding Winnie up by the back of her pinafore as she thrashed her arms at yet another display.

Good luck, baby girl. Papa's melodic voice fluttered through her head.

She blew him a kiss, then waited eagerly, watching Jason, then Brigit go into a special room for their marvel light stapier test. She was ready. She closed her eyes and remembered her summer practice routine. Each morning before she'd head off with Gran to the conjure pharmacy, she sat on the edge of her bed, took a deep breath, and sang until a tiny ball of twilight appeared in her palms. The little purply black light would shine like a plum drenched in moonlight.

"Number 239!"

Ella jumped at the sound of her number.

Mama appeared at her side, took Ella's hand, and kissed it. "You ready?" her voice croaked.

Ella could feel the upset still inside Mama and couldn't bring herself to look up and into her eyes.

"You don't have to come with me," Ella whispered.

"You think I'm letting you out of my sight?" Mama's eyebrows lifted, and Ella knew there was no getting out of this.

Ella handed the store clerk her ticket.

He read her name and his eyes bulged. He looked up and squinted so hard at her, Mama, and Gumbo, she thought he might be able to see their insides.

Mama tsked her tongue.

"Y-You . . . you may go in for your test," he stammered. "Mr. Khorram is waiting."

Mama eased open the door. "Hello?" she called out.

Mr. Khorram startled at the sight of Mama and Gumbo. A

flush brightened his light brown cheeks. "Umm . . . we don't allow parents to watch, usually."

"Well, consider this an unusual exception to the *usual* policy," she replied, taking a seat in the corner. "I'm staying."

Gumbo sprawled out at her feet. Ella swallowed a groan.

"Very well." He gulped and motioned for Ella to sit across from him at the table. She tried to pretend Mama and Gumbo weren't in the room. She tried to ignore the pressure she felt. She tried to ignore the tiny sounds she heard, Gumbo's tail slapping gently on the floor and his tiny snores, and Mama's labored breathing. She tried to focus on the task she'd done hundreds of times.

Mr. Khorram's eyes, owl-like and curious, blinked at her.

Shouldn't I be the nervous one? Ella thought.

Mr. Khorram placed the most beautiful stellacity sphere Ella had ever seen between them on the table. It was a miniature version of the massive one in the window, the ornate rings etched with the paragon symbols and thick veins of blue stellacity. More advanced than the ones they'd practiced with last year in Dr. Bearden's class.

"Are you ready?" He flicked a small knob, and the rings began to spin.

"Yes," she said.

"Begin."

Ella took a deep breath. She closed her eyes and called the conjure inside her, asking it to wake up. She began to sing. "Little light, shine bright . . ." Her voice croaked at first and she hiccupped, then started again despite the uncomfortable noises she heard Mr. Khorram make. Her head grew dizzy as she yanked at her gift like a cord and demanded it obey.

A tiny ball of light appeared in her palms. But not bright—instead a flickering sphere of twilight with deep indigos and violets. She focused as hard as she could to keep it strong, but a headache punched her temples, and her gift felt a little fuzzy. She tried to push away the anxiety and the questions about why her conjure felt like this right now and stay focused on the task at hand.

Mr. Khorram jumped with surprise as Ella slipped the light through the rings and into the center of the stellacity sphere. It flared and hissed as it drew strength. "I've never seen anything like this."

Ella smiled up at the perplexed man. "Conjure light."

His eyes stretched wide as he stared back and forth from the sphere to Ella and then at Mama in the corner. He scribbled into his notebook, then handed Ella a paper slip. "Take this to the cashier." He paused, pursed his lips, then took several breaths. "I must say, even though I shouldn't, that your light is marvelous and unique. I'm glad you're here with us."

"Thank you." She tried to hide the giddiness in her voice. She took the slip and walked out of the room with Mama, the buzz of triumph flooding through her.

As they rounded the corner and reentered the main showroom floor, Mama froze. Ella finally looked up at her. Tears streamed down her cheeks and her chin quivered as she struggled to swallow.

"Mama." Ella squeezed her hand. "What's wrong?" Deep down, part of Ella already knew the answer to this question, and she'd been too chicken to say it out loud.

"It's really happening. You're becoming a Marveller." The rest of her reply was a deep sob.

The Star Weekly

THE ACE OF ANARCHY SIGHTING!

Sarah Mallard-Garrison

Gia Trivelino, the Ace of Anarchy, was spotted in Betelmore. Evading Marvellian coppers, the criminal exposes the soft spots in the government's plan to deal with rising crime. Before long all the Aces will be back and fully operational.

Does anyone remember when they wreaked havoc on our world? Those five notorious criminals and their monstrous marvels. No city was safe. Their network of evil shops, shows, and entertainment. No one wants to see that circus back . . . And now, there's more of them. Gia's full-on in recruitment mode . . . and from what I'm hearing, she's more than doubled her deck.

While you all argue about the Conjurors, the fae, and starfolk, consumed by your bigotry, the Aces will return and rise again. Then it won't matter if Conjure folk end up buying a house next to yours or more of their children enroll at the Arcanum Training Institute, because there will be nothing left to protect from the wrong threat.

WANTED!

Gia Trivelino wore the most beautiful fascinator and veil she could find, making sure the thick black net hid her current face. She was, after all, headed to her version of a funeral.

Her stellaric car snaked down Betelmore's high street, avoiding hordes of excited children no doubt shopping in preparation for the new Arcanum school year. As a student, she'd never been that joyous about returning to that place; it'd meant missing out on helping her father with his commedia dell'arte shows and drifting from his sphere of influence to her mother's at the start of each Institute year. Schoolwork. Early bedtimes. Punishments for not meeting expectations. Daily behavioral reports from Dean Nabakova to her mother—and surprise visits. She'd hated being a child.

A small kid in white darted across the street.

"Stay steady, Volan. Last thing I need is a copper pulling us over because you almost hit someone."

"Yes, my lady. I'm sorry." Volan flinched, his fur standing on edge.

"Don't be sorry. Get us where we need to go." She nodded at her most loyal servant.

Gia tried not to stare too hard out the window. The groups of kids reminded her of her very own child out there somewhere. Any flash of pale blond hair set her teeth on edge. The memory of that not-so-distant night burned. The look of betrayal and anger in her child's blue eyes. They were identical to the way hers looked so often. All those questions. All that loneliness. All that upset. Gia knew it well. Now . . . Brigit knew it too.

She thought about the little famous Conjure kid Ella and her friend Jason, who'd foiled her plans and ruined all her hard work. She could still hear the crash of her precious glass bottles, the melody of failure. The news-boxes had valorized them all summer as if they'd truly ousted her.

If Ella had only known that her plan would help Conjurors too. But she'd deal with those meddlesome children soon enough. She'd have the final laugh. She always did.

The high street thinned out, the lanes narrowing and bending into a crooked curve as they descended into the second layer of the city. Darkness flooded the car, and the stellaric bulbs inside flared on as the low street spread out before her, just as busy as the other with people moving in and out of shops.

They made their way to her family's Commedia Close. High street newsies swarmed with low street ones as a construction crew dismantled just the thing she'd come to see. Gia seethed as she watched three Marvellers with, no doubt, incant marvels break through her veil and destroy all she and her father had painstakingly built. The once diamond-shaped signs. The gorgeous Trivelino Troupe's Circus & Imaginarium of Illusions sign.

The canal of mirrors. The gondolas. She watched the removal of the family pet, her baby leviathan, Poco, in a tank.

Coppers tossed the contents of her dressing room into the street, all her faces and garments piled up like rotten fish set out for trash pickup.

She closed her eyes, remembering when she was a little girl sitting in her father's office as he explained how to sew life-like costumes ready to fool the Marvellian eye with his clever channellor—handmade knitting needles. Powerful enough to tame the unique marvel they both shared. A marvel labeled *monstrous*. The ability to manipulate the strings of matter. She could still hear the deep texture of his voice as he slipped between English and Italian, explaining the importance of the threads and earning a big response from the crowd.

Gia balled her fists, watching them snap her very last thread. "Fetch my needles and anything else of value you can rummage from that pile."

"Yes, my lady." Volan parked the car nearby and slipped out it unseen. He eased into the chaos of onlookers, coppers, and cleanup crew.

She marveled at him, often envious of the starfolk's ability to hide in plain sight and move at a frequency unseen by Marvellers. Volan had worked for her since her father died and remained a loyal employee through her trial and stint in the Cards of Deadly Fate. After Marvellians moved into the skies and destroyed the starfolk population, the one good thing her mother ever did was set up her organization, the Starfolk Welfare, to aid in getting them work and housing. She'd never needed siblings growing up because the starfolk in the house had been plentiful.

She cracked the car window and listened to the street chatter.

"Heard the so-called mighty Gia Trivelino's really dead, and all of this is a front."

"She probably wants everyone to think that. She's hiding out somewhere for sure. Waking up the other Aces. We're done for if she gets them all back together—or worse, adds even more to her ranks."

"All a distraction from the *real* threat, if you ask me. Those Conjurors! The fae folk too. They're starting to move in. They're starting to forget their place."

"What does she even want? Her whole experiment failed. She can't take people's marvels. It's unnatural."

Gia nodded her head as they spun their theories. "It's time to teach this world a lesson . . . and that little Conjuror, Ella Durand. I will punish her too, for causing all this."

CHAPTER FOUR
THE SOCK & BUSKIN

Ella kissed her parents goodbye in front of her new dormitory, the Azure Dragon Tower. Other Level Two students whizzed past with their marvel-valises, zipping through the doors and up to their rooms. She couldn't wait to set up her new room with Brigit and investigate how different it must be to Ursa Minor.

Mama gazed at her with bloodshot eyes. Ella's stomach flip-flopped. She wanted to look away. It was hard for her to wrestle with the fact that her decision to attend the Arcanum had caused so much upset and yet so much joy at the same time. How can something taste bitter and sweet at once?

Ella gazed all around at the new Arcanum walls, now bright red instead of celestial blue. Tiny star-lanterns drifted overhead, dusting them all in soft crimson light.

"It's so different," Mama remarked.

Ella could still hear the tears in her voice. She didn't have the heart to remind her that the Arcanum changed what it looked like every year.

"You ready for all of this again, baby girl?" Papa asked.

"Yes, sir," Ella said, then held her breath, waiting for Mama to change her mind and march her straight into the dormitory, insisting on unpacking each and every item in her juju-trunk or fortifying the bottle tree she'd have to conjure in order to bless and protect the room for the year. Or worse, tell Ella she was too upset for her to stay, and discuss disenrolling her from the Arcanum Training Institute altogether.

But this time, Mama just sighed, tired. A deep crease appeared along her brow, and her voice still sounded wobbly. "More star-posts this year, little girl." Mama ran shaky fingers across Ella's hairline, then touched the back of Ella's neck where her conjure mark had blossomed from a lima bean to the size of a peach pit from all the work in the conjure pharmacy with Gran. Long roots stretched along her collarbone like a tiny necklace. Ella was excited to see how big it might get this year.

"Yes, ma'am."

"And listen to your aunt Sera. No ifs, ands, or buts about it, okay?" Mama added.

Ella nodded.

Papa leaned down and kissed her nose. "Stay out of business that isn't yours, you hear? No trouble. Period."

"Yes, sir." Ella secretly crossed her fingers behind her back. She didn't know if she could completely and totally do that because she had investigating to do. Investigating that could maybe prove Conjurors belonged here, and Mama didn't have to worry so much about her.

"And most of all remember, every shut eye ain't sleep. Be careful." Papa squeezed her hand.

Mama handed Ella a fresh jar of twilight stardust. "Keep this close." She kissed Ella's forehead. "And you sure you can conjure the tree on your own?"

"Of course, Mama. You're the one who taught me—and you're the best."

"Trying to butter me up?" Mama laughed a little, and it made Ella feel better about the stress of the day.

"I think Gran would argue with that." Papa took Mama's hand in his, kissed it, and squeezed tight. "Our little girl's growing up. She's got this and we'll have to trust her."

Mama put her other hand to Ella's chest, checking for her conjure-cameo. "Be safe. I couldn't bear—" Her voice cracked in half.

"She will," Papa replied, his gaze finding Ella. "Right?"

"Yes, I promise." Ella wrapped her arms around her mother's waist.

"Conjurors keep their word." Papa tapped his top hat and its skulls grinned down at her, as if they too were holding Ella to her promise. "We should get going." He tightened his jacket. "Can feel the hawk up here already. That sharp wind is coming off the cold sea."

"See you later, Ella!" Winnie grumbled before dissolving into another fit of tears.

Ella said a quick goodbye before turning on her heel and darting through the dormitory doors. She tried not to run, but her legs filled with excited tingles as she entered the huge lounge.

A Chinese dragon constellation slithered along rich red walls. Tiny star-lanterns floated through the ceiling, leaving crimson-tinted light over plush couches and ornate tables. A fireplace crackled in the center; the flames hissed, changing from brilliant reds and oranges to blues and golds.

Her heart lifted in awe. The Azure Dragon dormitory looked

and felt so different than the Ursa Minor one from last year. She couldn't wait to explore.

Ella and her juju-trunk climbed the stairs, dodging past other classmates, including Samaira and Luz and Anh. She waved at them, then looked from door to door until she found her name right beside Brigit's at the end of the hall.

She knocked, then opened it a smidgen. "Brigit?"

Ella found her friend and a tornado of objects on the left side of the room. She couldn't even get mad at the typical Brigit-style mess and instead burst out laughing. Feste backflipped on the bed, his tinkling bells echoing. He waved his tiny harlequin hat at her.

Ella reached down to hug him while her juju-trunk parked itself beside her bed.

"I messed up the incant. Now my marvel-valise won't unpack itself right. It dumped everything out instead." Brigit's face flushed pink with panic. "Where's your mom and dad—and Winnie?"

"They went back home."

Brigit's eyes filled with surprise.

"I know. I was shocked too." Ella unpacked her clothes, putting her mantles away, and spread out her quilt. Then she swept the room for bad spirits with her broom and arranged the saints on her nightstand.

"Ahh—glad to be out of the darkness," St. Phillip exclaimed.

"Oh, I see we'll be looking after you and Brigit again this year. Must keep our eyes sharp with you two." St. Catherine shook her head.

"We weren't that bad last year," Ella said, even though her words felt a little bit like a lie.

Brigit giggled from her side of the room.

The saints burst out with more chatter. She didn't mind them so much this year. She'd just have to make sure they didn't snitch to Mama.

"Time to get on with the bottle tree. It's cold up here. We'll need protection from the wind this year," St. Christopher said.

Ella conjured the bottle tree just as her mother had taught her. But her spell created a huge Spanish oak with a golden hue this time, its bark almost glowing as the night-balloons puttered in and out of the room, lending their light. And as she inspected it, she noticed a few brown leaves and some bald spots among the branches. Golden death moths perched on the branches. *Weird*, Ella thought. This wasn't how the one from last year turned out. She swallowed a pesky worry about her conjure.

"Wow." Brigit gazed up at it, running her fingers along its gilded bark. "It's so different. Why?"

"I don't know." Ella reached for one of its leaves and it leaned to meet her fingertips.

"It's beautiful." Feste perched on one of its thick roots.

She didn't have time to investigate because her juju-trunk wiggled, reminding her that she had one final item left inside. She dug out a leather tube. "I have to show you that secret *thing* I wrote to you about." She plucked the top off and flashed Brigit the blueprints.

"Wow!" Brigit took a step closer. "How—"

An announcement-balloon puttered into the room. "All Level Twos in Azure Dragon, please come down to the lounge in preparation for the midnight assembly."

"I'll tell you later." Ella put the lid back on the tube, then reached for one of the bottle tree's branches. She sang a concealing spell: "Hide what is sacred and keep close what is treasured."

The tree shook with recognition and reached out to pluck the leather tube from Ella's grip. It tucked the precious secret deep in its branches, blanketing the cylinder with moss and spiderwebs.

"Ready?" Ella whipped around to ask Brigit, and surprised, found her side of the room neat and tidy.

"One sec." Brigit sat her world-egg on her nightstand, a tiny full moon casting its glow over the desert oasis.

"The malyysvit is still alive?" Ella asked.

"Ten-year guarantee. That's what it says on the back. The desert's pink now. It's been storming for days, then suddenly it changed."

Maybe this year would be like that. Start out stormy but would end up revealing something beautiful in the end.

✦ ✳ ✦ ▮ ✦

ELLA AND BRIGIT ENTERED THE DORMITORY HALL, RUNNING straight into Lian, Clare, and Abina.

"Guess we're neighbors." Clare's harsh gaze brought back all those awful memories from last year, but Ella kept smiling. A fresh start, a clean slate, or at least she'd try to give that to everyone. But Clare always made things hard.

"Guess so," Brigit spat back.

"Hey," Abina said to Ella. Her long braids click-clacked against her shoulders, the beads sparkling in the star-lantern light. Before they reached the staircase, Abina pulled Ella to the side. Ella's pulse raced. "We're going to be friends this year, okay?"

Ella's eyes widened, and she couldn't do much more than nod and say okay before Abina ambled down the stairs. One of Ella's wishes for the year was already coming true.

They piled into the lounge and met their new Tower Adviser, a wizened Mrs. Francesca, a Paragon of Sound with an opera marvel, and heard the same rules as last year about making sure to wear their translation crystals and about being good Arcanum citizens with one another.

"Don't be alarmed if you see our most loyal and trusted Marvellian coppers posted about. The Head of Marvellian Law Enforcement, Mr. Sherwood, has a plan to ensure our safety while that . . ." She cleared her throat. "That evil criminal is still on the loose. One of my own pupils years ago."

Questions about Gia filled the space. Ella felt Brigit flinch beside her. She held Brigit's hand.

"Never you mind that, piccole stelle. Out of sight and out of mind. She can't get anyone here. Trust me." Mrs. Francesca handed out Azure Dragon scarves, their cerulean blue threads stitched with the golden image of a Chinese dragon. "We're expected in the Arcanum courtyard. Bundle up! Put on your translation crystals. It's already cold out there." She led the group into the hall.

Ella gazed around at the changes to the Arcanum Training Institute. She'd been waiting all summer for this. Her stomach wiggled with excitement. Star-lanterns fluttered overhead, their red paper bodies burning bright. The trolleys sparkled in radiant ruby, rich gold, and glittering jade with the Paragon symbols glowing along their sides. The ceilings curved into pointed slopes with constellation maps shimmering; four colorful animals skulked around the stars—a black tortoise, a white tiger, a vermillion bird, and a blue dragon.

"They're the twenty-eight Chinese lunar mansions," Lian proudly explained, then dove into a lesson about how each animal guarded sections of the sky and the seven groups of stars that lived there. Ella couldn't wait to learn more about these constellations even if it meant suffering through talking more to Lian Wong this year.

Oohs and *aahs* echoed as everyone took in the new surroundings. Skywells gave glimpses of snow clouds and revealed yellow roof tiles. Wooden columns and wall panels boasted paintings of animals, fruit, and good fortune talismans. Every few seconds projections of three bearded Chinese men appeared overhead, waving down at them and doling out blessings:

"We wish you good fortunes."

"Much prosperity for the year ahead."

"May you have longevity in your life and scholarly endeavors."

"The three stars are present."

Terracotta busts of the Arcanum founders waved at them as they passed. Ella felt like the Institute had morphed into an ancient Chinese palace.

"It's so different," Brigit whispered.

Different felt too simple. It was *transformed*. She had so much exploring to do. She'd need a new Arcanum map.

A nearby elevator opened, and more kids spilled into the hall. The sight of it made Ella wonder where the RESTRICTED LIFT ended up now that the building had shifted around. She'd add it to her list of things to investigate.

"This way!" Mrs. Francesca led them through a gate and into the new Arcanum courtyard. Enclosed by paper screens and other Institute buildings, Ella gaped at an enchanting pond, a grove of bamboo and moonflowers, a blossoming Greeting Pine tree, and endless pavilions. Various pathways bore signs to the new locations of THE LIBRARY, THE DINING HALL, THE ARCANUM MENAGERIE, THE PARAGON TOWERS, and more.

The space swelled with trainees, and Ella looked out at the Level Ones, tiny and dressed in all white, and wondered if they too had looked so small last year. She searched the crowd, hoping to find another Conjure student. Ella tightened her scarf as a cold wind wrapped itself around her.

Jason and his roommate Miguel bounded over, out of breath and excited.

"It's freezing already." Jason's teeth chattered while Miguel made clouds with his breath.

"We're in the White Tiger dorm, and the tiger roars stars," Miguel said, rattling off all the cool new things about their Level Two dormitory and their room, while Ella spotted some of the usual kids from last year—Pierre, Ousmane, Pilar, Brendan—and even Bex. They waved at her, snowflakes gathering in their mohawk.

But before she could wave back, she felt eyes on her. She looked left, finding the same girl she'd seen in the Vellian Port. The one who turned the fountain water black. Her gaze burned into Ella.

Ella wished she were close enough to ask her what she wanted. Instead, Ella stuck out her tongue, hoping to earn a laugh. But the girl didn't move, almost like she'd been frozen in place, her punishment to stare forever.

A rottie popped its head out of Jason's mantle pocket, startling Ella. She patted its head, and when she glanced back up, the girl was gone.

"They've already found you," Ella said to Jason as she nuzzled the rottie's nose.

Jason grinned. "Sweet Pea showed up five minutes after I unpacked."

The noise of a gong silenced the students. The midnight assembly felt like a whirlwind. The Headmarvellers stood on their floating platform and greeted everyone. Headmarveller Rivera waved and smiled, her papel picado burning red and orange as if she'd turned a setting sun into a crown. Headmarveller

MacDonald's tartan boasted beautiful dark greens and blues. They went through their usual announcements, even reminding everyone about the coppers who'd be at the Institute every day.

Ella thought this would never get old.

Headmarveller Rivera put a hand to her heart. "This is a special year, my beloved pupils, and cause for much celebration year-round. A commemoration of three momentous things. Good fortune comes in threes. Firstly, it's the start of the Tricentennial, our three hundredth anniversary of the community's decision to live in the skies together. We'll be hosting several events so that our trainees can get even more acquainted with our marvelous history." She paused for a short round of applause. "Secondly, we welcome our new Level Ones, especially three new Conjure students hailing from Cartagena, Colombia; Bahia, Brazil; and Harlem, New York, USA."

The clapping thinned out, awkward patches of silence filling the courtyard.

Ella pushed down the tiny twinge of fear as she turned to the Level One area, eyes combing through the crowd, determined to locate the new Conjure students. She would introduce herself immediately and make sure they knew she was here for them. She spotted three embarrassed-looking kids and waved. They flashed her shy smiles.

"Thirdly, the Arcanum is also hosting our special biennial exchange program. Every other year, Indigenous students from tribal nations across the world come to study with us. This year we're hosting five students from the Navajo Nation. We welcome you to our community. Our dynamic and diverse student body is growing." Headmarveller Rivera clapped so hard it felt like a command, and the crowd obeyed, parroting her.

Ella found students with beautiful squash blossom necklaces

draped over their mantles. Questions flooded her mind. Why didn't Indigenous Marvellers attend the Institute every year? She wondered how she'd missed this last year. She'd add it to her list of questions for Masterji Thakur. She couldn't wait to see him again.

Headmarveller MacDonald leaned down to the microphone. "On a more serious note, as you all no doubt know from the endless news-box cycles, our world is in a bit of disarray with a criminal on the loose. But rest assured, danger will *not* find us here. This is the safest place in the world for you to be. We are thrilled to be back together again."

The courtyard grew so quiet Ella felt like she could hear both her and Brigit's hearts thudding. She reached down to hold Brigit's shaky hand.

"Now, let's celebrate!" Headmarveller Rivera's papel picado transformed into a joyous tornado. "As Level Fours make their way around with our lanterns, prepare for a fun surprise. Make glorious wishes for a very lucky year."

The students screamed with joy as a troupe of Chinese acrobats poured out of nearby pathways. Dressed in red and gold, they backflipped and somersaulted through the crowd. Many flapped fans, and others held poles and spinning plates. Fireworks exploded overhead in bright reds and golds.

"Chinese civilization created fireworks. Did you know that?" Lian exclaimed.

As they watched, Jason elbowed Ella and pointed at Brigit, who stared all around as if looking for the nearest escape.

They pulled her closer.

"You okay?" Ella asked.

"I just . . ." Brigit looked left, then right, before whispering, "I don't want anyone to know . . . or find out about you-know-what."

"They won't." Ella clutched Brigit's hand. "We were the only ones there."

"And Masterji Thakur," Brigit added.

"He's a great secret keeper," Ella reminded her, thinking about how he'd been able to keep one of the biggest secrets of them all—he was a former Ace.

Brigit nodded, then stammered out, "Do—do you think people can tell?" Her cheeks turned as red as the light show above.

Ella shook her head no and assured Brigit, but if she was honest, the kind of honest Mama always warned her about, they did look alike. Gia Trivelino's wanted poster flashed in her head. The way their reluctant smiles tucked into the corners of their mouths. That gave it away. But you'd have to look closely.

"We won't say anything, right, Ella? We promise," Jason added before Miguel walked up with their wish-making supplies to share.

Ella nodded. "I promise."

"What if she . . . tries to . . . ?" Brigit said.

Ella didn't even want to think about what might be at the end of that sentence. "We wouldn't let her get to you." She hugged Brigit. "We will protect you."

Ella turned to her wish lantern and wrote her greatest desires for the year on the slip of paper—*Find out the blueprint's secrets, make Mama feel better, and keep Brigit safe*. She thought she might've made too many wishes, but like Headmarveller Rivera said, good luck came in threes.

Snowflakes began to fall, and the whole school cheered. She released her lantern, smiling as it dodged snowflakes and joined the others in the sky. Brigit helped Jason dig a wayward rottie out of the snow while Ella watched the rest of the acrobat show.

The performers backflipped and contorted themselves into various shapes. Ella watched with awe.

As the show finished, one acrobat snaked through the crowd, stopping in front of her. Unlike the others, the person didn't wear traditional Chinese theater makeup; instead, an odd mask covered half the person's face with a frown and the other half with a smile. They looked out of place amid the troupe.

Ella startled backward.

The acrobat presented her with an envelope. "For you, a reminder."

Ella tore into it as the performer disappeared into the crowd. The message read:

I'm watching you, little Conjuror.
You will pay for the mess you made and the plan
you ruined.
A debt is owed.
I will collect.

Her pulse raced. She knew the sender. Gia Trivelino. How did she get in here? Ella searched the crowd, looking for the acrobats, but they were long gone.

"What is it?" Brigit asked while wrestling Sweet Pea back into Jason's mantle pocket.

Ella pressed the threatening letter to her chest. Despite the cold wind, a hot bead of sweat skated down her back. She couldn't show Brigit this. Not after Brigit had just panicked about Gia finding her. She'd have to keep this secret. "Nothing," she replied. "Nothing at all."

★—★—★— **STARPOST**—★—★—★

My brilliant goddaughter,

Please come see me. I've missed you and need to lay my eyes on you.

Love,
Aunt Sera

★—★—★— **STARPOST**—★—★—★

Ella,

I hope you're settled into the Arcanum for Year Two. Enclosing an appointment card. Can't wait to see you and catch up on your summer. I have no doubts you've been busy.

Best,
Masterji Thakur

The Arcanum Training Institute for Marvelous and Uncanny Endeavors

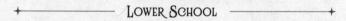

— Lower School —

ADDENDUM TO STUDENT HANDBOOK
SECURITY UPDATE—TRAINEE PLEDGE

New security procedures and policies have been implemented at the Arcanum for the safety and security of all trainees. The following rules and commitments are meant to keep the community safe. All students pledge to do the following:

- Follow all policies and procedures as outlined without question or hesitation.
- Adhere to instructions from each Headmarveller, Arcanum doctor, and visiting copper security member.
- Refrain from inviting unauthorized guests onto Institute grounds, into dormitories, etc., without the proper guest paperwork.

Trainee Signature   *Star Ink preferred

CHAPTER FIVE

STAPIERS

Life at the Arcanum was just as marvelous as Ella had remembered . . . once she'd figured out where everything had moved to.

The trolleys navigated symmetrical corridors like a maze. The Arcanum courtyard sprawled through the very middle. It reminded her of a family trip they'd taken to the Forbidden City in Beijing, China. The dining hall introduced a new food cart with stews to battle the cold, and Ella made a list of all the ones she wanted to try: Haitian joumou, Brazilian mócoto, Romanian ghiveci, Korean gamjatang, Palestinian freekeh, Ethiopian doro wat, and more. She'd heard each one gave you different dreams. She'd tried to catch the flying tea cart too, so she could try the Moroccan mint and Japanese matcha, but she always missed it by thirty seconds before it flew to another location. The weather balloons forecasted endless snow, and tiny float-fires drifted throughout, keeping the building cozy and warm.

The only strange thing about the Institute so far was the coppers who patrolled the pathways. Their heavy-soled boots reverberated through the open halls and galleries. She thought they might make her feel safer after receiving that threatening note, but she still looked over her shoulder all the time.

Her first day of Level Two classes was a whirlwind—Dr. Huang fortified their fire jars with heat and water in his dragon kiln during Global Elementals, they each received a news-box and historical reels in Marvellian Theory, and Dr. Goldblum helped them set passwords for their incant journals. But the biggest difference, the one she wasn't sure how she felt about just yet, was the fact that she didn't have *all* her classes with Jason this year. The fourth session, after lunch, turned out to be a Paragon-specific one, where she and Brigit had Future Forecasting II with Dr. Al Sayed and Jason had Animal Communication Fundamentals with Dr. Choi.

And right now, it was weird waiting for him to march into Intermediate Marvel Light Channeling.

Ella and Brigit found a three-seater desk, and Ella watched the doorway. She busied herself with inspecting the room. Last year, Dr. Bearden's Channellors' Chamber felt like a cluttered museum of bobbles and bits—but Dr. Yohannes's classroom felt like an art gallery. A stellacity sphere sat at the very center and soared high above, its base as thick and wide as the Arcanum Cardinal, and its rings so big Ella thought they could circle the moon. Projections of stapier parts and procedures filled the ceiling. The walls held posters boasting the history of Stephan Stadler, the original inventor of the instrument. Technique charts showed the connection between stapiers and one's marvel light. Beautiful vases filled with violets flanked her desk and made the whole space smell like a garden.

The staring girl from the midnight assembly sauntered down the aisle with Clare, her dark hair still in those two braids.

"Who is that?" Ella whispered to Brigit.

Brigit barely glanced up from a new pair of mittens she was knitting. "I heard everyone talking about her in the lounge. New student from Paris, Noémie. Clare's *obsessed* and won't stop blabbering about her new best friend."

"I don't think she likes me."

The girl looked up as if reading Ella's mind. She scowled, and Ella looked away. Weird.

"She's one of my roommates."

Ella turned around to find Siobhan. Her tangled brown hair still had a life of its own, and her cheeks held their usual red flush. She flashed Ella a weak smile, and Ella felt bad about everything that had happened the previous year with her naughty pixies. She hated that they'd been making mischief because they'd been trying to keep other kids from being mean to Siobhan.

Ella hugged Siobhan before she sat at a nearby desk.

"Everyone already loves Noémie," Siobhan reported. "She has people in the room all the time. Even after curfew. All she does is—"

A small creature popped out of Siobhan's satchel. Plump in the middle and with toothpick legs, he wore a tiny red hat and had leathery skin. "Stay focused, Siobhan! Tend to your own affairs!"

Ella jumped back and Brigit laughed.

"Don't mind this hobgoblin spy!" Siobhan tried to wrestle him back into her bag. "This snitch was sent by my ma to watch me day and night."

"Don't call me that." He jammed his tiny hands on his hips and tapped his foot. "I am Oraan. Charged with ensuring the well-being of this young girl prone to delinquency."

Siobhan shook her head, embarrassed. "Our family brownie

has come to spy on me for the semester. Ma is *so* worried I'll get into trouble again."

The little hobgoblin began to fuss about her previous track record. Ella tried not to laugh as he aired his grievances with her: the bed she never made, the lack of starposts she wrote to her ma and pa, and how many naughty books she read. Ella thought Jason would hate to have missed this. Eventually, Siobhan convinced Oraan to go back into her satchel, and their conversation returned to the new Level Two girl, Noémie Lavigne.

"I didn't know someone could go to the Arcanum if they weren't here for the first year," Brigit said.

This ignited a curious question inside Ella. Maybe Reagan could still attend (*if* she could convince the Marsalis family). Ella could even tutor her and get her up to speed.

"She was homeschooled and passed the Level One exams," Siobhan added. "She's not very nice. It's like last year rooming with Lian all over again."

Ella's gaze found Noémie again, and they glared at one another.

"No one wanted to room with me, so I got the kids who didn't know what happened last year." She motioned at one of the visiting kids from the Navajo Nation. Luci Tsinigine. Her hair spilled across her mantle, and Ella couldn't wait to ask her about the turquoise beads threaded into her braids. She'd love to teach her braid-hands to do that.

The star-lanterns flickered, sending students to their seats for the start of class.

Just as Dr. Yohannes walked to the front of the classroom to begin, Jason barreled in, plopping down beside Ella, out of breath and clutching a handkerchief to his nose.

"Where were you?" Ella whispered. "And what happened?"

He shrugged. "Nosebleed and a headache. I had to see Nurse Peaks."

Worry rushed through her. His eyes were bloodshot, and she thought he might've been crying.

"You okay?" Brigit asked.

"It was weird, I couldn't hear the rotties this morning or the wombies when I served them breakfast." His voice sounded shaky.

Ella didn't have a chance to reply. The star-lanterns dimmed, and a projection of a massive stapier stretched over their heads.

Dr. Yohannes smiled at them. Her mantle sparkled, trimmed with gorgeous patterns that Ella had seen on one of her mother's best friends, Auntie Bezi from Ethiopia. Gorgeous gold jewelry dangled from her ears and draped across her neck.

"Good afternoon, trainees, and welcome to Intermediate Marvel Light Channeling. I'm Dr. Liya Yohannes, a Paragon of Touch with a lapidary marvel, which means I use gems and gold to channel my light." Her delicate hands swept across her collar. "The hand has no fear!"

Several students mimicked her.

"Take out your slips from Sakamoto's Stapier Showroom, have them ready for collection, then place your stapiers in front of you. I'll be making rounds to ensure everyone has followed instructions," Dr. Yohannes ordered.

Ella grabbed her stapier box and slip from her satchel.

"In this class, you'll refine your ability to summon your inner light. The stellacity sphere has taught you the precision required to move to the next step—the stapier. Our very own universal channellor. Anyone know why Marvellians use this instrument specifically?" Dr. Yohannes moved from desk to desk.

Hands waved. Ella didn't know the answer to this question,

and she gulped. She'd have to check out a library book on the topic immediately.

Dr. Yohannes called on Anh.

She stood up and clutched the book *The Stapier Scoop* to her chest. "In the past, Marvellers from all over the world used different things to channel their light—which is why we still have our channellors too. But the founders believed that trainees needed something that connected us and helped us refine our light together."

"Very good. Exactly that. Our great founders wanted to unite all Marvellers," Dr. Yohannes replied. "I know many of you will come to this class with delusions of grandeur from watching Marvel Combat. Yes, our sport showcases how powerful our stapiers can be and how diverse our channellors are, but that will not prepare you for the task at hand. Your objective in this course will be to learn to control your light so that you'll be ready for your unique channellor at the end of the year."

Ella felt lucky that she already knew what her channellor would be. She had a cartomanic marvel. Fortune cards would be her tool if she could earn them. For the first time, she felt ahead of her peers.

Dr. Yohannes returned to the front of the room. "And let me make myself crystal clear: If I catch you with anything other than a Sabrewhizz 1.5, you'll go straight to Dean Nabokova."

Ella remembered that woman's terrifying face. She'd planned to never have to see the Dean of Discipline again if she could help it.

"All right, everyone, unpack your stapier and set it in front of you. We'll go through its parts."

Giggles mingled with eager sounds of paper ripping.

Ella tore into her box and removed her stapier. She gripped the handle and admired all the sparkling labels identifying the various parts—the knuckle guard, crossbar, pommel, forte, the two edges, and the sharp point. She held it upright, admiring how it soared over her head like a long staff, and compared it to the stapier projection above.

With hesitant fingers, Brigit examined hers. "Sort of like a fatter and super long version of my needles." She whipped out her trusty ones and compared them.

"I can't wait to get a Sabrewhizz 3.0," Jason said.

The classroom star-lanterns went out. Darkness engulfed the room.

"When you become proficient, your light will become a tool, and when you master it, a reflex." A tiny ball of light appeared between Dr. Yohannes's palms, then grew to resemble a bright sun.

Ella covered her mouth. *Oohs* and *aahs* crackled. She thought of her tiny ball of twilight. Would she be able to do that too one day?

Dr. Yohannes looked sun-drenched. She clapped her hands. Her gigantic light ball sailed over their heads and into the classroom's stellacity sphere. The rings spun faster and faster, making her marvel light grow bigger and bigger. She lifted a stapier. Light climbed up the slender rod, then her jewelry sparked like firecrackers.

In that moment, Ella knew she wanted to be like that, to have light as strong.

"All these objects work in tandem. Versatility is the key," Dr. Yohannes called out. "You will learn to master your gift in all its forms."

Dr. Yohannes's stapier darkened again. The stellacity sphere slowed. The star-lanterns blazed brightly.

"Wow," Jason muttered.

"How can she do that?" Siobhan whispered. Even her hobgoblin Oraan now sat speechless on the edge of her desk.

"Incredible," Brigit whispered.

Ella had been unable to take her eyes off her teacher.

Dr. Yohannes pointed her stapler in the air again. "Follow after me."

The entire class scrambled to mimic.

"Slide your hand into the handle—the grooves will automatically adjust for precision and comfort, the material memorizing your grip."

The class followed her instructions as she moved through the aisles, correcting students' forms. "Now squeeze tight. Think of the light inside you. Your marvel itself. Call it to your fingertips as if you were getting ready to use it."

Clare's stapler shot into the air like a rocket. Miguel's stapler turned bright red, almost igniting into flames. Samaira's stapler disintegrated, and she burst into tears. It all kept Ella from her task. She didn't want that to happen to her.

"Gentle! I didn't say shove all your marvel light through the thin blade," Dr. Yohannes said. "It takes control—and balance. Samaira, go get a replacement stapler from the front cabinet. I'll have it billed to your account. Try again. Practice makes better."

Ella clutched her stapler with her right hand. She squared her shoulders and held it out. She closed her eyes and started to hum. She ignored the prickly sensation of people watching her. She'd done this a million times, calling her marvel light and placing it in the stellacity sphere, and she'd just done it a few days ago to earn her slip.

This couldn't be that hard.

But it was.

She could see the violet twilight in her mind's eye, and feel it just at her fingertips, but it felt stuck. She heard Dr. Yohannes's footsteps getting closer. "Slow and steady. The metal is a conduit. Showing proficiency with a stapier will build the foundation for your unique channellor at the end of the year."

Sweat beads covered Ella's forehead.

Ella took a deep breath and sang to herself. But nothing. The blade stayed the same.

She opened her eyes, frustrated. Not even Jason could get his stapier to glow.

"My head hurts," Jason complained.

Brigit's stapier glowed to her right.

More annoyance bubbled up inside her. She gulped down tears and tried again, knowing Dr. Yohannes's gaze was directly on her. She tried singing louder, despite drawing more attention from her classmates. Her jaw clenched. Her head throbbed. Her eyes snapped open and she glared at the stapier.

C'mon, light, she thought to herself. *I need you to work.*

But nothing happened.

Ella looked up, finding Dr. Yohannes's disappointed eyes. "If you can't get your stapiers to work, trainees, you won't be eligible for your channellor, and won't last here very long," Dr. Yohannes warned.

Defeat piled up in her stomach. She'd never failed like this before. The new girl, Noémie, smiled at Ella as her stapier shone perfectly.

Her thoughts spiraled. The weird light sputtering during her marvel light test in Betelmore, then her bottle tree turning out strange, and now this. What was happening to her conjure? Why couldn't she do this?

CHAPTER SIX
GAG ORDERS

After Dr. Yohannes's class, Ella said goodbye to Jason and Brigit, and she sprinted all the way to the Paragon of Taste Tower holding her blinking appointment card, nearly earning her first demerit for the year from Dr. Choi. But she didn't want to be even one minute late in seeing Masterji Thakur. She wanted—and needed—to put as much distance as possible between her and what had just happened with her stapler.

The Taste Tower had moved all the way east, and she had to take the Jade trolley to the end of the line, and it had been running late too due to snow. She dashed into the tower, racing under the mechanical mouth and heliogram of founder Femi Ademola and his steaming bowl of truth soup. Her pulse raced, blocking out all the delicious sights and scents in this tower. She couldn't even look at the new edible wallpaper or inspect the sweet-balloons. She dodged kids eager for sugar snow to drop from them.

Too impatient to wait for the elevator, she darted up the winding staircase to the top floor, evading other trainees and

Arcanum doctors, and tumbled into Masterji Thakur's lair out of breath.

The ceiling held its usual peacock blue, and the walls now contained cut-out windows and projections of beautiful Rajasthani landscapes. She spotted elephants and tigers, gorgeous palaces, and a bustling market in the distance.

Masterji Thakur stood at his desk, a cane in his right hand. "Ah, if it isn't the brilliant, the most famous, *the* Ella Durand here to see me at last."

Ella's heart froze as her eyes combed over him. "Are you okay?" He wore a long tunic and a gorgeous pearl-laden turban, in his usual vibrant colors. But there were more creases around his eyes, a few silver streaks disrupted the pitch black of his beard, and his hands held a tiny tremor. Her mind replayed the terrible night she, Jason, and Brigit found him in that cage, bent over, bruised and in pain. Her anger at Gia hardened even more and made her wonder how he could've ever been friends with a person who'd do something like that. She still didn't have the courage to ask him how he became an Ace when he was her age in the first place.

"Healing slowly, but I think the cane makes me look quite dapper, don't you agree?" He did a little twirl, then motioned for her to take the seat across from him. "Have a little chai with me." He lifted a tea tray and slid it between them.

Ella plopped into the chair.

Masterji Thakur lit a tiny fire under a teapot. A dish of spices floated up and dumped themselves into the teakettle net. She spied ginger, cardamom, cloves, peppercorns, star anise, and a cinnamon stick. The scent stretched between them as the water boiled. Her heart started to slow.

"I have so much to tell you." Ella inched forward in her chair. "About the—"

Masterji Thakur put his hand in the air. "One second." He plucked a tiny satchel from the tray and spilled the contents on his desk. He waved his hands over them, and they sparked and lifted high overhead. He whispered, "Chupana." The spices exploded, the scent and color engulfing them in a glittering canopy.

"How . . . wow . . . what is that?" She gazed around as the beautiful spices pulsed.

His kind eyes found hers. "Lots of listening ears in this place. Any eavesdroppers will hear us merely discussing the weather. It really is quite snowy." He gazed up at the skywell in his room and smiled. "You'll learn all about protective veil incants this year with Dr. Goldblum. Now, taste this delicious chai and tell me everything about your glorious summer."

Ella nodded, still in awe. He poured her a cup. She took slow, careful sips. The tea soothed her, almost like it knew she needed comforting after the disappointment with her stapler.

"As you were saying . . ." He motioned.

Ella rattled off all the details of her summer, and what she and Reagan discovered at the Griotary.

"The griots couldn't accept that my great-grandfather Jean-Michel Durand would've ever had anything to do with Marvellers. He was one of the most important early Conjurors, helping our people fortify their neighborhoods and protect themselves from Fewels," she reported.

"No one believed me when I said it at your discipline hearing," he reminded her.

"My parents don't even want to talk about it."

"Given how invested Jean-Michel was in Conjure communities, it does feel strange . . . or a little out of character. I'd be asking similar questions about why he'd want to send Conjure folk into the skies. It is very curious indeed." Masterji Thakur rubbed his beard.

"The griots said that he disappeared, and no one knows what happened," Ella added.

"Do you believe them?" he asked.

"The blueprints have me questioning everything."

"It's good to have an inquisitive nature." He poured milk into his tea.

"Not if your mama is Aubrielle Durand."

He chuckled quietly, then went solemn. "I'm afraid we'll have to return those blueprints soon."

Panic shot through Ella. "But . . . I still need to study them and see if the architect left anything Conjure-related behind . . . like more than the blueprints themselves."

"With the Tricentennial happening, the Headmarvellers—and the world—will be pontificating about the greatness of the Arcanum. They'll want to parade those blueprints about. Remind our world of its achievements. There's an exhibit arriving soon. The artifact will be added, and the whole thing will make its victory lap through the Marvellian cities this year."

"When? And why can't the fake ones work? They have so far."

He riffled through official-looking papers. "They won't hold up to scrutiny, I'm afraid. We've gotten lucky so far. The exhibit arrives . . . on Halloween."

She gulped. It was already the end of September. She didn't have much time left. She'd have to work faster. "Do you think something bad happened to him?"

Masterji Thakur inched his tunic collar down where the branded *M* still scarred his clavicle.

The Muzzle.

The sight of it again made Ella's heart seize.

"The things . . ." He cleared his throat. Ella braced for the strangled sound he'd made last year when they attempted to discuss Conjure history at the Arcanum. He took a sip of chai. "The things I've told you are contested by the Marvellian government. Even what I said at your hearing is being challenged. Marvellian historians consider some information not okay to discuss." He swallowed and wiped his mouth. "And it is in the process . . . of . . ." He coughed. "Being erased. I don't want to alarm you, only to tell you the truth . . . or as much of it as I can. Later this school year, I will be facing a government inquiry that will either allow me to have this"—he tapped his neck—"removed or require that it be left permanently."

Ella's stomach flipped. Was this all her fault? Had she caused this with all her questions—or even her presence? Could she help fix it? She started to speak, but her words lodged in her throat too.

"I may have to leave the Arcanum depending on the outcome," he said with a long sigh.

"But you can't!" Ella almost shouted.

His eyes softened. "I am just as fond of you as you are of me. I would not be going willingly; I'll have you know that. And I'd leave with a bang!" He laughed to himself, but Ella couldn't find humor in any of this. She'd be losing her favorite teacher, her mentor, the one person at the Arcanum that made sure she never felt out of place.

She balled her fist and struck Masterji Thakur's desk. The

teacups rattled. "All the things you told me are true. I know it—and I'm going to prove it! I'm going to tell everyone."

He patted her hand. "My inquisitive Ella, I have no doubt you could solve life's greatest mysteries if you put your mind to it. But in this world, the truth is malleable. There are some who look at blue sky and want the world to say it's green because there's power in getting people to follow you without question . . . even if it's a lie."

Talk of power caused Ella's thoughts to turn back to Gia. She bit her bottom lip, wanting to ask a question she knew she wasn't supposed to ask.

"Out with it," he said.

"How . . . ?"

"Yes? You know you can ask me anything, and if I can answer it, I will do my best." He took another sip of chai.

"How could you be friends with *her*?" The question felt hot and disrespectful on her tongue.

He rubbed his beard. "I knew this question would eventually come." He inhaled. "We aren't always the same people we are when we're twelve." He winked at her. "And when I first got to the Arcanum, I was ostracized, an outsider, much like you. South Asian Marvellers struggled to be accepted, and instead of being more like you—attempting to build bridges and understanding—I got angry. I wanted power to make the hurt go away. I wanted to fit in. The Aces—"

The word made her jump. He smiled at her.

"It's just a word," he reminded her. "You need not be afraid."

Ella nodded.

"They gave me a group. Protection. Belonging. People who said they cared, said they'd do something about the bullying.

And most of all, they, *we*, became feared. No one messed with me anymore. I'm not justifying any of our behavior, and I wish kids—and frankly, adults too—didn't feel the need to do this. Gia was—"

A heavy knock rattled the room.

He waved his hand in the air and muttered, "Shanti!" The spice canopy dissolved, leaving behind the most delectable scent. "We shall have to resume our conversation soon, it seems." He stood. "Come in."

Headmarveller Rivera appeared in the doorway, her papel picado a ring of sunshine around her head. Her cane sparkled. "Mitha, we have another student complaining about a weak marvel and a nosebleed—" She jumped after noticing Ella. "I didn't see you there, dearest Ella." Headmarveller Rivera smiled down at her. "I hope you're settling into Year Two."

"A weak marvel?" Ella asked, curious.

"Never you mind that. I came to catch up with Masterji Thakur. Would you excuse us?"

Ella wanted desperately to like her and to be liked by her, but deep down, she knew Headmarveller Rivera had secrets. Behind Headmarveller Rivera's constant smile was something she didn't want Ella to know.

Ella quickly slipped out of Masterji Thakur's lair and into the hallway. Her pulse raced as she hurried back down to the first floor, a determination in each step she took.

She would solve the puzzle of the Arcanum blueprints and prove to the world that Conjurors had always belonged here, and that Masterji Thakur shouldn't have to leave the Institute.

She wouldn't let them tell more lies.

AN ANGRY WALKER

You're the last person I expected to hear from." Gia sat across from the Grand High Walker himself, Sebastien Durand, in Rameau Billiards Hall. He didn't wear his signature skull-rimmed top hat tonight. He could almost blend in with the Marvellers, his conjure marks expertly hidden by a tailored suit, but he had the type of power that radiated like a sun. A reminder of the burn you'd receive if you crossed him. "Seems you're still making good use of the travel coins I provided."

His handsome face remained expressionless, and she noticed that both he and his pesky child Ella shared the same intense gaze. A waitress set a drink before him, and he cracked his knuckles before tasting it. "I'm here to warn you."

Gia's eyebrows lifted. She wasn't often surprised. "About what? Have you seen an ill omen in my future?"

"My offices of spirits told me about your intentions. Your plans." He sucked his teeth.

"I don't know what you're talking about." Gia made sure to sound clueless about his gift of communing with ghosts. "Your dead?"

"My ancestors," he corrected.

"They're telling you what now?" Gia tried not to laugh as his voice deepened with frustration.

"That you plan to harm my daughter because of what happened last June."

Gia let his accusation stretch between them as the angry vein in Sebastien's forehead flared and his frustration rose. "Do you know what she did? How she ruined my enterprise?"

"You were keeping Masterji Thakur against his will," he reminded her. "Do you make that a habit?"

"You shouldn't throw rocks." She smiled as he gritted his teeth. "There are people who know about your past. Things that might lose you the powerful title Grand High Walker."

"You don't know anything about me other than what you've read in *The Conjure Picayune*," he spat. "Or one of the dozen Marvellian newspapers printing their lies."

Gia smiled. She loved when she knew something others claimed she didn't. He had no idea that his very own sister-in-law, his wife's long-lost twin, was one of her most trustworthy Aces and best friends. Celeste Baptiste had told her all she needed to know about this powerful man. "I know, in your younger days, that you went looking for answers in the skies and that the Marvellian government tortured you . . . and that's why you wanted to be Grand High Walker."

He cleared his throat.

"I know you were threatened. That's how Marvellers do their bidding. What did they say they'd do? The Muzzle? Imprisonment in the Cards of Deadly Fate? Take your memories?"

His eyes narrowed.

"You're too powerful for that, though, aren't you? Your dead would help." She licked her lips. "Ah, worse, is it? Must've been their favorite punishment . . . to strip you of your gifts, all but turning you into a bird with its wings clipped."

Sebastien's jaw clenched, and she knew she'd uncovered the right answer.

"So you sent your child instead. How clever. She'd be a spirited distraction while you worked behind the scenes."

"You don't know what you're talking about." His voice lowered. "My child is not a pawn in some game."

"Oh, but I think she is. Your pawn, rather." She leaned forward. "And your wife would hate this sort of information . . . probably the entire Conjure world would roast you if they discovered it."

Sebastien loosened his tie. "Are you threatening me?"

Gia smiled. She had him just where she wanted him now. "Not if I don't have to. I'm not like my fellow Marvellian counterparts, which I think you know."

"I'm done with this conversation," he said. "You know what you did to that Arcanum teacher and why my daughter intervened."

Gia cackled. "I will not discuss my methods and my relationships with my former Aces with you. They're my business."

"Well, Ella is mine."

"She shouldn't have done what she did."

"She's a child."

Gia let her eyes burn into his. "I worked hard on the elixir she destroyed. She owes me a debt—and debts require payment." She drummed her fingers on the table. "Shouldn't I be compensated for my loss? What will you do to make this right? To protect your daughter—and your secrets?"

An angry silence crackled between them. Gia could wait him out.

A gamekeeper clicked on a newsreel and the wall illuminated with the *Marvellian Times'* late-night report. One of the four presidential candidates for the summer election appeared. The sight of him knocked the wind out of her.

The image of a man from her past stared at her. Slicked back, almost paper-white hair and a smile that could convince anyone to walk to the very edge of Betelmore and leap into the Cloud Nests. His voice, once a distant memory, grated over her skin. The projection of his cold eyes seemed to find her sitting there.

Johan Fenris Knudsen I.

His political slogan flashed—*A Time for Marvellian Greatness Is Here!*

"Gia . . . ," Sebastien said.

"Gia!"

She ignored him; the current row between her and Sebastien felt like a distant memory as she watched this old enemy trying to convince the Marvellian public to vote in his favor.

Sebastien slammed his hand on the table, yanking her out of her stupor. The whole billiards hall stared in their direction.

Gia pulled down her veil. "I have to go. If you don't want Ella harmed, then make me a deal worth my while; otherwise, I will collect what I'm owed in whatever way I see fit."

★—★—★— **STARPOST** —★—★—★

Ella,

   Did you find out anything about you-know-what yet? Tell me everything. I've been researching at the Griotary again too. There's a lot of things happening here. People upset about you returning to that school and exposing your conjure gifts. Read the *Conjure Picayune* article I included.

   I'm worried. Write to me.

Love,
Reagan

★—★—★— **STARPOST**—★—★—★

Little Conjuror,

   I'm still watching you.

The Conjure Picayune

THE TROUBLE IS COMING FROM INSIDE THE HOUSE

OP-ED by Kenyatta Gibson

The *real* threat facing the Conjure folk around the world isn't Fewels who can't hear the rhythm of our rootwork or see the fruits of our spells . . . or even the Marvellers who took to the skies to selfishly ensure their everlasting peace, leaving us behind . . . It is our own doing us in.

The Durands of the New Orleans Delegation, and the Grand High Walker himself, elected by all Conjurors, introduced this trouble by sending their child into the mouth of a beast, and her aunt too, the infamous Sera Baptiste. They're spilling our secrets, exposing our conjure work to others. Even letting their divine light outside for everybody to see. It's unnatural to expose it. What's going to happen when there's Marvellers parading around with conjure marks like they've earned them . . . like they understand where the roots *really* come from? Or crossing into our Underworld as outsiders? Or, even, being able to steal—our memories? Our gifts?

What will we do then?

Now more Conjure delegations have sent their kids up into the skies to follow in Ella's very dangerous footsteps. Lord help us!

★—★—★— **STARPOST**—★—★—★

My Dearest Goddaughter,

I'm so sorry I missed our appointment. Everything here has been so . . . let's just call it complicated. One of my countless curriculum meetings went long and I couldn't get word to you. My apologies if you were waiting for me.

I'll send another date for us to have tea. I can't wait to hug you and get a good look at you.

Love,
Aunt Sera

P.S.: I saw your note about your conjure feeling weird. Mine does too. I think it's the cold up here. Let me know if you want a sizzle stone to carry in your pocket. Might help keep you warm.

CHAPTER SEVEN
ARCANUM VERSIONS

A snowy September tumbled into an even snowier October. Ella had been saddled with double the assignments from last year and found it hard to make progress on anything other than homework, reading, and projects. At every turn she'd felt thwarted from her investigation of the blueprints with mile long to-do lists, more classes to get to (and the new building shifts making the journey longer), and distractions around her stapler not glowing. All of it took up so much space in her head that she started to wonder if the Institute itself didn't want her nosing around about the blueprints, and maybe it conspired to keep her occupied.

But today she met a still sleepy Brigit and a very hungry Jason outside the Arcanum menagerie, determined to find out something, anything, to help her unravel this mystery.

"I'm missing the American breakfast cart," Jason whined as they walked through the archway.

"Your pancakes will be there tomorrow," Ella replied.

"It's really the bacon I want. Chef Oshiro said that cart will only be out on Wednesdays."

"This is more important than your grumbling stomach." Ella guided him forward, ignoring his groans.

They climbed the stairs, ducking around a sleeping gryphon. At the end of a tiny passageway, Jason's new hideaway loft felt like a cozy closet with two large windows—one overlooking Head-marveller MacDonald's Cloud Loch and waterhorse, Edi, and the other, a great view into the inner workings of the menagerie itself. Unfortunately, it smelled like the animal habitats below too.

"It stinks in here." Brigit waved a hand around.

"A natural smell," he corrected. "You'll get used to it."

Ella's ears filled with a crackle and pop. A massive bluish-black bird sat on a nest of tangled lightning above them. The fine hairs on her arms stood up. A warning. She felt the current. "What's . . ."

"It's Izulu, the impundulu. A lightning bird." He greeted her. "Remember last year, she helped us? Told us the original architect made the restricted lift. She's the oldest resident of the Arcanum. Used to be a presidential bird. The protector of the first Marvellian leader. Then she came here to retire. She's lived a long time. Over two hundred years."

Ella bowed her head and thanked the bird for helping them. She wondered if Izulu could help them again.

Lightning bolts stretched over her feathers like a stellacity current.

Brigit plopped down as far from the impundulu as possible, and Ella and Jason sat in front of her.

"Okay, y'all ready?" Ella plucked the tube from her satchel.

Everything tumbled out: all the things Masterji Thakur had told her, the details about their trip to the Founder's Room last year, the court case against him, the reminder about the Muzzle. Ella tried to keep the sadness out of her voice because she didn't want to cry today, not when she had a plan, not when she felt like she could fix it. "The government doesn't want him talking about those things."

"Why didn't any newspapers mention what he said at your hearing?" Brigit's brow furrowed. "It's, like, a huge thing—and they reported everything else."

"I bet they censored it. Marvellers erase what they don't want others to know," Jason said. "Granny Eugene said so."

"But how can you keep people from saying things—or thinking about something?" Brigit asked.

"By making them forget," Jason said. "My brother Allen said there are whole government jobs where people delete things from newsreels, documents, and some say . . . even conversations. There are people with marvels that can pluck a thought straight out of your brain."

Both Ella and Brigit gaped at Jason. Ella couldn't even fathom this. What about someone's privacy? Were they not allowed to think what they wanted? Is this why her mama and papa couldn't really remember what Masterji Thakur had said about the architect at her discipline hearing last year?

"That's scary," Brigit said.

Ella gently removed the blueprints from their tube. "More reason for us to find out what happened to the architect. I need to prove to my mama and the world that Conjurors were here, that they were always supposed to be here. Especially because they think Masterji Thakur is lying."

The thick iron-blue paper unfurled between the trio, then lifted just off the ground as if it knew the room was a bit too dusty for its liking. The blueprints' subtle blue glow washed over the loft. The paper flickered like a stellacity bulb powering on. It started to fill in: each miniature tower, every trolley, the various session rooms, and all the dorms (even the ones she could never see).

"Whoa," Brigit whispered.

Jason's eyes opened as wide as possible. Even each animal in the loft paused to look.

A word crawl appeared over the paper: VERSION 251.

Ella's heart raced. This hadn't happened when she'd inspected it back at home. Had she done something wrong?

The blueprints sparked. The towers shifted, moving to opposite corners. The Arcanum library traveled north. The dining hall headed south. The Arcanum courtyard stretched through the center. Chinese fu dogs appeared at the entrance. A glass shell enclosed parts of the grounds, and a soft snow began to fall.

Ella gazed up at the skywell to find flurries. "It's . . . it's . . ." The words wouldn't form in her mouth.

"Updating," Jason finished her sentence.

The surprise of it caught Ella off guard.

"How?" Brigit asked.

Jason leaned in. "It's so cool." He craned his head. "I've never seen Marvellian paper like this. Not something that could hold on to so . . . so much."

"That's because it's conjure paper," Ella said, then sang the spell to reveal its scribe: *Reveal your secrets, tried and true; my heart is here to hear them too.*"

The blueprints stretched, then the silhouette of a Black man projected from the paper. They gazed up at his stoic face. Long, neat locs hit his shoulders, a short top hat rested on his head, a pencil peeked out behind his ear, and tiny, distinguished spectacles sat on his nose.

Jason inched closer. "He's got an owl on his shoulder."

"His companion," Ella said with pride.

"And he looks like your dad," Brigit remarked.

"He's my papa's great-granddad but, like, many generations back," Ella said.

"Will anyone find out that these are missing?" Brigit reached for the projections, letting the blue light wash over her fingers.

"Masterji Thakur helped with that. But he said I'll have to return before Halloween because of the Tricentennial celebrations."

Jason squinted at the blueprints. "Why would they hold on to these? Especially if someone could unlock the secret architect like you just did?"

"Well, they probably didn't think there'd ever be any Conjurors at the school," Brigit replied. "So, no one here would've known how to do what Ella did."

"Right. But there's got to be something else," he added. "Like why keep them right here for someone to find?"

Ella stood and paced around the small space. "You think it's not real?"

"It's definitely *real*. I just think these are hiding more than just the architect. I bet the founders had no idea Jean-Michel made these on conjure paper and left this signature behind. How would they? Marvellers are clueless when it comes to conjure. Think they're better and don't pay attention," Jason said. "I bet it has all the different versions of the Arcanum. Can I try one thing, Ella?"

Nerves buzzed through Ella. "I don't want to mess anything up."

"It's a conjure spell my mom taught my dad. Helps him keep all his map versions in one place. She called it a weird word. A palimp . . . palimp . . ."

"A palimpsest." Ella remembered Masterji Thakur telling her how history was like a palimpsest manuscript, a layered book in which words have been written on top of others.

Brigit gawked at her until she explained it.

Jason leaned over the blueprints. "I have a feeling there's more here. I promise the spell doesn't do anything bad."

Ella gulped, then nodded. She pressed her hands together to keep them from trembling. If something happened to these, her only proof would be gone.

Jason stood up, the blueprints floating near his waist. He took a deep breath and sang. His voice was beautiful. She'd never heard this spell or him sing before. She swelled with surprise as he tapped into his Conjure roots; her bubbling nerves subsided.

The projection of Jean-Michel Durand disappeared, and another word crawl appeared. The numbers looked like huge buttons begging to be pressed.

Ella leaned closer. "What's happening?"

The word crawl flashed.

"This is probably every change the Arcanum ever made or will make in the future." Jason pointed at different ones.

VERSION 29.

VERSION 133.

VERSION 8.

"Bet we could see the *original* version. His first design," Jason said.

"Maybe there'd be more evidence of conjure? Something still around to prove that the school had been meant for both Conjure and Marvellian students together." Ella's ideas rattled out.

"What do you think will happen if we press one?" Brigit reached a finger out.

"Wait!" Ella's nerves got the best of her. There had to be secret protections on this valuable historical document, right? Could she mess it up . . . or worse, somehow destroy it? What if they all got caught—and in trouble? "What if there's some sort of alarm?"

"We'll never know if we don't try it," Brigit said.

Ella's stomach roiled. She thought about what she'd do if the worst happened: They'd push one of those buttons and an Arcanum doctor would come marching into Jason's loft, finding them with the stolen blueprints, and they'd be in trouble. So much trouble the three of them would probably be on the first sky-ferry home with expulsion letters. Ella's heart thundered, but her curiosity beat harder.

"We have to," Brigit said.

The trio exchanged tense glances, each waiting for the other to reach out and push a flickering button.

"You do it!" Brigit said to Jason.

"No, Ella, you do it," Jason replied.

Worries threatened to consume her. She felt more than afraid. Petrified. Her fingers trembled.

Ella wiped her clammy palms on her mantle, then held her breath as she reached out. Jason guided her hand and nodded with encouragement. The word crawl felt thick and tangible, not like the flickering projections of the buildings below, as she pressed it. The button click echoed. The noise of it hit her in the chest as she scrolled back to the very first version of the Arcanum Training Institute for Marvelous and Uncanny Endeavors.

"Together," Ella said, eyes fixed on the number one.

The three of them put their fingers side by side, and Jason counted down.

"Three . . ."

"Two . . ."

"One . . ."

They pressed it at the same time, then leaped back. The blueprints writhed, their blue glow turning red. Ella gasped. The word crawl reappeared with a message:

UNAUTHORIZED LOCATION DETECTED.

RETURN TO FOUNDER'S ROOM TO PROCEED!

They exchanged panicked glances. The image of a tiny elevator blinked three times on the blueprints.

"The restricted lift," Ella said.

"It's beside the Touch Lounge," Jason said.

An announcement-balloon sounded from the belly of the menagerie, reminding trainees to get to their first morning sessions on time.

Ella gulped. "We have to find the Founder's Room again—as soon as possible!"

CHAPTER EIGHT
DEEPEST, DARKEST SECRETS

After curfew, Ella obsessively pored over the blueprints again. Feste paced across her quilt, staring up at them too and waiting for Brigit to come back from wherever she'd gone.

"You see there"—Ella pointed for Feste—"that's the restricted lift I mentioned. We've got to take it to the Founder's Room." Ella explained what happened the first time the elevator had accidentally taken her, Brigit, and Jason there, and then the second time she'd gone with Masterji Thakur to get the blueprints in the first place.

"But I don't see that room anywhere." Feste waved his tiny hands in the air. "Where could it be?"

Ella didn't have an answer. She hadn't been able to locate the Founder's Room yet either, but she felt like maybe the Institute looked so different she couldn't recognize everything. Like her eyes were playing tricks on her. She perched over the blueprints, determination buzzing through her. She needed help.

"Where's Brigit?" she asked.

"With Siobhan in the library—" He covered his mouth like he was pressing a secret back in.

"Homework?" Ella asked, mostly proud of Brigit if that was the case.

Feste shook his head. "I'm not allowed to say."

Ella felt a hot pinch in her stomach. What was Brigit doing—and why couldn't she know? She thought best friends weren't supposed to have secrets. And it felt surprising that she was hanging with Siobhan. Were they best friends now too?

The door snapped open. Both Ella and Feste startled. Brigit barreled in, arms full of paper and trailed by an angry automat.

"All right, all right. I know. I shouldn't have stayed out past curfew," Brigit replied.

Ella scrambled to cover the blueprints. The bottle tree lowered its branches, the leaves providing cover. Ella and Feste watched through a gap in the foliage.

The automat shook its metallic finger at Brigit. "You've still earned a demerit for being out after curfew and one for trying to cause me bodily harm."

"You don't have a real body—how could it have hurt?"

The automat scoffed. It presented her with two blinking demerit cards, then puttered out.

Brigit slammed the door. Another demerit slid under it. She grunted.

The bottle tree receded.

"You okay?" Ella asked.

Brigit jumped. "Yeah, fine." She raced to her desk and shoved papers into the top drawer.

Ella wanted to ask what those were, but one look from Feste

and she gulped down the question. "What happened? Where were you?"

"Nothing and nowhere," she grumbled.

A lie. Why was her best friend hiding things from her?

Ella gazed at Feste again. He shrugged sheepishly before climbing off Ella's bed and sauntering over to Brigit. He hugged her leg, and she lifted him into her arms. They whispered while Ella's stomach knotted.

"They're always watching me," Brigit complained. "I swear Dean Nabokova hates me."

Ella bit her bottom lip. She wanted to press Brigit for more answers, but a phrase Mama always said drifted into her head: *If someone doesn't want to tell you something, then it's none of your business.*

Brigit's eyes found the blueprints. "Find anything new?"

"No," Ella admitted.

"What do you think the original version of the Arcanum will show?" Brigit changed into her pajamas.

Ella vomited out all her theories: a conjure pharmacy as part of the elixir labs, a conjure garden near the greenhouse, and even maybe a door to the Underworld to work on crossing. Saying her ideas aloud made them feel more possible. "I hope it's big enough that no one can lie about it."

Brigit climbed into bed. "We have to find something so they can't try to explain it all away."

A soft knock echoed.

They froze. Maybe it was Mrs. Francesca with a lights-out warning.

The knock came again.

"One second," Brigit called out, while Ella rolled up the blueprints and eased them back into their container.

The person knocked a third time, then Ella heard her name from a voice that didn't sound like Mrs. Francesca. Ella handed the bottle tree the tube. "Keep it safe!" she directed, then bounded off the bed.

Ella and Brigit eased the door open together.

No one was there.

They craned to look out.

"Psst!" came a voice.

Ella spotted Abina hiding around the corner.

Abina waved them forward. "Come on!"

"Where?" Ella whispered.

"What's happening?" Brigit asked.

"A game in Noémie's room." Abina grinned.

Ella bristled. "But she doesn't like me."

"That's just the way her face is. She sent me to get the two of you," Abina assured them.

Ella and Brigit exchanged a glance.

"Might as well," Brigit whispered, to Ella's surprise.

They tiptoed behind Abina. She knocked a rhythm on the door, then it eased open, and Ella saw Siobhan's panicked face.

Siobhan surveyed the hall before letting them inside.

"What's going on?" Ella asked.

"Another one of Noémie's games," Siobhan answered with a shrug.

Ella gazed around. The room looked so different than hers. Three beds were tucked in opposite corners. A shamrock quilt blanketed Siobhan's bed, and her brownie's habitat lurked on her headboard. A giant mural of the Eiffel Tower loomed over Noémie's nook. And lastly, one bed sat on a high platform above the rest with a beautiful canopy of woven blankets, and a clay chiminea oven blazed bright beside it, and Ella knew that was for Luci.

In the center, a gaggle of girls sat in a circle around Noémie, who held a large basin in her lap. Ella spotted many girls from the other dorm, Vermillion Bird, as well as Anh, Luz, Samaira, Lian, and Clare. Her stomach twisted as they walked closer. What were they up to? And would they be nice?

Noémie smiled at Ella and motioned for them to join the circle. "We were just starting." Her voice was full of unexpected warmth, catching Ella off guard. Maybe she'd misjudged Noémie after all.

The other girls made space, and Ella eased down beside Anh. Clare dumped out a satchel of candy. The girls scrambled to grab Marveller-bars and milk dragon eggs.

Noémie clapped her hands. "We're going to play I-Spy-A-Secret."

"What's that?" Brigit asked.

Clare rolled her eyes. "Only the best game *ever*. Everyone plays it."

"It's the best when you use your marvels," Lian added. "Are we doing that?"

Noémie grinned. "Of course."

"Can someone explain already?" Brigit barked.

Everyone giggled. Even though Ella needed an explanation of the rules too, she wished Brigit would soften a little.

Abina cleared her throat. "Okay, so you have to guard your

deepest, darkest secret. Use your marvel to block people from discovering it."

Ella squirmed. She wanted to ask how to use her marvel that way, but she felt too embarrassed. They hadn't learned protective incants in Dr. Goldblum's class yet, but everyone else seemed to already know how to use them. She felt like a sitting duck, her secrets about to be plucked right out of her. What if everyone found out about the blueprints? What if everyone found out something was off with her conjure? Could she trust anyone besides Brigit in this room?

Ella and Brigit made eye contact. Ella felt Brigit's body stiffen.

"I don't want to play—" Brigit started to stand.

Noémie and Clare laughed.

"Have something to hide?" Clare teased.

"No," Brigit lied.

"Everyone has secrets." Noémie set the basin on the floor.

Ella held Brigit's hand. She knew they should get up and go back to their room, but part of her wanted to belong with these girls despite the risk. She still couldn't believe Noémie had even invited her. Part of her liked that. "Let's see what happens. We can run out of here if we need to," she whispered, and Brigit nodded.

Noémie opened a small box. Ella noticed strange vials of liquid. They reminded her of the bottles she'd seen in Gia's workshop.

"These perfumes will unlock your deepest and darkest secrets." Noémie smiled. "Scent is a powerful experience. Similar to music with notes. It can tell a story. It can preserve your fondest memory."

"How does it work?" Anh leaned forward.

Noémie winked. "You'll see." She flashed one vial in the air before uncorking and pouring it into the basin. Thick purple clouds exploded around them. Everyone oohed. Then she thumbed the next one, adding it to the bowl. A thick plume of blue shot through the purple like a gorgeous peacock feather. The last vial made the concoction turn white like a ribbon of smoky snow. "This recipe is made to unlock the hidden. The perfume will re-create a secret from one of you in this room. You'll see it as clear as a newsreel projection."

"Who's first?" Abina asked.

"Whomever the perfume chooses," Noémie replied as the thick clouds stretched between the members of the group. "I can't control it. It has a mind of its own."

Brigit yanked Ella's hand. "We should go *now*."

But Ella couldn't move, her eyes transfixed, her nose too infatuated by the scent to move an inch.

The perfume began to storm. Thunderous lightning and tiny rumbles made the girls squeal. It reminded Ella of a firecracker.

"Shh, or we'll get caught," Clare reminded them.

The room went silent. Luci checked the hall. "No sign of Mrs. Francesca."

"Good." Noémie turned back to her perfume cloud, waving her hands over it, making it grow bigger and bigger. "I wonder who will be first. It'll latch on to the strongest secret that's here in the room."

Ella felt Brigit gulp.

The perfume cloud made its way around the circle as if examining each girl.

Don't stop at us, Ella thought, willing it away. *Keep moving.*

The beautiful vapor paused right in front of them. Ella looked at Brigit. Guilt flooded her as she watched Brigit's eyes glaze over with tears. She started to stand, but the clouds rumbled and wrapped themselves around Anh.

Anh coughed and sputtered, waving her hands around. The perfume transformed. Ella watched as gorgeous, tropical trees appeared, then a long stretch of sand and Anh under a beach bungalow writing starpost after starpost with a big smile on her face.

The girls giggled as the name Jonathan Yang appeared on the envelope.

Anh squealed. "Make it stop!"

"Do you have a little crush?" Abina teased.

Clare made kissy noises. Lian laughed.

"Use your egg. Trap the perfume like you'd do a dream or a nightmare," Siobhan urged.

"I don't know how to yet." Anh scrambled, removing a tiny egg from the pocket of her robe. She jammed her eyes shut. Ella held her breath as she watched her try to pull the perfume into one of her paddy eggs. She knew Anh, a fellow Paragon of Vision, could hatch dreams and nightmares, but she didn't know exactly how her marvel worked. "It's not working." Panic made Anh's voice wobbly. "I can't feel the egg. I can't feel—"

"Admit your undying love for Jonathan Yang, Anh. The perfume doesn't lie," Noémie interrupted.

Ella didn't like the way Noémie grinned as if she enjoyed watching Anh struggle. Goose bumps covered Ella's skin, and she put a hand over her nose. She also didn't like how powerful this perfume was. What else could it do?

Anh's face went pale. "My head hurts. Please stop."

The perfume thickened around her. No matter how many times she swatted at her secret, it re-formed.

"You're just embarrassed," Clare replied.

"Just tell the truth," Lian goaded.

A knot of worry formed in Ella's stomach. Something felt wrong. Beads of sweat coated Anh's forehead, and she swayed left and right as the perfume engulfed her. Ella sat upright; she could barely see Anh's body.

"Maybe we should stop," Ella said.

"Yeah," Abina replied. "Anh looks sick."

"It'll move on," Noémie exclaimed with glee. "Give it another second."

The tension in the room crackled. Ella's pulse raced. The girls chanted: "Secrets, secrets, secrets!"

The perfume cloud finally lifted. Anh's eyes fluttered. Blood streamed from her nose and she crumpled.

LEAKED

TO: [redacted]

FROM: Automat #19

Trainees E. D. and B. E. were seen leaving the dining hall early and riding the Ruby trolley. The transcript of their conversation is attached.

CHAPTER NINE
THE MEMORY-CASK

The next morning, Ella and Brigit lurked in the Touch Tower entrance, waiting on Jason so they could go find the RESTRICTED LIFT. They should've been headed in the opposite direction to study hall, but the latest development with the blueprints couldn't wait. They had to get to the Founder's Room and unlock the original version of the Arcanum Training Institute before any of the Arcanum instructors found out. Ella swore with every bit of Conjure in her that the architect was trying to tell her something through the blueprints.

"You think Anh's going to be all right?" Brigit asked.

"She's still in the infirmary. At breakfast, I overheard Clare say that Anh's allergic to perfume. Everyone's mad she didn't say anything," Ella said. Last night she'd had terrible dreams about that perfume cloud and Anh fainting. She sent a get-well-soon starpost, but her stomach had been unsettled all morning thinking about how she could've done something in the moment. Stood up for Anh, stopped the whole thing.

Jason ran toward them out of breath. One of the rotties, Brownie, perched on his shoulder, smiling at them.

"Glad to see she delivered the note and didn't just eat the praline I gave her." Ella bopped Brownie's nose before the rottie tucked herself into Jason's mantle.

"We've got ten minutes before we have to be in study hall." Brigit pointed at a nearby clock-lantern. "I refuse to get detention again and be forced to scoop poop. I already have too many demerits. I'll die, I swear."

The trio raced beneath the heliogram of founder Indira Patel the Brave and her floating daggers. They lied to every passing automat who asked them what they were doing and ducked out of view of the mischief-balloons when they came too close. They held their breath passing the lapidary labs and dance studios, praying not to be spotted.

As they approached the Touch Lounge, a copper stood in between them and their destination. They froze. The copper perched over three Level Ones struggling with nosebleeds.

"You think she'll stop us?" Brigit crossed her arms over her chest.

"Hope not. She seems too busy anyways," Ella said.

"It's like last night with Anh," Brigit said. "Her nosebleed."

Jason looked puzzled, and Ella quickly explained Noémie's game of secrets.

"My sister used to play that during her boring sleepovers. I used to snoop. Her best friend Nour has a water marvel, so they'd use that," Jason said. "But it never made anyone sick. Embarrassed them mostly."

Ella tried to think through everything that had happened last night again. What could've really made Anh ill? Perfume felt harmless.

"I had a nosebleed too. Remember that day I was late to Dr. Yohannes's class? I smelled something weird after getting off the Pearl trolley. My nose was all itchy, and I got a headache so bad I had to sit down. Then I couldn't hear the rotties. Like my kindred marvel had turned off for a few seconds."

"Hmm." Ella's brain buzzed. "When I met with Masterji Thakur, Headmarveller Rivera showed up, and she mentioned weak marvels and nosebleeds before she realized I was there. She shooed me out so fast."

"Weak marvels?" Brigit's eyebrow lifted.

"But it went away," he said. "And I feel fine now. I can hear the animals again. My dad thinks it was the headache."

"My nose bled too," Brigit said. "When my marvel went away . . ." She swallowed hard, and Ella could tell she was reliving what happened with Gia and that marvel-stealing elixir all over again.

Ella rubbed Brigit's shoulder. Headaches, nosebleeds, weak marvels. What was happening? Could something be making them sick?

But Ella put her questions to the side as they moved closer to the copper. Her feet became antsy. The heaviness of the blueprint tube in her satchel a constant reminder of what they needed to do.

"Sit with your head forward," the copper said. "That should help."

Ella watched as the trickles of blood freckled the kids' white mantles. All the confusion made her heart race a little. Could this happen to her? Was it only a matter of time? Something strange was already happening to her conjure. Would her nose bleed too? Was it all connected? But she wasn't ready to confront that or talk about it out loud just yet . . . especially with Brigit and Jason. That would make it feel too real.

"There's no way we're getting past them," Brigit whispered.

"Just a few more steps," Jason replied.

As they eased forward, Ella thought up excuses in case they were questioned. She'd tell the copper Brigit had left her satchel.

A clock-lantern floated overhead, reminding them of the time.

"We just need a distraction." Jason lifted the sleepy rottie from his mantle hood. "You up for a task, little one?"

Jason nuzzled Brownie's nose, promised a mountain of sweets, then set her on the ground. They waited while Brownie gathered speed, running through the hall before leaping in the air, bouncing off the wall, and landing right on the copper's hat.

The copper screeched. Her wolf barked and took off to try to catch the rottie. The chaos gave Ella, Jason, and Brigit just enough time to get to the end of the hall unnoticed.

Ella spotted the RESTRICTED LIFT ahead, and her heart soared with relief. "There it is!" She ran at full speed. But as they drew closer, she noticed the door sat ajar, and its glass windows held cracks. Cobwebs stretched over its entire frame. The floor was covered with broken levers and smashed buttons.

"What happened to it?" Brigit said. "It looks . . . dead. Or at least made to look like it."

Jason bent down, inspecting every angle. "Definitely not working."

Ella panicked. What had happened to the lift? It reminded her of a wrecked Fewel car she'd seen in an alley once.

Jason's eyes found hers. "Someone wanted to make sure it couldn't be used again."

"But who?" Ella's mind raced as she tried to comb through who would do such a thing and leave it for them to discover. The Arcanum Training Institute was never dirty. The starfolk and automats kept everything in pristine condition. She didn't think anything could look this unkempt here. Why would this be left here unless someone wanted them to find it?

"I think it's the Headmarvellers," Brigit said, arms crossed. "I don't trust either of them."

"But the Headmarvellers wanted Ella here. Wanted more Conjure kids to enroll. They made sure of it," Jason said. "So, why would they do this?"

Theories exploded in Ella's head. What if someone was trying to get to things before she did? What if they were destroying her ability to find conjure objects or proof? Was this some weird game? But who would know, besides Masterji Thakur, that she was looking for it? A wave of paranoia set in. She thought of the threatening note too. She was being watched. But by whom?

An automat appeared at the end of the hall, holding up three blinking slips in its metal hand. Ella knew the cards had their names on them. They'd just earned themselves three spots in the first Saturday detention of the year courtesy of skipping study hall with Madame Madge. She'd broken her promise to Papa . . . and they were no closer to finding the Founder's Room.

It'd all been for nothing.

✦ ✷ ✦ ✷ ✦

LATER THAT AFTERNOON, BRIGIT TRIED TO CHEER ELLA UP WITH A new plan as they headed for the first Conjure class of the year.

They stumbled off the Jade trolley and climbed the stairs to the eighth floor of the Spirit Tower. Aunt Sera's Conjure Atelier had moved from the fourth floor. That entire Institute level seemed to just disappear from each building this year. "Everyone knows the number four is bad luck," Lian Wong had told them.

"Let's go to the library and ask Madame Madge if they have a record of Arcanum maps. They've got to have that, right? Kids would've needed to know how to get around," Brigit said.

"You really think they'd make a map with something *off-limits* on it?" Ella rolled her eyes as more frustration bubbled up inside her. And she wanted to add, "Plus, you've been spending a lot of time there without me and not telling me why . . . ," but she knew a fight with Brigit would only make the day worse.

"It's still a good idea," Jason replied. "And it's *something.*"

"Madame Madge has been helping me with—" Brigit swallowed the rest of her sentence, blushing.

"With what?" Ella said, her anger loose and ready to pummel Brigit.

"Nothing. It's nothing." Brigit glanced down.

Brigit's response hardened Ella even more. Now her roommate and best friend was continuing to keep secrets from her. Did she not trust her?

Ella scoffed, then marched into her aunt's Conjure Atelier. Two new bottle trees sat at the entrance, waiting to welcome those who crossed the threshold. The trees shuddered, greeting her. Echi, Aunt Sera's snake, lurked above, licking her tongue out and hissing at them.

Ella ran straight for her godmother. "Aunt Sera!"

Her godmother leaned over a long table, her hair in twists that brushed her waist, and her flowing dress kissed the top of her feet. "It's about time I got to lay eyes on you." Her face filled with joy as she hugged Ella. The warmth of her conjure marks, raised and puffy from a recent spell, no doubt, comforted Ella and helped erase her bad mood.

Aunt Sera turned to Brigit and Jason. "It's good to see you both too."

"You have desks this year." Brigit pointed at the rows of two-seaters.

"Ah, so many new rules. 'Conjure must adhere to our standards,'" she said, mimicking Headmarveller Rivera's voice. "There's a new curriculum specialist here . . . and let's say, we haven't seen eye to eye. That's why we're starting our Conjure lessons so late. It's almost mid-October, and here we are again, just like last time. I have so much ground to make up while the other teachers are well into their second units."

"You will," Ella assured her.

Bell-blimps flooded the room as if helping to chase students to their desks.

Aunt Sera waved her hands in the air. "Settle down, everyone."

Ella walked straight to the first row. Brigit slid in beside her, and Jason sat behind them, keeping a seat open for Miguel.

Ella secretly hoped that this year would be better for her godmother, and that she wouldn't have to deal with the same nonsense. Maybe now that everyone had been around both her and her aunt, the suspicions, and the questions about the Conjure Arts, would disappear.

Aunt Sera began to sing, and the candles inside her tree lanterns illuminated.

The classroom went silent with awe.

"Welcome to Conjure Arts II." Aunt Sera took roll, noting

Anh's and Pierre's absences as both in the infirmary. "Last year, we studied the origin of conjure and its emphasis on crossing. Can someone recap what I mean? Let us dust some brain cobwebs from a long summer off."

Ella's hand shot into the air like an arrow. Aunt Sera smiled down at her. "Someone who isn't my dearest goddaughter?"

Brigit raised a tentative hand, and Aunt Sera nodded at her. "It comes from crossing oceans from West Africa, and having been put under the pressure, horror, and realities of slavery, and all that followed." She gulped, then continued: "Conjurors' light, their twilight, can cross into things."

"Excellent. Can you explain more by providing us with an example?"

Brigit's cheeks pinkened. Ella nodded at her with encouragement. "They can make plants grow by crossing into their wills."

"Great job, Brigit. Can I have another volunteer to fill in what else Conjure folk can do?" Aunt Sera gazed at the other students.

Ella's hand shot in the air again.

Aunt Sera called on Abina.

"They can cross into the Underworld." Abina winked at Ella.

"More? Jason?" Aunt Sera asked.

Jason almost leaped from his chair. "They can . . . cross into people's minds."

Whispers spread.

"There has been much said about this particular Conjure talent. We will demystify it this year. Many have labeled Conjurors nosy or believe that they enter the minds of others against their will or somehow turn people into poppets and dolls to be controlled. But the mind itself is very important to Conjure folk, as we've had to exhibit mental strength to endure. Speaking of minds . . . " She pivoted on her heel and went to her worktable to retrieve a covered object. "Miguel, will you assist me?"

He raced up the aisle to stand beside her. "Please hold this." She handed him the item.

"It is often said the mind is a terrible thing to waste. Well, Conjurors believe this, literally." Aunt Sera slid the silk handkerchief off the object.

The object glowed. Gasps exploded. Ella felt the deep drumming of the crossing tug at the sight of it.

"Is that a . . . mini-grave?" Luz called out.

"Or an urn?" Samaira replied. "Or lantern?"

"A weird dollhouse!" Lian added.

"It's a crypt," Jason said.

Aunt Sera grinned. "It's all of those things and none of those things at the same time." She took the object from Miguel, thanked him, then ushered him back to his seat. "It's a memory-cask." She held the small mausoleum in her hands. A miniature version of the graves that often freckled Fewel city cemeteries with their dead aboveground. Indestructible wrought-iron curled around its frame, protecting it and beautifying it with conjure-roses.

Ella had never actually been allowed to study a memory-cask up close and had only seen her family ones tucked away in their crypt at St. Louis Cemetery No. 1. She knew Gran had prepared her own, and neither her nor Winnie were allowed in the family conjure room while she did it. Part of her didn't want to know about this particular conjure object because it meant the Conjuror was preparing for death.

"This one is mine." Aunt Sera earned a bunch of *oohs* and *aahs* from the class. "It is where all my memories, my knowledge, and my secrets live."

"They're not in your head?" Lian said. "I don't get it. How is that possible?"

"They're in both places. This is a living replica," Aunt Sera explained. "And when I pass on, it'll crystallize and house all that I know, all that I've experienced, and all that I want to share with those who are left behind. My ancestors will be able to use a spell to review all its contents anytime they need to."

"Why would anyone do this? It's so bizarre," Clare interjected. Ella cringed.

"It's so that nothing will ever be forgotten, which is useful because the past helps us navigate the present and the future. Not one story, not one memory, not one wise saying, not one experience—good or bad—is lost. Everything can be passed down in a family. Like many Marveller families save incant books with special knowledge, this is our way." Aunt Sera sang again, and the bottle trees' branches reached down to retrieve the memory-cask from her hands. The trees cradled it, slowly moving the object through the class, allowing kids to have a closer look. Ella watched their faces, how their eyes opened wide with awe, how she could feel all their questions (and fears).

"It's imbued by our ancestors and bloodline to preserve it," Aunt Sera added. "Unlike memory, it cannot be destroyed."

"Looks like it's made of bones," Lian commented.

Aunt Sera chuckled. "Maybe it's made of the figurative bones of all those who came before me. All my powerful ancestors, my offices of spirit."

"This is why my mom calls Conjure people nosy," Ella heard someone whisper. She whipped around, looking for the culprit.

Aunt Sera laughed and winked at Ella. "Indeed, Conjure folk can cross into others' minds in various ways. From mere whispers, sharing secrets and important warnings, to providing a pathway for our conjure companions." She blew a kiss at Echi high above. "Lociambulism, as it's known officially, or the mind-walk. It's not about being nosy or going into someone else's mind without permission. That would be a violation of the Conjure Creed. You have to have something of importance that belongs to the person who you're mind-walking, which functions as a token of consent."

"What does it have to do with memory-casks, though?" Luz asked.

"Great question. A Conjuror must use the mind-walk to visit a memory-cask and unearth its contents," Aunt Sera explained. "A memory-cask contains the mind of the dead person after all."

Miguel raised his hand. "How is a memory-cask made?"

"From a special ingredient—twilight stardust—that you'll learn about soon," Aunt Sera replied.

Ella thought of the tiny jar sitting on her nightstand and the stars that filled the skies of the Underworld. Made for Conjurors and by Conjurors. Her favorite thing to see when she visited the Land of the Dead.

The bottle tree turned the memory-cask on its axis, flashing its contents. More gasps crackled through the room.

"Is that a . . . *house?*" Miguel craned out of his chair.

The interior of a beautiful French Quarter mansion from Ella's hometown of New Orleans sat inside.

"Indeed. That's my home. Memory-casks take the shape of a location that's of great importance to you." Aunt Sera motioned and the bottle tree returned the memory-cask to her. "We will continue—"

A bell-blimp floated above them and announced the next

period. Students didn't wait for Aunt Sera to dismiss them before bursting out of their seats and back into the Spirit Tower.

Ella told Brigit and Jason she'd meet them in the library after lunch and try Brigit's plan. She guessed it wasn't such a bad idea after all. She lingered behind to talk to her godmother.

"Aunt Sera. That was a great class. I needed it."

"You think so? I can never tell with these kids. When I taught Introduction to Plant Crossing at Madame Collette's, y'all were always pleasant, and so respectful. I could tell you were happy to learn. Here, I'm never quite sure." She pursed her lips. "But I must believe what Headmarveller MacDonald keeps telling me. Things will settle into place so that the pressure will be worth it." Aunt Sera placed a warm hand on Ella's cheek. "Ready to face another year?"

Ella nodded. "I think everyone will like learning new conjure skills." She'd maintained hope that maybe, just maybe, she and Aunt Sera would find more acceptance.

"My eternal optimist. I wish I could guard your heart from disappointment. The Marvellers are always a problem, baby girl. But I fear this year they might not be the only problem we've got. We have other fish to fry from back home." Aunt Sera sighed. "Will other Conjure folk be excited I'm teaching up here again? More of our traditions out in the open. Or that the Arcanum might add a conjure marvel to their Paragons?"

Ella hadn't thought about what would happen if a Marveller got a conjure marvel. She tried to imagine someone who wasn't like her or her family with conjure roots growing across their skin. How strange it might look.

"There's a lot to figure out." Aunt Sera began to tidy up the room. "And no one has any good answers they can live with right now. Conjure is as much a tradition of work and sacrifice and survival as it is a heritage."

The questions piled up inside Ella as she helped Aunt Sera reorganize the plants in her tiny conjure greenhouse. She thought about Brigit and what would've happened had she been given a conjure marvel by the Marvel machine. What would her white skin look like blossoming with roots . . . and how would that make other Conjure folk feel? The strangeness of it all settled over her. It felt like a tangled-up ball of yarn impossible to fix.

Aunt Sera kissed her forehead. "This is for me to worry about. Go have fun with your friends."

Ella left the Conjure Atelier as Headmarveller MacDonald entered. She headed for the library. The ceiling above her clouded over, grumbling and whirling before four starposts dropped into her palms. Her heart froze. What if it was another threatening note?

The four envelopes felt warm in her grasp. Her frantic eyes combed over the handwriting on the outside. One from Mama. One from Reagan. One from Gran. And one from someone whose handwriting she didn't recognize at first glance. She held her breath and braced herself for another threat as she tore into that one first.

Ella,

This is a secret starpost. Burn it in the Azure Dragon fireplace as soon as you're done reading it. If someone else, like your roommate, finds out, we'll know you're responsible, and then I'll hate you forever because I put you on the list when everyone else didn't want to.

You're invited to the Underground League. A secret stapier group to get you ready for spring Paragon tryouts.

WHERE: Greenhouse
WHEN: Tomorrow!
TIME: Thirty Minutes After Lights-Out!

Abina

P.S.: I told my mom I'd be your friend this year because I think you're kind of a hero. Don't make me regret this. I mean it.

Ella pressed the starpost to her chest. Her heart thudded for two reasons—firstly, that there was such a thing as a secret student Marvel Combat League, and secondly, that Abina Asamoah had invited her to something special. Maybe she really meant that they'd be friends. And maybe this day didn't completely suck after all.

CONJURE CENSURE

Mme. Sera Baptiste

c/o United Conjure Congress

American Congregation

New Orleans Delegation

Orleans Parish

Dear Sister Sera Baptiste,

This is a formal notice that you are breaking Conjure Commandment #3 in the sharing of trusted secrets in a formal setting outside of the global Conjure community network.

We implore you to cease and desist and continue to guard our most treasured traditions. The Marvellian world contains many of our adversaries.

Sincerely,

Hattie Marie Jenkins

Secretary to the Honorable President of

the United Conjure Congress

★—★—★— **STARPOST** —★—★—★

Ella,

    The house is always too quiet when you're gone. Winnie misses you terribly—like all of us. Please try to send her a starpost. She checks the box every day.

    Also, I am writing to apologize to you for being so upset on our trip to Betelmore. Your papa and I have differing opinions on all of this, as you know, but I realize that it could've made you worry unnecessarily.

    I'm okay. Love and miss you, baby girl. Use your conjure-cameo soon so I can hear your voice.

Love,

Mama

OLD STOMPING GROUNDS

Gia stood at the edge of the Arcanum campus and leaned against the greenhouse. She inhaled. It still smelled the same, the wild iron with its sweet metallic scent. She closed her eyes for a moment as a soft snow collected on her shoes. She'd spent so much time out here, away from the other students, when they'd teased her about having a monstrous marvel, plotting her revenge among the plants.

"I'll only be able to keep it open for a few more minutes." Volan held back the clever veil the Headmarvellers and coppers installed to shield the Institute from intruders. But luckily for her, using starfolk magic to protect the school meant she had a way in.

Gia pulled a device from her pocket and turned a dial. "We'll need more than that if the automat is deep in the Institute." She pressed two buttons and a light flickered, then the word RETRIEVAL blinked. "All of these corridors might delay it."

As they waited for her special automat to make its way outside, Gia thought maybe she should just break inside herself and take what she needed. But then she might not be able to make a door and leave. She'd bet a thousand stellas that they'd fortified the place to make sure she couldn't get in or out with her particular marvel. "Have you ever wanted to see something burn, Volan?" Gia gazed up at the Arcanum Cardinal nearby, its tenet almost teasing her.

THE ARCANUM CARDINAL

THIS TOWER REPRESENTS THE TENET OF SCHOLARSHIP IN OUR GREAT MARVELLIAN WORLD.

Only by all committing to the pursuit of knowledge may our society continue to rise above the rest.

"Not particularly, my lady," Volan replied with a grunt.

"Even though Marvellers ruined your cities and crowded you out of the sky?"

Volan's paws quivered and his ears perked up.

Gia noticed how slick his fur turned as he struggled to hold the veil open. For a fleeting moment, she felt bad about the toll her mission had taken on him, but she'd rewarded him and would continue to do so for his loyalty. He'd never be homeless or hungry on her watch.

She craned to look for her automat and clucked her tongue with joy as she found it puttering down the path. "It's here!"

The automat wore a little hat made of snow. It parked itself at her feet. Gia brushed it off. "Retrieval mode," it said.

Gia stared into its metallic eyes. "Report."

The automat detailed every movement Ella Durand and Brigit Ebsen had made since returning to school, including what they ate for breakfast, lunch, and dinner, their bedtimes and grades, and even the current scene in Brigit's malyysvit on her nightstand.

Gia dug out a starpost and a tiny bug from her pocket. "Deliver this letter and plant this listening beetle somewhere on her bedside table. Keep both out of sight." She had faith the little bug would keep an even closer eye on the two girls and their conversations. She needed to know more.

"I will do as you command," the automat replied.

Volan's arms trembled. "I can't . . . hold . . . it for . . . much . . . longer."

"Coppers are approaching on their nightly round," the automat announced.

"Just in time." Gia plucked a gentleman's pocket watch from her jacket. She remembered how Fabien Fournier had used it before she'd taken the object from him. Her new marvel buzzed inside her, waking up, ready to be used.

She clicked open the timepiece.

The coppers and their wolves froze on the path like angry toy soldiers.

Gia smiled; a spark of excitement flickered in her chest. She liked how this new marvel worked. She'd have to use it more often.

She turned to Volan and touched his arm. He blinked, then shuddered, his ability to move restored. "It's time to go home," she told him.

He nodded.

Gia removed an intricate card from her pocket. The beautiful conjure card glittered with the image of a gorgeous town house from the canals of Venice, Italy. Gia flicked it and the card sparked alive, the window shutters opening in anticipation of her arrival.

She cleared her throat and butchered the spell Celeste Baptiste had taught her. "Tuck me far away . . ." She'd never had a talent for singing.

"You know what to do," she told Volan before reaching into the card and tumbling headfirst inside.

The Institute grounds woke again. The snow resumed falling. The coppers strode forward. Volan released the veil, tucked the card into his pocket, and hid out of sight.

★—★—★— **STARPOST**—★—★—★

Ella,

    Don't forget about you-know-what. It's tonight. Meet me behind founder Femi Ademola's statue. We can go together.

    Burn this too, just to be safe.

Abina

CHAPTER TEN
TRAVEL COINS

As Gia Trivelino hid inside a conjure card, Ella bent over her desk writing a note full of lies to Brigit. She'd waited until Brigit slipped into the bathroom before sneaking out of their room. She crept down the stairs and through the Azure Dragon Tower lounge, where other girls worked on homework and Mrs. Francesca, their Tower Adviser, hovered explaining the differences between dream decoding and nightmare analysis.

Ella lied to her too, asking to go see Nurse Peaks to get medicine for a headache. She figured she could use whatever sickness was going around to her advantage in this moment.

"Hurry back." Mrs. Francesca handed her an infirmary pass. "I don't want to have to send an automat after you."

Ella eased into the hallway and flashed her blinking little card at every automat who approached her with pesky questions about why she was in the hall after curfew. But instead of heading left toward the infirmary, she went right, darting past the library and the dining hall, hoping not to be spotted by a photo-balloon.

Ella sneaked into the Headmarveller's Wing. The terracotta

statue of founder Femi Ademola the Honest stood ahead, lifting his truth bowl up and down every few seconds and saying the phrase "The tongue tells truth!"

She ducked behind it, knocking right into another person.

"Hey, watch it!"

Bex. Their mohawk sparkled with glitter, and they had tiny rainbows painted in the corners of their eyes.

Ella grinned. "Sorry, didn't see you."

They laughed until Dr. Choi entered the hallway. Ella and Bex pressed themselves against the wall. Ella hoped with all her might the huge statue would hide them both. She held her breath as Dr. Choi paused to investigate. Once the hall went silent again, they both looked at each other and burst into giggles.

"I heard she's a gumiho," Bex said.

"No way. That's a rumor."

"That's why she teaches Marvellian-Adjacent Beings: Creature Study and she's always wiping her mantle. Trying to get the orange fur off and hide her secret."

Ella wondered how Dr. Choi could hide all her foxtails if that was the case and why she wouldn't have told them. But she figured that Dr. Choi might've dealt with some prejudice.

"Heard that too!" Abina squeezed herself into the hiding spot. Her braids were laced with gorgeous new beads. "Had to dodge Mrs. Francesca. I swear, she can smell a lie."

"You're late," Bex said.

"Am not!" she replied. "You're early."

"How are we getting to the greenhouse?" Ella asked, concerned. "There are coppers at all the doors and I hear the stone fu dogs from the entrance prowl at night now."

Abina dug into her pocket and produced three peculiar-looking coins. Ella didn't recognize them. The usual Marvellian coins were much smaller.

"Aren't those illegal?" Bex asked.

"Only for Marvellers under eighteen," Abina said, smug.

"Hate to break it to you, but we're twelve," Bex quipped.

Ella leaned forward to get a closer look. The coins' inscription read *Travel Well, Travel Blessed.*

"What is it?" Ella asked.

"A travel coin—takes you wherever you want. West African Marvellians—Nigerians, specifically, though my Baba said Ghanaians helped—made them back when they weren't very welcome in the skies and needed to travel back and forth quickly . . ." Abina's voice trailed off.

A rush of surprise hit Ella. She never knew they hadn't been invited with open arms into Marvellian cities. She wanted to ask more questions, but Abina started talking again.

"These belong to my older brothers. I might've . . . borrowed them," Abina said.

"How do they work?" Ella asked. The process made her think of the intricate conjure maps and hatpins Mama and Papa used to move between Conjure towns to avoid Fewels, and how similar they might be. She wanted to know everything.

"You clutch it in your palm, think of where you want to go, say the incant. The coin will go first, and you follow. It kind of feels like fainting, but you get used to it."

That seemed simple enough.

Bex frowned. "You forgot the most important thing."

"What?" Abina said, annoyed.

"They're totally and completely and one hundred percent dangerous." Bex threw their hands in the air.

"We're not leaving the grounds. What's the big deal?" Abina said.

"Wait, so what are the dangers?" Ella asked.

Bex turned to her. "You have to really know where you're going so your coin arrives in the right place. I've seen so many newsreels about Marvellers ending up in the living rooms of clueless Fewels. Or the middle of the ocean. Or worse, trapped in jars because the coin got moved by a mischievous person who recognized it when it showed up in a public place."

Ella's stomach twisted. She wanted to go along with Abina's plan and to hang out with her. But deep down, this made her scared.

"I'll make my own way." Bex stood. "You coming with me, Ella?"

Ella gulped and looked back and forth between the two of them. But she couldn't make herself move. She was too curious. She was too eager not to make Abina upset with her when they'd just decided to be friends this year. But she felt terrible about abandoning Bex. They'd been nice and saved her from getting in trouble with Headmarveller Rivera last year and she wanted to be their friend too.

Bex shrugged.

"Don't be such a baby," Abina called out as Bex tiptoed away. She slung her beads off her shoulders, then turned back to Ella. "Their loss. You ready?"

"Yes." Ella plucked one of the weighty coins from Abina's palm. It was heavier than conjure coins and warm with strange, new energy she'd never felt before. Abina reminded her of how it worked and made her pronounce *Irin Ajo* a few times.

Ella let the travel incant roll over her tongue until she felt ready. She held the coin as tight as possible.

Abina whispered the words and disappeared. Ella did the same and tumbled into the darkness behind her.

✦ ⚔ ✦ ⚔ ✦

ELLA CRASHED WITH A THUD BESIDE ABINA. THEY BOTH STARTED to laugh.

"You'll get used to it—and stick the landing next time." Abina picked up their travel coins from the greenhouse doorstep.

Ella rubbed her stomach and tried to get her ears to pop. That didn't feel like conjure travel at all. Instead, she felt like she'd been put through one of those old mangles at the Mississippi house to squeeze water from the laundry.

Abina handed her the coin back. "Keep it for next time."

Ella tried not to grin too hard as Abina turned to knock on the greenhouse door. Fresh snow trimmed the glass panes, and a frost obscured the view.

The door creaked open and a hand appeared. "Invite."

Abina placed a starpost in the palm.

"Come in!"

Ella entered the packed greenhouse behind Abina. Thick heat hit her. A mechanical sun oscillated through the ceiling, and weather balloons dropped a mist over the plants.

She perched on her tiptoes, trying to see above the crowd and watch as banners projected heliograms. Two golden stapiers sparked with fireworks. A message flashed: MARVEL COMBAT IS A WAY OF LIFE—MAKE YOUR PARAGON PROUD!

Excitement coursed through her.

Within all the thousands of plants, a suspended X-shaped platform floated above. Two trainees crossed stapiers. Their Paragon symbols blazed bright on their uniforms. One a Paragon of Spirit and the other a Paragon of Touch. They sparred, their stapiers glowing big and bright. The crowd raged as they each struck each other's paneled jackets, lighting them up.

"Ugh, we've missed the start of the match dealing with Bex." Abina zigzagged in and out of the crowd. Ella followed close behind her, trying not to get separated.

"Wow." Ella gazed up at the fighting opponents.

"This is nothing. The Marvel Combat tournament in the actual arena is everything," Abina replied. "You'll see at the end of the year."

Ella watched the two trainees strike each other's jackets, amassing points to move forward on a competition scoreboard.

"We could've signed up if we weren't so late. The Level Twos get to go in the first practice round. Those are Level Threes," Abina said.

"What happens if you strike someone with your stapier and you're not wearing the uniform?" Ella realized she didn't know as much as she wanted to about the mechanics of the sport.

"It's like putting your finger in a stellacity socket. Not a good idea. Stings," she said. "But you'll get used to it. I'll sign us up for the next one. Now that you know how to use the coin, we won't be late."

Ella's stomach rumbled a little. She still couldn't get her stapier to glow yet. She couldn't get her conjure light to push through the blade no matter how many times she'd practiced in her room or met with Dr. Yohannes after class. There was no way she would be ready. But she didn't have the courage to tell Abina not to write her name down on the sign-up sheet.

They made their way to the sitting area. Long benches stretched along the platform. Ella saw Lian and Clare. She braced herself to have to sit with them, but to her surprise, Abina moved in the opposite direction. Ella thought about asking if everything was okay with her group, but she also didn't want to ruin the moment. Abina had chosen to bring her along and to sit with her. It was best not to ask questions.

"Competitors come forward!" a Level Four boy with locs shouted from a referee box. "I need a Touch and a Spirit."

"Eugene! Eugene! Eugene!" Someone started a chant.

Allen waved. One of Jason's older brothers. They both shared a slight gap in their front teeth and a mischievous grin, but Allen had a set of dimples that looked like two perfect holes pressed into a dark chocolate Marveller-bar.

Was Jason here too? Ella looked around. She felt Lian and Clare watching them but tried to ignore it. A hand touched her shoulder. Ella glanced back, finding Jason's smiling face. In that moment, she realized they'd both kept this a secret from one another (and from Brigit), and that made her feel kind of weird. Did best friends keep secrets? Did it mean something had changed between them? She thought of leaving Brigit alone in their room. She thought of Brigit visiting the library without her.

Another match began before she could say anything to him. Her attention returned to the competitors.

Two Level Fours climbed the staircase to the floating platform. They nodded at Allen, then marched to opposite sides.

"Channellors round! You know the rules. First one to score a point by hitting the other wins," Allen called out.

Each competitor pulled down their foil mask and bowed.

"En garde!" Allen shouted.

Ella held her breath as one student threw a diamond, and it transformed into a shield. The other held a rod in the air. The sizzle of lightning crackled as the other student summoned it and directed the bolts at her opponent. The diamond shield lit up, blocking the bolts. The trainees dodged each other left and right.

"This is so amazing," she whispered to Abina. "Better than I ever thought it could be."

"Right? Marvel Combat is truly the best." Abina beamed. "I'm going to be a Sound champion, I know it. I'll be able to summon every spider to swarm my opponent."

Ella desperately wanted to be able to duel like this. She would learn all she could from this Marvel Combat club. She was determined to figure out whatever was keeping her from making her stapler glow so she could compete.

She had to be a champion too.

❖ ◆ ❖ ❖ ❖

AFTER THE FINAL MARVEL COMBAT MATCH, ELLA AND ABINA USED their travel coins to land themselves right outside the Azure Dragon Tower. Night-balloons puttered about, and a fire in the hearth flickered as they tiptoed back inside. They eased up the dormitory staircase, hoping not to make a sound. The Azure Dragon constellation snaked along the walls, following them to the third floor. Abina went right and Ella went left.

Ella waved good night, but as she turned toward her door, she found Noémie sneaking out of her room clutching one of her perfume bottles to her chest. Ella watched as she slipped down the staircase and out of the dormitory. Where was she going?

Ella thought about being nosy and following her, but a clock-lantern flashed the late hour. She turned the doorknob so it wouldn't creak, then tiptoed into the room. Ella practiced a new lie to tell Brigit in case she was still awake. The Azure Dragon constellation filled the ceiling and gazed down at her as if it too knew she was about to lie to one of her best friends.

The twilight star on her nightstand left a light trail to her bed. As she inched closer, soft sniffles echoed. Ella's heart plummeted. Did Brigit know already where she'd been? Was she devastated?

Feste waved Ella over.

She took a deep breath. "Brigit . . ."

No answer.

Ella's stomach knotted. How could she make this better? "Are you okay?" She crouched beside Brigit's bed.

Brigit tried to rub away the tears, but they kept falling. Ella prepared to say she was sorry, prepared to offer some sort of explanation. She'd never seen Brigit so emotional before. Brigit's feelings always felt buried deep inside her.

"I just can't believe." Her words tangled with a storm of tears.

"I'm . . . I . . ." Ella never imagined she'd be this upset, especially since half the time, Brigit hated group activities. The word *sorry* felt thick on her tongue.

Brigit pointed to her nightstand, then burst into tears again. A starpost sat beside her malyysvit toy. "Read it."

The little moon from her desert world-egg bathed the envelope with light. The name Beatrice was scrawled across the front. Ella's hands quivered as she opened it and began to read.

My daughter,
   You may not want to hear from me, but there's much to say. You must have questions. I think we owe it to each other to meet and clear the air. I know under the current circumstances that can feel impossible, but if you agree, I will arrange it.

Send word. Use the return courier post provided. It'll find its way to me without having to go through the starpost box.

G.T., your mother

Gia's evil cackle crushed in her thoughts. The memory sent a cold shiver down her spine. She thought of the threatening notes she'd gotten over the past few months, her eyes cutting to the drawer where she'd hidden them. Should she tell Brigit about them? *It might make it worse*, she thought.

Brigit sobbed.

"You don't have to answer it," Ella said.

"Part of me wants to know, and the other part of me doesn't. How is the person everyone in the world hates . . . my mom? Why me? Why can't I have one *normal* thing?" More tears flooded Brigit's cheeks.

Ella pulled her close and hugged her. "What's normal, anyways?" She rubbed her back.

"You don't have to do anything you don't want to. You don't even have to talk to her. I have something that might make you feel a little better." Ella darted to her bureau and grabbed a stick of Bayou Blues Bubblegum, one of her favorite conjure candies that always brightened up bad days. "Here, chew this."

Brigit took a piece. Her cries lessened and she wiped her face. "What took you so long?"

Ella gulped, a lie rolling around on her tongue. This wasn't the right time to upset her more. "I went to the library, then had to help Abina with her braid-hands. But you should go to bed."

Brigit nodded as Ella tucked her in the way her mama always did back home. She put the starpost back on Brigit's nightstand beside her malyysvit. Inside the desert world, a camel was already asleep beside the sand dunes, and a tiny beetle buried its head in the sand. Ella still wished she had one of her own, preferably a jungle landscape with a sloth.

"Good night," Ella whispered to Brigit. Guilt filled up each part of her as she went back to her side of the room and got ready for bed. Brigit's sniffles quietly continued as Ella eased under the covers.

"Lying is not good for one's moral fiber," St. Thomas whispered to her.

"I know." Ella turned over, burrowing herself. She couldn't even face the saints tonight. The bottle tree bloomed with belladonna, a sign of danger on the horizon, but Ella was too distracted to notice as her mind churned over ways to figure out how to get Brigit an invitation to the secret student Marvel Combat League and feel better.

She'd have to do whatever it took.

TO: His Excellency Sebastien Durand, Grand High Walker

Mansion of Death

Underworld

Conjure Quarter

Congo Square, New Orleans

Dear His Excellency, Sebastien Durand,

   Have you determined the proper payment for the
debt owed to me by your eldest daughter? I would hate
to think you've forgotten about our meeting. This is my
final polite request for you to make this right.

   I await word.

                                        Best,
                                        G.T.

★—★—★— **STARPOST** —★—★—★

Ella,

    I need to speak with you. Please use your conjure-cameo when you get a chance. And most of all, I need you to be very safe. Usually Mama's the one issuing the warnings, but I need you to listen to me now. Please stay on the Arcanum grounds no matter what. Please reply to this message as soon as you get it. I need your word.

Love,

Papa

CHAPTER ELEVEN
THREE HUNDRED YEARS

On Halloween, the Arcanum halls swarmed with strangers, and none of them were in festive costumes. Mostly, they were stuffy and boring-looking with their starched collars and stiff pants.

"Who are they?" Brigit asked as they waited in line to enter the Grand Assembly Hall for the special Institute-wide meeting.

"People from the government." Jason motioned at the crests on their blazers.

Heady perfume and pipe tobacco choked the air, and the automats seemed to be in overdrive cleaning, shining, and sweeping everything. The Arcanum teachers were on high alert, correcting even the tiniest behavior issues.

Mrs. Francesca's words from this morning's dormitory meeting echoed in Ella's head: "Piccole stelle, please be your best selves. It's the kickoff of our Tricentennial celebration. I know that it is also Halloween, and we shall stuff ourselves with sweets later tonight, but right now, you are to be representatives of our great training institute."

As the Level Twos shuffled through the entryway, the star-folk herded them into their proper section, helping everyone find their seats. Ella saw Aries for the first time since school had started back. He winked at her, his kitten-like ears perking up. She wanted to make sure to ask if he'd gotten her thank-you gift this summer. He'd helped them so much last year when they sneaked out to rescue Masterji Thakur by breaking the rules and driving them in the Arcanum cable car down to Betelmore. He could've turned them in but he didn't.

Paragon banners decorated the walls. Striped balloons sporting the A.T.I. initials sailed across the high ceiling. Looking around, Ella couldn't figure out why her nerves felt on edge, but the peach fuzz on her arms stood up. Ella found Masterji Thakur and her godmother seated beside one another at the long teacher table. She waved at them, and they smiled.

Headmarveller MacDonald silenced the room. "Good morning, trainees!"

The room answered, "Good morning, Headmarveller Mac-Donald and Headmarveller Rivera!"

"I know for most of you, today is merely Halloween or the night before el Día de los Muertos, and we will get to those activities soon enough. But first, this year, we're celebrating a momentous milestone. The three hundredth year of us living in the skies together. No doubt you've seen new faces around the Institute, as we're hosting members of the Marvellian Historical Society. They're here to present to you. Let's relish this learning opportunity."

The Grand Assembly Hall doors snapped open. Ella watched as Madame Madge led a procession forward. A stodgy-looking man tugged a cart, its wheels grunting and wheezing under the weight of a shrouded object.

Ella sat straight up. She felt the crossing tug as it drew nearer and nearer down the aisle.

"What's wrong?" Jason whispered.

"I feel the crossing tug," she replied.

"What's that?" Brigit asked.

Ella explained the pull in her heart whenever she'd enter the Underworld or a conjure object came near.

"Wow," Brigit muttered.

"I've never felt it before. But maybe because I haven't been to the Underworld yet," Jason said.

"I'll take you both," she replied, her eyes fixed on the object. What was under that cloak?

Headmarveller Rivera started a round of applause as the procession made its way to the front of the room for all to see.

One of the visiting historians stepped forward. His brown skin glowed beneath the star-lantern light. "I am Dr. Laga'aia, and I'm so glad to be here with you all." He mopped his forehead with a handkerchief. "We are here to share our Tricentennial exhibit with the Arcanum Training Institute for Marvelous and Uncanny Endeavors' Lower School." He pulled the beautiful drape off the hulking object.

It was the same exhibit Ella had seen at the Vellian Port, and now the Arcanum blueprints fluttered beside the other items. She took Jason's hand, then Brigit's.

The crossing tug yanked her forward so strong she could barely stay still.

"Look," she whispered hard.

They both gasped, noting the Arcanum blueprints too. Were those the ones from her bottle tree or the fake ones Masterji Thakur had left behind?

The noise in the room drained away, her ears filling with the sound of her own heartbeat. Could they have gotten them from her bottle tree? Did they already know? Would she be in trouble the moment this assembly was over?

She looked up at Masterji Thakur, who didn't meet her gaze.

Dr. Laga'aia droned on, describing each of the exhibit objects, from the cups and bowls to an ancient-looking stellacity lamp, noting their significance to Marvellian history.

"Now we shall invite each student level to come take a closer look. Teachers, please prepare to escort your groups forward when called," Headmarveller Rivera directed. "A few of our most accomplished trainees will assist. Beatrice Eugene, Johan Fenris Knudsen II, and Moussa Diallo, please take your places."

Ella turned to Brigit. "Can you get a bathroom pass, go back to our room, and check the bottle tree for the tube? You know the spell?"

"I can do it," she said with a nod.

"I just want to make sure."

Brigit rose from her seat.

"Jason and I will get a closer look," Ella said.

"They couldn't have just taken them, right?" Jason's eyes filled with worry. "Someone would've said something. Or at least given you detention, don't you think?"

Ella closed her eyes for a second, thinking about how she'd seen the blueprint tube tucked safely away in the branches of her bottle tree just this morning. It would be impossible. They didn't know the conjure spell to release the tube from the branches. They wouldn't harm the tree. Right? But she still didn't understand the depths of Marvellian magic just yet. "I hope they're the fake ones."

Ella watched as each student level got to visit the exhibit. She whispered to Jason how she'd just seen the display while at the Vellian Port that day they went shopping, and how she'd felt the crossing tug then too, but she couldn't figure out why.

"Bea feels it randomly sometimes too," Jason replied. "Though she doesn't like to admit it."

Ella's mind was a storm of questions; his voice blended into the noisy room.

"I hope to one day feel it," Jason admitted.

Ella couldn't even acknowledge his statement or be excited that he wanted to be more invested in his Conjure roots. Her eyes remained fixed on the floating blueprints in the exhibit ahead.

Her stomach coiled tighter and tighter until it was their turn to approach. She almost jumped out of her seat to join the line and follow behind Samaira.

Just as they approached, Ella saw two of the Level Four helpers—Johan to the right and Beatrice to the left.

"Here, take one." Johan handed her a pamphlet.

She couldn't stop staring at him. He felt . . . familiar. His intense blue eyes and pale blond hair. But there was something else, something she couldn't put her finger on.

"Two at a time to approach the exhibit," Dr. Laga'aia directed.

Ella scanned over the multitude of historical objects until she found the floating blueprints. As she got a closer look, she noticed they didn't illuminate. Not like the real ones. They were the decoys Masterji Thakur had left behind. Her eyes found Masterji Thakur, and he nodded as if he knew exactly what she was thinking.

Relief rushed through her. "They're not—" Ella started to say to Jason.

"Bea, what's wrong?" Jason raced out of the line.

Ella looked at Beatrice Eugene. Sweat covered her forehead. Her eyes watered and blood rushed down her nose. Samaira screamed.

Jason held his sister's hand.

"My marvel, my marvel," Beatrice whimpered over and over before she fainted and hit the floor.

Ella felt frozen in place.

AFTER GETTING READY FOR BED, ELLA READ A STARPOST FROM Masterji Thakur over and over again, hoping it might change its message if she read it enough times.

> Ella,
>   The time has come to return what I have lent you,
> I'm afraid.
>
>   Best,
>   Masterji Thakur

The weight of his words sat like an anchor in her stomach. She gazed at her bottle tree, the blueprint tube still tucked between the golden leaves and belladonna. She'd already been on edge all day after seeing Beatrice faint during the assembly. Now she didn't know what to do. She slammed herself back onto her pillow and tried to fall asleep. Maybe she'd wake up with an answer.

But Ella tossed and turned all night, her dreams a tempest of unanswered questions and complicated feelings. She could see Aunt Sera's upset face, worry lines etched in the beautiful brown of her skin. The wailing sound of her mama's cries from that day in Betelmore echoed. The solemn expression of the architect, Jean-Michel Durand, projected from the blueprint. She felt like they were all begging her to find a way to unlock this story and fix everything.

Hail plinked the windows, and the hard whistle of wind found its way inside. A float-fire crackled and flared, working hard to keep the room warm. Ella struggled to stay asleep.

"Wake up!" St. Christopher whispered.

"There's trouble afoot, Ella," St. Catherine added.

Ella kicked her quilt off. She glared at the ceiling. The Azure Dragon constellation stared back. "Guess you can't sleep either," she mumbled at it.

She glanced over at Brigit, who was a small lump beneath her beautiful quilt. Tiny snores echoed in between the melody of more hail.

The dragon constellation pointed its snout at the bottle tree.

"What is it?"

She'd never seen the constellations behave this way, always assuming that they were merely clever decorations made by the starfolk.

Ella skulked to the edge of her bed and glanced up into her bottle tree. Light pushed through the seams of the blueprint tube. Fear vibrated through her, and she scrambled into the tree to grab it. Was something wrong with it? She yanked off the lid and took out the now glowing blueprints.

They unfurled, the outline of buildings filling in as usual. She waited for those buttons to appear again. VERSION 251 projected above.

"Why are you glowing right now?" she asked.

The blueprints shook with recognition as if understanding her. Ella leaned in closer. A small rectangular-shaped object began to blink. Ella watched as it sharpened, the rest of the building projections dimming ever so slightly.

"What are you trying to show me? What are you trying to tell me?" She squinted, finding a tiny door tucked behind the founder statues in the Headmarveller's Wing.

She gasped.

A staircase and a sign: THE FOUNDER'S ROOM.

The very place that would allow her to access VERSION 1 of the Arcanum Training Institute. A realization fell over her.

The blueprints were helping.

★—★—★— **STARPOST**—★—★—★

Jason,

    Is Bea okay? Are you okay?

From,

Ella & Brigit

★—★—★— **STARPOST**—★—★—★

Ella & Brigit,

    She's in the infirmary with Nurse Peaks. She's going home early for winter break because she can't get her nose to stop bleeding and she's freaking out. I'm freaking out too, but I don't want her to know that. My mom says I need to be strong for her and not let my worries make her worries worse. She also is having trouble with her marvel. It's scary. My dad's on the way to pick her up.

Jason

The Arcanum Training Institute for Marvelous and Uncanny Endeavors

Lower School

TO: Headmarveller MacDonald & Headmarveller Rivera
FROM: Nurse Peaks

Dear Headmarvellers,

To date, we have twelve trainees with nosebleeds, headaches, and rashes. We've seen a rapid uptick in the first few days of November. Many complain about their marvels feeling fuzzy. Enclosed please review my initial findings on the nosebleeds. I'd like for there to be a thorough cleaning of the Institute air ducts, especially in the dormitories and session rooms, and then a discussion with Chef Oshiro about possible food allergens to start eliminating potential culprits for the unusual symptoms.

Best,
Nurse Peaks
Head of Infirmary
Arcanum Lower School

HEADQUARTERS

Gia walked through the halls of her secret house. She still felt in awe that it was tucked inside a very clever conjure card. Made by her favorite Ace, Celeste Baptiste, though she wouldn't admit if asked, the hideaway became convenient in the days she'd been on the run after the notorious night when she'd murdered her rival Phineas Astley. It was one of the few things she treasured.

Gia inspected every bedroom, one for each of her beloved Aces to stay when times got tough. She ran her fingers over their doors, finding the intricate etchings she had carved back when constructing this little pocket universe. Each one of her Aces' names were laid out in gorgeous calligraphy. The original members.

The Ace of Mischief. Benjamin Mackenzie. Her club.

The Ace of Illusion. Victoria Baudelaire. Her spade.

The Ace of Machination. Linh Nguyen. Her diamond.

The Ace of Destruction. Mitha Thakur. Her leaf.

The Ace of Perception. Celeste Baptiste. Her wild card.

The Ace of Influence. She couldn't bear thinking of his name. Her heart.

She'd only had six to start. And she was the Joker. But her enterprise had grown in the upper school and beyond, and others had proved themselves loyal and worthy, so she doubled her deck. Collecting new blood.

She lingered in front of Mitha Thakur's room the longest. "My sweet, sweet friend. Lost to me . . . for now."

"My lady." Volan stood at the end of the hall. "Your guests have arrived."

Gia returned to the first-floor dining room, where many of her Aces sat. She'd forgotten what it felt like to have almost a full table. Six faces stared back at her. Almost all of those who were left.

She gazed out with pride. Her newest—the Ace of Intellect, Hernando Ali-Balthazar nodded at her while her Ace of Brawn, Leo Cruz, cracked her knuckles.

A tense quiet fell over them.

Before taking her seat at the head of the table, she gazed at two empty seats. Left open for her missing members. Her Ace of Influence and her Ace of Destruction. She ground her teeth. She'd get them back—or they'd pay for leaving her.

"It's good to have you home," Gia said. "There's work to be done."

The dinner began.

Linh Nguyen pushed her food around. "I'm retired, Gia. I don't want to play this game."

Gia breezed right through Linh's statement, turning to Celeste Baptiste. "My Ace of Influence couldn't bless us with his presence?"

"The campaign has him busier than anticipated." Celeste

locked eyes with Gia. They both knew that there was more to it than that. He didn't respect her authority anymore. But she'd be sure to remind him of his everlasting pact soon enough.

"He should just use his charm and be done with it," Gia replied.

"He wants to win this election fair and square," Celeste added. "We've been working hard to do so."

"He can't spell the word *fair*." Gia slammed her goblet on the table. Volan jumped in the corner.

The tension crackled.

Gia rapped her fingers on the table. "Momentarily, I will have the funding to bring our operation back and start recruiting. But our first objective will be to disrupt this election." Her eyes burned into Celeste's until the woman cast her beautiful eyes away. "And second, I have a few people who owe me debts."

"Who?" Leo rubbed her shaved head, then took a notepad from the interior of her jacket. "I'll prepare to collect."

"Ella Durand is up first."

PART II
CONJURE CONUNDRUMS

CHAPTER TWELVE
LOCIAMBULISM

Over the next few days, whispers about students getting sick filled every trolley Ella rode. "I saw one kid running out of the gem lab with a nosebleed," a Level Four said.

"The girl who works at the Institute store said her marvel was gone."

All day she'd caught snippets of gossip about the kids getting sent to the infirmary to see Nurse Peaks as she'd made her way to her classes. She thought of Jason's sister, Bea, at home a whole month and a half before winter break.

"Two Level One students puked in the Headmarveller's Wing earlier," someone reported.

"Four kids in my weathermancy class had to leave halfway through our rain experiment," another added. "They couldn't manipulate the clouds. Their marvels just stopped."

Some tried to blame Chef Oshiro's new dining carts. Others pointed to the cold weather caused by the Norwegian Sea. But

Ella remained suspicious. Hadn't the school been in cold areas before? What could be making people sick?

Her conjure-cameo warmed against her chest. She pressed her hand to it, knowing her parents were trying to get in contact with her. She pulled it out. The cameo portrait of her papa stretched as if waking from slumber.

Ella hustled off the trolley before answering him.

Papa's eyebrows furrowed. "What took you so long?"

"I was on my way to see Aunt Sera for my conjure lesson," she replied.

His tiny portrait seemed relieved. "Did you get my starpost?"

"Yes, sir. I meant to write you back but I got behind."

"I just wanted to reiterate our need for you to be safe."

"I know, Papa." She'd never heard this kind of worry in his voice before. That was usually Mama's job.

"Please don't leave the Arcanum Training Institute under any circumstances, you hear me?"

"Yes, sir." She wanted to tell him that none of the cities were even close to the school right now, so there was no place to go, but he didn't seem like he was in the right mood for reminders.

"Also, your mother and I heard about some nosebleeds or something happening there. You all right?"

"I'm fine. Some kids are having them."

"Do they know the cause?"

Ella shrugged. "The teachers aren't really talking about it. Most people think it's the cold. It hasn't stopped snowing once since I got here."

"You stay safe. Mama is sending you a salve to protect your nose. Keep us posted."

"I will. I promise."

"And remember—"

"I know, Papa. Conjurors keep their word, and I'll stay at the Arcanum."

"That's my girl. Just what I wanted to hear. Love you and miss you."

Ella's appointment card blinked. "Papa, I have to go see Aunt Sera. I'm late."

"Love you, little girl."

"Love you too."

Papa's cameo portrait froze once more, and she turned to head into the Spirit Tower. But as Ella passed the Arcanum faculty lounge, she caught a flash of red hair. Clare Lumen. Ella watched as Clare looked left before ducking into the off-limits room, clearly ignoring the flickering sign above the door: NO STUDENT TRAINEES ALLOWED. PULL THE BELL AND SOMEONE WILL BE WITH YOU SHORTLY.

What was she doing in there? Ella felt tempted to peek despite the nearby clock-lantern reminding her that she was very late. A tiny part of her *had* to know. She reached to open the door.

"Excuse me! What do you think you're doing?"

Ella spun around. A Marvellian copper towered over her. His thick mustache twitched.

"I—I . . . ," she stammered out, unsure of what exactly to say. Should she snitch on Clare and let her get caught? Which would make Clare hate her even more than she already did? Or should she admit that she was just being nosy and take whatever consequence?

Her skin grew hot, and sweat skated across her brow.

"Did you see the sign? It's clear as day." He scanned her, his eyes landing on the new conjure roots growing across her collarbone.

His entire body hardened. She'd seen that happen before. The realization that she was a Conjuror. "Were you going to take something?"

Panic flooded her. She couldn't get in trouble again. She'd promised Mama and Papa no mischief reports, and she had already gotten detention. It would be worse if one came from a copper. "I was looking for—"

"Dr. Huang," came an unexpected voice.

Ella looked left to find Lian and her fu dog, Jiaozi, at her side.

"He told us to meet him here," Lian lied. "I came to find you, Ella. The plans changed." She played with the thick blue streak in her hair. "We have to go to the Spirit lounge instead."

Ella nodded with relief. "Yes, I'm—well, we're—meeting Dr. Huang like she said. I must've written it down wrong." She flashed her godmother's angry appointment card at him, hoping he didn't ask to inspect it. "But the plan changed. I was just in the wrong place."

He scowled. "Is that so?"

"Yes," Lian replied. "If you have a problem with it, you can contact my dad. You know, Dr. Wong, the Supreme Head Judge of the United League of Marvellers, our government, the people who pay for you to be here."

Ella tried to hold a fake smile as Lian insulted the copper. They'd never been friends or even friendly, but she was grateful to Lian in this moment. Maybe she wasn't just snobbery and meanness all the time.

"Get to where you need to go. No more detours." The copper shooed them away and marched back to his post.

Ella and Lian waited until the copper turned the corner, then burst out laughing. The fu dog licked Ella's leg until she bent down to pet him. "Hi, Jiaozi." She rubbed his thick, curly mane. "I missed you."

"You remember his name?" Lian's eyebrow quirked.

"Of course. He's not exactly forgettable." Ella nuzzled her nose against his snout. "And thanks for the help back there."

"No problem. I don't like the coppers here. The ones that follow my dad around are way better. Also, I think the whole thing is for show. The Arcanum is totally fortified. My dad said there's protective incants. Can never be destroyed."

She wondered if the architect dreamed that up and if the "incant" was really a conjure eternity spell.

"That's a month's worth of detentions for going into the teachers' lounge." Lian scooped Jiaozi into her arms. "What were you doing anyways?"

"Thought I saw my godmother go in there," Ella said, not wanting to snitch on Clare to one of her best friends. "We have a meeting." Ella's appointment card blared. That satisfied Lian and she took off down the hall.

But before Ella entered the Spirit Tower, she glanced back, watching Clare sneak out of the Arcanum faculty lounge with papers. What was she really up to? Mama's ever-present warning played in her head: *Mind your business so nobody's minding you.* The appointment card vibrated again with her final warning.

When she turned back around, Noémie stood right in her face.

"Umm, hello?" Ella stumbled backward.

Noémie's intense glare made her stomach knot.

"What do you want?" Ella shifted left to let Noémie pass. But she didn't move. She went right, but Noémie blocked her path again.

"You shouldn't be so nosy," Noémie said, her voice a low growl. All her niceness from the game night was long gone. Ella couldn't read her.

"What?"

"You heard me!" Noémie replied.

Ella gulped. She balled her fists. Frustration built up inside her.

"Are you going to hit me?" Noémie asked, then flashed a smile.

"I've never hit anyone before." Her pulse raced.

"I don't think anyone would believe that." Noémie gazed up at one of the photo-balloons, then finally moved to the side to let Ella pass. "Stay out of our business."

Clare called out Noémie's name, and she spun around and sauntered away.

Ella's stomach knotted. What had just happened?

✦　◼　✦　◼　✦

ELLA STARTED RUNNING THROUGH HER LAUNDRY LIST OF LATENESS excuses the moment she crossed the threshold of Aunt Sera's Conjure Atelier.

Her godmother waited, arms crossed, standing over a conjure pont, the beautiful plant cocoon Conjurors used to recover from their work. Ella wondered what they'd be up to today to warrant it.

"Sorry, Aunt Sera. I didn't mean to be late. One of the coppers stopped me." Ella hoped that would soften her.

Aunt Sera put her hand up, and Ella gulped down the rest of her excuses. "You ready to get on with it, then?"

Ella gazed around. Candles burned, an incense bundle left

trails of smoke, the worktable wore a purple cloth and held her godmother's memory-cask and a jeweled box of powder bundles. She eased into a chair. She had to be on guard. She didn't want her aunt finding out about the blueprints or that her conjure still felt weird and her bottle tree looked different. Conjure women had ways of finding out things you didn't want them to know. Especially the women in her family.

Aunt Sera went to her cabinets and returned with a jar of liquid. "Take this. It'll give you some mojo. You seem scattered, and I need you focused." She placed a cold hand on Ella's forehead. Ella thought she should tell her about the run-in with Noémie, but she knew it would mean a meeting with the Headmarvellers about being bullied. She didn't want any trouble like that this year.

Aunt Sera held out a glass. Ella scrunched her nose at the liquid's dark color. "It has sugarcane in it. One of your favorites. Drink it down."

The beverage smelled like it was straight from the sun tea pitchers Gran would leave in the house windows on hot days. Ella drained the glass. A warm flush oozed through her, and she felt like she'd just woken from a satisfying nap.

"Better?" Aunt Sera asked.

"Yes."

Aunt Sera sat across from Ella. "Ready for your lociambulism lesson?"

"Really?" Surprise made her jump.

"Your mama says you're ready to learn since this will connect so much to our study of memory-casks. Also, because that machine of theirs said you have a cartomanic marvel. She's concerned you don't really know what that means."

"I'll be able to tell the future—like Brigit and her knitting—but with cards." She'd looked up the word in all different kinds of books trying to make sure she knew exactly what it meant.

"Not exactly, baby girl. If you were just a Marveller, then yes, you'd be able to use cards to divine the future. But you're a Conjuror. This skill manifests differently in our community." Aunt Sera took Ella's hand and flipped her palm upright. "You'll not only be able to glimpse someone's past and see their future, but when you get strong enough, you'll also be able to change their fortunes at times."

Ella's mouth dropped open. "Wait! What?! Mama and Gran never told me this."

"Well, you're still learning." Aunt Sera stretched her hand out palm up beside Ella's. It'd been marked with black ink like a tattoo: three lines beautifully drawn. "We Conjure folk disguise our divining gift by wrapping it in palmistry and card reading." She pointed at the dark lines. "Most people are familiar with those practices, so it keeps our *true* gift safe. Lociambulism—the mind-walk—is a unique blessing."

Ella had heard some of this from Gran. The scary part was sitting in readings, and the way people had tear-streaked cheeks, desperate to know about their futures. She didn't like the pressure to be right, to give someone a kernel of hope they needed to push on, and if dark things appeared in their readings, she didn't know whether to be honest. Gran had always said to send customers out with a bundle of good and only a pinch of the bad, whereas if one got a reading from Mama, someone had to be ready to hear it all.

She'd have to learn the right way for *her* to do things. And what did it mean to change someone's fortune anyway? And when it came down to passing her channellors test with the cards, which way would she have to do it—the Marvellian way or the Conjure way? She felt a pinch, not wanting to have to wrestle between the two.

"But how can the mind-walk help tell the future?" The realization of how hard this would be washed over Ella.

Aunt Sera fanned her conjure cards across the table. Ella admired how intricate they were: the card backs with a skull trapped by a gilded snake and conjure-roses. Ella swore they were alive, and she had memories of watching Gran feed them with tiny pearls of her own blood. She couldn't wait to earn her own set. She reached out to touch them, then pulled back, knowing you're not supposed to touch another Conjuror's deck if you can help it.

"Okay, let's review. Name the three ways that a Conjuror can tell the future," she challenged. "Maybe the logic will reveal itself."

"You can tell fortunes with the cards." Ella pointed at Aunt Sera's deck.

"Yes, and?"

"Gran said the ancestors can tell you things. So, you can appeal to the spirits with offerings." Ella glanced over her shoulder at the tiny doors scattered along the wall. Flower petals and bits of food sat at the small doorsteps, and she thought of the hands of her ancestors reaching through to help do Aunt Sera's bidding.

"Well done. Didn't think you'd get that one. Underworld work might be my favorite. And lastly?"

Ella knew Aunt Sera wanted her to bring up the mind-walk, but she didn't really understand. "I don't know how lociambulism fits." The word garbled in her mouth, much like her understanding of this skill.

"Lo-key-amb-u-liz-um." Her godmother stretched out the syllables and Ella mimicked her. "So let me try to explain it. If you needed to help uncover a secret, what would you do?"

"Could you ask the ancestors?" Ella asked.

"You could, but there's a price for asking favors of the dead. The more expedient way is the mind-walk or the art of lociambulism. It's less drama," Aunt Sera replied. "You need not be afraid of it. Sometimes it can save lives. Years ago, someone was terrorizing the Third Ward of Houston, Texas, and Conjure folk decided to try to figure out who was burning the buildings and breaking into their stores by mind-walking suspects. It saved the city. The man was going to do worse and set off a bomb. They prevented a major tragedy."

Ella nibbled her bottom lip, thinking through the magnitude of the skill.

"The future lies within," Aunt Sera said. "And lociambulism gives us an advantage. We can examine someone's past." She tapped her temple. "And in trying to understand their memories, we can gather clues about their future, discover things they must look out for inside themselves. Their own monsters. The mind holds it all. Even beyond death, for us." She rested her hands on her memory-cask.

The importance of the mind-walk and the act of lociambulism started to crystallize for Ella. It was another way to know what needed to be known. But she couldn't help feeling scared of the whole thing. Going into someone's mind? She was a curious kid, too curious for her own good according to Gran and Mama, but this felt like too much even to her. An extra level of nosiness.

"Do you know why my memory-cask is here?" Aunt Sera ran her fingers over the wrought-iron casing.

"No."

"It's the same spell."

"But I don't understand." Ella stared at her, confused.

"You can mind-walk the living and the dead. Remember, a memory-cask is essentially the mind of the deceased, containing all their memories, wisdom, et cetera. It's the same act."

Ella felt in awe of the depth of conjure work.

Aunt Sera opened her box. Bundles twinkled in the candle-light. "What are these, petit?"

"Crossing powder." Ella admired them. She'd seen Gran make it with twilight stardust. Took months to get it just right, and she knew there were numerous ingredients in it.

"What does it do?" Aunt Sera quizzed.

"Helps protect the Conjuror as you cross into the Under-world," she answered, thinking of the little ladies who hovered at the feet of the deathbulls at the Underworld gates, ready to wipe the palms of those wishing to enter.

"Where else?"

Ella didn't know. "Ummm . . . I guess it also helps with mind-walking or visiting a memory-cask."

"Exactly! Think of it like our Conjure passports that give us access to Marvellian cities, but instead it's a passport into the mind." Aunt Sera opened one of the bundles and spread powder on Ella's right palm. "You must let your connection to another person's mind or their memory-cask open like uncorking an elixir bottle."

"I've never done that before."

Aunt Sera chuckled. "I suppose not. Point being, it must be

slow, unrushed. If you try to pull the cork from a bottle too soon, it can break and fall into the liquid, ruining it. Same for mind-walking. You want to ease into it so you're in control." She added powder to Ella's other hand too. "Another tip for beginners, we often use a recovery pont." She motioned at the one in the center of the room. "It can help make the journey smoother and not deplete your energy in the process."

"Oh." Ella didn't realize they were used for anything other than reenergizing. She'd helped her mama and gran make a thousand of them from roots, plants, and oils. Their husks scattered throughout the family conjure room during peak fortune-telling season after New Year's Day.

"We don't have time to do all that today, so we will just practice entering and exiting my mind."

As much as Ella wanted to learn more about this conjure skill, she wanted to get back to the blueprints. Impatience bubbled up in her. "But—"

"Nope, stay focused." Aunt Sera patted her hand. "You're traveling through the palace of someone's memory. I'll teach you how to enter and exit and how to understand the symbols that appear. Items that—once analyzed—will help you decipher their fortunes."

"Will you teach everyone this?" Ella asked.

"This is something for *us*, and us only. Has to be," Aunt Sera said. "Our unit on the memory-cask seems sufficient enough for the non-Conjure folk." She wiped sweat from her brow. "The United Conjure Congress continues to be upset that I'm still here. So many angry starposts—and if you could see the *Conjure Picayune* and the things they're saying. Whew!"

A cold trickled over Ella's skin, and she wondered what they must be saying about her too.

Aunt Sera took Ella's hand and placed it on top of her palm. "You ready to practice?"

Ella didn't feel ready to mind-walk. The weight of it sank like a boulder in her stomach. She didn't get a choice. She'd have to master conjure skills *and* train to be a Marveller. No matter how hard.

Ella nodded.

"Once you enter, the first thing you should do is note the weather. It gives the lociambulist their first clue about the state the person is in. A thunderstorm here"—she waved a hand above her— "is the same there. Full of hot, angry lightning that can strike, or a downpour that can flood, so be aware, and take cover."

Ella swallowed her worried questions, like *What if I drown from the rain in someone's mind?*

"Don't forget, you'll see repeated symbols. I'll explain what they mean during our next lesson." She put a finger in the air. "But in a living mind, never ever touch an object. Repeat after me. Never—"

"Touch anything."

"No matter how tempting. This is the key difference between mind-walking the living and the dead. In the first, you can touch nothing, and in the latter, you're meant to touch everything. The living mind is fragile. If you taint the symbols, you can hurt someone, or worse, get trapped inside. One of my cousins—a silly, silly woman—got stuck in a man's mind."

"Who?"

"It was before you were born, so you never got a chance to

meet her. Marianne. She was nosing around to see if her boyfriend loved her. Not minding her business. Saw something she didn't like, touched it, and could never get out. We lost her for good."

Despite Ella hearing much of this before, today it all felt different—urgent. "I'm nervous."

"It's healthy to be that way. The fear will keep you careful."

Ella didn't feel ready. Couldn't she think a little more about this before having to do it?

"You're a Baptiste and a Durand. Two powerful Conjure bloodlines in you. The most powerful of the original Conjure families. You can do this."

"But—" Ella started.

"No more buts." Aunt Sera squeezed Ella's palm.

Her vision went black and her body tilted forward, pitching headfirst into a tornado of color and shadow.

BAPTISTE LOCIAMBULISM POWDER RECIPE
Makes: *A batch for one traveler*

2 tablespoons of Kananga water

A pinch of tobacco

1 teaspoon of Mullein

2 cups of Hyssop

4 tablespoons of saltpeter

1 Adder's tongue

3 thistles (blessed)

2 Verbena leaves

1 Solomon's Seal Roots

5 Snake Weeds

¼ teaspoon of cumin

1 ounce of lye

2 Butterfly bushes

1 ¼ tablespoon of dried deathbull blood

1 silver dime or 3 mercury dimes

1 Ash Tree Root

1 pinch of salt (purified)

1 Five-Finger Grass leaf

3 cups of twilight stardust

THE SCENT OF MEMORY

As Ella tumbled into the mind of her godmother, Gia sat in one of the private scent rooms of Mrs. Victoria Baudelaire's Perfume Atelier awaiting her host. She sniffed the air, filling her nostrils with the scent of lavender and Parisian rain. Part of her wished she'd stolen a perfume marvel so she could have at least one Paragon of Taste in her arsenal—a keen nose was a valuable thing. It allowed one to untangle a city by deciphering the thousands of odors that made up its invisible stew. She'd be able to find whomever and whatever she wanted.

But Gia knew better than to be greedy, hearing the words of her Ace of Perception in her head. *Pigs get fed and hogs get slaughtered*, Celeste always told her. If she took too many marvels, she could mess up their delicate properties and their balance with her primary one. Plus, she hadn't quite mastered how to use her new marvels effectively. Each one vibrated inside her at different frequencies. When using them, she had to tune in, pluck the right one, and sharpen her instincts.

The room around her vomited pinks and creams, and the look

of it started to grate her nerves. Gia slammed her hand against a bell on the table. She'd been kept waiting too long. Volan flinched, clutching tight to her winter coat.

Mrs. Victoria Baudelaire appeared from behind a curtain, wheeling a cart of glass bottles, vials, and atomizers. "Your perfect perfume awaits." Her voice held on to its cheery tone as if Gia was just one of her typical customers in search of a new, signature scent.

Gia cackled.

The woman's smile turned into a scowl. "Aren't you supposed to be good at playing along?"

"Only when I feel the need to put on a show."

"If you don't, my Fewel husband might suspect something," Victoria replied.

"And discover you're my Ace of Illusion, and not merely his doting wife."

Victoria scoffed. "I'm different now. I told you that at your dinner."

"No one truly changes. We're all the same versions of ourselves, the ones we think we can hide."

"Let's get this over with. I'm tired of the debt you're holding over me. You need to ensure my daughter's safety."

"Speaking of which . . . what's the latest report?" Gia asked.

"It has begun. We're being cautious, but it is slowly taking effect." Victoria sat a long, rectangular box on the table and proceeded to flip open the heavy lid. Inside the velvet-lined box sat three compartments filled with fat bottles no bigger than a row of eggs.

"Glad to hear that." Gia ran her gloved fingers over the bottles as if they were tiny candies in a box. "You never told me how you were so adept at procuring these memories, my dearest V. I've been away from you for so long. Tell me."

"I don't share the inner workings of my marvel."

Gia grabbed Victoria's wrist, squeezing until the message was received; this was a demand and not a request.

"I've always been in the business of secrets; you know that, Gia." She yanked her arm away. "The perfume encloses the memory. Some give their secrets to me willingly, others just to hide them from government-leaching incants."

Gia grinned at her. When they were young girls at the Arcanum, she'd love to watch Victoria take the secrets of their classmates and use them as collateral to get whatever they wanted. She'd helped make the Aces so powerful. She'd do whatever it took to get her back permanently at her side. She was one of her greatest weapons.

"I'm nothing more than a thief, now," Victoria admitted, her hazel eyes glazing over with hate. "Hired to siphon secrets from the sick, the dying, the unwilling, and those dead and gone."

A smile broke out on Gia's face. Not so noble after all. "Tell me the truth. How did you procure all of these secrets and memories?"

Victoria gritted her teeth. Gia didn't care if it was taboo to ask.

"Every person I create a perfume for, I take memories that could be helpful for me. A second payment for safekeeping."

Gia gave her an applause. "You've done well with your monstrous marvel." She lifted each little bottle one by one, examining the tiny, handwritten labels detailing the names and dates of collection. She held out one of the vials. The very one she'd come so very far to see. "Did you find the first thing I need? The correct parfum de mémoires."

"Yes," Victoria spat; her white cheeks flushed red. "I'm working my way down the list."

Gia sank back in the chaise lounge as if preparing for a show, and Victoria handed her a bottle.

The label read: CLARA TRIVELINO.

Her mother.

Victoria set six bowls in a circle. Starting at the top of the circle, she poured water into the first two and cast petals into them. They resembled fat blood drops and swirled on the surface for a moment before dissolving. She blended the contents of both bowls together into a jar, turning the solution a deep indigo, the color of the wintery twilight sky over Paris right this very moment.

The next two bowls combined into a perfectly clear liquid, like fine blown glass. And the last two blended into a solution blacker than black, the darkest of shadows.

"What are you doing exactly?" Gia leaned forward.

"Preparing a conduit to release the memory." Victoria lit a match, setting each bowl's liquid on fire. "This one was hard to get from your mother. She fought me to the very end."

Gia's heart pounded with excitement. She hoped her mother had suffered too. Just as she had.

Thick clouds bubbled up, and the fire turned to shadow. Shapes formed. Familiar ones.

Gia watched as the smoke sharpened into view; thinning out and turning into something like a newsreel projection. The memory unfolded: her mother taking her child that fateful night of her arrest, her mother changing the rules of opening the family vault, her mother hiding the child in the Fewel City of New York.

A smile consumed Gia's face. She knew where she needed to go now.

She knew how to get what she wanted.

Nothing could stop her now.

CHAPTER THIRTEEN

MADAME BAPTISTE'S PALACE OF MEMORIES

Ella's mantle ballooned around her like a parachute. The wind slapped around her twists. For a long, horrifying moment, it was like falling down a deep, dark hole until she felt solid ground, and the blurry shapes around her sharpened. She blinked until everything settled.

"Hello," she called out.

Her voice bounced back.

"Anyone here?" she said, then felt stupid. "Of course no one is here. I'm inside my godmother's mind." Sometimes conjure felt unbelievable and impossible.

Ella tiptoed forward into the great hall of Aunt Sera's consciousness. The walls were eaten away in spots, with crumbled piles of bricks and stone scattered about at various heights. Her mind felt like a run-down version of her beautiful house back in New Orleans.

A broken ceiling exposed veins of red lightning. They fired like a tapering storm, slow intervals illuminating a dark sky.

Goose bumps covered her arms. Ella put her hand to her chest and couldn't help feeling a little afraid.

She turned around and around as if there was some sort of door where she could exit. One of Mama's annoying phrases popped into her head: *Sometimes the only way out is through.* She took a deep breath, smoothed out her mantle, and walked forward.

Ella passed a myriad of wall portraits—some of family members, some of places, some of objects. She noticed repeated ones. Symbols, maybe? There were two of Headmarveller Mac-Donald. Strange. What was he doing in here? Was she worried about him . . . or her job . . . or something?

But the portraits changed before Ella could pin down exactly who and what the rest of them were. The wallpaper curled and the carpet became threadbare as if to push her deeper into the house. Shadows stretched in every direction. This wasn't the way she'd imagined her beautiful aunt's mind to be. Was she tired? She didn't look it. Was she sick? She hoped not.

A warm object brushed against Ella's leg. Ella screamed and jumped. She spotted a lithe creature, then she heard her godmother's gentle laughter.

"Didn't mean to scare you," the thing said. "It's just me." The speaker's words bled into one another.

"Who are you?" Ella inched backward.

"I've known you your whole life. I was even there when you were born." The creature rose to eye level. "You don't recognize me?"

Two familiar yellow eyes met hers, and the outline of a snake took shape in the subtle darkness. "Echi?"

"Yes," she answered.

Aunt Sera's boa constrictor. Echi licked Ella's cheek, and they giggled.

"What are you doing here?" Ella said.

"I'm her companion after all. We communicate in here," she hissed. "And I protect her mind from invasion. Though I will allow you to be here as a learning lesson, of course."

Ella realized there were so many details she didn't know about conjure. She'd been told she'd get a companion at thirteen. That it would find her somehow when she needed it the most. She didn't know it would be alive in her head too. Ella felt like the list of things she needed to learn was endless.

"Come." Echi zigzagged ahead. "Let us get your little test over with."

Ella couldn't help pausing at each door, wondering what was behind it. She almost turned one of the doorknobs.

"Don't forget," Echi started.

"Right. Don't touch anything. Sorry."

"Keep moving ahead," Echi directed.

She made her way to the end of the hall, then turned left, and the space opened into a great library. Books filled countless shelves. She couldn't see where they ended.

"Don't go in there," Echi warned.

"Why not?"

"Your godmother said to get used to things. Not snoop." Echi tried to block her path, but Ella leaped over her.

"I'm not being nosy. Just looking around." Ella didn't wait for Echi's response and barreled inside.

The library was chock-full of all manner of things—not only books but old files, a card catalog, leather map tubes, dusty albums, and so on. Ella walked through the aisles. Candelabras bathed the spines in a warm glow. Faded letters spelled words Ella had never seen before—*goofering, quincunx, hexes*. She was careful not to touch anything but noted the different books: some thin, some thick, and many too heavy to hold in her hands (even if she wanted to open them). The tables held towers of paperwork. Ella noted the Marvellian symbol on them and wondered how behind her godmother might be and if that was why she was so stressed.

Ella felt too curious and wanted to take a look.

White-and-black explosions clouded her vision. The falling sensation swept her away again.

When she reopened her eyes, she found herself back in Aunt Sera's conjure room, stretched out along a chaise.

Aunt Sera knelt at her side and pressed a hand to her forehead. "Are you all right? I pulled you out too fast. I'm sorry for that."

Ella panted. Aunt Sera put a glass of water in her shaky grip. "Maybe this was all too fast. Maybe I pushed you too hard today." Her godmother's delicate features tensed with worry.

"Are you okay?" Ella asked. "Your mind looked . . ."

"I'm fine. Don't you fuss over me."

Aunt Sera rushed Ella to her feet. "It's nothing. I'll make myself a mind-cleaning spell. Please rest for the remainder of the day, and I'll come check in on you in a little bit." She swept Ella from her lair like a dust bunny and locked the door behind her with a deep click.

THE CONCERNED ARCANUM PARENT INITIATIVE

Dear Headmarveller Rivera and
Headmarveller MacDonald,

The Arcanum Training Institute will pay for allowing
more Conjurors in and endangering all of our children.
Stamping out our scholars' bright light with their EVIL will
have deadly consequences no one can protect you from.
The new Conjure Arts curriculum presents even more
dangerous ideas and lambasts the original Marvellers,
challenging the one, true history of our civilization. Stop
letting them rewrite our valiant efforts and make us into
villains—and most of all, guilt you into presenting our
children with lies.

   We are WATCHING YOU! We WILL replace YOU
both!

From,
The Concerned Parents of the Arcanum Lower School

The Marvellian Times

BREAKING NEWS! NEWS ALERT! MYSTERIOUS ILLNESS BREAKS OUT AT ARCANUM LOWER SCHOOL

The editorial board has intercepted a verified report that the Arcanum Lower School Headmarvellers have attempted to hide a pandemic ravaging the student body—and several Arcanum teachers—of the Institute. Several students have been isolated in the infirmary with complaints of headaches, nosebleeds, rashes, and now, weakened marvels. Parents have been writing to the Headmarvellers with their outrage and shock at the lack of communication. Many are en route to pull their students out for the term.

★—★—★— **STARPOST**—★—★—★

Ella,

The next you-know-what is coming up. Wednesday. Get ready!

Abina

★—★—★— **STARPOST**—★—★—★

Abina,

What if I'm . . . not that great at using a stapler yet?

Ella

★—★—★— **STARPOST**—★—★—★

Ella,

Let's practice together.

Abina

★—★—★— **STARPOST**—★—★—★

Ella,

You better not tell anyone about Clare in the teacher's lounge. You'll regret it.

Noémie

CHAPTER FOURTEEN

THE ARCANUM LABYRINTH

Ella, Jason, and Brigit sneaked out of Dr. Choi's Marvellian-Adjacent Beings: Creature Study course as the whole class watched snippets of the first election season debate. Armed with bathroom passes, they went to find the Founder's Room.

First, Ella headed back to her dorm tower to grab the blueprints. The hallways were near empty. A few starfolk here and there fixing star-lanterns or cleaning windows or shoveling snow from the corridors. She tried not to give them any reason to stop her.

She skulked through the Arcanum entry hall and eased by the Tricentennial exhibit, trying her very best to ignore the crossing tug she felt. Two coppers patrolled the entrance.

"Keep walking," she whispered to herself, willing away her curiosity about whatever was inside that case causing this tug.

Ella spotted the Azure Dragon Tower ahead and raced up to her room. She plucked the blueprints from the bottle tree and made it to the founders' statues in the Headmarveller's Wing without further incident. Part of her felt afraid because it'd been too easy. But Masterji Thakur had asked for the blueprints back by today, so this was her last chance. The exhibit and the historians would be leaving tomorrow for the grand tour.

She found Brigit and Jason crouched behind the terracotta statues waiting for her.

"Took you long enough," Brigit said. "We've almost gotten caught a million times."

Jason lifted a rottie to her face. "Brownie says the teachers' meeting will be done soon and we need to hurry."

Ella gazed at the Dean of Discipline's office before turning to the animated statues. She looked at their terracotta forms and watched their repeated movements: Femi Ademola the Honest lifting his bowl of truth soup, Indira Patel the Brave throwing her daggers, Shuai Chen the Keen making lightning clouds, Louis Antonio Villarreal the Sage twitching his handlebar mustache, and Olivia Hellbourne the Patient playing her flute. She tried not to imagine how disappointed they might be about their hijinks. She tried not to imagine how much trouble they'd be in if caught.

Brigit ran her fingers over the stone wall. "I don't see a door."

Ella joined her, feeling for a crease or a tiny draft of wind. Nothing.

"Do we know an incant?" Brigit asked.

"Maybe the one for open?" Jason tried various words.

But nothing happened again.

"Wait!" Jason plucked Brownie from his hood. "What did you say?"

"What?" Ella and Brigit said in unison.

"She says there's a hidden button. It's not an incant that will open it. She saw the door opened when"—he paused and lifted the rottie to his ear—"those historians were visiting."

The rottie leaped from Jason's arms, her chubby bottom and long tail thwacking one of the stones. Lines of light appeared along the wall, taking the shape of a small door.

"It worked," Jason replied in awe.

A doorknob protruded out like a fat mushroom cap.

Ella planted a dozen kisses on the rottie's head, promising her conjure sweets.

"You ready?" Brigit asked.

Ella didn't know if she was, but she needed to be. She stepped forward and turned the knob. The door wiggled before opening.

They gazed down at the staircase, then took tentative steps into the dark. The pitter-patter of tiny feet made Brigit scream.

"Shh! It's just the rotties," Jason said. "They said to be careful."

"I hate it down here," Brigit grumbled. "We can't see *anything*. And what if these stairs stop and plunge us into the sky?"

"Don't you think we'd be able to feel the wind?" Jason replied.

Ella felt Brigit's angry stomp. Then a tiny ball of light illuminated the darkness. Brigit's marvel light.

"Thanks," Ella said.

Cobwebs clung to corners and locked doors hid their contents. They passed by rooms labeled STORAGE, STELLACITY HUB, and FREEZER. They walked and walked, minutes feeling like hours. They'd traversed up and down many sets of staircases and ventured through what felt like a million halls.

"I feel like we've been down this way before," Brigit complained. "We already passed by this Paragon closet. I remember."

The desperation piled up in Ella, and they were no closer to finding the Founder's Room again. This felt like her last chance to unlock the blueprints before having to return them to Masterji Thakur. She couldn't let him down or get him in any more trouble because of her. She felt like the Institute itself was keeping her away from the truth and playing some sort of elaborate game.

"Wait," Jason called out, then he dropped low to the ground. He pressed his ear to the wall, then a panel slid open. "The rotties said we keep passing it. They'll show us."

Brigit lowered her hand. Her marvel light washed over five tiny rotties eagerly smiling up at them.

"They want sweets after, though. I promised them a milk dragon egg," Jason said.

Ella would give them just about anything right now. They'd saved the day. The rotties took off in the opposite direction, and the trio followed like there was a tornado at their heels. The blueprint tube became slick, her sweaty hands threatening to drop it. Ella's eyes blurred and her muscles ached, but she kept going until the rotties stopped in front of the black door labeled FOUNDER'S ROOM.

The rotties picked the lock. The door opened. It was just as she'd remembered it: the wall portraits of the founders, the majestic circular table and five chairs.

"Wow." Jason did a lap around the room, looking up at each one of the founders. "Did you know that they all died weird deaths?" He slipped a book from his satchel and flashed the cover, *The Founders' Magic: The Unauthorized Biography of the Fastidious Five.*

"Strange," Brigit replied.

"When I first came down here with Masterji Thakur, the blueprints floated over that table," Ella said.

"Let's see what they say now." Brigit thumped the container.

Ella eased them out. The thick paper unfurled and stretched as if it were a cat returning home to its warm bed.

Ella and Jason worked quickly to access the Arcanum version buttons and scroll back to the very first one. Sweat poured down her forehead as she pushed the floating button. This was it. This was where she'd find her answers about the first iteration of the Arcanum Training Institute for Marvelous and Uncanny Endeavors and what her great-grandfather had designed.

The blueprints illuminated. The buildings began to transform. Five towers went to three. The trolleys changed into self-pulled carriages. The library floated high above, moving every few seconds. The Arcanum Cardinal sat in the very center emanating twilight stardust. She knew that deep purple glow anywhere. Same as the twilight inside her.

She gasped.

"What is it?" Jason said.

"See the Cardinal?" Ella perched on a chair and pointed.

"Yeah, so what? It's in the courtyard," Brigit replied.

"It's pulsing." Jason leaned as close as possible, the subtle blue light washing over his deep brown skin.

"Twilight stars." Ella marveled at it. She couldn't believe it. She thought her eyes were deceiving her.

There's no way Marvellers would be able to get that anywhere but the Underworld. This was her proof. This was why she felt the crossing tug when she went near it. Just like the blueprints themselves . . . and even the one in the Vellian Port. The Arcanum Cardinal and the Vellian Port Cardinal were Conjure made. All five must be.

"They're from the Underworld skies. Conjure folk use the

fallen dust in spells. It's my gran's favorite ingredient to work with. Only a Conjuror could work this material." All the stories Papa told her about those who tried to steal it or use its properties without proper Conjure authorization raced through her head. There was no explaining this away if they were still using the twilight stardust. "This proves—"

The door shot open. The historians marched in with Dr. Huang, Dr. Yohannes, and Aries.

Ella's heart sank into her stomach. She rolled up the blueprints.

"Now what do you think you're doing?" one of the historians asked.

"Tampering with a historical document!" another added. "And touching something so fragile and valuable without the proper gloves."

"Did you compromise our exhibit—and bring those down here?" a third pressed. "Why in the world would you do that?"

"We're going to need some answers." Dr. Yohannes gazed at Ella, then Brigit and Jason with disappointed eyes.

Ella tried to find the words to explain, but she couldn't. Her pulse thundered, and she felt like she'd swallowed an earthquake. It reminded her of the last time she'd been busted in the Founder's Room after she had to call for help with Masterji Thakur. She could still feel Dr. Slade's sharp gaze on her, and this time it felt a little worse because she liked Dr. Yohannes so much. Both Brigit and Jason stared at the ground.

They'd lost the blueprints for sure now.

The Marvellian Times

"WHO GETS TO LIVE WITH US?" THE ELECTION QUESTION SENDING VOTERS TO THE POLLS!

OP-ED by Joseph Lyons

The big-ticket issue come the summer election season will be immigration. If the Ace of Anarchy isn't put back in her cage by then, most will try to blame the government for the dangerous criminal on the loose . . . but we all know what the election will come down to . . . the skeleton in the closet, the elephant in the room . . . the inclusion of Conjurors and near-human creatures in our society. That's who will be blamed. Star folk, fae, gumihos and kitsunes, and more will bear the brunt.

Will we accept them? Can they become *true* Marvellian citizens? This happened years before they stopped erasing our history books. West African Marvellers had a hard time. Caribbean Marvellers faced their own bans. Asian Marvellers dealt with quotas and had to petition for the translation crystal and pioneer the technology themselves. And so on . . .

One might call this resistance to change the *true* Marvellian Way. Heck, most Indigenous Marvellers from the Americas don't even trust us enough to live in the skies alongside us.

An immigration bill is headed to the Supreme Courts of Justice, but will it pass the Assembly?

We shall see, dear readers. Outlook is not good.

FIREWORK!

Gia put the finishing touches on her masterpiece while ignoring a chorus of frustrated sighs from Victoria Baudelaire as well as the *Star Weekly* newsreel report on the presidential election in the background. A replica of the very first stellacity lamp sat between them like the one that would soon be on display in the Tricentennial exhibit in Astradam.

Gia's eyes volleyed from the sketch to the object before her, a cross between an hourglass and a lamp. "You'll put on a beautiful show, won't you?" She crouched beside the worktable, admiring the object's glass veins, pathways for stellacity that would fill with her secret weapon. "My pretty little firework. My little flower."

"Isn't there another way?" Victoria grumbled.

"You know there isn't." Gia looked up at her. "Now, fill it—and explain it again. I need to hear every detail. Don't leave anything out."

Victoria carefully placed a tray beside the lamp. With shaky fingers, she filled its bulbous body with a sandy mixture that tickled Gia's nose. Gia could identify saltpeter, charcoal, and sulfur.

Victoria nestled lavender perfume blocks into the sand. "Once the sand is heated, the wax will melt and the lamp will explode. The fumes should have their desired effects on any who breathe it in. There's enough here to fill the streets of Celestian City and probably Betelmore too."

Gia smiled to herself. She loved it when a plan came together. While Victoria prepared the lamp, she turned her attention to the presidential candidates deep in debate.

The first: current president Al-Nahwi in a gorgeous hijab and wearing a blinking button that read—CHANGE WE NEED, CHANGE WE CAN BELIEVE IN.

The second: a Black man named Sir Walter Tull, repeating his slogan—A NEW DEAL FOR MARVELLERS—over and over again with his thick British accent.

The third: Jefferson Lumen, with his liver-spotted white skin, and his gaudy blinking signs—MAKE THE MARVELLIAN WORLD LIGHT AGAIN!

The last: Her enemy, Johan Fenris Knudsen I, with his perfect smile and his charming message, A TIME FOR MARVELLIAN GREATNESS IS HERE!

The arguments swarmed: President Al-Nahwi reminded listeners of all she'd done to make the Marvellian community more inclusive. Sir Walter Tull discussed the changes the cities needed to survive in the skies. Jefferson Lumen complained about everything the current president had accomplished. Johan Fenris Knudsen I spoke about the society needing to focus on its own protection and isolation.

"I never thought Johan would make it that far," Victoria said. "Certainly not without you."

Gia turned off the news-box. "He won't for much longer. He'll pay." She looked back at the lamp. "Now, how do I detonate it?"

Victoria pulled a vial from her pocket. Inside, a cluster of fire-bugs climbed on top of one another. "Pour these into the sand. As it churns, they'll ignite and warm the sand. Then—"

"BOOM!" Gia said with a laugh. "The greatest light show in the skies."

★—★—★— **STARPOST** —★—★—★

I'm still watching you, Ella.

CHAPTER FIFTEEN
INDEFENSIBLE INCANTS

lla followed behind Aries with heavy feet. As they got closer
and closer to the Headmarveller's Wing, she'd practiced what
she planned to say. She could hear Jason's anxious breathing
and the tiny stomp in Brigit's feet. She felt even more terrible.
Now she'd gotten her friends in major trouble and she'd lost
the blueprints, her one piece of evidence . . . and might've gotten
Masterji Thakur in even more trouble by accident. She'd been so
close . . . and now, poof, *nothing*.

Her thoughts churned over and over again in her head, and she
could hear the lies she'd told to Dr. Yohannes, Dr. Huang, and the
historians. That they'd merely found the blueprints in that room
and didn't know what they were. She didn't know what would happen when they discovered the blueprints in the exhibit were fake.
She hadn't had time to think through that part.

"I don't know why the three of you were in the bowels of the
school," Aries said for the third time. "Last year you were also
always in a mess."

"And it saved everyone," Jason blurted out.

"If that's what you call it," he replied. "I got fined three months of wages for helping you."

Ella swallowed hard. She didn't think she could feel worse, but she did. "I . . . we . . . didn't know that happened to you, Aries. I'm sorry." She had so much to make up for, and she wished she could just tell him the whole truth about the blueprints, the secrets, and what they'd been up to. She knew he'd understand, but she didn't want to put him in any danger or invite any more trouble his way by knowing.

"I just don't understand." He shook his head, disappointed.

"Maybe we should . . . ," Jason started, then stopped.

"Maybe you should do what?" Aries questioned.

The trio exchanged tense glances.

"Tell you the truth," Ella replied, fighting the fear inside her.

Aries paused, then led them into a small nook. "What's going on?"

The story poured out of Ella. She told him everything and almost cried when she mentioned how Masterji Thakur might be in trouble with the government because of her.

Aries's jaw dropped, then his brow furrowed. He started to pace. Ella held her breath. Would he tell the Headmarvellers—or the historians? Would he get them in even more trouble? Would he spill their secrets?

"The starfolk used to whisper about things like this." He leaned in closer. "Marvellers have a lot of things they're desperate to hide. Between us and the rotties, we know."

"ARIES!" The Dean of Discipline, Dean Nabokova, stood a few feet away. "Have you lost your way to the Headmarvellers' offices? Shall we demote you—or better yet, replace you?"

Aries shuddered.

"Ugh," Brigit groaned.

Ella panicked. Had she overheard them?

"My apologies, Dean Nabokova." Aries bowed. "I was waiting for—"

"Me," Ella interrupted. "My head hurt, and I needed a minute. You know, like how the other kids are getting sick?"

Dean Nabokova's lips flattened into a straight line. "Let me make sure you don't lose your way any longer. There's much to discuss." She waved them forward. Her long frock coat dragged behind her like a pool of darkness and made Ella think of the Bayou of Death in the Underworld.

Before Ella could collect herself and get her story straight, the Headmarveller's Wing stood before them. She was out of time. How would she explain their behavior? Or why they were down there in the first place? What had Dr. Yohannes, Dr. Huang, and the historians already told them? Would they message Mama and Papa? Ella thought she might faint with every step forward.

She heard Brigit muttering her frustrations and Jason's nervous gulps.

Aries deposited them in the Headmarvellers' office. Outside the large window, Headmarveller MacDonald's waterhorse, Edi, shook her head with disappointment, then turned her back to them. A fat tear rolled down Jason's face, and the sight made a sob claw its way up Ella's throat. She swallowed over and over again to keep it down. She'd gotten Brigit and Jason into so much trouble.

The Headmarvellers appeared at the top of the staircase, gazing down at them with disappointment.

"I didn't think I'd see the three of you in here this year," Headmarveller Rivera said, taking careful steps down with her glittering cane. "I'd thought you three learned your lesson."

Ella avoided her eyes.

"I cannae say I'm pleased either, you three." Headmarveller MacDonald rubbed his beard. "Who wants to explain?"

A tense silence spread. Ella felt like she might suffocate in it.

"Perhaps some time spent digging trenches in Siberia might help loosen their tongues," Dean Nabokova said. "I can prepare transport."

Ella flinched. "It's my fault. They shouldn't have to pay for it. I'll take the punishment."

"No," Jason protested.

"We all did it," Brigit added.

Headmarveller Rivera's eyebrow lifted. "So, who wants to explain why you were in the Founder's Room?"

"And how did you get down there in the first place?" Headmarveller MacDonald asked.

Ella opened and closed her mouth a few times, trying to form the right lie. How could she get them out of this? She heard Mama's favorite phrase in her head: *Why tell a lie when the truth is an option.* But she didn't feel like the truth was something she could share. Telling the truth right now would affect everything. She needed more time. She needed to figure out her next move, the next plan.

Aries stepped forward, a paw to his chest. "It was my miscommunication, dear Headmarvellers. I take full responsibility. I asked them to help me collect the rotties out of that area. They owed me after all the hubbub at the end of last school year. But I'd already told Dr. Huang and Dr. Yohannes I'd assist them with the tour for the historians."

The shock of Aries's lie made Ella's heart flutter. Aries's eyes burned into hers, and she nodded. She turned to Jason and Brigit, who stared at her in shock. She wished she could whisper inside their minds like Mama did to her and tell them to play along.

"Right," Ella said, prompting Brigit and Jason to nod their heads in agreement.

Dean Nabokova scoffed, then glared at Aries. Ella spotted the sweat slicking the fur around his ears.

Headmarveller MacDonald rubbed his red beard. "That doesn't explain how they got into the bowels of the Arcanum." His eyes narrowed with suspicion. "Those are restricted areas. How would they even know?"

"I left the entrance open for them. They were supposed to wait for me, right?"

The trio nodded.

"We got too curious," Ella said, then apologized.

Aries put his paw in the air. "I will take the consequences for them."

"Hmm." Headmarveller MacDonald sat back in his chair. "And the historians said you were messing with the blueprints. That you had them in your possession. Did you take them from the exhibit, Ella? Why would you do that?"

Ella gulped.

"My fault again," Aries chimed in. "I'd found them on the ground. I fear one of the other students might've been pulling a prank on our *very serious* visitors. You know how kids are these days. Very pesky." He released a fake chuckle. "I was cleaning up yet another blood splatter from the nosebleeds . . ."

Ella noticed how both Headmarveller Rivera and Headmarveller MacDonald squirmed.

"I didn't want any liquids to ruin such a valuable artifact, and I didn't know how to put them back in the exhibit . . . sometimes us starfolk can be so clueless, so I asked Ella to bring them with her to our meeting point. I'd get them back to the Founder's Room safely until the historians could re-install them in the exhibit. I didn't want to make a mess of things."

Ella couldn't tell if the Headmarvellers bought Aries's story, but she couldn't believe how effortlessly he told the lie.

"Thank you for your work, Aries. But you know we'll have to fine you again." Headmarveller Rivera shook her head. "And we might have to have a deeper discussion, Aries, about your place here. This is the second infraction. The Arcanum Training Institute might not be the right fit for you."

Ella's heart sank. Aries could lose his job because of her. "But—"

"The fault is entirely mine." Aries spoke over Ella. "I will take whatever consequences you see fit, madam."

"As for the three of you"—Headmarveller MacDonald turned to them—"you'll serve the Saturday detention with Madame Madge, then an additional one with Dr. Silvera in the Arcanum menagerie. That brings your total to three. Not a good way to start off November."

"Now, I believe you have Global Incants with Dr. Goldblum. Get to it, and I don't want to see you in places you don't belong," Headmarveller Rivera said, escorting them out. The huge doors closed behind them, and Ella's panic about what would happen to Aries made her hands quiver.

✦ ✳ ✦ ✳ ✦

ELLA, JASON, AND BRIGIT LEFT THE HEADMARVELLER'S WING. AS soon as they got far enough away, Ella stopped; her emotions bubbled over, and she couldn't stop crying. She apologized over and over again for landing them in detention. "We can't let Aries get in trouble for us. What if he loses his job here? What will he do?"

A few rotties appeared. They climbed up her mantle and into her arms, trying to comfort her. Both Brigit and Jason hugged her and told her it was going to be okay, but she struggled to believe them. "What are we going to do?" Ella asked.

"We have to tell everyone," Jason said.

"We can't let anything bad happen to Masterji Thakur or Aries. Not when everyone here is lying." Brigit scowled. "When people know the truth, it'll change everything."

"That's what I'm afraid of," Ella admitted. She hadn't thought through how she was going to share all these Arcanum secrets with the world quite yet. "What if they don't believe me?"

"We'll make them." Jason balled his fist.

An announcement-balloon reminded them that the next sessions would begin in less than five minutes. They took off to the Sound Tower, zipping beneath a huge mechanical ear and floating instruments from every corner of the world. Sitars, pianos, trumpets, trombones, and guitars played a tune every few minutes while founder Olivia Hellbourne called out: *The ear hears all.*

They whizzed past other trainees, navigating through a flurry of mantles, as students hustled to avoid being late. They tumbled into their Global Incants class three minutes tardy.

Posters projected the root words of popular incants, while interactive maps traced their origins. Balloons carried banners explaining the Marvellian incant laws, like ALL MARVELLERS AND THEIR INNER LIGHT ARE CONSIDERED EQUAL, and MARVELLERS SHALL NEVER USE INCANTS TO HARM OTHERS.

Dr. Goldblum stood in front of the room. Tall and reed thin, he held a long staff, and a yarmulke sat nestled between the soft curls of his hair. "More dawdling stars! Please find your desks and prepare to expand your incant capacity."

Ella, Brigit, and Jason scrambled to find seats, but they had to split up. Brigit plopped down beside Abina and Siobhan before Ella got the chance, while Jason got a spot next to his roommate Miguel. The only seat remaining was between the new girl Noémie and her worst enemy, Clare Lumen.

Ella felt like a wrung-out sock after what had happened with the Headmarvellers and Aries, and she wasn't prepared for a fight. She shrugged, easing into the seat as if it were a scalding bath.

Clare gawked at her like a dragon had joined their shared desk. She smoothed her red hair, then played with her blinking necklace, tracing her fingers along the letters of her name. Noémie stared so hard Ella thought maybe her marvel allowed her to see people's skeletons. Her intense eyes made Ella's skin crawl, and she smelled of heady perfume.

Ella sneezed.

Clare rolled her eyes, and whispered, "Keep your germs to yourself. People are getting sick; don't you know that?"

Ella rolled her eyes but didn't get to challenge her, as Dr. Goldblum walked to the front of the room.

"Now that we're all settled, we can get down to business. We've finished our refresher unit on basic universal incants and their origins. Hopefully, we're ready to build upon that foundation." Dr. Goldblum flipped over a massive chalkboard. "Incants connect us to our marvel light. The words set our intentions. Otherwise, we would be lost to the pure chaos of our emotions.

When you focus your light and send it through your stapier, or eventually your unique channellor, it helps make it more precise. This is the foundation of our practice of the Marvellian Arts, or light science, as I like to call it."

He tapped the chalkboard with his staff and said, "Tichtov."

A fat piece of chalk rose from his desk and hovered close to the board. It wrote: HELLO!

"Can anyone tell me how I just did that?" he asked.

Hands waved in the air. Ella sat back in her chair, thinking. She felt terrible she couldn't remember the assigned reading from *The Incant: Form and Function, the Science of Allurement and Figments*. Her brain felt overstuffed after everything that had happened, her singular focus on losing the blueprints and Aries taking the blame for them.

Dr. Goldblum called on her desk mate Noémie.

"It's an allurement. You're enchanting the chalk to write by itself—and do something it's not supposed to do," she replied, then turned to Ella with a smug grin as if she could hear Ella's racing thoughts. Noémie's strange gaze made her stomach twist again.

The chalk wrote the word ALLUREMENT.

"And how did I get it to write the word *hello?*" he followed up.

"You thought about what you wanted it to say," she added.

"Yes, very good. I gave the chalk a command, then held the message in my mind, my intention." He nodded with approval. "But does it last forever?"

Noémie didn't turn back to Dr. Goldblum to answer, instead continuing to stare at Ella. "Depends on how strong you are. Forever if your will is powerful enough."

Ella felt stubborn. She wouldn't look away until Noémie did. What was her problem? Why was she staring at her?

"Very good, Noémie." Dr. Goldblum turned back to the board, and shouted, "Convierte!"

Suddenly, the chalk sprouted wings and fluttered over their heads like a white butterfly. Ella broke eye contact with Noémie to follow its path.

"Now, what have I done, my stars?" Dr. Goldblum asked.

More hands raised.

He called on Lian.

She cleared her throat, smoothed the front of her mantle. "A figment," she replied, confident. "You changed the chalk's appearance—or its form."

"Very good, very good. I also held the image of a butterfly in my head while I said the incant." Dr. Goldblum beamed. "A great understanding of the fundamentals. Maybe one of you might join the United League of Marvellers in Celestial City, and work on creating new incants for all of us to enjoy someday."

The chalk flew back to the board, writing the word FIGMENT below ALLUREMENT.

The class clapped with delight. It wasn't so different from the way Conjurors interacted with the world. But they sang their spells instead of cramming actions into one word.

They could also do more than produce a temporary allurement like having chalk write by itself. Mama could cross into the will of any object, leave her commanding song behind, and it'd be permanent for as long as she wanted. She thought of the house broom that swept on the hour and Gran's iron that made its way into everyone's closets on Sundays to put a pleat in every pant leg and starch every collar. And Conjurors could do more than create a figment, not only making an object grow wings for a single flight, but rather crossing into its essence and changing it forever.

The Baptiste family home in New Orleans had been brought alive by one of their ancestors, and it sometimes shuffled rooms around and redecorated itself based on the seasons.

"As you improve your incant work, you can use figments and allurements merely by thinking them." He pursed his lips. The chalk danced. "Or by signing." He moved his hands in rapid succession, spelling the word in sign language. The chalk back-flipped.

Oohs and *aahs* exploded.

"But before we get too excited, we must understand the rules and limitations," Dr. Goldblum said.

The chalk wrote the words INDEFENSIBLE INCANTS beneath the other two words.

A hush fell over everyone.

"I see we all seem to know what these are as well."

Ella heard several gulps and awkward shuffles.

"Shanti!" Dr. Goldblum called out, and the chalk settled back on his desk. He pointed his long staff at one of the overhead blimps, and it sailed through the air. The banner read:

THE EIGHT INDEFENSIBLE INCANT USES

Marvellers shall not use incants to permanently alter matter.

*Marvellers shall not use incants to manipulate
the natural growth of living things.*

Marvellers shall not use incants to mislead and manipulate.

Marvellers shall not use incants to harm any living being.

*Marvellers shall not use incants to impede
the will of other living beings.*

Marvellers shall not use incants to steal.

*Marvellers shall not use incants to
torture themselves or other living beings.*

Marvellers shall not use incants to kill any living being.

"With great incant work comes great responsibility. Use of incants in any of these ways will land you in hot trouble."

"A trip to the Cards of Deadly Fate," someone blurted out.

"You make it seem like a vacation," Dr. Goldblum said. "It's a life-long sentence without appeal."

Whispers exploded. Ella caught snippets:

"Madame Baptiste can make things grow!"
"My mother said Ella's mom can walk around in your head."
"They also unnaturally control their pets."

Ella's cheeks went hot. She heard Jason and Brigit attempt to argue with the whispering voices, but she couldn't turn around to face them. Anger swelled in her. It made her think of last year when they ransacked her room and sent her those anonymous notes. She didn't want to go back to those feelings.

Just watch the board. She kept her eyes fixated on Dr. Goldblum.

He shushed the class, but the gossip grew louder as he tried to push through his lecture.

Her jaw clenched. The whispers weren't wrong. Why did

Marvellers think these things were bad? Why did these Conjure skills violate the rules of Marvellian light science?

Ella wanted to raise her hand and ask, but it felt like last year all over again—her having to explain that conjure wasn't scary or bad . . . but a different tradition.

They all stole glances at her. She sank deeper into her chair. Usually, she would've returned every glare and stare with an equal one, but today, she felt too tired after all that had happened earlier. She couldn't shake the look in Aries's eyes and Head-marveller Rivera's threat to remove him from the Arcanum because of what they'd done. She couldn't stop obsessing over what would happen to the blueprints, and if Aries's lie would hold if they discovered the fake ones. She swallowed hard, pushing away the tears. All her emotions were too close to the surface for her liking.

An announcement-balloon puttered into the class. Its chime disrupted Dr. Goldblum's lesson: "Arcanum trainees, we have an important message for you all. We regret to inform you that the Institute will be closing early for winter break due to the ongoing illness plaguing our student body. Your parents and guardians have been notified. Arcanum instructors, please share the approved information with your class. All activities have been postponed until further notice."

Ella turned to Jason and Brigit. They looked equally confused. The Arcanum was closing. What did this mean?

LEAKED

The Arcanum Training Institute for Marvelous and Uncanny Endeavors

+ ——————— Lower School ——————— +

Dear Families of Trainees in the Lower School,

We regret to inform you that the Arcanum's Lower School will be closing early for winter break on November 6 due to the ongoing and contagious illness spreading among the student body; our desire is to help contain the outbreak.

Please make arrangements to pick your students up from the Vellian Port or the Stardust Pier tomorrow at 6:00 p.m. GMT.

If you have any questions, please send an urgent starpost to our offices.

We are sad not to be able to finish our term, but we have full confidence that our community will be back together soon. Your scholars have been given assignments to complete and send by starpost back to the Arcanum. Be sure to adhere to the schedule.

All the light and good marvelling,

Headmarveller Rivera and Headmarveller MacDonald

Pandemic at Arcanum Institute Caused by Outsiders!

Integration has brought disease to our door!

Our government is shrouded in darkness and so worried about non-Marvellers that they've forgotten to take care of their own.

PROTECT OUR CHILDREN

Make the Marvellian World Light Again!

Vote Jefferson Lumen for President

CHAPTER SIXTEEN
THE JOURNEY HOME

irls! Girls! Up to your rooms and pack up, quickly now," Mrs. Francesca, their Tower Adviser, shouted. "Take only what you need. I have been assured by our noble Head-marvellers that we will be back here before you know it." She clapped her hands and rushed everyone up the stairs. "The sky-ferries leave in ninety minutes."

Ella's heart fluttered as she packed her juju-trunk. Brigit slung everything in her marvel-valise without folding despite Feste's protests about being tidy. Brigit mumbled under her breath and clenched her jaw like she was two seconds from blowing up. Ella was upset about leaving the Arcanum as well, but she thought she'd never live to see the day when Brigit did not want to go home to New York City.

"You all right?" Ella let the question ease out as she packed her saints away in their carrier.

"No," Brigit barked, her cheeks bright red and her eyes glazed over with frustrated tears.

"Want to talk about it?" Ella carefully made her way to Brigit's side of the room.

"No." Brigit threw a scrapbook on the top of her messy clothes and yarn, and it exploded everywhere. Pictures, newsreel film, and photocopies scattered along the floor. She dropped to her knees, scrambling to gather everything up.

Ella picked up a strip of newsreel film. She made sure not to be nosy and hand it straight back to Brigit. "What is all this?"

"What I've been doing in the library with Siobhan." She showed Ella the scrapbook. Ella spotted pictures of Gia Trivelino and the commedia dell'arte circus, newsreels about the murder of Phineas Astley, papers about her grandparents, and more.

Ella's eyebrow lifted. "Oh." An instant wave of guilt hit her. She'd been so upset with Brigit for not telling her about the after-curfew visits to the library with Siobhan . . . even though she never told Brigit about the Marvel Combat practice league in the greenhouse with Abina and Jason. The hypocrisy of it all made Ella feel even more terrible.

"I wanted some of my questions answered. Like who's my dad? And what happened to me the night . . . when my . . ."— she stumbled over the word *mother*—"was arrested. Siobhan was helping me. And I didn't want to tell you because I was embarrassed."

"Why would you be?" Ella crouched down beside her.

"I am the daughter of the worst person in the world. You have the best family in the world." Tears streaked down Brigit's cheeks. Feste climbed into her lap and tried to wipe them away. "Siobhan gets it because everyone whispers about her family. Her ma and pa are always in trouble and in the newspapers."

"They say things about me too," Ella reminded her.

"Yes, but it's different."

Ella didn't understand how, but Brigit was too upset for her to ask another question. "None of this is your fault. Who Gia is and what she's done."

"It doesn't feel that way. When everyone finds out, they'll think I'm just like her . . . and maybe I am. Maybe I'll be just as bad." Brigit kicked away some of her research and sobbed. "I needed to find out if I had at least one good parent, but now I won't be able to finish looking because we're going home."

Ella didn't have the answers. Instead, she sat and held Brigit's hand until she calmed down.

A reminder-balloon puttered into their room with a five-minute dismissal warning. They hustled out of the Azure Dragon Tower. Mrs. Francesca led them to the Arcanum entrance. They stood in dorm groups as each level exited to the docks. The Level Fours marched out into the snow first.

"Ella!"

She whipped around to find Masterji Thakur near the wall. He waved her over, and Mrs. Francesca gave her permission to leave the group.

He gazed down at her with concerned eyes. "I heard what happened with Aries and the Founder's Room and the blueprints."

Shame spiraled inside Ella. She wanted to explain, but there were too many people around. She opened her mouth to speak, but Masterji Thakur shook his head.

"Did you find what you needed to find?"

"Yes, but I don't know what to do with the information. How to . . ."

"I'm sure you'll figure it out during your unexpectedly long winter break," he mused. "I want you to enjoy your time at home and try not to worry."

"I don't want to go home."

"You'll be missing Saturday detention." He winked, but Ella couldn't match his enthusiasm. He put a hand on her shoulder. "It'll be okay."

"But what if . . ."

"Don't allow your mind to reach for darkness. Stay positive." He lifted her chin, and she nodded. He flashed her his signature smile, and the pearls on his turban wiggled. "The replicas have been put away, and borrowed items have been returned. None are the wiser. The exhibit is making its way to Astradam."

She nodded. Her proof was so far away now.

He gave her a hug. "The truth always finds its way out. Safe travels. Try to enjoy the time back home. You might uncover something useful. I promise you that the Arcanum Training Institute—and I—will be here upon your return. I'll make sure of it."

She made him pinkie promise before rejoining her dorm group.

"Stay to the left!" a copper yelled at the Level Three trainees preparing to exit.

"Make way, make way," another one barked to the Level Two group.

The Arcanum doors swung open, and a series of bodyguards marched in, making a wall between the students and a very important man. He wore a perfect gray suit with buttons that matched his white blond hair. He had a smile that was hard to look away from. A curved scar ran from his forehead, over his eyelid, and down to his lip, like somebody had tried to carve a crescent moon into his face.

A masked copper dressed in all black stood beside him. The Headmarvellers raced over to greet him.

He was one of the Marvellian presidential candidates. Johan Fenris Knudsen I.

"Mr. Knudsen," Headmarveller Rivera said with a little curtsy. "What an unexpected visit."

Whispers buzzed around Ella.

"Look at his enforcer." Jason pointed at the masked copper at Johan's side. "His shadow."

"All that fancy copper security means he's super important." Miguel inched up on his tiptoes.

Ella felt a strange force gluing her in place, making her stand there and watch this man's every movement. The masked enforcer scanned the crowd, and Ella felt his eyes land on her.

Johan Fenris Knudsen I surveyed the crowd. "I'm here to pick up my son."

"We were just dismissing everyone to the ferry docks. We sent a notice—"

He put a gloved hand up and Headmarveller Rivera squeaked. The sound surprised Ella.

"Johan Fenris Knudsen II, where are you?" the man shouted. "Hurry up—I have a press junket in Celestian City."

A Level Three boy with identical blond hair and blue eyes stepped out of the crowd of students. She'd seen him before. He'd been Bea's partner to help students view the Tricentennial exhibit. Her eyes volleyed between him and Brigit. The resemblance was uncanny.

"He kind of looks like . . ." Jason trailed off as the man and his enforcer turned in their direction. His eyes found the three of them.

Ella flinched. Could he hear them? What sort of marvel did this man have? What sort of marvel did the masked enforcer have?

Johan's head cocked to the side as he continued to stare, and Ella felt Brigit squirm beside her.

"What's your problem?" Brigit spat.

The kids around them chuckled.

Johan took a long moment before slowly smiling.

"I guess manners isn't on the curriculum this year . . . but perhaps it should be." He turned back to a panicked Headmarveller Rivera. "Clean up this school or you'll have no students left to teach." He strode forward, the masked enforcer finally turning his attention away from Ella.

"This way!" Mrs. Francesca shouted. "Level Two is up next! Single file please."

As Ella passed under the Chinese lunar mansions in the entry ceiling, she whispered goodbye to the Azure Dragon and exited the school. A tug of fear had replaced the crossing tug in her heart now. She tried to bury the worry cropping up inside her: *Would she ever get to come back?*

CONFLICTING REPORTS

Gia hid among reporters at the winter press junket in Celestian City's Assembly House arena for the third presidential debate of the election cycle. Lindsay Oliver's face, press badge, and too tight skirt that she'd stolen helped her fit right in. No one took a second look at her. It even helped her pilfer a few coin purses without detection.

Onstage, the four candidates sat in high-backed chairs and looked as if they were getting ready to have a fireside chat. A moderator stood in the middle fielding questions from the press corps and giving directions to the news-blimps hovering just above, ready to send their fresh newsreels around the globe.

Gia waited while they peppered the candidates with questions like "What will the new immigration policies be?" or "What is your vision for adding a fourth jewel to the skies for Marveller city expansion?" or "How do you plan on fixing Marvellians' fraught relationships with Marvellian-adjacent beings?" before asking hers. She even let Malcolm Eugene go through an entire sermon about the treatment of magical creatures in Marvellian society and how Marvellers had a responsibility to protect them.

She raised her hand, prepared to use her most innocent voice.

"Yes, Lindsay Oliver from the *Star Weekly*," the moderator said.

"This question is for candidate Johan Fenris Knudsen I." She eased out the syllables in his name, careful not to let her anger and disdain leak through . . . or her true identity be discovered. He'd know.

He turned to her, the intensity of his blue eyes once having the power to make her do anything. "Yes," he replied.

"I wonder if you—and I suppose the other candidates—would speak about your marvels and talents. I read somewhere that you have one of the notorious monstrous marvels the government has tried to weed out over the years. Is it true?"

The press box exploded at the accusation. But Gia didn't take her eyes off Johan. Not even when those around her jerked her shoulders or chastised her for such a rude question.

Johan rubbed his chin and smiled. "There have been many things said about all of us." He motioned at his fellow candidates. "Isn't that the game of political theater? Discredit and destroy with lies." He pressed a hand to his chest. "I am a Paragon of Sound. *The ear hears well.*" He waited for other Sounds to mimic him before continuing. "I have merely an oratory marvel and the ability to problem-solve and lead. No problem is a match for me." He flashed his smile, earning claps. "It's why being governor of Astradam came so naturally to me."

Gia struggled to fight against his power. She could feel his marvel like heat, softening her, trying to force her into submission.

"You shouldn't believe everything you see in the newsreels, my lady." He earned chuckles from those around her.

Gia let him have this laugh—she would have the last.

CHAPTER SEVENTEEN

CHRISTMAS IN NEW ORLEANS

Ella usually loved being in New Orleans at Christmastime. The wrought-iron house galleries draped with holly and lights, the streetcars and steamboats decked out, the bonfires on the levee to guide Papa Noël to the city, the carolers making their way through the streets, filling it with songs, and their big Réveillon dinner tonight.

But it all felt different right now.

She'd been at home for far too long, and she still hadn't heard any news about the other sick students or when the Arcanum would reopen after the winter break. Each day, she checked her starpost box and waited for her daily subscription reels from the *Marvellian Times* to arrive, but there were no new reports. Her worried starposts to Aries and Masterji Thakur had also gone unanswered. And Mama started talking about re-enrolling her in Madame Collette's Conjure École so she wouldn't miss out on learning after the weeks continued to pass by. And worse, Mama had her on a daily medicine regiment, filling her with all sorts of tonics to protect her from (and prevent whatever) "Marvellian disease" she might've been exposed to in the skies.

Conjure folk kept their distance. Fewer people dropped by the conjure pharmacy for their usual holiday gifts, and the amount of visitors who usually stopped by the house had dwindled to zero.

Even her dreams were a mess. She kept waking up with nightmares about the Arcanum, the blueprints, and the Marvellian Tricentennial exhibit. She couldn't get the images to go away, not even with Gran's special nighttime tea and Mama's sleep sachet under her pillow.

And lastly, a weird black bird perched on her windowsill each morning. Surely, it was a bad omen that winter break would continue to get worse.

Ella felt like a bone knocked out of its socket. With the blueprints gone, the Institute closed, and faced with the impossibility of proving Conjuror involvement in the creation of the school, all she could manage was to sit on the couch and stare outside every day. She couldn't even unpack her satchel or practice using her stapler. She was barely making progress in the latest book she was reading, *The Conjure City: Keeping Our Neighborhoods Safe*, to scan for mentions of the architect . . . and reading was one of her favorite things to do.

"Get your nose out of that window, sugar, and help me season these skillets," Gran called out from the kitchen. "Grab some twilight stardust from the conjure room on your way."

Ella turned away from the front window and the Christmas parade making its way down the street. Usually, she would've jumped at the chance of helping Gran prepare the skillets for holiday conjure work, but today her heart wasn't in it. She had to drag herself out of the chaise.

"Turn that frown upside down, baby girl." Gran tapped her foot. "Hop to it! We'll be getting ready for dinner soon, and there's work to be done."

Gran's companion, Paon, clucked at Ella as she dragged herself to grab bundles of twilight stardust. The sight of it reminded her of the Arcanum Cardinal and how it glowed on the blueprints. A few flakes coated her fingers. "What exactly can you do?" She still hadn't gathered the courage to ask Papa or even Gran about it yet.

"Ella!"

She hustled to the kitchen, and Gran planted her at the counter. Ella busied herself with all her grandmother's demands—seasoning skillets, tying ribbons around sachets, and pruning holiday luck roots—until it was time for the Marsalises to arrive for Réveillon dinner.

The house sparkled around them. Two Christmas trees twinkled, the fireplace held wiggling stockings and a small fire, the saints on the mantelpiece doled out good tidings and Christmas blessings, and the altar overflowed with gifts for the ancestors. Ella even put on the frilly dress Mama had laid out for her without complaint. She would try her best to have a good time, especially since she got to see her best friend Reagan tonight.

Hours later, the Marsalises and her family sat around a table covered with ham, oyster gumbo, shrimp and mirliton dressing, stuffed bell peppers, and dirty rice. Mr. Marsalis kept getting food in his beard, while Mrs. Marsalis tried to clean him up every two seconds.

Mama smiled a real smile for the first time in weeks. Mrs. Marsalis was always able to make her laugh. Papa entertained with stories of pesky haints and spirits trying to escape past the death-bulls. Gumbo and Mrs. Marsalis's companion, a gray fox, chased each other, while Greno and Mr. Marsalis's mockingbird had a chirping contest. Reagan's older twin brothers, Louis and Laurent, played Christmas songs on their trumpets and told hilarious stories about Fewels who wandered in and out of the family's famous jazz club on Frenchmen Street. Their identical companion tarantulas tussled along the table. Winnie and Reagan's little brother, Remi, played checkers in the corner.

Laughter filled the room and Ella felt herself relax for the first time in weeks. It felt like every other Christmas. Maybe everything would be okay after all.

Reagan dropped her fork and everyone laughed.

"Bet a hungry man's coming to dinner," Gran announced.

A heavy knock cut through the laughter. The family dirt dobbin shuddered, spewing dust everywhere and squeaking with concern.

"Tuh, I was just joking! Who could that be? And at this late hour on Christmas Eve?" Gran said. "Your parents planning on visiting, Sebastien?"

"Not yet." Papa went to answer the door. "Joyeux Noël—" He swallowed the rest of his greeting. "How can we help you, Officers?"

Ella spotted a trio of Marvellian coppers. The brass *M* on their uniforms caught the candlelight. Fear mingled with the food in Ella's stomach. What were they doing here?

A hush fell over the room. Mama's eyes narrowed.

"We're investigating the illness breakout at the Arcanum

Training Institute's Lower School, and we have a few questions for your child, Ella Durand, and you," one said.

Ella's pulse raced. Reagan held her hand under the table.

"What's going on?" Reagan whispered.

Ella couldn't form words, her ears working so hard to eavesdrop.

Mama rose from the table and joined Papa at the door. "I know y'all are not here on Réveillon interrupting our meal with this nonsense."

Papa slid his arm around Mama's waist. "It's Christmas Eve and after midnight. If you want to talk to me—or my daughter—please send my office an official letter and we'll make an appointment."

One of the coppers gritted his teeth and his red-eyed wolf barked. Another one stepped forward with a pad and stylus. "And you wouldn't happen to know where Sera Baptiste might be right now? We went to her home and she's not there."

"You do know people travel during the holidays, yes?" Mama replied.

"Aubrielle." Papa leaned down to kiss her cheek. "Officers, we don't know what her winter plans were, so we can't help you. Have a wonderful season if you're traveling. Good evening to you." He closed the door before they could respond, then slowly turned back to face those at the table.

"What was that about?" Mrs. Marsalis asked.

Mama crashed back into her seat, anger radiating off her. "They think we're to blame. I knew it."

"About what?" Ella eased her question out.

"They think their grand school in the sky has closed due to you and the other Conjure kids . . . and now, apparently, my cousin Sera too. They're going to find a way to blame us like they always do."

Ella's stomach flip-flopped. "But I didn't do anything."

"It doesn't matter. You were there. You're the scapegoat." Mr. Marsalis rubbed his temples.

"By hook or crook, they always find a way to pin it on us." Gran shoved her plate away. "They'll blame those sweet Navajo students too. I read an article about it yesterday in *The Conjure Picayune*. They're looking for anything to make sense of why *their* children are sick. They wouldn't have cared if it had traveled to any Conjure towns. Or made us ill."

"The arrogance"—Mama shook her head—"to think Sera's teachings had anything to do with this."

"It's the easy answer," Mrs. Marsalis chimed in.

"And it's something that will make it worse here. With more and more Conjure folk mad about our kids being at the Arcanum," Mr. Marsalis added. "This will be more fodder for them."

Papa took a deep sigh. Ella's stomach twisted with anxiety.

"I'm just going to say it. I think they want an excuse to occupy," Louis said. "To send their coppers down here to terrorize us twenty-four seven or to impose their rules."

The tension made Ella feel like she was drowning. She bolted from the table and headed straight to her room. She dove onto her bed in a fit full of tears. All of this was her fault. Her parents were hated, the Conjure community was turning on them, and now Marvellian coppers and the government thought she and her aunt were to blame for the sick students. What would happen to them?

A soft knock echoed.

"Go away," she mumbled, but the door opened slowly.

"Ella?" She heard Reagan's soft voice.

Ella buried herself deeper in her quilt. She felt Reagan get into bed next to her.

"It's okay," Reagan whispered.

Ella faced her. "It's not—and you know that!"

"Then we'll fix it," she replied.

She wanted Reagan's words to make her feel better, but the tears kept pouring out. "How?"

"The Griotary will reopen after New Year's. We'll research more and add to what you already discovered. We can prove to the world, to both Conjure folk and Marvellers, that Conjurors designed that Institute, and that they did *not* start any illness."

"No one's going to believe us." Ella turned over again. "I lost the blueprints. The one thing that could prove it all." She went through everything that had happened before the Arcanum closed early. She admitted her failure. Hearing the defeat out loud made it worse.

"Remember when Madame Collette didn't believe us when that firebird had gotten into the attic? She thought we'd lied to get out of class. We set that trap for it. We showed her. She was stunned."

Ella laughed despite her frustration.

"We can do it again." Reagan's eyes burned into Ella. The determination. The confidence.

She let her friend's bravery settle into her.

"They'll never know what hit them." Reagan held Ella's hand. They had to fix this; otherwise, both their lives would change forever.

The Conjure Picayune

MARVELLIAN COPPERS CRAWLING THROUGH CONJURE TOWNS

Marcus Williamson

Beware, fellow Conjure folk. Take precautions. Marvellian coppers spotted in Conjure towns from Harlem to Havana asking questions about our gifts and their side effects for non-Conjure folk.

Don't tell them anything. United front, always. We shall overcome.

★—★—★— **STARPOST**—★—★—★

Ella,

Stop ignoring the bird at your window. Talk to it.
There's a surprise.

Jason

★—★—★— **STARPOST**—★—★—★

Ella,

I'm having strange visions about you, your parents,
and Gran. Is everything okay? I'm sending you the
things I've knitted to see if you can make sense of them.
There's one with your family standing in front of some
angry-looking people . . . like a trial. It feels like trouble.
Miss you.
Be careful.

Love,
Brigit

★—★—★— **STARPOST**—★—★—★

Jason,

How'd you know about the bird at my window?
That's weird. My mama says some birds are bad
fortune and everything sucks right now. She wouldn't
want me talking to any birds.

Did you get my starpost about what happened at
Christmas? The Marvellian coppers are still here—and
they keep asking to meet with me. Ugh!

Ella

Luci,

   I hope it's not weird to send you this letter, but the
Conjure newspapers say we're being blamed for the
sickness at the Arcanum. I wanted to make sure you
were ok and the coppers weren't bothering you at
home.

Ella

P.S.: I plan to prove them wrong. Want to help?

CHAPTER EIGHTEEN

THE GRIOTARY

After New Year's Day, the number of Fewel visitors in New Orleans swelled even more as the Mardi Gras season ramped up. In between family outings, Ella and Reagan had spent hours and hours on the phone talking through all the evidence Reagan had gathered, and Ella filled the notebook she'd gotten for Christmas with all their theories.

"Don't wear out your welcome, little girl," Mama warned as she dropped her at the Marsalises' before her afternoon errands.

"Yes, ma'am." Ella bounded across the lawn. She waved at Reagan's little brother, Remy, as he threw rocks at the family bottle tree, aggravating it into swatting at him.

The front door crept open before Ella could knock. The Marsalis family dirt dobbin appeared. Her droopy eyes scanned Ella from head to toe, and Ella hoped she wouldn't start spewing dust and making trouble. The pesky spirits found their way into Conjure attics and rarely left if the family was nice enough. But they were always good luck . . . and Ella and Reagan would need that today.

"Hmph, it said!" she grumbled. "Here to make more trouble for my girl."

Ella rolled her eyes. "Not more than you."

It cackled and let her pass. Ella loved walking into the Marsalis foyer because it always spilled over with sugar and music. A piano played a melody on its own in the front room, and a wall of trumpets chimed in every few seconds. Ella giggled as plastic stretched over antique chairs and couches at the sight of her. The family broom swept her feet, reminding her to remove her shoes.

Mrs. Marsalis poked her head out of the kitchen. "Hey, sweetie! In the middle of a big catering order." Her voice always sounded like the most beautiful wind chime. "Reagan's in her room. Go on up." Flour coated her light brown cheeks, and she looked tired. *Maybe she'd burned one of her legendary King Cakes,* Ella thought as she climbed the stairs.

"Reagan," Ella called out.

The door was snatched open and a hand yanked her inside.

"What took you so long?" Reagan asked, exasperated.

Her usually tidy room looked like a tornado had barreled through. Most times, everything had its place: her craft area with every item put away, her neatly made bed perched inside her bottle tree like a tree house, her puzzle table filled with her latest accomplishments. But today, messy blankets hung along the tree's branches; the walls were covered with a sheet; her craft section was a mess of paper, yarn, and thumbtacks; and her favorite detective novels were strewn about.

"What's going on?" Ella asked.

"I can't stop thinking about this." Reagan darted to the wall, pulled a string, and revealed a collage of *Conjure Picayune* articles, transcribed newsreel reports from the *Marvellian Times,* all their starposts and notes, photocopies of pages from books, and the rough sketch of the blueprints Ella had made from memory. Everything Ella had given her or shared with her lived on the wall.

"Whoa." Ella's eyes scanned everything, taking it all in. She felt like they'd transformed into detectives from one of Reagan's favorite mystery novels, ready to solve a perilous crime.

Reagan dove into her theories: "Since we know the architect was a famous Conjuror and the founders erased him, I think they must've had a big argument or something. Why else would they pretend there was never a sixth founder?"

Ella considered it for a moment. She'd only ever learned how amazing the founders had been and how much they loved each other and worked in harmony to build the Arcanum community. "But everyone loves them."

"Doesn't mean they didn't do anything wrong. And they didn't do a perfect job cleaning up whatever it was because they forgot to get rid of his Conjure work in the building itself."

Ella nodded. "The blueprints themselves and, now, the Arcanum Cardinal too. The first version of the school showed the tower covered in twilight stardust."

"What does twilight stardust *really* do that Marvellers would want it?" Reagan nibbled her bottom lip. "Madame Collette hasn't taught us much about it yet. Only that it comes from the stars in the Underworld and to season our skillets with it for the best spell results."

"And that it's in the crossing bundles to enter the Underworld," Ella added.

"And to mind-walk and deal with memory-casks." Reagan paced in front of her wall.

"We need to add it to the research list." Ella wrote it in her notebook.

"We also need to find out more about the architect and what happened once he returned from the skies. Like what happened after the five of them sent him away."

Ella wrote down their list of questions thus far. "We need to go back to the Griotary." She filled with possibility like she could put the pieces together. "Do you think they'll take us seriously this time?"

"I think we don't ask the griots. I think we do the research ourselves. Tell them it's a project for Madame Collette."

"Where is it right now?"

"At the corner of Burgundy and Bienville. They reopened yesterday." Reagan pulled on a sweater. "I've been tracking it."

Ella hadn't exactly gotten permission from Mama or Papa to go anywhere other than the Marsalis house, but the Griotary and its current location wasn't very far. They'd only have to take one Conjure streetcar. She'd be back in plenty of time for Mama to pick her up after her hair appointment and errands.

As Mrs. Marsalis continued to curse at her fussy oven, Reagan and Ella sneaked out of the house.

They darted across Reagan's lawn, ignoring Remy's threats to snitch on them, and went around the corner to catch a streetcar. The beautiful black streetcars floated through the city like glittering stars. Conjure folk climbed on and off, and they didn't have to wait long for the Rose Line headed to the Griotary. Ella and Reagan deposited their small black coins in the meter and found an empty bench.

They rode four stops, exiting at Dauphine Street. They

navigated through crowds of Fewels and turned down Bienville until they reached the Griotary.

The building towered over the street, only second to the triple spires of St. Louis's Cathedral. Conjure-roses and ivy tangled with the wrought-iron gallery porches and crawled over the brick like armor. Older Black folks sat in rocking chairs with books piled high and floating beside them.

Ella missed when the library was on her block in the Conjure Quarter, but it had to move every time Fewels started their endless construction.

Three levels of bookshelves ringed the room. When Ella was smaller, it had always felt grand and majestic, but now that she'd been in the Arcanum library, it felt so tiny in comparison. A glass ceiling let in a blush-pink sky.

Reagan marched right up to the research desk. A squat Black man in a suit gazed down at them. "Hello, sir! I called this morning about a research project," she said.

His eyes drifted over to Ella, and she flashed him her biggest smile.

"Hmm," he replied. "You have to let me see." He lifted a piece of paper from the desk. "Is your name Reagan Marsalis?"

"Yes, sir," she replied.

"I see you called six times about this."

"Well, Madame Collette has standards," Reagan lied.

"Now, does she?"

Ella froze. She recognized that voice. Her old headmistress, Madame Collette of Madame Collette's Conjure École, towered over them. Tall and elegant, with honey-colored eyes and delicate hands, she felt like a beautiful giant. The most decadent purse floated right beside her. She was just as Ella remembered her.

"Well, get over here, ma petite, and let me have a look at you." Madame Collette waved Ella forward.

She gulped and inched closer. She'd known this woman her entire life. She'd learned how to build a starter conjure garden and crush herbs and sing spells at just six years old sitting in her classroom. But she couldn't figure out what made her hesitate, what caused her skin to cover in gooseflesh. Maybe it was Mama's incessant threat to send her right back to the school and give up on Ella returning to the Arcanum Training Institute. Maybe it was wondering how Madame Collette might really feel about her choosing to go study with Marvellers rather than stay in New Orleans with her.

Madame Collette wrapped Ella in the tightest hug, and she smelled the same, a little clove, a little honey. Once she released Ella, she pulled back and began her inspection. "You're all legs now. Growing up on us." She peeked at the conjure mark growing down Ella's neck. "Need to be sure all my work didn't go to waste with you up there in the sky." She winked, then turned to a now very sweaty Reagan. "What are my two brightest pupils up to?"

"Nothing," Ella lied.

"Just researching," Reagan said.

Madame Collette sucked her teeth, and Ella could tell she didn't believe them for a second. "It better be nothing that'll land you in trouble."

Ella hoped she wouldn't linger or ask more questions. She was impossible to fully lie to.

"You know what they say about curiosity and cats." Madame

Collette touched a finger to each of their noses. "And you"—her eyes burned into Ella's—"need to be careful in everything you do."

Ella's pulse drummed. Madame Collette's words felt heavy. She glanced around before whispering in her ear, "They're watching you, ma petite. You, your mama and papa, Gran, Sera, your Nana Durand and PopPop Durand, and even little Winnie. Don't give them anything else to be angry about."

Ella didn't know who *they* were, but she knew it couldn't be good.

"Be wary the questions you ask and the secrets you share," she warned.

Those words made Ella shudder. Reagan stared at her, puzzled.

Madame Collette kissed both of their foreheads. "Don't be a stranger, Ella. Your desk is still open if you want to return." She sauntered out with armfuls of books and her designer purse following her.

Reagan flashed Ella a panicked look before turning back to the Griotary clerk. A stack awaited them on a small cart. He sent it (and them) on its way.

"You'll be in research alcove three." He pointed. "It will show you the way."

Ella and Reagan followed the cart as it shuffled down the hall and parked itself in front of a tiny room. As soon as the door closed behind them, they giggled.

"That was close," Reagan said. "You think she'll tell my mom?"

"What about mine?" Ella asked.

"What did she whisper to you?"

"That *they're* watching me."

"Who?"

Ella didn't know, and thinking about it made her head hurt. "Let's look at these books. I don't want to think about it anymore."

The cart unpacked itself before leaving. A news-box and newsreel film sat on the table alongside eight books all tabbed and fluttering open to specific pages.

Reagan dove into the books. "We should split things up so we can read more of them before we have to get back to my house. You look at the reels."

Ella loaded old newsreels from *The Conjure Picayune* and *The New York Conjure Globe* into the news-box. She cranked the lever and the reports began.

JEAN-MICHEL DURAND DESIGNS HELP
PROTECT CONJURE TOWNS FROM FEWELS

NEW ORLEANS CONJURE ARCHITECT INNOVATES WILD IRON,
HELPING CONJURE BUILDINGS ADAPT TO CHANGE

DURAND TO OUTFIT EVERY CONJURE CITY AND TOWN
WITH LEGENDARY PROTECTIONS FREE OF CHARGE

Ella listened to the reports, waiting for any mention of Marvellers or the Arcanum, but she could find nothing but the greatest hits of his accomplishments. She tried another one, learning that he pioneered different kinds of wild iron. A third mentioned that he helped Freedmen's Bureaus and later helped build all-Black towns throughout the American South. Frustration built up inside her. She wanted all the answers to her questions to just appear at once, but she knew deep down that the world didn't work that way. She'd have to dig for it.

Ella loaded up more newsreels, and this time she got to see old footage of her papa. She watched him stand in the Marvellian Courts of Justice and argue the case for her to attend the Arcanum Training Institute. She couldn't believe she'd never seen this before. His voice boomed: "To separate the children of Conjure folk from the children of Marvellers solely because of the differences in their gifts will create an inferiority and division so vast and so deep, it'll harden both sides beyond repair."

She smiled at the little heliogram of her papa winning his case and paving the way for her.

"Ella?"

But Ella didn't hear Reagan through her deep focus.

Reagan shook her shoulder. "I found something." She slammed the heavy book—*The Unexplained: Unsolved Conjure Mysteries* by Franklin Turner—in front of Ella. "Look." Reagan traced her finger across a page. "It says, 'the body of a missing Conjure architect was returned from the skies to his beloved wife, Vivian Durand, under suspicious circumstances.'"

Ella's eyes combed over the page.

Notable and beloved Conjure architect Jean-Michel Durand— son of the Grand High Walker, Jean Paul Durand—went missing for years. After huge press about his venture into the skies with Marvellers and his desire to bring the two communities together, his disappearance rocked the global Conjure community. The Conjure Force searched for him until all resources had been exhausted and the United League of Marvellers banned them from their cities and passed more Conjure Codes and restrictions. Then, ten years later on Mardi Gras eve, his body was found on Freedom Isle, perched on a bench in the middle of the Conjure immigration hub. Workers and witnesses say he appeared out of nowhere.

Ella's heart raced. "What does this mean?"

"I found this too, but I don't understand the symbol." Reagan held up another book and pointed at four sentences that discussed the missing Conjure folk in the Marvellian cities. A tiny pulsing *MV* blinked beside the text.

Ella brushed her finger over the symbol and the sentences redacted and reassembled into the warning CONTESTED BY THE UNITED LEAGUE OF MARVELLERS. "They censored it. I found books in the Arcanum library just like this."

Reagan frowned. "I didn't know Marvellers could change *our* books, though. How powerful is their magic?"

"I don't know." An angry knot formed in Ella's throat as she flipped through other books, finding more and more of that Marvellian symbol.

Reagan's eyes grew big with concern. "Something really, *really* bad happened. I can feel it. We have to find out—"

"And just what do the two of you think you're doing?"

The girls whipped around to find both their mamas, arms crossed, angry expressions marring their beautiful faces. Little Remy peeked out from behind Mrs. Marsalis's leg with a wicked smile.

They were in big trouble now.

★—★—★— **STARPOST**—★—★—★

Ella,

I need to tell you something. A secret I can't write down.

We're in Japan. Dad's trying to convince more ryū to build dragon lairs in the Astradam canals so Marvellers can help keep them safe from Fewels.

Best,
Jason

P.S.: Stop ignoring the bird on your windowsill.

★—★—★— **STARPOST**—★—★—★

Ella,

Thanks so much for your letter. My grandmother doesn't want me to come back to the Arcanum even if it reopens. The Navajo Nation is very upset with the lies. I can't believe someone would think it's us (or you). My dad thinks we're being set up by angry parents who don't want us there. What do you think it is?

Luci

★—★—★— **STARPOST**—★—★—★

Brigit,

   Thanks for the package. I don't know who those people are in your vision, and I'm too scared to ask my mama about it. She'll think we're up to something. I wrote down all the new things I've figured out while at home. I wrote them in code, though. The key is in the next starpost.

Best,

Ella

CHAPTER NINETEEN
A MESSENGER!

Ella had been punished until the very end of winter break and possibly beyond, if winter break never ended and she never got to return to the Arcanum Training Institute. Not only was she forced to help Gran with every single thing she needed, she wasn't allowed to leave the house if it wasn't with one of her parents or Gran . . . and worst of all, she also would be starting back at Madame Collette's Conjure École this very Monday morning until the Institute opened back up.

"I don't want to have to come back in there," Mama hollered down the hall.

Ella had a staring contest with her old uniform. The conjure apron, the crossing rings, the headwrap, and the long skirts. She didn't hate it . . . She'd just thought she'd never have to put it back on again after getting into the Arcanum Training Institute. Her eyes kept cutting to her Arcanum satchel in the corner and her stapier poking out of it. That life felt like it was about to be erased.

The Baptiste dirt dobbin lurked in the corner, chuckling at

her. "No more fancy school in the sky, hehe haha," she teased. "Feet back on the ground where you belong."

Ella shooed her away. She much preferred the Durand dirt dobbin at the Mississippi house. He was less rude and nosy. She turned her back to it and pulled on her clothes so slowly you'd think they were full of ants.

Mama knocked on the door. "You better be ready."

"I am," she replied, trying to keep the frustration out of her voice. She didn't need to add more days to her punishment.

The door swung open.

Mama beamed at her. "That's more like it. Looking like my baby girl again. A young Baptiste woman." Ella hadn't heard this much joy in her voice in a long time, and that made her part happy and part sad. A reminder that Mama preferred her at the local conjure school.

Ella tried to do everything her mother requested. She rustled Winnie out of her room, grabbed their lunches from Gran, and headed out to the car. Mama drove them to Madame Collette's Conjure École at the edge of the Conjure Quarter instead of taking a streetcar.

Ella gazed up at the blush-pink mansion with its wraparound galleries and wild garden. The flowers greeted her as she passed. She'd walked this path a million times. Her feet felt heavy. She'd thought she'd never have to walk it again.

The doors opened. Madame Collette stepped out, all smiles. "Look who the cat dragged in."

Ella cringed as Mama eased her forward.

"One of your old students eager to resume her studies," Mama said proudly. "At least for the time being."

Ella's cheeks warmed. She wanted to emphasize *time being*

because as soon as the Arcanum reopened, she'd be out of here again.

"We'll take good care of her like always." Madame Collette patted her back.

Mama's voice fluttered into Ella's head as she prepared to leave: *Be my good girl, you hear me? Don't give Madame Collette any trouble or any attitude. I'll be asking for a full report.*

Ella was too frustrated to acknowledge the warning, and instead just nodded and stepped across the threshold. A truth root waited on the foyer table. She touched its petals. Madame Collette ensured that not a single lie would be uttered under her roof.

As Madame Collette sent Winnie off to her classroom and walked Ella to hers, she didn't know how to feel about it all. She had to drag herself forward. The pretty wallpaper flickered at her. The gilded mirrors flashed beautiful views of the Underworld. The conjure garden climbed along the walls. She gazed up at the bottle tree that cut through the house, its branches and bottles filling the ceiling of every single room.

This used to be her reality. This used to be one of her favorite places in the world. But now she felt different, *it* felt different. She wondered if she still fit. That question alone made her feel terrible. She was a Conjuror . . . and a Marveller. But a Conjuror first. This was home . . . so why did it feel so weird? Why was she so worried about how other kids would treat her?

"You'll be with your old class. You should have no problem sliding right back in. It'll be like riding a bicycle. Reagan is in Mrs. Toussaint's room. You'll recognize it because your aunt Sera taught in it." Madame Collette planted her in front of the door, then headed off to greet more students.

Ella took a deep breath and stepped into the classroom. Chalkboard walls contained detailed plant diagrams and herb profiles. A model of the Underworld sat in the far corner. The bottle tree's branches held gorgeous glass that twinkled in the morning sun.

Everyone looked in her direction. She felt their eyes comb over her, finding the Arcanum satchel on her shoulder. She'd known each and every one of them since she was six years old and started school. She could recite their first and last names by heart. However, she couldn't feel more different from them right now. Ella fussed with her conjure apron and kept twirling her crossing rings.

"Welcome back, Ella." Mrs. Toussaint, a squat Black woman covered in moles and freckles, ushered her forward.

Reagan raised her hand. "Ella! Over here."

Ella weaved in and out of desks and plopped down beside Reagan.

"You okay?" Reagan asked.

"I don't know yet." She wished she knew a conjure spell for disappearing because that's what she wanted to do right now.

The house shuddered. Crystalline tones echoed as glass bottles nudged each other and quieted the room. It was time to begin.

Mrs. Toussaint raised her hands in the air. "Good morning, class."

"Good morning, Mrs. Toussaint," they replied in unison.

The class stood.

"Let us prepare to lift our voices and sing the Conjure anthem to start our day," she said.

The intercom crackled on and the familiar melody played.

Ella's voice folded into the others, and the song poured out of her from memory.

Madame Collette gave her morning message, and Mrs. Toussaint resumed her lesson on the care and feeding of conjure hot plants.

Ella's day felt like a flash of lightning: She recharged her crossing rings, learned how to properly make a conjure pont, discussed the architect over a lunch of steaming hot gumbo with Reagan and recorded more theories and plans in her notebook, and refreshed her memory on deathbull etiquette and Underworld crossing procedures. By the end of the day, Ella didn't know if she actually wanted it to end. She loved being with Reagan and the fact that she didn't stick out. Her conjure felt renewed and she couldn't wait to practice with her stapier again. There were no whispers about her gifts being strange or weird looks when she talked about conjure. She hated that Mama might be right about how it felt to be back home with her own folk. All her fears proved to be unfounded.

As the class prepared for dismissal, Ella slid Reagan a note about them staying after to ask Mrs. Toussaint about twilight stardust.

Ella waited until the classroom emptied. "Mrs. Toussaint, I have a question."

"And I have an answer. Well, I hope to." She waved Ella and Reagan up to her desk. "And I must say, it's so good to have you out of those skies. Back down here where you belong. You did good today too. Haven't missed a beat."

Ella flashed her a tentative smile. Reagan fidgeted beside her. "Now, what can I do for you ladies?"

"I have a question about twilight stardust." Ella tried to make sure her words didn't prompt any further questions. "Besides crossing into the Underworld and seasoning our skillets, do we use it for other things?"

Mrs. Toussaint mused. "Oh yes, sugar. How you think our streetcars float around? Or we fortify the Conjure Quarter to protect against Fewels? Or the Griotary can move about? Mixed with wild iron, it's Conjure folk's little secret. Our ability to adapt, to move when the road gets rocky and unsafe. Given to us from our ancestors."

Ella and Reagan exchanged glances. In that moment, they'd unlocked one piece of the puzzle. Ella's great-grandad was the reason the Arcanum Training Institute could move through the skies.

✦ ✶ ✦ ✹ ✦

AFTER DINNER, ELLA SAT AT THE KITCHEN TABLE WORKING ON assignments about herb-drying processes with Gran and trying to work up the courage to ask her more questions about twilight stardust. Mrs. Toussaint's words rolled around in her head on repeat.

The ping of the doorbell reverberated through the house.

"Who could be coming here this late?" Gran's eyebrows lifted. "People these days don't have any manners left. It's long after dinner."

"Mama!" Ella heard her own mother call out.

Gran's brow furrowed. She hobbled out of the kitchen. Ella followed, wondering what all the fuss was about.

Mama and Papa stood in the hallway. Were the Marvellian coppers back?

Greno jumped up and down on Papa's shoulder, sounding the

alarm with furious ribbiting. Gumbo paced, his long tail slapping the floor.

Papa turned around, a somber expression on his face. "A messenger." His eyes cut to the floor, and a black snake slithered forward. It carried a crimson envelope in its fangs.

The United Conjure Congress emblem flared. Ella's heart leaped into her throat.

Mama retrieved the envelope. Gumbo snapped his teeth at the snake. Greno ribbited angrily. "Thank you, and good night."

The snake hissed, then nodded. The house broom ushered it back outside.

"Might as well grab the paper too," Gran called out. "No use in avoiding it."

"What did it bring?" Ella took tentative steps forward. She couldn't take her eyes off the envelope.

Winnie ran out of her room like there was a dog chasing her. "Do we have guests? Is someone here to play with me? Can I stay up later?"

Mama whipped around. "Both of you to your rooms immediately!" The boom of her voice punched Ella in the chest, and she jumped.

Winnie squeaked and turned right around. Ella didn't even fight. Her pulse drummed as she walked up the stairs. She felt Mama's eyes on her the entire way. But she slipped just out of view, then found a corner to watch from. Winnie nuzzled in beside her.

"We have to be quiet," Ella whispered. "So we can find out what's wrong."

Winnie nodded.

They leaned close to the railing, watching as their parents and Gran hovered over the letter.

"Go on with it," Gran urged. "Let's see what they want now."

Mama broke the wax seal. Billowy smoke escaped, and the letter wrenched itself out of the envelope like a writhing worm.

"Some of their associates have been bothering me at the pharmacy while y'all have been back and forth to Rose Hill. I told them that we'd have no more of it." Gran waved her fists in the air. "We won't be bullied."

Papa stepped onto the porch, then returned with the evening edition of *The Conjure Picayune*. Ella spotted one of the headlines:

TRAITORS! DURANDS KEEP DAUGHTER AT THE ARCANUM DESPITE RECENT ATTACKS ON CONJURORS!

Her stomach roiled. What else had they said about her? *Do they hate me?*

"Out with it. What do they have to say for themselves?" Gran squinted.

The floating letter turned as if listening. It unfolded itself. Words written in bright red ink burned like embers in a fire.

Mama scanned it. "We've been summoned by the United Conjure Congress. We have to face several charges."

Ella's heart plummeted, and she remembered Brigit's quilt squares and her mention of a trial. They were in trouble all because of her.

Dear Aubrielle Baptiste-Durand, Sera Baptiste,
Ava Baptiste, and Sebastien Durand,

You have been summoned to appear before the
United Conjure Congress on February 1. We wish to
discuss the recent choices made by your families that
put our way of life at risk. Please see a list of charges
and prepare your responses.

You are to report to the Freedom House in New
Orleans, Louisiana, not a moment after midnight.

If you refuse to appear, the Conjure Force will be
sent to fetch you. I do hope you oblige, as there is
much to discuss, and you owe your community at
least that.

Blessings!

Adelaide Adieux

Head of the United Conjure Congress

★—★—★— **STARPOST**—★—★—★

Ella,

I have an idea! I can't believe I didn't think of it earlier. What if we could visit the Underworld and talk to the architect? We could find out what happened to him that way.

Reagan

★—★—★— **STARPOST**—★—★—★

Reagan,

But then my papa would know. He'd never let us. But let me see if there's something else we can do, like a summoning jar. I'm going to try to talk to Gran about it. Wish me luck.

Best,
Ella

CHAPTER TWENTY

ST. LOUIS CEMETERY NO. 1

O ver the next couple of weeks, the entire Durand
household pretended the snake messenger hadn't
shown up. Whenever Ella asked about it, she was met
with "Stay out of grown folks' business," or worse, silence. She
tried to get in the mood for Mardi Gras by putting up more decorations and starting a countdown. She helped clean the house
(especially shooing the black bird from her windowsill) to usher
in good fortune. She went with Gran to the Marsalises' Sweet
Box Shop to place an order for King Cake. She repotted the luck
roots in the window boxes. But it did nothing to lift the spirits in
the house or lighten her punishment. Ella was still relegated to
helping Gran with whatever she needed without complaint and
going to Madame Collette's for lessons every day.

And now she was dragging Gran's old lady cart to the streetcar stop so they could visit the pharmacy. A small black pavilion
shielded several elderly Conjure folk from the sun.

"Papa could've driven us," Ella said.

"And miss out on people watching on this fine Saturday

morning? No, baby. This is my favorite part." Gran reached down and scooped her companion, Paon, into her big bag.

A black streetcar floated up, its trim the indigo color of twilight stardust. Ella still couldn't believe twilight stardust helped it move. How had she missed this detail her entire life? How did it work? She didn't have time to investigate as she helped Gran up the stairs. They eased their way onto cozy benches. Gran ignored the lingering stares and whispers that filled the space, while Ella grimaced. She tried not to think about the newspaper headlines about her and her family.

The streetcar floated through the Conjure Quarter, dodging Fewel cars.

Ella tried to enjoy the ride, but her mind raced on a constant loop. She couldn't stop thinking about the summons or the sound of her parents' arguments finding their way into her bedroom every night since. Or how many questions she still had about what happened to Jean-Michel Durand and how she'd never be able to prove anything now that the Arcanum blueprints were gone. Or how she hadn't been able to continue her research while punished. But today, she would resume her plan—or at least give it her very best try. It was the perfect opportunity to get Gran talking without Mama nosing around.

"You thinking real loud, little girl. A penny for your thoughts." Gran kissed Ella's forehead, startling her out of her tornado of thoughts.

"It'll cost you a Conjure dollar," Ella teased.

"You drive a hard bargain." Gran smiled, slipping her a crisp black bill. "Now out with it."

Ella appreciated her not automatically crossing into her mind. She could never tell Gran what was *really* going on because she'd stop her right in her tracks, but she could share some things. "I hate that Mama and Papa . . . and even Aunt Sera are in trouble because of me. Because I wanted to go to the Arcanum Training Institute."

Gran's eyes softened. "It's not just because of that, sweetheart. It's never just one thing. And your papa wanted you to go to that school too. Don't you forget it."

"I know."

Gran took Ella's hand.

"Everyone's upset with us." Ella tried to make her voice even lower so the nosy people on the streetcar couldn't hear her.

"What other people think of you is none of your business," she said.

But Ella wanted to be liked.

"Trying to prevent the bad, baby girl, is like trying to tame lightning. It's impossible. And you can't always get everyone to agree." She pursed her lips. "I didn't want you to go to that school at first. I made my feelings known—and I have my reasons. But I've come around to it. Like the others will." Gran smiled. "Change ain't easy, and our folk have a lot of trouble with it because we've always had to bend ourselves around the shape of others. Fewels we have to hide from. Marvellers who decided to save themselves and never look back."

Ella knew that not everyone would want her to go to the Arcanum Training Institute, but she never thought it'd get her family summoned before the United Conjure Congress. She never knew that it'd get them in trouble. But she thought maybe her discoveries would help things. If she could reveal that a Conjuror designed the school, that it was originally concepted as a place that included them, and that there was proof left behind in the building itself, maybe people wouldn't be so mad at her . . . and her family. Maybe this could heal the rift between the two communities. Or at least start to.

Ella let her next question ease out slowly between them. "What if Conjurors and Marvellers could live together . . . or were supposed to from the very beginning?"

Gran's eyebrows lifted with surprise. "Never thought about that. I know many Marvellers live in Fewel cities instead of their big fancy sky ones—but they're never in Conjure neighborhoods or towns. They act like they're too good for us."

"I know, but what if they weren't? What if we were supposed to all be together and away from Fewels?"

"Hmmm . . ." Gran rocked back and forth, considering it. "That would be something, wouldn't it? It'd change *everything*." Gran patted Ella's knee. "Time to get off and get busy. There's customers already waiting on us. You see? That Baptiste luck ain't run out yet. Not everyone hates us, after all."

Ella tugged a chain and the streetcar pulled over in front of their store, THE CONJURE ROSE: GROCERIES AND GOODS OF THE OTHERWORLDLY KIND. Gran waved at her loyal patrons and assured them that they'd be ready in a few minutes.

A bell chimed as they crossed the threshold. The entire space sparked to life. Hooded lamps clicked on, their warm glow freckling over all the items for sale. The shutters flew open, letting the morning sun rush in. The ceiling fans whirled. Shelves spilled over with Mama and Gran's legendary potions and tonics and curios.

Paon took his perch in the window, and the sign flipped from CLOSED to OPEN as Gran got settled behind the counter and greeted her ancient cash register. Ella visited every shelf to make sure the displays were in order. She rearranged the horseshoes and skeleton keys, then alphabetized the potions that had some-how gotten out of their proper place.

Customers filed in and placed orders for abundance baths and good luck candles for Mardi Gras or made appointments to have their fortunes read.

The shop went quiet, momentarily empty.

"Come on over here, sugah. Idle hands make for a too curious mind. Isn't that what they say?" Gran ground her mortar into her pestle. "Grab the bay leaves."

Ella gladly obliged. "What are you making?" She gazed down into the shallow bowl as the paste took shape.

Gran motioned at the order slip nearby. Ella lifted it up to read: *Bad spirit in the attic.*

"How do you know how to make all these things?" Ella asked.

"Now, why you being silly? You already know the answer."

"Your mama taught you." Ella tried to ask about summoning jars in a way not to make Gran suspicious.

"That's right, and my own gran too," she said. "I visit them monthly in the Underworld, and if they don't feel like talking spells, I go to the cemetery and visit their memory-casks. I just perfected this one because Meme told me I was adding too much goofer dust." She chuckled to herself. "Nothing is ever lost. Con-jure is good."

"All the time." Ella tried to hide her grin. This was just the entry she needed to get Gran talking about their ancestors. "Can you visit anyone?" Ella realized she'd never even asked her papa this question before.

"The Underworld Walkers would prefer you had a connec-tion. Otherwise, the living could terrorize the dead on a whim, pulling them out of their rest even for strangers. There are lots of rules about it," Gran replied.

Ella felt Reagan's idea slip away. "What if they're family?"

"Same rules apply." Gran added more herbs to her mortar. "All special requests would need to go through your papa for approval."

"What about summoning them? Estelle Broussard said she called the spirit of her great-aunt right in her bedroom with a summoning jar," Ella said.

Maybe she could conjure Jean-Michel's spirit back and speak with him about what happened? Would the Marvellian Courts of Justice accept the testimony of a ghost? Would they write it off as a conjure trick?

Gran pursed her lips. "So many questions this morning. What are you up to?"

"Nothing. Papa just hasn't told me much yet." It wasn't a complete lie. She knew better than to outright lie to a Conjuror as powerful as Gran.

"Well, summoning is dangerous—and disruptive. You'd have to have something of the person you want to bring forth, and it often yanks them from the Underworld without warning, so they often aren't too pleasant upon arrival," she explained. "And you never know what else can slip through with those you bring forth. Sometimes bad spirits attach, and you get more than you bargained for. It's best to go for a visit. Your papa arranges it all wonderfully."

Ella felt like a deflated cake. Papa would ask too many questions, then Mama would find out and put an end to it all. And it was probably unlikely she'd be able to find something that belonged to the architect now that the blueprints were gone. He was alive hundreds of years ago. The weight of the task started to press down on her. How would she learn what happened if no one was alive to tell it and she couldn't visit him in the Underworld? Ella just needed to know what happened in a way that she could prove to others.

"But what if you wanted to know a distant relative's life? Learn about their memories and their accomplishments. Like for a research project."

"You'd visit their memory-cask for all of that," Gran said matter-of-factly before returning to her grinding and humming. "One day you'll be visiting mine and learning all I know and all I've seen."

A chill rushed over her skin. The excited prickle of an idea rushed through her. The Durand family crypt. The architect's memory-cask had to be there.

Gran's words rolled around in her head: *It'd change every-thing.* Maybe she could do that.

✦ ✹ ✦ ✹ ✦

IT TOOK SOME EXPERT STRATEGY AND A FEW WELL-PLACED HALF-truths, but Ella and Reagan weaseled their way into tagging along with one of Reagan's teenage brothers, Laurent, to run a Mardi Gras errand.

"Do I even want to know why you have me bringing you here?" Laurent shook his head as he led them through the gates of St. Louis Cemetery No.1.

Ella's satchel spilled over with candles and flowers; a carafe of chicory coffee, plus a tiny piece of hummingbird cake fluttered above her shoulder. The crypts spread out before them like a city of death. Little white houses to hold urns, caskets, and memory-casks, if they belonged to Conjure folk. A few Fewel mourners walked along narrow paths, with arms clutching votive candles and flowers.

Reagan started to explain again, but Laurent put his hand up. "Actually, don't tell me 'cause when Mama comes looking for answers, I'm not getting in trouble with Ms. Aubrielle or her. I want to be a High Walker one day, so I need Mr. Sebastien to like me," he said.

Ella smiled at him. "He already likes you because Reagan is my best friend."

"If you say so." He turned down another path.

The whole graveyard felt too quiet. Not how she wanted to think of the dead. Not like the vibrant noise of the Underworld with all the chattering spirits and walkers. But she figured a place with only the bones and the ash of the dead would be silent.

The Durand crypt soared over them, slicing into the late January sunlight. The cold shade settled over them. Ella sang the entry song, and the wrought-iron gates opened. Gas lamps ignited as they stepped inside. Laurent removed his Low Walker hat to show respect, and even his tarantula companion bowed. The flickering light left a warm glow across the white interior. An ancient bottle tree spread out from its very center, stretching toward walls of shelves that held beautiful sarcophaguses, caskets, and memory-casks labeled by name and year. A marble table encircled the base of the tree.

Ella couldn't stop smiling. The feeling of being around all these ancestors made her heart flip. They created a small altar at the base of the bottle tree, and Ella prayed that Jean-Michel would be okay with her opening his memory-cask even though they never knew each other.

"Wow." Reagan walked around. "Our family crypt doesn't look like this."

"It definitely doesn't," Laurent added.

Ella finished her prayer and scanned the walls. There were generations and generations of memory-casks going back one hundred years, then two hundred years and beyond. How could they possibly find the one belonging to Jean-Michel Durand? Her eyes grew tired. Reagan sighed too, no doubt becoming exhausted.

"You know there's a faster way, right?" Laurent chuckled.

Ella glared at him. "What?"

"A locator spell? Like baby conjure stuff. How do you not know this? Madame Collette must have changed things up." He shook his head.

Ella should've known that. She'd done a type of locator spell, a hot foot last year to find Masterji Thakur after he disappeared.

"Who are you looking for—and why?" Laurent asked.

Reagan jammed her hand to her hip. "I thought you didn't want to know."

"Call me curious," he replied.

"You can't snitch, Laurent." Reagan stuck out her pinkie to force him to promise. "Mama says you can never hold water."

"Can too. That's Louis." Laurent scoffed, then looped his pinkie into hers. Ella also forced him to do the same with her to reinforce it. "I promise. I'll even hide it from him. Block him from my mind for a little bit."

Reagan looked at Ella. "Okay, tell him."

She explained everything from the architect to the blueprints to the pandemic at the Arcanum being blamed on Conjure folk to the summons showing up.

His eyes went wide. "This can't be true."

"It is . . . "

Laurent paced. "This will change everything if anyone finds out."

"I know," Ella replied. "So will you help us?"

He moved toward the oldest wall in the crypt, put his arm in the air, and began to sing. "Let us find what we seek . . ."

Two memory-casks slid off the highest shelf. Ella held her breath as they floated down to the table.

"Why did it bring down two?" Reagan asked.

"I don't know. Maybe they're linked," he said.

Ella examined the ancient-looking objects. Wrought-iron curled around the stone and revealed the first name, JEAN-MICHEL DURAND, and then the other one, VIVIAN DURAND.

She remembered that name from their research at the Griotary. His widow. This was it. The answers to her questions a spell away. She placed gentle hands around Jean-Michel's memory-cask. She tried to keep them from shaking.

"Do you know how to open it?" Reagan asked.

Ella realized that she never saw Aunt Sera open her memory-cask during her conjure lesson. "I . . . I . . ."

Laurent shook his head and sighed. "But did she teach you how to enter it?"

"Yes," she replied. "Well . . . um, she let me visit her mind. That counts, right?"

"Did you bring crossing powder?"

Ella and Reagan exchanged panicked glances. They'd forgotten.

"Ugh, are you serious?" He took Jean-Michel's memory-cask from Ella's hands. "I'll open it, but I'm not entering it. That you'll have to do on your own."

"But we can't take this memory-cask out of here," Ella complained.

"Guess you won't be entering it, huh?"

"Come on, Laurent," Reagan begged.

"Some plan, if you aren't prepared." He rolled his eyes and retrieved his hat. He fished a small packet from the lining. Crossing powder.

Ella clapped and Reagan grinned.

"You both are lucky that Walkers never travel without it." He took a deep breath and sang again.

The wrought-iron unfurled. Ella's heart thundered as the three of them leaned over to look inside the architect's cask as it opened.

Ella gasped.

It was empty.

"I don't understand." Ella looked up at Laurent and then at Reagan.

"You think someone stole it?" Reagan asked.

"I don't think any Conjuror from here to Colón could get past the protective spells on this place," Laurent replied. "No, it's got to be something else."

Ella gazed at the insides again as if it was just hiding out of sight. But the interior looked smooth and brand-new, even after two hundred plus years.

"Nothing has ever been placed in here," Laurent said.

"What about his wife's?" Ella picked up the other one. Conjure-roses bloomed in the wrought-iron, guarding the entrance.

He put his hands out to block Ella, and even his tarantula protested. "I've already helped you enough today."

"C'mon. You've already opened one, what's the harm in another?" Reagan hugged Laurent's middle. "We need to see what's inside this one too. You won't even have to mind-walk."

"How?" Ella asked.

Laurent sighed. "Walkers can touch anything of the dead and see its secrets."

Ella's mouth dropped open. "My papa never told me that."

"He wouldn't because it's Walker business." Laurent glared at Reagan. "And I don't even know how my little sister would know something like that unless she's been eavesdropping on my conversations with Louis or reading my handbook . . . things she's *not* supposed to do."

Reagan cowered a little.

"Is this why you asked me to come with you?" he pressed.

"Maybe," Reagan admitted sheepishly.

Ella grinned at her clever friend. She'd made sure they had a backup plan.

"Just this once, please. Can you find out?" Reagan slipped her hand into her big brother's and begged.

"Yeah, please," Ella added. "It's really important."

Laurent rolled his eyes and took a deep sigh. "You can never tell anyone. Ever. You hear me?" His glare burned into Ella's eyes, and she gulped, then nodded.

"We promise," they said in unison.

Laurent put his Low Walker hat back on, then held Vivian Durand's memory-cask to his chest. His eyes snapped open, his once hazel pupils now snow white. He hummed, and the baritone of his voice sent a shiver over Ella's skin.

The memory-cask wiggled, the wrought-iron cage releasing and conjure-roses blooming. The lid opened. Warm light drenched his sweaty skin like moonlight.

Ella heard her own heartbeat thudding. The seconds felt like hours as she waited and wondered what he saw in the memory-cask.

Laurent's eyes cleared, then he shuddered.

Ella bubbled over with anxiety. "What did you see?"

Laurent set the memory-cask down. "It was so . . . strange. Her memories are so painful. I can hardly breathe." He mopped his face with a handkerchief. "Her husband, Jean-Michel, went missing after creating the blueprints for that Marveller school like you said. They made him think he was going to be a founder. After his body was found on Freedom Isle, his wife prepared his memory-cask, just as our tradition demands. She wanted to find out what happened, but before she could consecrate and prepare to enter it, someone stole it—and the body. She didn't get to honor him. She didn't get to bury him. She died of a broken heart."

Ella's thoughts raced. "Why would anyone do that? It's—"

"Sacrilege. It's offensive to steal a memory-cask—or a body for that matter. It prevents a spirit from entering the Underworld or finding peace. It cuts you off from communing with your ancestors both living and dead," Laurent replied. "No Conjuror would ever do that to another. The punishment is brutal. To be eaten and regurgitated by the deathbulls at the gates of the Underworld forever."

Both Ella and Reagan shivered.

"But a Marveller wouldn't know that . . . ," Ella said. "And they didn't want anyone to know he was the Arcanum architect."

"Maybe even more than that," Laurent challenged. "He'll never be at rest without both his memory-cask and some part of his body in the Underworld. But one thing's for sure, they didn't want his memories found."

"A memory thief," Ella said through gritted teeth. A resolve hardened inside her. She had to find the missing memory-cask by any means necessary.

★—★—★— **STARPOST**—★—★—★

Masterji Thakur,

I found out so many things about the Arcanum blueprints and the architect.

There's a cover-up. Something bad happened to him after he worked with the other founders, and his body weirdly showed up on Freedom Isle. That's like the Conjuror's version of the Vellian Port for those traveling between Conjure cities. Then his body and memory-cask were taken again by the Marvellers before his wife could finish preparing him for burial.

What do you think could've happened to him? As a Conjuror, for him to be at rest, we'd need to find his missing memory-cask or whatever is left of his body . . . which might be nothing at this point because it's been so long. Maybe bones . . . Anything would help. I don't even know where to start. I can't wait to tell you everything if school ever reopens.

Best,
Ella

HARLEM NIGHTS

Gia navigated a busy Harlem street in New York City, snaking through crowds of Conjure folks (and a few Fewels out of place uptown). A late January snow had started to fall, and even the Conjure canopy stretching over the block couldn't keep it all from hitting the sidewalks.

Annoyance bubbled in her chest with each step she took. Every part of her plan had taken longer than she'd wanted, and her coin purse had grown too light for her liking. She moved with purpose, hat cocked, as she looked for her favorite spot in this strange city, the Twilight Rooster. Besides filling her belly with their legendary chicken and waffles, she knew it'd have the rest of what she needed. Celeste Baptiste always steered her right.

She took one of the vertical taxis up to the 200th floor, found an open seat at the counter, and listened as the Conjure folk around her complained of Marvellian coppers prowling through the neighborhood.

"Bet those coppers ain't really looking for the cause of their little sickness. Bet they're trying to figure out how to take over our neighborhoods," one woman claimed. Her beautiful church hat contained a gorgeous blue bird asleep in a nest. "I've seen more and more Marvellers down here buying fancy skyscraper apartments and shopping at our stores."

"They left, so they should stay gone." Another person tapped their glass against the wood. Gia added hers to the chorus of knocks. She agreed with them. Marvellers had long left Conjurors down here to deal with Fewels, and they shouldn't be welcomed back.

"The skies are getting crowded. New York City is practically half in the sky anyways now. They booted the starfolk out and think they can have whatever they want," a third chimed in while petting his hawk companion.

The man behind the counter directed corn bread skillets across the counter. "They're no better than some of our own. Take those Durands down South. Sent their little girl up there, and now we have all the heat on us. Our own Grand High Walker a sympathizer and sellout. Encouraged the Hughes to send their boy up there too. They live over on 127th and Five Avenue." He shook his head. "We need to get our own community right. Clean up our own yard."

Gia cleared her throat, and they turned to look. The woman with the bird hat scowled at the interruption. "Ever thought this is exactly what they want? You turning on each other?" Gia wasn't particularly a fan of Sebastien Durand right now, after he'd threatened her, but she hated to see the Marvellian government and its propaganda department win. "They manufacture controversy to get what they want."

"And what would you know of it? You aren't a Conjuror

anyways. You should mind your business," the man with the hawk replied.

"That's right," the lady in the hat agreed.

Gia laughed as they went back to their conversation, all but erasing her from the room.

A tall man slid into the seat beside her. He ordered a wailing waffle and hot honey chicken before turning to her. "A friend told me you were looking for help."

Gia glanced over at him. Freckles covered his brown skin like chocolate chips in a freshly baked cookie.

"Yadiel Herrera, at your service."

He was more handsome than Celeste had mentioned, the slight accent to his words giving away his Dominican heritage.

"A question first," she said. "Are all the houses here veiled?"

"Uptown, yes. The Bronx, the Heights, Harlem, and Spanish Harlem, for sure. Conjure folk in Brooklyn and Queens do other things," he replied.

"And you're good at detecting them?"

"I'm in the business of making them and removing them. What might you need—and most importantly, what are you willing to pay?" His eyes searched hers, and she knew he was looking for information about who she might be.

She slid the last of her money to him. "I need to be able to see a very important house."

"I'm not a thief. I don't organize robberies."

A slight smile tucked itself into the corner of Gia's mouth. She loved when people had a moral compass. It made her eager to push them to the very edge of it. "I can't say I'm not going to steal, but the thing I need has no value to anyone but me."

His eyebrow lifted. "Like I said, I'm not a burglar. Celeste didn't say anything about—"

"I need to see my daughter. She's being kept from me. She has something I need." Her words weren't untrue, but she made certain they landed just right, adding a touch of desperation to ensure he folded. She watched as the crease in his forehead softened and his once suspicious eyes filled with pity. A mother without her child always played upon the heartstrings of men. "Will you help me?"

He nodded. "I can do that."

Gia hid her triumphant smile, then placed conjure dollars on the counter and left the restaurant with Yadiel.

KEEP THE MARVELLIAN WORLD KIND!

The Marvellian world is a
place for all with magic.

We are a people made of many.

We were all strangers once, and we built
a table big enough for all of us.

**Vote for Noor Al-Nahwi, the Change
We Need, the Change We Can Believe.**

Little Conjuror,

Just because you're home doesn't mean I'm not watching.

CHAPTER TWENTY-ONE
SUMMONS

The first of February came faster than Ella had wanted. Summons day. She was still in the middle of piecing together all she'd learned from Laurent Marsalis about the architect's wife, and she wasn't ready to try to prove her case to other Conjure folk just yet if need be. There were still too many unanswered questions. She also didn't have time to think about who kept sending her anonymous notes. They'd appeared outside of her starpost box now, tucked here and there and full of threats. She should be worried, she probably should tell Mama and Papa, but her focus was singular.

A cold humidity slapped against Ella's cheeks as they rode in Papa's car headed for the Freedom House. They passed by beautifully decorated houses: statues of court jesters, columns laden with pearls, balconies dressed in purple, gold, and green lights, garlands draped from galleries. Usually all the Mardi Gras decorations made her heart soar even more than Christmas ones. This was Ella's favorite time of year in the city, but she couldn't even get excited. Too many things were going terribly, and she was in the worst mood.

Winnie squirmed in the seat beside her, asking question after question as Mama grimaced.

"Where are we going again?" Winnie asked.

Gran pulled Winnie close. "We've told you a thousand times, baby girl, and you know I don't like reruns. The Freedom House."

"In Jackson Square?" Winnie asked.

"That's what Fewels call it."

"It's Durand Square," Papa corrected. "Named after one of your great-grandfathers, Vernel Lucien Durand. He was the very first Grand High Walker. Folks say his spiritual strength after slavery opened the door to the Underworld itself. Be sure to call it that—and never forget it."

"Yes, Papa," Winnie whispered.

Ella drifted in and out of listening to the conversation in the car. Her stomach twisted as worries piled up inside her. The summons replayed over and over again in her head. The snake. The embers. The threat. Conjure folk were mad that she attended the Arcanum Training Institute, and now her entire family was in trouble because of her desires and choices. She felt terrible—and helpless. She still didn't have the answers she needed yet to help herself, her family, or even Masterji Thakur.

"You have nothing to fear, baby girl. Chin up," Gran said, and Ella never understood how her gran could figure out her feelings without reading her mind. "You're a Baptiste and a Durand. Neither of your bloodlines frighten easily. We'll humor them with this little meeting of theirs and then go about our business, you hear?"

Ella felt like Gran's message wasn't just for her but for her parents as well.

But Ella did feel afraid. What would they say to her about

going to the Arcanum Training Institute? How would they treat her parents and her godmother? Would they be punished? How bad could it get?

Ella caught Gumbo's reflection in the window. He lifted his head from the very back seat and winked at her. She wished that made her feel better. She wished that made her feel like everything was going to be all right.

Papa parked his car on Decatur Street, near the entrance to Durand Square. Horse carriages gave way as they piled out. Ella followed her family into the park as the iron gates opened and gold filigree appeared beneath their feet. They walked along a path toward the St. Louis Cathedral and the Freedom House. Ella glanced back at the water and the riverboats lined up like floating candles. She wished she could whisk her family away in one of them tonight to avoid this meeting.

"Ella, keep up," Mama called out.

She tried not to drag her feet, but even they didn't want to take this walk right now.

Bottle trees and conjure-roses circled the park, catching the moonlight. A moving statue of their Durand ancestor stretched high above, lifting his Grand High Walker hat up and down every few seconds. Papa tipped his own hat and Mama and Gran blew kisses as they passed by. Conjure teahouses and cafés ringed the perimeter, with late-night patrons flooding out and fortune tellers and merchants awaiting them at the steps of the cathedral.

The Freedom House sat to the left of the cathedral. The gorgeous black brick caught the moonlight. Sconces flared as they approached. A plaque warned: BEWARE TO THOSE WHO ENTER WITH HATE IN THEIR HEARTS FOR THE PUNISHMENT SHALL BE ETERNAL.

Ella spotted Aunt Sera waiting. She took off running and dove headfirst into her. She had to swallow hard to keep from crying.

"Missed you too, my sweet niece," she replied, and Ella could hear the presence of tears in her voice.

"Are you okay?" Ella looked up at her.

"I will be."

Winnie leaped into her arms, requiring Mama to peel her off Aunt Sera. The grown-ups whispered for a while. Ella tried to distract herself by people watching, but it was no use.

Finally, Mama put her hands on Ella's and Winnie's shoulders, then leaned down, looking into both their eyes. "I need you on your best behavior. No matter what happens or what is said. Please, no talking, outbursts, or reactions, okay?"

Winnie nibbled her bottom lip. "Okay, Mama."

"And you, my oldest girl?" Mama's eyebrows went up. "Will you follow instructions?"

"I promise." Ella's stomach was too much of a mess to even think about doing anything but focusing on not throwing up. Fireflies fluttered in her belly.

Papa kissed both of their foreheads. "Nothing to worry about."

"That's right." Gran ambled forward.

The Freedom House doors opened like a great mouth ready to swallow them whole. Two men stood guard.

An attendant greeted them. "Please come with me." He led the way down a long corridor.

Black walls held portraits of famous Conjurors. Doors led to various chambers and the largest altar Ella had ever seen in honor of the Lost Folk.

The hall emptied into an assembly room. A stained-glass

ceiling cast colorful shadows upon a sea of beautiful hats and scowling faces.

The Head of the United Conjure Congress, Madame Adelaide Adieux, sat in the center, flanked by important-looking Conjurors from all over the diaspora. Their conjure jackets boasted their delegation and congregation pins. Ella noted people from Brazil, Colombia, Cuba, Cape Verde, and more.

As they walked down the aisle, they were met with upset faces. Their attendant led them to a pew in the very front.

Papa removed his hat and smiled. His charm earned more sour expressions. Ella's stomach tightened.

Madame Adieux stood, and the room went quiet. Elegant and poised, she looked like the perfect doll to Ella. Her white gown without a wrinkle. Every fold of her headscarf crisp. "Good evening, everyone, and thank you for assembling on such short notice. Conjure is good."

"All the time," everyone replied.

Mama stood. "Why don't we cut through all the pleasantries and get to it? You've summoned us—well, more like, threatened us—and we're here."

Ella flinched and Winnie held her hand. She didn't think she'd ever heard Mama this angry before, and she'd seen her plenty mad.

Madame Adieux perched over the dais. "Sister Aubrielle, respectfully, I don't think you're in any position to rush our proceedings."

Worry stormed inside Ella, but Gran patted her shoulder. She heard her honeyed voice drift through her head: *This is the game, sweetheart. Don't worry. Your mama knows how to play it well. She learned from me.*

Papa put an arm around Mama's waist. "I'm unsure of why you've brought us here on this very fine night. We haven't broken any laws."

"We beg to differ, Brother Sebastien." Madame Adieux garnered a chorus of *umm-hmm*s from the crowd.

"Well, please enlighten us," Papa said.

Madame Adieux pursed her lips. "If this is how you want to go about things, Sebastien, then we shall. It seems you want me to waste my breath."

"This whole thing is a waste," he replied, still smiling. "A waste of everyone's time and effort."

Chatter exploded. Madame Adieux put her hand in the air. Silence spread. "The entire Conjure world is at risk with your Marvellian experiment, and we've had enough. I've looked the other way while you sent your precious child, one of our beloveds, up into the skies with our enemy." She pounded her fist on the wood, and Ella gripped the pew. "And even worse, one of our brightest teachers, Sera Baptiste, to expose our ways to them. To actually teach them conjure work. Our traditions, our secrets, our history. Giving them an opportunity to learn—and worse, copy—what we can do." She took a deep breath. "I heard they made your daughter show her divine light *outside* of her body!"

"But—" Ella started to protest before Mama shot her a look.

"It's an abomination to do such a thing," Madame Adieux declared.

Many in the crowd shook their heads, agreeing.

Ella felt her skin prickle. She wanted to explain so badly how she called her light. She wanted to explain how it wasn't as awful as they were making it out to be. She wanted to explain how it wasn't dangerous, it was just different.

"You exposed our entire community with your lawsuit and your dangerous game. The Conjure Black Belt of America is being overrun by Marvellian coppers asking questions about our work and if our spells can cause nosebleeds or take away someone's marvel. We've heard rumors they're moving into Central and South America next. Our offices are overwhelmed by complaints. You and Aubrielle represent two of our oldest and most notable bloodlines. Why choose this path when our own folk have so much more to offer?" Her eyes narrowed. "What do you have to say for yourself?"

Papa cleared his throat. "You mischaracterize and miscast our intentions. Let me explain." He put a hand on Mama's shoulder and another on Aunt Sera's. "I believe that in order for Conjure folk to survive, they must know both worlds—Conjure and Marvellian—to be truly safe."

"You would have us live in the skies? Away from our ancestors?" a council member asked.

"I would have you have a choice." Papa stepped forward. "I sued the Marvellian government because their hands are unclean. They have kept us monitored, subjugated, and frankly unsafe in their cities. What happened to the Lost Folk has never been acknowledged." He paused for a moment, and everyone followed to give respect to the Lost Folk and the dead. "It's time to dig out their skeletons."

"And you suppose our children belong on the front lines of this? And we're supposed to let them see our work—"

"It's always been like this," Gran interrupted. "Each generation making a way for the next. Some of us having to do the hard things. Some of us have to lose things for the community to learn how to be safer and wiser. I lost a whole child to the skies." She stamped her foot and Mama reached out to hold her hand. "But for my granddaughters"—she motioned at Ella and Winnie—"I've come to believe it's knowing how to navigate all worlds, Fewel, Marvellian, and Conjure, that's the key. But trust and believe, I don't like her fooling with Marvellers—and neither does my own daughter, Aubrielle. Sebastien knows we don't. I want my grandbaby down here with me where I can keep my eyes on her and teach her our ways. So she can grow into one of the best Conjurors of her generation."

Ella beamed with pride. Part of her wanted that too.

Madame Adieux bowed in respect as Gran made her way back to her seat. Gran kissed Ella's forehead, and a calm settled over her.

Papa pressed his hat to his chest. "My daughter isn't the first to try to bridge the gap between the two worlds, and she won't be the last. I knew it would be hard. Maybe a little harder than anticipated because of the decades of strife between the two communities. My goal isn't that my children fall in love with the Marvellers in the skies and leave us here, rather that they learn how to survive anywhere. That they know what the other is like and are never afraid."

Madame Adieux gritted her teeth and looked madder than a wet hen, as Gran would say. Ella worried none of this had worked to change the council's mind.

"While we understand and can honor the reasons why you'd take such action, we disagree with you, Sebastien Durand." Madame Adieux's voice was almost a growl. "Consider this your formal notice. Your family and Sera Baptiste are under investigation for breaking Conjure Commandment Number Five—*All Conjure work shall be protected from outside eyes*. If found guilty, the punishment is expulsion from New Orleans and excommunication from the Conjure community. Then you can go live with your beloved Marvellers."

Aunt Sera burst into tears. Mama shook with anger. Gran wailed.

A pit burned in Ella's stomach. This was all her fault.

Dear Ella Durand,

    The correspondence you sent to Masterji Mitha Thakur last Thursday has been intercepted and monitored. It has been found to contain false information in relation to a pending case in the Marvellian Courts of Justice and thus destroyed.

    If you believe you've received this message in error, you may appeal by writing to the address on the back of the envelope. Please cite case #478911 in your correspondence.

Best,

Henry Rutherford

Head Inspector

Marvellian Postal Inspection Service Unit

Celestian City

PART III
HARD TRUTHS

BLOOD IS THICKER

Gia stood at the end of Sylvan Terrace in Washington Heights with Yadiel. Wooden town houses stretched along the block and looked like they'd been made of gingerbread in a city full of iron and brick.

"There's one missing on this block," she said to him.

"How do you know?" he replied.

"The house numbers go from nine to ten to twelve. Where's eleven?" She glared up, knowing one was hiding from her. Had to be. Her Ace of Machination, Linh Nguyen, never supplied false information.

"Could be a mistake."

"Fewels don't make mistakes like that," she spat back. "Now, are you going to lift the veil like I paid you to or stand here and argue with me all night?"

Yadiel began to sing beautiful words in Spanish. As he reached the chorus, little by little the cloaked house peeked out from behind the conjure veil.

Gia clucked her tongue. "Mother, you hid her well." She didn't know whether it bothered her more that she'd gone so long thinking her only child was dead or if it was that her mother had successfully kept something from her—and let her believe a lie.

"Thank you." Gia watched him disappear down the block. She waited until there was a small lull in the foot traffic on the street before letting her thread marvel wake up inside her. The power of her primary marvel warmed her skin. She reached a hand for the iron railing and turned it to string. She removed knitting needles from her satchel and used them to stitch the metal into a door. One that led straight into the foyer of the Children's Village.

"I wondered how long it'd take you." A person waited in the darkness. The subtle glow from the streetlamps washed over them. Ms. Mead. Her mother's best friend.

"If it'd been up to you, forever."

"Those were your mother's wishes."

"Well, she's dead. And you let me think my child was dead too." Gia cracked her knuckles. "Hiding her all these years." She gazed around at the meager house. "Then sending her up to that school all year long. Letting them infect her."

"Well, well, well . . . you just told on yourself." Ms. Mead laughed. "But you knew just what to do, didn't you? I had a feeling you might be responsible for all that sickness at the Institute. That you'd be unable to get to her while she was in their protection. That you needed her isolated. You set this trap."

Gia didn't mind the woman unraveling her plan. Listening to it aloud let her hear just how brilliant it turned out to be. It had proved successful. One of her more genius plans to get what she needed from her daughter and mess with the Arcanum Head-marvellers at the same time.

"What can I say . . . I'm creative."

Ms. Mead stepped forward.

"And I suppose this is the part where you say you're going to stop me." Gia pursed her lips.

"If you try to take her or harm her . . . ," she threatened.

The fireplace behind Ms. Mead flared and a ceiling candelabra ignited.

"A fire marvel. A Paragon of Spirit." Gia admired the woman's gift and made sure the parcel she carried remained away from the flames. She didn't need her firework displaying its wonders too soon.

"I won't let you take her," she warned. "And I won't let you hurt any of the other children in this house. Just turn around and walk right out. She's not yours anymore."

Gia removed her hat, then her mask. She wanted the woman to really see her face. "And she was never yours. You did my mother's bidding without a second thought of me. That I might want to know what happened to my child."

"You were never fit to be a parent." she spat. "Look at you now."

"Marvellers love to sit on high and judge. And you may be right. But you don't get to judge me."

"Brigit doesn't want to have anything to do with you. Now LEAVE!" Ms. Mead lifted her arm and an angry fire engulfed her.

Gia slipped her timepiece from her pocket. "I'm tired of the lecture." The lid sprang open and the room froze.

She walked past Ms. Mead's flaming body as she made her way up the stairs. She peeked her head into various rooms, eyes scanning over a multitude of sleeping children, until she found Brigit's room. The KEEP OUT sign on the door should've been her first clue. Part of it made her smile a little. They had much in common after all.

She crept into the room. A miniature house sat on metal stilts, pressing right up against the windows, and beside it, a bed.

Tiny snores filled the space. Brigit's pale hair spilled over the pillow. The sight of it made Gia think of Brigit's father, a man she never wanted to think about again.

"It would be so easy to take you," she whispered, then came to her senses. She pulled a small canister from her jacket's inner pocket and released the tiniest glass insects, no bigger than ladybugs. The hum of their tiny gears echoed through Brigit's snores as they flew over her sprawling limbs.

They landed on her quilt and quickly got to work, climbing on to her arms and neck and face to take tiny bites. Their glass shells filled with Brigit's blood as Gia watched.

The sight of the red liquid made her heart race. The end of her money problems, right there. Finally, it'd all come together.

Brigit squirmed. Gia waited for her daughter's eyes to open, but she turned over. The tiny bugs left her skin and found their way back into her box.

Gia turned to walk away.

"Who's there?" Brigit asked, groggy.

Gia didn't stop. She doubted Brigit would recognize her current face anyways.

"No one. This is all a dream."

CHAPTER TWENTY-TWO
LET THE GOOD TIMES ROLL!

The dead are coming! Wake up! Wake up!" The sounds of the Skull men drifted through Ella's bedroom window, waking her on Mardi Gras morning.

She groaned. The sun hadn't even risen, and the house started to fill with sound. She glanced at her little grandmother clock and it showed 5:00 a.m. Usually, Ella loved Mardi Gras morning. The sound of the drums waking the Conjure Quarter, the scent of Mama's bananas foster French toast, Paon's festive cock-a-doodle-doo. They'd stuff themselves, then Gran would pack provisions and they'd head to watch the parade floats on Canal Street.

But none of it felt exciting this year. The meeting with the United Conjure Congress still haunted her, and she didn't know when (or if) the Arcanum would open back up. The starpost from the Marvellian postal inspection made her terrified to send another starpost, afraid that everything she'd sent to Jason and Brigit might've been intercepted too. Everything was too different, too out of control, too scary.

Tap, tap, tap. Ella gazed at her window. The bird was back.

"Shoo!" she called out.

Tap, tap, tap.

"Ugh," she replied. "Why won't you leave me alone?"

Sizzle. Pop. The sharp crack of lightning made Ella jump. The bird's wings illuminated.

"Izulu?" She raced out of bed, wondering if it was the impundulu from the Arcanum Training Institute, but that would be . . . impossible.

Ella opened the window. "What are you doing here?"

"I thought that would get your attention."

Ella stumbled backward. How was Izulu talking to her? She didn't have a kindred marvel. She wasn't a Paragon of Sound.

"It's me."

"Who?"

"You don't recognize my voice?"

Realization washed over Ella as the bird cocked her head. "Jason?"

"Yes."

"But . . ."

"I told you to stop ignoring the bird."

Ella put her hand over her mouth, too shocked to reply.

"I sort of . . . well, my mom calls it a kindred-walk."

"But how?" Ella asked.

"Since I'm both a Conjuror and a Marveller, she says that some of my gifts will change. I can enter animals' minds, see what they can see, travel with them, and even control them. But my mom says not to tell anybody that part because it'll scare Marvellers."

Ella examined Izulu as if she was looking for traces of Jason. Izulu nuzzled into her hand and hopped inside her room.

The bird flew around. "Nice stuff."

"Uh, thanks."

"So how does it work?" Ella asked.

"Just like mind-walking or entering a memory-cask except it's an animal. I have to form a relationship with them first to build trust."

"It's amazing!" Ella thought this might be the coolest marvel of them all. It made her curious about how the other conjure skills might change if blended with Marvellian marvels.

"I've been trying to talk to you for weeks." The bird perched on her canopy. "But you've been shooing me away and ignoring my starposts."

"I know. I just thought you were bad luck."

The bird chittered. "Stereotypes. Black birds should be celebrated and not feared. Izulu agrees." The bird swooped beside Ella. "I have to tell you something . . . something I couldn't send in a starpost. I got in trouble for having a messy room, and my dad made me clean out the attic. I found—"

Ella's door opened. Mama appeared. "You ready for Mardi Gras breakfast, baby girl?" Mama saw the bird before Ella could explain. She wrenched her house slipper off and sent it flying.

"Mama, wait!" Ella tried to stop her, but Mama chased Izulu (aka Jason) back outside, then locked the window and pulled the curtains shut.

"No bad omens today," Mama said, out of breath.

"Ugh!" Ella slammed herself back on the bed. She didn't even know how to explain to her that it was Jason and not a bird of misfortune, and she didn't feel like trying. Everything felt impossible right now.

Things had changed between them since she returned from the Arcanum Training Institute. Not outwardly, for Ella had everything most children needed: clean clothes, a full belly, all the books she'd ever wanted, the perfect dollhouse, several handmade dolls, a devoted litter of cats who kept her quilts warm, and so on. But none of this really mattered to her.

Ella remembered a time when Mama would whisk her away for the day just to go shopping in Havana or to hunt for rare books in Harlem at the largest Conjure bookshop in the world. Or they'd venture out to the bayous and forage for rare and temperamental conjure plants, just the two of them. They no longer did this. As winter break came and went, and the Arcanum didn't reopen, December turned into January, and January turned into February, and the fun disappeared. All her mother did was worry and fuss over her.

Mama's strong hands rubbed Ella's back. "What's wrong?"

"Everything," Ella replied.

"What's everything?" Mama coaxed Ella into rolling over.

Ella didn't want to cry or be upset, especially on Mardi Gras. She gulped hard. "Everyone is mad at us because of me. Sometimes I think even you're secretly mad at me too."

Mama lifted Ella's chin. The sunrise poured in, splashing across one of Gran's quilts. "I might have not agreed with your papa about you going up to that school in the sky, but I'd never be mad at you for wanting to go. The truth is, I'm not as brave as you." She kissed Ella's cheeks. "I have always been a bit of a chicken and hesitant to change."

Ella could've never thought of her mama as afraid. That felt impossible.

"I like the food that I like, the clothes that make me feel most comfortable, and being home. I feel safest in the things I know. Gran always wished I was more adventurous, but that was my sister, Celeste. She was the bold one. I was mostly scared of my own shadow."

"You're the bravest person I know," Ella said.

"You think that because I'm your mama. I make sure you don't see those parts of me. But when I was your age, I don't think I'd have had the courage to attend the Arcanum and face all those Marvellers."

"Now it's gotten us all into trouble." Those words made Ella's heart hurt, and she couldn't help a tear from falling. "Maybe I shouldn't have gone in the first place. Everyone hates us now."

"Or . . . everyone is using this as an excuse to let out their true feelings about us. These things don't just show up overnight. All it takes is one opportunity to reveal someone's true colors. We aren't going to let anything ruin our Mardi Gras or the time we have left together."

"What do you mean?"

Mama slipped a glittery starpost from her robe pocket.

Ella's heart fluttered as she reached for it, her name scrawled in celestial blue ink and the Arcanum Training Institute seal on the back. She tore into it, her eyes scanning the words with excitement:

Greetings of the most marvelous kind, Ella Durand,

After several months of disinfecting, cleaning, and working with Dr. Rodriguez, who let us borrow his magnificent wind marvel to release gales for expert air circulation throughout the Arcanum Training Institute for Marvelous and Uncanny Endeavors, we are ready to welcome you back. Our afflicted students have recovered.

We look forward to welcoming you back for sessions tomorrow. The Vellian Port has added additional sky-ferries headed to the Arcanum as well as a sky-ferry for you and three Conjure students to travel back. It will be waiting at West End Point tonight at 7:00 p.m.

Good marvelling to you and yours,

Laura Ruby

Executive Assistant to Headmarveller Rivera and

Headmarveller MacDonald

Ella thought she might faint from the sudden excitement.

"That's the first real smile I've seen from you since break started," Mama said. "And I'm glad to witness it."

Ella dove headfirst into her mother's arms. She'd get to go back now and finish what she started.

"Now, let's get ready for Mardi Gras before I have to say good-bye to you again." Mama swept Ella out of bed.

After a big breakfast and a cleansing bath, Ella and her family boarded a Conjure streetcar headed to Canal Street. Ella finally let the Mardi Gras magic wash over her. The city swelled with people, Fewels and Conjure folk alike. Jazz music filled the air, and the scent of jambalaya, crawfish étouffée, fresh beignets, and King Cake had stomachs growling.

Along Canal Street, watch-boxes hovered high above. Conjure families settled in, preparing to see the first flying floats. Umbrellas shielded Conjure folk from the sun.

Ella and her family climbed the staircase up to their box. She couldn't wait to cheer on the Marsalises' legendary float. Reagan kept their theme top secret.

Ella could see the entire city up there.

Winnie leaned over the box's edge despite Mama's protests. "Can the Fewels see us?"

"Of course not," Ella reminded her, thinking the Fewel parade looked so little and boring down on the ground and in comparison to theirs in the skies.

Mama grabbed the back of Winnie's dress. "They'll have their little parade below while we do our thing up here. You didn't think Marvellers were the only ones who could fly, now did you?" Mama handed them each a hot beignet. "We won't even notice them as soon as your papa lays down the veil."

The deathbulls howled as the gates of the Underworld opened and signaled the official start of the main parade. Papa's float emerged shaped like the Mansion of Death and made of skeletons. High Walkers and Low Walkers chanted and pounded their feet and reaping staffs as they made their way down North Rampart and to Canal. Their song washed over the crowd as they drew closer and closer.

Papa waved his skull-rimmed hat to thunderous applause. "Laissez les bon temps rouler! Krewes, let's go!"

The crowd erupted. The first parade floats made their way down: a swamp dragon spewing twilight stardust, a court jester waving his cap and bells, an underwater seascape, and more. Ella joined the joyous screams and started throwing beaded necklaces into other watch-boxes.

A few families turned their backs away from her as he passed by.

"What's wrong with—"

Mama patted her back. "We don't pay attention to any of that, you hear?"

But Ella couldn't stop looking at them and wondering how upset they were with her . . . and her papa.

Gran slid a slice of King Cake into her hands. "Eat up, you'll miss it in a few hours when you're back in the skies with all that bland food."

"I found the baby!" Winnie held up a tiny figure covered in cake crumbs. It wailed like an actual infant. "I'm going to be the luckiest."

Ella smiled down at Winnie, who'd grown almost to her shoulder now. She'd been home so long, she thought about how much she'd miss it once she was back at the Arcanum. A small part of her felt sad, and another part of her felt excited to get back.

The day wound down so fast Ella thought she'd lost minutes. The parade ended. They stuffed themselves with a big Mardi Gras meal. She repacked her juju-trunk and Arcanum satchel. But before she placed her stapier inside, she tried to get it to glow again for the first time in months. She slipped her hand into the grip and held it out. The handle adjusted to her fingers. She took a deep breath and closed her eyes.

Sweat coated her forehead. Her wish bloomed, the darkness turning to twilight, as she willed her conjure to cross into the stapier. Her fingers tingled and her body flushed with heat. She felt so different than the last time she'd attempted this in her dorm room.

Ella's eyes snapped open. A deep indigo sparked at the stapier's base, then climbed the rod to the very tip. The purple light washed over her room. A smile consumed her entire body. She'd done it.

Her bedroom door crept open, and Papa's face appeared. "Ready to . . . oh, look at you, the next Marvel Combat champ in the making." He clapped.

Ella beamed at him, then explained how she couldn't get it to work for months.

"I wonder if that strange sickness at the Arcanum had anything to do with it," he said.

"But I didn't get sick or have any nosebleeds. My conjure—" She swallowed the rest of her sentence as his eyebrows lifted. She didn't want him . . . or really, Mama . . . to know that she'd had issues with her gift back at the Institute.

"Go on . . ."

She admitted to conjure feeling fuzzy at the Vellian Port, the strange look of her bottle tree, and the struggles she had in Dr. Yohannes's class and afterward attempting to use her stapler.

He rubbed his chin and she braced herself, waiting for him to holler for Mama. "You feel better now?"

"Yes, sir."

He touched her forehead, pretending to examine her. "I think whatever was going around up there did have an effect, but after all this time at home, you're back right again."

"You're not going to tell Mama, are you?"

He chuckled. "It'll be our little secret." He tapped her temple. "If you can guard it from her."

She wrapped her arms around him and inhaled his scent, a little cologne, a little pipe tobacco, and a little of the spiced coolness of the Underworld.

"Let's go," he said.

An hour later, Ella was standing at the West End Point Pier with her juju-trunk and her parents, saying goodbye.

"You've got everything, right?" Mama rubbed her hand across Ella's collar to ensure the conjure-cameo was still tucked there.

"Yes, Mama." Ella hoped she wouldn't worry but knew that was an impossibility.

You sure you still want to go? Mama whispered in her mind.

"Yes," Ella replied, though if she was in an admitting mood, it felt a little harder this time around. She was surprised neither of them insisted on coming with her up to the Arcanum, but she felt grateful for the trust they instilled in her.

"We'll be okay down here, baby girl." Papa kissed Ella's forehead and swept her forward. "Don't you go worrying."

Ella waved at her parents, then turned toward the sky-ferry sitting on the water. She took a deep breath and walked down the pier. She didn't turn back and look at them for fear she might change her mind. She'd been home so long, it felt weird to be going away again. It was everything she'd dreamed of all winter break, but part of her felt a little afraid. Did Marvellers still think Conjure folk started the sickness? How would people treat her?

The sky-ferry door opened, and inside sat three Level One Conjure students looking like scared little mice.

Ella waved and sat down.

"Buckle your seat belts, please," an announcement crackled through the speakers. "We are taking off momentarily."

She stared out the window, watching as the Mississippi River and its boats disappeared as they climbed into the sky. Angsty feelings mingled with her fear. There was so much for her to do once she got back, so much to prove.

The sky-ferry's ceiling began to storm. A starpost dropped into Ella's lap. She flinched, hoping it wasn't another threatening letter. But the harried handwriting on the envelope made her heart slow down. It was Brigit's scrawl.

Ella tore into it.

Ella,

Gia visited me. I thought it was a dream, but it wasn't. I kept knitting her over and over again, and then I put it all together. I'm freaking out.

I'll be waiting for you as soon as you get back.

Brigit

Ella gulped. Never a dull moment.

★—★—★— **STARPOST**—★—★—★

Ella,

Welcome-back party in Noémie's room tonight after curfew. You're invited. You can bring Brigit too. Noémie said it was fine.

Abina

★—★—★— **STARPOST**—★—★—★

Ella,

I have a theory about the illness, but I don't want to write it down. Let's talk. I convinced my grandmother to let me come back.

Luci

CHAPTER TWENTY-THREE
THE JOKER

The next morning, Ella could barely inspect the Arcanum for any new changes or investigate how many students were wearing face masks or protective shields because she and Brigit were bolting to the dining hall to meet Jason. Ella had the longest checklist in her notebook of things they needed to do: deal with the note Gia sent Brigit, tell Masterji Thakur everything she'd learned while at home, visit the Arcanum Cardinal and ask Aries about twilight stars and make sure he was okay after lying for them, find Luci and ask her about her theories about the weird illness, and go to the library and research the history of the Institute construction. But as she and Brigit rounded the corner to the entry hall, they passed Noémie and Clare headed for the front door.

Ella pulled Brigit into a corner to hide. "What are they doing?" Ella asked, and wondered if it had anything to do with the party they'd skipped last night. She didn't even know why Noémie had invited them in the first place, as mean as she was to Ella every other time she saw her.

"No time to care." Brigit yanked her straight through the massive dining hall doors.

Ella gazed around. It all felt so different. There was no sushi constellation floating around. Blimps replaced it with banners full of safety rules about spreading out at the tables, wearing gloves to get food from the carts, and being mindful of germs. The level-specific areas felt empty, with fewer students than usual. Did they split up the breakfast times now? Or did fewer people come back?

"Ella, hurry up!" Brigit walked toward the Level Two area. Luz and Anh waved at her, then she saw Abina, who smiled.

"He's over there." Brigit pointed at Jason holed up in a corner with an audience of rotties at his table sharing in his megameatballs and endless pasta bowl.

They rushed ahead. He smiled, and the rotties gave them kisses. "We need to talk," they said in unison.

Brigit slid him the note from Gia. His eyes grew wide as he read it. "We can take shifts. Make sure you're never alone."

Ella still hadn't told them about the weird person she'd seen at the midnight assembly and the threatening notes she'd received. She definitely couldn't tell Brigit about them now; it would make her even more panicked. "Tell us the whole story." Brigit had gone through some of it last night, but she needed to hear it again when she wasn't so sleepy.

Brigit recounted how she'd woken up with three strange bug bites, then she'd started knitting terrible images of Gia towering over her. She fought away tears and the rotties nuzzled her cheeks.

"What do you think she wants?" Jason asked.

"I don't know, and worst of all, Ms. Mead has been sick, and I haven't been able to talk to her about it."

Jason sighed. "We have even more problems."

Ella braced herself.

"My dad said they're *still* trying to blame the sickness and the school closing on Madame Baptiste's lessons, the new Conjure students, and the visiting Navajo students. That there's some hearings or something in Celestian City. Investigations."

"That must be why Conjure II isn't on my timetable anymore." Brigit riffled through her satchel and retrieved a piece of paper.

Ella's eyes scanned it, then she went to look at hers. Sure enough, her godmother's class was missing. Her heart crashed into her stomach. "I don't understand. The Institute is back open and everyone is okay. Why would they think we had anything to do with this? Or the Navajo students?" She needed to see her godmother and Luci as soon as possible. She had to figure it all out. Part of her wondered if this was all somehow connected.

Jason shrugged. "They need someone—or something—to blame."

"But why us?" Ella knew the answer as soon as the question left her mouth.

"I have to show you both something else." Jason fished an old heliogram from his pocket. "I tried to tell you, Ella, when you were back home. But your mom shooed me away."

"Shooed?" Brigit stared at him, confused.

"I can kind of . . ."

"He can mind-walk animals. It's the coolest thing ever," Ella blurted out.

Brigit's eyes widened. "You can what?"

"It's called a kindred-walk. I can cross into their minds and go places with them. I just started learning how to do it." He cradled one of the rotties. "But I'll explain later." He leaned forward with the heliogram. "I got punished and had to clean out the attic, but I found this."

He placed the heliogram in front of them and pressed it. A tiny projection of six Level Three students illuminated. They stood outside the Marvel Combat Arena in their uniforms, their names scrawled along the edge—Barbara Williamson, Mitha Thakur, Johan Fenris Knudsen I, Victoria Baudelaire, Camille Bell, and Gia Trivelino. Ella found Jason's mom, then she gasped.

"There's Gia." Brigit pointed. "They knew each other."

"The other Aces too," Jason added. "Even Masterji Thakur."

"Was your mom an Ace?" Brigit asked Jason.

He shook his head. "No. She said she just knew them. But it's all weird, you know?"

Ella couldn't take her eyes off the woman to Mrs. Eugene's right. Her heart pounded. "Who is Camille Bell? She looks just like my mama."

But Jason didn't get to respond because Headmarveller MacDonald's voice commanded their attention and silence. Jason motioned for Ella to put the heliogram in her pocket.

"Welcome back, distinguished students. We are thrilled to see you. So much has transpired over the last few months. I'm so grateful to the starfolk and staff who have readied the building for your reentry. A school should be filled, and this strange illness has robbed us of many weeks together, including our coveted Marvel Combat tryouts, which I know you're keen to learn more about. We have a plan in place for you to make up the lost learning opportunities. Your Tower Advisers will have more information on this, but Headmarveller Rivera has a few important announcements first."

Ella could barely pay attention. The heliogram flickered in

her mind, the young woman who looked identical to Mama. That could *never ever* be her. Then who was it?

Headmarveller Rivera stood. "You'll see some changes around here, my little stars, for the safety of our student body. Meals will be happening in smaller groups, session transitions will look different, and there will be many handwashing and cleanliness procedures in place. We ask that you heed all the new protocols to help us all stay safe and move forward."

"What about Marvel Combat?!" a student shouted.

Headmarveller Rivera chuckled. "Ah, yes, the important things. Marvel Combat tryouts will be at the end of the year this year, and we'll have our usual tournament then. It does mean that our newest competitors won't get to compete until the next year, but we'll be sure you see plenty of dueling action."

A few boos trickled through the room.

"I can cancel it altogether, if you wish," she threatened.

The hall silenced.

"That's what I thought. This is the only way to ensure that we are safe and healthy. Until I see that we can follow the new rules, this is the plan. Understood?"

The entire room shouted, "Yes, Headmarveller Rivera!"

After the Headmarvellers toasted to an auspicious and healthy rest of the school year, Ella turned back to Jason and Brigit. "We have to find out who that person is!"

✦ ✼ ✦ ✖ ✦

ELLA TRIED HER BEST TO PAY ATTENTION IN HER CLASSES, BUT she'd earned a demerit in Dr. Choi's Marvellian-Adjacent Beings: Creature Study for scribbling theories in her notebook instead of watching snippets of the election season's fourth debate.

She'd accidentally scorched her fire jar in Dr. Huang's Global Elementals class because she hadn't been watching close enough during their lesson on harnessing blue fire. She'd accidentally let the chupacabra loose during her Marvellian Monsters workshop with Dr. Silvera in the Arcanum menagerie.

And now, she could barely focus on Dr. Al Sayed's future forecasting lesson on Marvellian tarot, when this should be her favorite lesson because she has a cartomanic marvel. Her thoughts looped back to her list of questions and her overwhelming desire to see Masterji Thakur and tell him everything she'd discovered while back home. She was worried about sending starposts to him since she'd gotten that notice, so she needed a moment to get to his classroom. He would also know the woman from the heliogram Jason found.

"Marvellian tarot consists of seventy-eight cards, and they're divided into two groups." Dr. Al Sayed raised her delicate arms as heliogram projections of each card filled the classroom ceiling. Light from the skywells made them twinkle. "There's the major arcana, which has twenty-two cards. Please note this. It'll be on your next quiz. You must memorize. The minor arcana has fifty-six cards. You will have to know the meaning of each one."

Ella slouched forward and put her head on her desk. Brigit poked her arm with a knitting needle right before Dr. Al Sayed snapped her fingers. Ella straightened up and resumed taking notes. She groaned. She'd never had this much trouble before. She always loved to learn all she could, but on her first full day back at the Arcanum, she felt scattered.

"Those who have cartomanic marvels—like me—should be paying *extra* attention to this lesson so that they can be eligible to earn their channellors at the start of Level Three. Without this information and passing my assessments, I won't be able to recommend they get to use their channellors." Her eyes landed right on Ella.

Ella looked away and shifted in her chair.

Dr. Al Sayed walked through the aisles, inspecting notebooks as she continued, "Brought to us by Italian Marvellers long ago, this fortune-telling instrument can be very powerful. The cards have been translated into many different cultures and have taken many different forms."

"But how can you use them for Marvel Combat?" Pierre blurted out. "Seems like it'd be a terrible channellor to have."

Ella glared at him. She didn't know how it worked during Marvel Combat, but she didn't want to think that she wouldn't be able to compete and win.

Dr. Al Sayed plucked a deck from her pocket, fanning the cards before her face. Their backs contained intricate tessellations in turquoise, sandy brown, and gold, reminding Ella of the gorgeous tiles she'd seen in Morocco during a spring break trip. Dr. Al Sayed shuffled the cards, then tossed the stack in the air.

They swarmed Pierre until he giggled.

Dr. Al Sayed flicked a finger. The cards transformed into a dragon and flew in circles around the classroom to *oohs* and *aahs*.

Ella gasped. It was an allurement.

"If I wanted to, I could sharpen the cards' edges . . . make them as deadly as daggers or cut as deep as jagged glass. Or I could use them to change the outcome of the match itself—though that's outlawed by the Marvel Combat Federation." She smiled.

Pierre's eyes held awe.

"I hope there are no further questions about the viability of a cartomanic marvel. It's one of the most powerful." Her eyes landed on Ella again, and she gulped. "Now, back to the task at hand." The cards returned to her perfectly manicured hands.

Brigit leaned close to Ella. "Will you be able to do that?"

"I hope so." Ella couldn't keep her eyes off Dr. Al Sayed's card deck.

"Since many of us have been struggling to focus today, we'll play a game and test what we know." She took another tarot deck from her desk. "You'll hold a question in your head, take a card, then attempt to interpret the answer based on what you pick. Let's see who's been paying attention."

As Dr. Al Sayed made her rounds, Ella smoothed her paper and tried to read through her notes as fast as possible. Her classmates plucked cards with magicians, hermits, chariots, and stars on them, and eagerly answered questions like, will the snow ever stop, what would go on Chef Oshiro's dinner menu, and how many kids would fail the next test.

But when Dr. Al Sayed paused at Ella's desk, she felt nervous. Tremors worked their way up her legs, and she tried to will her hands not to shake. Her mind raced with too many questions: What really happened to the architect? How could she prove that a Conjure architect designed the Arcanum Training Institute in the first place without the actual blueprints? Where did his body and memory-cask disappear to? Would Masterji Thakur still get in trouble for helping her? Did Aries get in trouble for helping them? Would Brigit (and she, frankly) be safe from Gia? Would the United Conjure Congress throw her family out of the Conjure world? Who was the woman who looked like her mama in the heliogram? Why did kids get sick at the Arcanum? She didn't want to say any one of these questions out loud, though she desperately wanted to know the answers.

Dr. Al Sayed said her name, and when Ella glanced up, she realized by the look on her teacher's face that her instructor had probably said it a few times. "Please hold *one* question in your head and draw a card."

Ella took a deep breath and thought, *What was wrong with the Arcanum?* Then she pulled a card from Dr. Al Sayed's deck. The weight of it felt so different than a conjure deck. Thin paper. Muted colors. Thick calligraphy. She turned it over. A harlequin in a checkered jumpsuit danced across the card. Diamonds pulsed along the edges.

Her heart accelerated. It reminded her of Gia's circus. The Trivelino Troupe's Circus & Imaginarium of Illusions. The harlequin stomped on the word FOOL.

"Ah, the Fool," Dr. Al Sayed said.

"Because she's a Fewel," someone called out.

Dr. Al Sayed snapped her fingers. "Be quiet. We'll have none of that."

Heat rushed through her, but she didn't turn around to look for the culprit. She couldn't keep her eyes off the card.

"What does it represent?" Dr. Al Sayed asked.

Ella glanced down at her notes. "New beginnings. Faith in the future. Luck. Being inexperienced."

"Well done, you—"

The card flickered. The words scrambled and changed, FOOL turning into JOKER. The little painted harlequin revealed a strange double mask from behind its back, one with a sad face and a happy face.

Brigit grabbed Ella's hand. Sweat skated across her forehead.

"Well, look at that." Dr. Al Sayed held the card up for the class to see. "Ella's question must've been complex for the Fool to reveal the Joker."

"What is that mask?" Ella had seen it before on that person at the midnight orientation.

"A sock and buskin. Ancient symbol of Greek theater for tragedies and comedies," Dr. Al Sayed explained. "So, what was your question? It's very rare that this card reveals its hidden alter ego."

As Ella pondered whether to share, her eyes snapped shut and her mind filled with images. Two faces playing peek-a-boo behind those masks. Noémie and Gia. Fear stormed through her.

A hand touched her shoulder and Ella startled. The faces disappeared.

"Did you hear my question?" Dr. Al Sayed's face held concern, and she felt the heat of everyone's curious gaze on her. "Are you okay?"

"Dr. Al Sayed!" a shout came from the back of the classroom. "Luz's nose is bleeding."

The whole class turned to look. Part of Ella was grateful to have Dr. Al Sayed's attention off her, but now the illness was back.

Marvel Combat Tryouts!

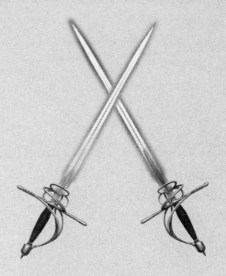

Level Twos and Threes only.
Bring Sabrewhizz 1.5 edition!

LOCATION: Marvel Combat Arena
DATE: Last Day of School

★—★—★— **STARPOST**—★—★—★

G.T.,

I got your message. The debt has been paid. My daughter did what was asked of her . . . and now you're asking for more. The school closed. You got what you wanted.

We're done.

Victoria

The Arcanum Training Institute for Marvelous and Uncanny Endeavors

Lower School

DAILY ILLNESS REPORT

Reported Cases: 8

Symptoms: Recurrent nosebleeds, headaches, complaints of weakened marvels

Recommendations: Increase starfolk cleaning schedule, add more clouds to classrooms, potentially build outdoor pavilions for classes with over twenty-five trainees.

Nurse Peaks

★—★—★— **STARPOST**—★—★—★

Victoria,

    We're done when I say we are. She has one final task. I'll be in touch with the instructions.

    You owe me.

G.T.

CHAPTER TWENTY-FOUR
A SPY MISSION!

Tell me everything you saw again." Brigit paced around Jason's lair in the Arcanum menagerie. They'd sneaked out of dinner early to meet before curfew. The rotties piled in their laps, sharing in the fighting falafel at war with each other.

Ella retold the story about the sock and buskin mask and seeing Gia and Noémie together. "But I'd seen that symbol before."

"Where?" Brigit asked.

Ella bit her lip. She hadn't wanted to tell either of them about the threatening notes. There'd been so much going on already. Her eyes cut to her satchel, where she shoved the notes to the very bottom so they'd never be accidentally found. "I've been getting . . ." Her voice trailed off, and she dug them out. She handed them to Brigit and Jason.

Jason's eyes bulged. "Whoa. These are bad."

"Why didn't you say anything?" Brigit's cheeks turned bright red.

Ella shrugged. "There was also a person wearing this mask at the midnight orientation. They were hidden with the Chinese acrobats."

"I can't believe you didn't say anything." Brigit crumpled one of the notes.

"I didn't want to worry anyone or for my parents to find out. They would've pulled me out of the Arcanum even before it shut down." Ella heard how ridiculous she sounded and flooded with regret. She should've said something. They were a team, after all.

"Those notes were obviously from Gia," Brigit replied.

"You shouldn't have to deal with this alone." Jason patted her shoulder and placed a smiling rottie in her lap.

"I hate her," Brigit almost hissed. "And your vision is so weird. How would the two of them even know each other?"

"Maybe they don't. Maybe my vision was wrong. I haven't exactly had one before. Not like you." Each time Ella closed her eyes, the images flashed like a newsreel and it sent a tingle across her skin. But she didn't know how to trust anything right now. Everything felt confusing and overwhelming.

"What question did you think of before you pulled the card?" Jason asked.

"I asked what was wrong with the Arcanum," Ella said.

Both Jason's and Brigit's eyes widened.

"Do you think Gia or Noémie have something to do with it?" Jason scratched his head. "That can't be a coincidence."

"Luci said she had a theory too. But I haven't seen her yet." Ella nibbled her bottom lip. "I think there's something to it. Has to be . . . Because—"

"Wait!" Jason threw his hand up, then perched low to the ground. More rotties swarmed him. "Sweet Pea said Noémie stays up all night almost every night. Sometimes she leaves the school."

Ella looked at Brigit. They'd seen Clare and Noémie slip out the front door of the school earlier today. What were they doing? Where were they going? "We have to find out what she's up to."

"And if it's connected to Gia," Brigit added.

"How?" Jason asked.

"We follow her." Ella churned over a plan in her head.

"But we need to know what's in her room too." Brigit balled her fists, and Ella could feel her anger. "We should ask Siobhan and Luci for help. They're her roommates."

"Let's do both." Jason scooped up another rottie.

Ella nodded. "Okay, Brigit, let's stay up late and keep watch."

"The rotties say they'll help." Jason lifted Brownie and Sweet Pea.

"Once Noémie leaves her room, Brigit, you go in, and I'll follow her."

"I'll meet you, Ella," Jason added. "I told the rotties to keep an eye on her and come to your room when she's left. They'll tell us where to go. I'll meet you as soon as they show up."

They solidified the plan and went back to their dorm rooms. Ella could barely do her homework, fixating on their clock-lantern and trying to go through all their theories with Feste. When Mrs. Francesca came by to remind them about lights-out, Ella didn't even argue or get frustrated. She and Brigit pretended to get ready for bed.

"What do you think Gia's up to?" Brigit asked.

"I don't know." Ella stared up into her bottle tree. The golden leaves caught the moonlight, and she wished the branches still held the blueprint canister. Her mind jumped around in a thousand directions. She felt like everything had to be connected—the illness, the blueprints, Gia. She tried to ignore the fear that rose inside her. They'd figure out Gia's plan. They had to.

Brigit cleared her throat, and Ella knew it was to keep from crying. "What if Gia is trying to get me again?"

"We won't let that happen. I promise."

"Same," Feste chimed in.

"But—"

A tiny squeak echoed.

Ella sat up. Four rotties perched on the edge of her bed.

"Time to go." Ella leaped up and Brigit followed. "You know what to do?"

"Yeah. I'm going to look for anything weird in her room. Siobhan and Luci said they'd help." Brigit grabbed her satchel.

"Good luck," Feste said.

They crept into the hallway, looking left and right. Photo-balloons drifted about and night lanterns left soft balls of light on the staircase. The Azure Dragon constellation stretched along the ceiling, snoring. Stars shot from its nose.

"Meet you in a few minutes," Brigit said.

"Yes, the rotties will bring you to us."

"We can do this, right?" Concern flooded Brigit's eyes.

Ella saluted her. "Yes, yes, we can—and we will."

They separated. Ella tiptoed down the stairs, following behind two rotties. She sprinted out of the dorm and into the hall. The rotties helped her dodge automats and led her to the Touch Tower.

Ella waited under the massive mechanical hand now frozen in a wave. The heliogram of Indira Patel the Brave and her daggers left shadows on the ground. She thrummed with anxiety as she waited for Jason. Every noise, every movement, every speck of light made her jump. She listened for coppers' boots or the sound of their red-eyed wolves or worse, the flutter of their ravens. Her mind raced. What would she say if she was caught? Her excuse didn't hold water, as Mama would say. She really should be back in her room. But she practiced a lie: *She was looking for her missing notebook because she had a test in Marvellian Theory with Dr. Mackenzie.* It wasn't a complete lie.

"Psst!"

Ella found Jason in the far corner. She sprinted over to him.

"The rotties said she's in the greenhouse," he reported.

They took off behind the tiny creatures, following the flick and swish of their tiny tails. The good thing about the Arcanum layout this year was that everything existed inside the same compound. If they took the right corridors, they'd remain undetected and avoid the main gate and copper patrol.

They sneaked through open galleries and passed the art studios and lapidary labs. The rotties took a shortcut past the paper workshop. The Stariary shone bright and active, and Ella wished she could stop and see if Aries was in there tonight. But she kept moving. They cut through the Arcanum courtyard. The Cardinal soared above her. She thought of the architect's original plans and the twilight stars emanating from it, but she couldn't see anything but falling snow. She stopped to look, but Jason pulled her forward. "This way," he whispered. "No time."

They tiptoed around the greenhouse. Rotties perched on Jason's shoulders and helped him clean off the glass. Ella pressed her face to the panes, feeling the heat inside. She was desperate to keep warm. The mechanical sun blazed high in the ceiling.

"Look, there she is!" Jason pointed.

In the middle of the foliage, Noémie stood in front of a strange floating door. Ella craned to look. "Who is she talking to?"

"It's a tall woman with dark hair. It has to be Gia," Jason whispered. "She wears hats like that. I've seen the wanted posters."

Ella stretched on her tiptoes. The woman in question wore a large-brimmed hat that cast a shadow over her face. Ella listened hard.

She caught only snippets:

"You said it was over."

"You said I didn't have to anymore."

"They're going to find out."

A hand touched Ella's back. She screeched. Noémie whipped around. Ella and Jason crouched low. Brigit and three rotties stared back at them.

"Didn't meant to scare you," she panted. "But, but I found . . ."

"Breathe." Ella patted her back.

Sweat coated Brigit's face. She bent over, hands on her knees. "Look at these!" She took six teeny tiny bottles from her pocket.

Ella examined them. The vials of glittery liquid pulsed in the darkness. Each bottle marked with a name: Anh Nguyen, Pierre Dupont, Samaira Al-Nahwi, Hassan and Youssef Doumbouya, Clare Lumen, Brigit Ebsen, and Ella Durand. "What are these?"

Jason's eyes widened, and he put a hand over his mouth.

"I found a notebook with names listed in it," Brigit reported. "And Noémie isn't her real name. I saw starposts in her desk to *Amelie*. Luci said she found anonymous letters written to all the Marveller newspapers about the illness and it being caused by the Conjure kids, Madame Baptiste, and the Navajo students."

"How . . . why . . . ?" Ella's words garbled up as she thought about the bottles Noémie used during her game and how similar they looked to the fiery elixir Gia had last year. She perched back on her tiptoes to look into the greenhouse. It was empty. Door gone and no more Noémie. "We lost her. Do you think she saw us?"

"It doesn't matter if she did . . . she's doing what Gia did. She's stealing marvels. I bet that's what's causing everyone to get sick." Jason lifted the bottles up into the moonlight.

"We need to find out more about Noémie or Amelie or whoever she is," Brigit said.

"How?" Ella asked. "We can't just ask her. It's not like she's going to tell us the truth."

Jason cradled a rottie and brushed snow from his fur. "Her trainee file. That's got to have information in it."

"Aren't those in the Headmarvellers' office? We can't just march in there and look." Stress raged inside Ella as she tried to put together a plan.

"They're in Dr. Ruby's office. My sister Grace volunteers there," Jason said. "We should find out as much as we can."

Brigit nodded while shivering.

"We have to stop her *now*!" Ella balled her fists.

★—★—★— **STARPOST**—★—★—★

Ella,

Please come to my atelier for your conjure lesson.

Love,
Aunt Sera

★—★—★— **STARPOST**—★—★—★

Dear Masterji Thakur,

Can you send me an appointment card? I have so much to talk to you about. My starposts to you keep getting returned with some weird message. I want to show you. I don't know why it keeps happening.

Ella

★—★—★— **STARPOST**—★—★—★

Ella,

I am away in Celestian City still dealing with *that* matter. I hope to return soon. Don't send me anything else via starpost right now. I'll explain when I see you.

Masterji Thakur

★—★—★— **STARPOST**—★—★—★

Ella,

I feel like someone is watching me. Every time I try to come find you, I get stopped or interrupted.

like someone or something doesn't want us talking. I'll just write out my theory and hope no one is eavesdropping. I think the sickness is not natural like a cold going around. I could be totally wrong, but that's what my gut tells me—and my grandmother says to always trust it.

Luci

CHAPTER TWENTY-FIVE

THE ARCANUM ARCHIVES

The next afternoon, Ella stood in the center of Aunt Sera's Conjure Atelier gazing around at how empty it felt now that there were no classes held here anymore. Echi's snores echoed as she slept on a tree branch. White sheets covered the student worktables. The small library of conjure books was freckled with dust.

Aunt Sera fussed with the plants in her tiny conjure garden, cursing and mumbling under her breath, and Ella could feel the frustration radiating off her.

"I hate that you can't teach right now," Ella said. She still couldn't believe the Headmarvellers suspended her sessions until after a hearing. How could they actually believe conjure had anything to do with kids getting sick? This hadn't happened last year. If conjure was the cause, wouldn't it have started then?

"Well, lucky for you, I still get to teach you. Ready for your lesson?" Aunt Sera retrieved her memory-cask and set it on her table. "We're going to discuss the symbols you need to look for when you're mind-walking someone or visiting a memory-cask."

Ella looked forward to her lesson today despite feeling like there were a thousand things for her to do—make a plan to investigate Noémie's files with Brigit and Jason; figure out how to deal with waiting until Masterji Thakur returned from Celestian City; and figure out if there was something to Luci's new theory. But she felt eager to learn about this after watching Laurent enter the memory-cask of the architect's wife back in the cemetery. Part of her wanted to blurt the entire story out for Aunt Sera and get her opinion on what to do, but she couldn't trust that her godmother wouldn't spill the secrets to Mama and Papa . . . or worse, tell her to stop looking.

Aunt Sera lit three candles, then opened her box. Twilight stardust bundles glittered. "Now, let's continue part two of your lesson on lociambulism, the mind-walk. When you use this technique to either enter the living mind of another or venture into the memory-cask of an ancestor, you will encounter symbols. They're always repeated. Could be anything from keys to clocks to rattles to food to mirrors. Any—"

"I don't remember the ones in your mind," Ella interrupted, trying to remember.

"Sometimes during our first journey, we struggle to pay attention. Everything is so new that being awestruck can distract." She rotated the memory-cask on the table so Ella could have a closer look inside. "You're sifting through the doldrums of their mind for clues about who the person is, what they've been through, and where they're headed."

The interior of the memory-cask reminded her of a dollhouse filled with tiny passages leading this way and that way. It made her wonder what the architect's memory-cask might've been like. She filled with more questions.

"The objects are charged with energy that'll help you determine if they're related to the person's past, present, or future, and help—"

"Does a living mind feel different from a dead one?" Ella interrupted again.

Aunt Sera frowned. "Please hold your questions until I'm finished. Maybe I'll answer some of them along the way."

"Sorry!" But Ella felt about to bubble over. So many pieces of this very complicated puzzle swirled around inside her. Who stole the architect's memory-cask—and what memories were inside it that they didn't want people to know about?

Aunt Sera proceeded with her lesson detailing how the symbols could be intuitive. Sightings of blood or a bird of misfortune could signal difficult circumstances on the horizon. Gold coins and an abundance of food were often a sign of good fortune to come. Ella tried her best to pay attention, but as she fixated on her godmother's memory-cask, she couldn't keep the questions from coming. "What if someone stole your memory-cask? Can anyone enter it—even if they're not family?"

"Hush!" Her godmother's voice was so sharp it echoed. The candlelight froze and the flowers in the bottle tree tucked themselves away. "Just hush for a few minutes."

Tears pricked Ella's eyes. What was wrong with her today?

"Listen to me." Aunt Sera swallowed hard and took a deep breath. "This once, just listen. Say nothing. Let me tell you how it's done. Let me get it all out. Things have already been so stressful, and I need one thing to go right. I need to be able to tell your mama that I was able to do at least this." Aunt Sera wiped away the single tear that fell down Ella's cheek. "I'm sorry, my petit. I didn't mean to be so stern. I'm tired and upset and we must get through this."

Ella hiccupped, then nodded reluctantly. She felt terrible. She knew she'd been an interrupting chicken, as Gran called her when she got like this, but Aunt Sera had never yelled at her. Not once in all her twelve years.

Aunt Sera kissed Ella's hand. "It's going to be okay. We're going to be okay. Just let me tell you this last thing, and then I'll answer all your questions."

Ella forced herself to smile and swallow the rest of her sadness.

"When you get good enough at mind-walking, you can even invite others into your own mind and connect people. The way your mama is connected to you and can speak to you. You'd be able to allow others. This is all to prep for your companion."

"But what about crossing powder? She doesn't use it to talk to me," Ella said.

"She did when you were in her belly and first born. All Conjure parents do. It's tradition." She thumbed one of the powder bundles. "Even I got to meet you and talk to you some before you arrived here, before you were born."

That softened Ella, and she thought maybe her aunt's bad mood had passed.

"Now, on to your questions." Aunt Sera explained that a living mind and a dead mind felt the same to the lociambulist, but that visiting a living one had more consequences if something went wrong and nefarious people had ways of entering memory-casks if they wanted to. "Why this sudden curiosity?"

Ella opened her mouth to tell a half-truth when Headmarveller MacDonald appeared in the doorway.

"Oh, hello, Ella, and Madame Baptiste," he said.

"Hi, Eoin." Aunt Sera stood, smoothed her dress, and touched her face strangely as if to check to make sure she didn't have anything on it.

"Sorry to interrupt." His white cheeks pinkened.

"No, not at all. We were just wrapping up, right, Ella?" Aunt Sera's voice turned high-pitched and nervous. Ella stared at her, curious.

"I just wanted to remind you that we'd love for you to be a chaperone on the upcoming field trip to Celestian City for Election Night," he said.

Aunt Sera turned to Ella. "Petit, I need to discuss this with Headmarveller MacDonald. We're all done now. Next time we can discuss the making of the memory-casks themselves and go through the materials." She swept Ella out of the Conjure Atelier.

✦ ✖ ✦ ✖ ✦

DURING DINNER, ELLA AND BRIGIT WAITED AT THE ENTRANCE TO the Headmarveller's Wing. They watched as Jason talked to his older sister Grace from Level Three. They tried to eavesdrop but also not draw too much attention. Grace towered over Jason and she wore long braids. Ella's thoughts spiraled. What if Grace wouldn't help them? What would they do instead?

Brigit yammered on about her theories concerning what Noémie and Gia were up to, but Ella couldn't process it.

Jason turned away from his sister and sprinted back to them. "She's in."

Ella and Brigit followed Jason back down the hall. They thanked Grace.

"Just never mention it, okay? We don't know each other and this never happened," she replied, using her keys to open an office. "You have fifteen minutes. Dr. Ruby always comes back after dessert to prepare her to-do list for the next day. The archives are in the back. There's an alcove."

They eased into the executive assistant's office. A float-fire crackled in front of a large desk. Papers sat in perilous towers threatening to topple. A huge starpost box floated beside the door.

"Over there." Brigit pointed at a sign, ARCANUM TRAINING INSTITUTE ARCHIVES.

Jason pushed through the door. Cabinets soared to the ceiling.

Ella gulped. "How are we going to find anything?"

"Here." Jason lifted a clipboard. "Grace said you write down a name and the cabinets answer. Dr. Ruby has an archive marvel." He scrawled Noémie's name on the paper.

The cabinets shifted left and right, and up and down in a whirlwind. Drawers shot open. A file slipped out.

Ella, Brigit, and Jason huddled around it and riffled through the pages.

"Noémie's not even her real name," Brigit said. "Just like we thought."

"It's her middle name." Ella's eyes scanned the pages. "She's from Paris."

"Her full name is Amelie Noémie Baudelaire-Lavigne." Jason took a few pages. "Well, she's got good grades and every teacher seems to say nice things about her."

Frustration boiled in Ella. There was nothing unusual about anything in here. The plan suddenly felt stupid. What did she expect . . . for the Arcanum to have a piece of paper that said Noémie was working with the number one criminal in the entire world, Gia Trivelino, and under surveillance?

Brigit said her name over and over again until it became a mantra in Ella's head.

"Wait!" Ella took her timetable and looked at her name again. "I've heard one of her last names, Baudelaire, before . . . but where?" Her eyes found Jason's, and she removed the heliogram he'd given her from her pocket. The one that he'd found in his attic. She pressed it and examined the friend group. "Look at the names. She's Victoria Baudelaire."

"Wait . . ." Brigit rustled through the file again. "Look!" She pointed at an emergency contact form, and there it was again. "Her mother is an Ace."

"Then Noémie has to be working with Gia," Ella said. "This proves their connection."

Brigit grabbed her satchel and yanked out her pocket-box. She dug through it, then pulled out a beautiful thick blanket covered with faces. "I've been knitting her—and others." She ran her hands over the different sections. Each face sat in a playing card. "These are all the Aces."

"Whoa." Jason perched over it. Rotties flooded the room, having a look too.

Ella's eyes tried to take in all of them. "What are their names?"

"I'm still researching, but this one is her, Victoria. I'm sure of it. She's even holding a bottle like the ones Noémie has." Brigit smoothed the blanket.

Jason scooped three rotties into his arms. "The rotties said Dr. Ruby is on her way back. We have to go!"

Ella scrambled to put Noémie's file back.

"One last thing. I need to see Gia's file." Brigit scribbled her name on the clipboard and the cabinets shifted again.

"There's no time," Ella protested.

But the cabinets released a folder that looked like a hundred files smashed together. Ella knew they needed to leave quick, fast, and in a hurry, but curiosity overwhelmed her too. She dove into the file with Brigit. It burst with demerit ledgers, mischief reports, copies of starpost letters home, formal complaints, discipline board summaries, and more.

Jason held up one of her timetables. "She got almost perfect marks. Always fives."

Brigit scowled as she read through everything.

"How can you get in so much trouble but have perfect grades?" Ella wondered.

"I guess you don't have to be good to be smart," Jason replied. "The Arcanum doctors hated her. There are so many meetings about her behavior." He cleared his throat. "Listen to this from her Level Two report card . . . 'Gia Trivelino could turn out to be one of the most powerful Marvellers in all of history, but I fear there's too much evil in her heart, too much desire for power. From the questions she asks in class to the company she keeps. Mitha Thakur, Johan Fenris Knudsen I, Victoria Baudelaire, and Camille Bell, especially, her partner in crime, will hasten her downfall."

"Camille Bell . . ." Ella pressed the heliogram again and looked at the tiny projection of the young girl who looked identical to her mama.

"We have to go now!" Jason said. "The rotties said Dr. Ruby is rounding the corner."

They packed up the files and let the cabinets put them away. Brigit tried to erase the names from Dr. Ruby's clipboard to cover their tracks. "It's not working."

"We have to leave it." Ella pulled Brigit away.

They zipped back through Dr. Ruby's office and out into the Headmarveller's Wing.

"What are you three doing?" an automat yelled.

Ella, Brigit, and Jason looked at one another and took off

running. They raced through the halls, headed for their dorms. The noise of the automat made Ella run as fast as she could. Photo-balloons clustered overhead, and Ella tried not to panic about them no doubt taking their picture and reporting to Dean Nabokova. Her legs burned, and she felt like she wasn't going to make it to her room without being caught.

The Azure Dragon door glimmered ahead, the dragon constellation welcoming her and Brigit with a concerned expression. But automats swarmed the entrance. They looked left at Jason's dormitory, the White Tiger, and there more automats waited.

Ella's heart lodged in her throat. What were they going to do?

"Hey, over here!"

Ella looked left and found Bex peeking around a corner. "This way."

The trio followed down a narrow hall. Ella had never explored this nook of the Arcanum before. It was like she'd never really noticed it.

Brigit stopped abruptly. "I've never seen this dorm."

Bex smiled at her. "You can see it?"

"Yeah, can't everyone?" Brigit looked puzzled.

Ella and Jason stared around and around. There was nothing but a plain wall covered in heliogram projections of the Arcanum throughout time.

"It looks like real gold. What is that . . ." Brigit ran her fingers over the stone.

"I get three guest passes a month. No time to explain." Bex dug in their pocket, retrieving the glittering tickets. They pushed them into the wall and it sparked.

Ella jumped back. The heliograms melted away, giving way to

a golden door. The constellation of a creature Ella had never seen before greeted them with a bow. It looked like a cross between a giraffe and a Chinese dragon with antlers and beautiful scales that resembled fat stella coins. "What is that?"

"The Yellow Qilin." Bex led them through the door just as an automat entered the hall. They watched through hidden windows as the dormitory door disappeared again.

"This is amazing." Jason did a loop around the lounge. A rainbow stretched across the ceiling, and floating clouds dropped sweets every few seconds. Colorful couches stretched to fit everyone.

Ella gazed up, remembering last year when Bex helped her deal with Headmarveller Rivera catching them looking for Masterji Thakur and saying they lived in Chimera. Their words echoed in her memory: *Only those who need it know where it is.* This made her love the Arcanum Training Institute more and want to uncover all of its secrets. She felt like it contained thousands of contradictions.

"What were you all doing?" Bex asked.

Brigit shot Ella a look. "Investigating," she said.

Bex laughed. "Me too." They held up a strange plant in a vivarium. "Masterji Thakur has me looking after his night plants again while he's away."

"When will he be back?" Ella felt desperate to hear from him.

"I don't know." Bex shrugged.

"Without him, we're all in trouble," she said.

The Arcanum Training Institute for Marvelous and Uncanny Endeavors

Lower School

SECOND YEAR LEVEL TWO
MIDYEAR MARKS
Name: *Amelie Noémie Baudelaire-Lavigne*

CORE REQUIREMENTS

PARAGON REQUIREMENTS:

SCORING RUBRIC:

5 = Showing signs of mastery

4 = Showing signs of proficiency

3 = Satisfactory

2 = Needs Improvement

1 = Failing to Show Effort and Progress

NOTES: *Noémie shows great promise, and even though she was homeschooled, she shows no sign of struggle in her coursework or socially with making friends. She could do a little less socializing and improve her focus, especially when it comes to her homework. She has something she's hiding and keeps earning demerits for being out of bed after curfew. Our recommendation is she see Dr. Chin for one-on-one counseling because she's having trouble sleeping at night and seems paranoid and on edge at times. We've received a few complaints about her bullying others.*

INHERITANCE

After several long weeks of waiting for the copper patrols in Betelmore's cemetery to lessen, Gia Trivelino finally slipped inside undetected. The Trivelino vault stretched above Gia and Volan as she gripped the locket around her neck. She traced her fingers over her family emblem—the sock and buskin masks—one sad, tragic face and one happy, comedic one. She waited for her mother's clever riddle to appear again.

THOSE WHO SEEK ENTRY MUST BE PAIRS BONDED BY BLOOD.
ONLY TOGETHER SHALL YOU CLAIM WHAT YOU DESIRE.

As it took form in the stone, she pricked her finger and waited for a pearl of blood to rise from the wound. Then she removed one of the little glass bugs from her special canister and emptied some of Brigit's blood into her own. The mixture made her heart race. All the trouble she'd had to go to for these tiny drops. But she'd won.

She retraced the family emblem, giving the sock and buskin a bloody smile and a bloody frown. The gates opened with a sigh.

"Keep a look out, Volan," she ordered.

"Yes, my lady."

"Whistle if you see any coppers."

Volan nodded as she stepped forward.

A skylight window let in the moon's glow. The nondescript vault felt leeched of spirit. Gray walls, jagged floors, and little light, which made sense as there were no dead here. They were tucked away in the Underworld, for Marvellers would never tolerate the stench of the dead to pollute the skies. She opened several safes and filled numerous coin purses with as many stellas and lunaris as they could hold before turning her attention to files of papers from her parents' archives.

She went through her papa's things first, running a gloved hand over his commedia dell'arte costumes and play scripts, almost hearing his laugh echo through the cavernous space. She took some of his clever masks and disguises. They'd help her begin to rebuild those she'd lost. Then she turned to her mother's side of the vault and riffled through her papers. She uncovered details about her mother's charity, the Starfolk Welfare, and an unexpected item that made her heart race.

There were documents and letters from the Marvellian Temperance Union on the eradication of monstrous marvels for the betterment of Marvellian society. She scanned through them, finding work her mother had done in tracking families—like her own—that had ancestors with monstrous marvels. Lists of surnames and descriptions of marvels filled page after page. The group's plans on how to end the presence of such gifts from bloodlines were laid out in pamphlets.

Gia laughed out loud. She'd been given a surprise gift.

A whistle filled the space.

"My lady, you must go," Volan called out. "There's movement at the cemetery gate. A copper patrol."

Gia hustled out of the vault and into the moonlight.

"Did you get what you needed?" he asked.

"More," she replied. "Much more."

★—★—★— **STARPOST**—★—★—★

Jason,

　　We're going to mind-walk Noémie. It's the only way to know what she's up to. I need your help. Brigit is . . . in, but she's nervous. Can you help me get ingredients from my aunt Sera's room?

　　I've attached a list.

Ella

★—★—★— **STARPOST**—★—★—★

Ella,

　　I'll have the rotties do it. No problem. They're addicted to conjure candies, though, so I'll need some of your stash.

　　Let's do it after the stapier test.

Jason

★—★—★— **STARPOST**—★—★—★

Ella,

　　I asked Siobhan to help us. I know, I know . . . you said don't tell anyone, but she's already helped us before. She proved she can keep secrets.

　　She's going to make sure Noémie is sound asleep. Her hobgoblin has sleepy time powder. Because I'm scared Noémie will wake up and we'll get stuck in her mind forever.

Brigit

CHAPTER TWENTY-SIX
STAPIER TEST

"I t is time to test your ability to use a stapier," Dr. Yohannes called out. "Take them out. I'll be calling you up to my desk one by one to demonstrate."

A panic climbed through Ella. She had been so wrapped up in investigating Noémie and trying to put together the biggest puzzle in need of solving . . . that she'd neglected practicing using her stapier. The last time she'd used it was the day she'd left home to return to the Arcanum Training Institute.

She ran her fingers over the stapier handle, watching it match her grip. The worst-case scenarios ran through her head: What would happen if she failed? What if she'd forgotten how to make it work? How did she get herself to this place?

Brigit poked her. "What's wrong?"

"I forgot about the test. I didn't practice," Ella admitted.

"You'll be okay," Brigit assured her.

"But what if I can't. What if I fail?" Worry clawed at her heart.

"Then you don't do good for the first time ever."

Ella didn't know how not to do well. She was supposed to be

excellent. Perfect, in fact. Her parents didn't send her up here to make people think Conjurors couldn't do what Marvellers could.

"You'll be okay. I promise." Brigit rubbed her arm.

But Ella snatched it away. "You don't know that."

Brigit looked stung. "I could . . ." She lifted her knitting needles and yarn to remind Ella of her timesight marvel, but Ella turned her back.

Ella's thoughts raced. How could she prepare as quickly as possible while Dr. Yohannes called students to her desk? She'd just completed kids with last names starting with *B* and she'd be at *D* in no time. Ella cupped her hands under her desk. She took deep breaths and tried to at least summon her light.

She squeezed her eyes shut. She yanked it to the surface. The twilight blazed bright. Too bright.

"Ella!"

"Ella!"

Screams startled her and her eyes snapped open. Everyone in the classroom look stunned. The beautiful violets that usually sat beside Dr. Yohannes's desk now consumed the classroom ceiling, a gigantic canopy blocking the skywell. The star-lanterns blazed brighter to combat the darkness.

"Is everything all right?" Dr. Yohannes stared down at her.

Embarrassment and anxiety mingled in Ella's stomach. What had she done? What was wrong with her conjure?

Whispers crackled around her:

"Her marvel is out of control."

"What's wrong with her?"

"This is scary. I still can't believe they can do this."

Ella gulped and Brigit gazed at her with concern.

"Come with me—and bring your stapier." Dr. Yohannes led her forward. She turned Ella away from the class's nosy stares. "Want to tell me what's going on?"

Ella sighed. She didn't want to tell her teacher that she forgot about the test even after several reminders over the past few weeks. She didn't want to see the disappointment in Dr. Yohannes's eyes. She didn't want to face not being prepared and perfect for this woman's class. "I'm having a bad day," she lied.

"We all have them, and things have been stressful around here. It's hard to be back home for so long and get back into the Institute rhythm. That's understandable." Her kindness made Ella feel even worse. "So let's get your stapier test over with. Maybe it'll alleviate some anxiety, and you can go back to perfecting your light"—her eyebrows lifted at the violet canopy still over her head—"because clearly you have some work to do."

"Yes, Dr. Yohannes," she replied.

Ella took a deep breath and held out her stapier. The grip softened as she held tight. She closed her eyes again and pretended that no one was watching. She tried to ignore the prickle of everyone's eyes on her. This time she didn't grab for the light, she waited. She wanted to hum and sing to try to control her conjure, but embarrassment kept her quiet.

C'mon, c'mon, she thought to herself.

She waited for her wish to bloom inside her mind's eye. She waited to see the beautiful twilight. But it remained dark. Uncontrollable tears skated down her cheeks.

Her stapier blade remained lifeless. She'd failed.

The Arcanum Training Institute for Marvelous and Uncanny Endeavors

———— Lower School ————

Dear Parents or Guardians of Ella Durand,

We are writing to inform you that your student has failed their stapier test and will be ineligible to use a stapier and will not progress on to using their specific channellor at this time.

Due to the unusual pandemic closure, we will be offering all students a second opportunity to test in June, and we hope your student will be able to show improvement; otherwise, they will have to attend summer school or disenroll for Level Three training next year.

If you have any questions, please send a starpost to our attention.

All the good marvelling,
Laura Ruby
Executive Assistant to Headmarveller MacDonald and
Headmarveller Rivera of the Lower School

★—★—★— **STARPOST**—★—★—★

Ella,

What's going on with your grades and tests? What happened with your stapier? Please use the conjure-cameo and check in with us.

Do you need more help? Should we contact Aunt Sera?

Love,
Mama and Papa

CHAPTER TWENTY-SEVEN
THE CONJURE PONT

Ella poured all her angry energy into making three conjure ponts and preparing to mind-walk Noémie. She pushed away all the disappointed feelings about her stapier test. She tried her best to pretend it hadn't even happened, and she definitely ignored the warming of her conjure-cameo even though she knew her mama and papa wanted to talk to her. Her focus was singular.

She set all the ingredients in the middle of Jason's secret loft. Brigit and Jason sat beside her as she worked. Her eyes combed over the items. With determination, she listed everything in her head: valerian, golden seal, angelica root, blessed oil, sandalwood, vandal leaves, and an entire crab's eye bean plant.

"How does this all work?" Brigit asked.

She hadn't actually done it before and put her hands on her head. "Well, we're going to be in these pods to keep us safe as we mind-walk." She should be able to put these things all together and make it work. She'd grown up watching Gran and Mama do it after the long fortune-telling season at the beginning of every year. She'd have to just try at least. Even if it was wrong. "It'll be like being in a little cocoon."

Brigit gulped. "Okay."

"And all three of us are going to mind-walk her?" Jason asked. "Just like what Madame Baptiste talked about?"

"Yes." Ella emptied the jars. "Help me make three equal piles."

They placed all the ingredients in rows. She drizzled blessed oil over their fibrous stems. The mixtures writhed and wiggled.

"Whoa." Brigit jumped back.

"Don't be scared." Ella took the crab's eye pot, drew a circle in the dirt as a sign of respect, then yanked the whole thing out. Its roots squirmed when exposed from the soil. "Brigit, lay on this one and wiggle down into everything."

Brigit's cheeks flamed. "But it's messy?"

"It won't get you dirty, and I promise we're going to be okay." She wrestled with the angry plant. "Jason, grab the crossing powder bundle. Wipe it on your palms, then Brigit's, and then mine."

Jason scrambled to follow instructions.

"Now, you get on your pile," she ordered.

"Okay." He lay flat and crisscrossed his arms over his chest.

"Why are you laying like that? This isn't a coffin," Ella said, and Jason let out a nervous giggle.

"Just get it over with," Brigit replied. "Please. I don't like being in small spaces."

Ella worked quickly. She held the crab's eye bean over them, then closed her eyes and listened for the plant's heartbeat. She felt her conjure wake up inside her. A little sluggish but there.

"C'mon," she whispered to herself. She should be able to do this easily, but under pressure it was hard to focus. Her head filled with the noises of the Arcanum menagerie instead of the gentle hum of the plant's life force. Worries about what her mama and papa and gran might say if they knew she was doing this tugged at her focus.

Ella balled her fist in frustration. She had to do this. She tried again, listening hard like for the first raindrops at the beginning of a storm. She heard the plant's tiny hum. She set it on top of Jason's folded hands. Its little red seeds cracked open like chicks hatching from eggs. One by one, their roots pushed out and thickened like ropes. They stretched around Jason's body, then Brigit's, and just as they reached for her, she plopped on the ground. The three of them were encased in matching brown-and-green shells.

Ella pulled Noémie's perfume bottles from her pocket and sang the crossing spell, "*Send us yonder. Take us where we need to go.*" Her voice sent the three of them plunging headfirst into Noémie's palace of memories.

✦ ◼ ✦ ◼ ✦

ELLA EASED HER EYES OPEN AS NOÉMIE'S MIND SHARPENED around them. She found herself pressed onto the rocky side of a cliff. She looked down and instantly filled with fear. Her feet slid forward, barely able to fit on the ledge. Sharp waves hit a dark coast below her. Wind blew her hair all over. She didn't dare move a hand to wipe it from her face.

Brigit's screams rang in her head like a never-ending bell, and she gripped Ella's hand so tight she thought her fingers might be permanently smashed together.

"It's okay, Brigit. We're fine—and in one piece," Ella said, out of breath.

Brigit panted. "What . . . how . . . are we really . . . in her . . . ?"

"Yes, we're in her mind." Ella gazed around. The fine hairs on her arms stood up, warning her to be careful. "Where's Jason?"

"Up here!" He stood at the top of the cliff.

The sky was the color of a fresh bruise—purple, black, and greenish. Ella held her breath. Her stomach flip-flopped. What had she gotten herself into—and her friends? She'd never been to another mind other than Aunt Sera's. How did she *really* think she could do this?

"You have to climb." Jason pointed to a rocky set of stairs.

Ella tried to erase her fear. She didn't have a choice. They were here, and she needed to make sure no one panicked. She steadied her balance and inspected a series of brass grips went up the cliff. She scaled them like a ladder.

"This is so weird." Brigit followed. "I'm scared."

"I know." Ella didn't want to let on that she was afraid too. She'd gotten them into this, and she'd have to get them out safely and with the information they needed.

A stone path led to a small shop. As they got closer, a series of lampposts snapped on, and moths fluttered about like snow. The sign above the door read: AMELIE'S COLLECTIBLES, MEMORA-BILIA, AND VINTAGE PARAPHERNALIA.

The door sat ajar.

"Her mind is bizarre." Brigit spun all around. "I don't know what I expected . . . but not . . . this."

"It's kind of amazing. Is this her favorite store—or her dream to own one? Either way, it's cool." Jason turned around and around. "I wonder what mine looks like."

Ella yanked Brigit and Jason inside. Her heart quickened as she moved through the darkness.

Two oil lamps cast their yellow glow through the space like two great eyes watching for movement in the dark. The shop was a bleak, miserable place. A decrepit grandfather clock stood like a sentry guard. Its chime startled them. Why was her mind like this? Was she sick—or worried? Was she unhappy? Was that what this all meant?

"Remember, don't touch anything," Ella said. "We're looking for clues of what she's up to."

"Got it," Jason replied.

They tiptoed ahead. Vials floated down the hall, and they had to duck to dodge each one.

The hallway emptied into a workroom. Golden pins zipped through the air like lightning bugs with sharp stingers. They clustered in the ceiling, drawing Ella's attention upward. Life-sized dolls hung like pendulums.

"Look!" Ella covered her mouth.

They swayed back and forth to an eerie rhythm.

"This is so creepy," Brigit whispered. "How are we supposed to make sense of any of this?"

"I don't know." Ella's eyes scanned the room for anything that could help them so they could get out of there as quick as possible.

"It's getting weirder and weirder," Jason added.

Ella squinted to see in the dark. Heaps of unrecognizable objects took frightening shapes as they investigated. She desperately scanned for a repeated image, but Noémie's mind felt chock-full of meaningless things. Before she almost gave up, she noticed a series of tiny perfume clouds clustering around the back of the room.

"There, that must be something." Ella took off in the direction of the perfume. Her intuition told her it had to mean something.

They stepped into a world of glass and liquid where the walls held cupboards lined with bottles of every shape and size, liquids the color of honey, amber, and licorice, bulb-shaped vials, and vases of curious construction.

Ella weaved between boxes, careful not to touch any of them. She wanted to inspect every item on each table and in each cupboard shelf and read each cursive label and see if there was something, anything that would tell them what Noémie was up to. But she knew she couldn't touch anything, which made her job harder.

She didn't know exactly what she was searching for, but her discoveries came quickly: a long worktable with beakers, tubes, droppers, spoons; a mortar and pestle; newsreels on the Aces; papers filled with other students' names; a map of the school marked with star-lantern routes; notes from her mother full of worried demands about sticking to the plan; and a portrait of Gia Trivelino herself with a sock and buskin.

Ella put a hand to her stomach. "I think I found something."

Brigit and Jason rushed to her side.

"Noémie is definitely working with Gia," Ella said. "We were right. My vision makes sense now."

"How do you know?" Jason asked.

"Why else would her picture be here? And all these things on the Aces. Her mother also keeps sending her letters about doing some sort of plan and mentioning a debt. Has to be something, right?" Ella motioned at the papers. "She owes Gia."

Brigit leaned close to the portrait of Gia, transfixed. "You promise me that we don't look alike? That I won't be anything like her?"

"I promise," Ella said.

"But . . . I . . . just want to know . . ." Brigit reached out for it.

"NOOOO!!!!" Jason shouted. "Don't—"

The store rumbled like they'd set off an earthquake. An eclipse of moths swarmed them. The golden pins stormed down. Ella swatted them away.

"You weren't supposed to touch anything," Ella yelled.

Brigit dropped the portrait, looking panicked. "I'm sorry."

The floor cracked beneath them.

"RUN!" Jason hollered.

They darted back toward the entrance. Plaster and paint rained from the ceiling. The walls crumbled. The shelves dumped their contents. The dolls tumbled to the floor, and the ceiling ripped open. Wooden floor panels began to fall away.

They leaped onto the remaining ones, desperate not to fall through. Brigit's screams echoed as they sprinted down the hall. Ella could see the door ahead as the structure disintegrated behind them. She snagged her foot and tumbled forward.

Jason helped lift her back on her feet.

"We have to get outside," she panted.

The large hole in the floor grew bigger and bigger, threatening to swallow them. The trio scrambled, trying not to fall in, clinging to whatever they could. When Ella looked down, only darkness was under her, and panic set in. Aunt Sera never told her how to exit a mind . . . and with two other people.

"I can't hold on," Brigit screamed.

Jason stumbled forward, trying to help her. He crashed into one of the floating perfume bottles. It exploded, sending liquid and fumes all over him. Blood streamed down his nose. Burns appeared on his skin. "I . . . feel . . . weird!"

"Jason!" Ella called out.

She had to get them out of this. The last of the shop's roof blew off, and a midnight sky growled. Wind batted the sign, and a sudden cold left frost crystals on what was left of a window.

"Get us out of here!" Brigit yelled.

Ella let go, falling into darkness and bringing her friends with her.

PART IV

MARVELLIAN LIES

A SWEET VISIT

Gia blinked several times to make sure her eyes weren't deceiving her. Her old friend . . . well, now adversary after all that had happened . . . slid into her booth at the Blues Well, a Conjure restaurant in Betelmore. Mitha Thakur looked recovered. No longer gaunt, his face had plumped, and the persimmon turban he wore complemented the rich brown of his skin. The stitched pattern changed every few seconds, making Gia wish she could touch the ornate threads.

"Never thought I'd see you again. Well, not willingly," she said.

"Do you think what you did to me is a joke? Is that what this all is to you?" He rubbed his beard, and Gia knew that she'd struck a nerve.

"Have a Twilight 75 before the musician's next set. It's quite good." She shoved the frothy beverage across the table. "And if we're going to have a history lesson, then let me remind you of what you've done to me. Turned on me during my trial. Even broke our Ace code and testified. Allied with *him* after all I've done for you." She pursed her lips and nodded at the newsreel projection of Johan Fenris Knudsen I on a presidential candidate visit to the Arcanum Upper School. "Do you remember how I erased what you'd done—what he'd done—so you both could have new lives?"

Masterji Thakur sighed. "I'm pretty sure that was Victoria Baudelaire who helped with that."

"At my direction." She pounded a fist on the table. "I cleaned it all up. You got to teach, Johan got to be the governor of Astradam, and I got to sit in jail for eleven years."

"Does he know Brigit's alive?" Masterji Thakur's question was like a hot poker in her side.

"Should he? You think he'll be some great father?" The memory of her life with Johan invaded her thoughts. All the moments she'd forced Victoria to suppress blossomed back to life like the spring gardens now awakening after a snowy winter.

"He has other children. He could . . ."

She put her hand in the air.

"I admit, I didn't come here to overturn old stones." He fussed with the basket of peanuts between them. "I came here to make peace."

"That is something I've never known," she replied.

"Maybe it's time. You could change."

"Have you come to rehabilitate me or is there a true purpose to this meeting?" Gia still felt surprised by it all. When his starpost showed up, she thought it was some elaborate prank. Maybe even a setup. But she'd sent Volan ahead and couldn't resist seeing what he wanted for herself. "What do you really want?"

"A trade."

Gia perked up. "What could you have to offer me?"

Masterji Thakur removed an hourglass-shaped bottle from

his tunic. The liquid inside it writhed, crashing against the glass. The Elixir of Light.

Gia nibbled her bottom lip. Her ears filled with the memory of crashing bottles, her very own marvel-stealing elixir destroyed last year by those pesky kids. She'd wanted this recipe so badly. But her mission had evolved. She no longer wanted to steal other Marvellers' marvels right now. She'd amassed quite a few helpful ones to tide her over. Instead, she wanted to see how Marvellers would behave after their light had gone out, when they'd be no better than Fewels. Powerless. Ordinary. Useless. She wanted to prove that what made them marvelous, what made them think they were so superior could be snuffed out in an instant. She wanted to scare them . . . to humble them.

But as she stared at that glorious liquid, her palms warmed, and greed surged through her. She wanted it anyway. She might need it later. "What's the catch?"

Masterji Thakur pulled down his collar. A branded *M* sat on his clavicle. "Can you remove it?"

A grin tucked into the corner of Gia's mouth. "Yes, yes, I can."

CHAPTER TWENTY-EIGHT
A SPIDER'S WEB

The world slowed after the trio crashed back into Jason's loft. Ella felt like an automat, wound up and set off in one direction. One of her best friends was hurt, and she needed to help him. She and Brigit raced Jason to the infirmary to see Nurse Peaks. The rotties chased behind them. Blood kept gushing from Jason's nose, and he sobbed in pain.

Worries drummed through her. This was all her fault.

Nurse Peaks took Jason to a triage area, then turned back to Ella and Brigit. A wrinkle of concern marred her otherwise perfect brown skin. "What happened?"

They looked at each other, both trying to form the right lie.

"Practicing using our stapiers," Brigit said.

Nurse Peaks harrumphed. "We'll take it from here."

"Is he going to be okay?" Ella thought her heart might never slow down.

"I have every reason to believe. Now I must tend to him." She walked away, and one of the infirmary automats swept them out.

Days went by, and Ella hadn't heard anything about Jason.

She went to bed thinking about him and woke up worried. She'd sent him starposts each day—one in the morning and one at night—but had gotten no response yet. Even the rotties didn't have any news. She prayed to her saints, and they tried to send blessings and healing vibes Jason's way.

"What if he's really hurt?" she asked Brigit during lunch. "Nurse Peaks won't even let me visit him."

"I think we'd know," she said in between her argument with a jerk wing. "And it's only been a few days."

"We have to find out something." Ella gazed around the dining hall looking for one of his numerous siblings. Maybe they had gotten to see him. Maybe they could tell her. She spotted Bea with Johan, the kid whose dad was running for president. "Come on."

Ella and Brigit eased into the Level Four section of the dining hall. She willed herself forward, trying not to be afraid as trainees gawked at them or teased them for being over here in the first place.

"Hey, Beatrice," Ella said, her voice squeakier than she anticipated.

Beatrice looked up at her like she was a fly that had gotten into the house. She didn't even acknowledge Ella or Brigit with a word. Her friends chuckled.

"How's Jason?" Ella asked. "Nurse Peaks won't let me see him."

"He's a mess. No thanks to you," she spat. "He told me what y'all were doing."

Ella gulped. She searched Bea's eyes, trying desperately to determine what she knew. "Will he be okay?"

A kid beside Beatrice pointed at Brigit. "You two look alike." He motioned between Johan and Brigit.

Everyone at the table craned to look. Brigit blushed.

Johan shrugged. "She just has blond hair. Shut up, Nigel!"

"And the same eye color. And y'all scowl the same," another person added.

Beatrice looked Brigit up and down. "Could be your little sister."

Johan waved away the accusation, and Brigit twitched uncomfortably. She crossed her arms over her chest. "I'm not anyone's sister."

"Okay, you big baby," someone joked.

Brigit turned her back to the table.

Ella tried to get Bea's attention again. "Can you let me know when you see him?"

"He's been sent home. My mom's taking care of him like she did me when I got sick. He'll be fine. But steer clear of him. I know you did something." Bea shooed them away.

Ella grabbed Brigit's arm to keep from crying right there on the spot. As soon as they left the dining hall, Ella let the tears fall. "What if he's never okay again and it's my fault?"

"It's mine too. I touched the picture even though you told me not to," Brigit replied, tears welling in her eyes.

"We have to make sure he's okay," Ella whimpered. "We have to stop Noémie too."

ELLA LET BRIGIT SET THE PLAN THIS TIME. HER GUILT ABOUT MIND-walking Noémie and Jason getting sick sat like a brick in her stomach. She didn't even know if she could think her way out of this. Brigit assembled a crew and got them up to speed. With Siobhan's and Bex's help, they staged a stakeout after curfew.

"Tell me again how this is going to work?" Ella sat on the

floor of her room with Brigit, Siobhan, Luci, and Bex, hoping Mrs. Francesca wouldn't do another late-night bed check. A pile of random objects sat between them: one of Bex's glass bulb vivariums with a fat spider, Brigit's knitting needles, and a truth bean from Siobhan's hobgoblin.

"When she sneaks out tonight, I'm going to trap her. This spider"—Brigit pointed at the vivarium—"will give me the right silk."

"Clotho's from Masterji Thakur's night garden," Bex said. "Helps me tend to the plants." On the branch inside the glass bulb sat a snow-white spider.

"Then we'll try to get the truth out of her," Brigit said. "And if she lies, we'll use the truth bean."

"I'll send the hobgoblin when I see her packing up. He'll knock three times on the door." Siobhan glanced down at him.

Oraan crossed his arms over his round belly. "This is top-level mischief, Siobhan. The sort your ma said to keep you out of."

"But it's for a good cause," Ella urged. "We have to know what Noémie is up to—and stop her."

Oraan paced around the objects. "Maybe just this one time. I heard what you said. As long as you don't get caught. I gave my word."

"I'll make sure to watch for Mrs. Francesca," Luci chimed in.

Ella nodded, then looked at the clock-lantern. It was almost midnight. It was almost time.

"I used to wake up and think she was just using the bathroom. Sometimes she'd try to leave the water running, but now I've watched her tiptoe out the door," Siobhan said.

Bex coaxed the spider out of the vivarium. "You ready?"

They tiptoed into the hallway. Siobhan and Luci eased back inside their room while the rest of them hovered near the door.

Brigit closed her eyes and prepared to knit. The spider began to spin. Shocks of silk were expelled from Clotho's spinnerets, and Brigit used her needles to grab the soft fibers. Her hands moved faster than Ella had ever seen before as she weaved a nearly invisible net.

Ella and Bex worked to guide it over the doorframe. Once complete, Bex placed the spider back in the vivarium. "I'll wait up in my room in case you need me," they said. "And good luck. Keep me posted. Send a rottie!"

"Thanks," Ella said as she and Brigit tucked themselves out of sight to wait. While the minutes stretched to an hour, Ella told herself this plan would work over and over again. It had to. Adrenaline coursed through her veins, pushing away exhaustion and worries. The Azure Dragon constellation watched from above, and she wished she could tell it that this was all for a good cause. Their mischief had a purpose.

Three soft knocks echoed through the hall. Ella and Brigit craned to watch.

Noémie inched the door open and stepped straight into the silk fibers.

"What is . . ." She thrashed her arms around, getting more and more tangled.

"Let's go!" Brigit leaped out of their hiding spot, and Ella followed.

"We know what you're doing." Brigit held up her needles and grabbed hold of more spider silk. She began to knit even faster. The threads knotted and linked together until Noémie was left swaddled in a cocoon, only her face visible.

Ella and Brigit dragged a grumbling Noémie into their room

just as photo-balloons soared through the hall. They barricaded the door and placed Noémie in the center.

"You were sneaking out to meet Gia, weren't you?" Ella accused her.

"You better not scream." Brigit pulled some of the silk away from Noémie's mouth.

"Tell us the truth! Right now." An anger Ella had never experienced before flared inside her. She braced for Noémie to lie and fight . . . or worse, use her perfume marvel to hurt them both.

Tears filled Noémie's eyes and she sobbed.

Ella and Brigit looked at each other, puzzled. Ella thought she'd be mean as a junkyard dog, as her Gran would say. She had been before.

"She made me do it. I never wanted to," Noémie said between cries. "My mother owed her a favor. I didn't even want to attend this school in the first place. I was happy living in Paris and learning at home. But she forced me, then told me to put special perfume in the star-lanterns. She made it seem like we were testing out a new product for our store. But it started making kids sick, and I told my mom we needed to stop. She said we couldn't. That if we did Gia would hurt her, my stepdad . . . or me. They're all I have. So I kept doing it."

Ella softened as Noémie cried and told more of the story. The realization washed over her . . . Noémie and her mother were Gia's victims and not her conspirators. Brigit cupped a hand over her mouth and stood frozen in shock.

"After the Institute closed, I thought we were done. My mom said that's what she wanted."

Ella's mind whirled, the answers clicking into place like the needle in a compass, pointing her in the right direction. She turned to Brigit. "She wanted you."

Brigit gazed at her, confused.

"She couldn't get to you here"—Ella motioned around—"so she needed you home. Away from here. You hadn't been back to Ms. Mead's since before our Level One school year."

Brigit bit her bottom lip. "You're right. I was at summer school, then camp, and Ms. Mead came to visit me and take me shopping. But why?" Brigit began to pace. "When she came to see me, she didn't do anything. If she'd wanted, she could've taken me. Why just stand over me and watch me sleep?"

"My mom said she needed to get into her vault," Noémie said. "That she needed your blood. Your grandmother changed the rules of their inheritance or something . . ."

Brigit hugged herself. ". . . The weird bites . . ."

Ella rushed to her. "It's going to be okay."

"Not if Gia finishes what she started."

Ella whipped back around. "What is she planning? Tell us everything."

"She asked me to get certain kids' memories. I don't know why. I promise you I don't." More tears fell from her eyes. "She gave me a list, and I have to keep doing what she says."

Ella clawed through the spider silk and freed Noémie. Both her and Brigit sat in silence as Noémie continued to cry. Ella tried to make sense of it all; her thoughts felt like a kicked beehive. What was Gia *really* after? She'd gotten Brigit's blood and into the vault, and presumably the money she needed. What else was there left for her to do? What did she want with memories?

"I tried to warn you, Ella," Noémie said with a hiccup.

Ella gazed at her. "When?"

"At the Vellian Port. I turned the fountain water black. I wanted you to know that something bad was about to happen. I couldn't say anything because she has people watching me at all times."

"But black doesn't mean evil," Ella corrected. "No one should think that." She frowned at her. "And why were you mean to me one day and nice the next?"

More tears filled Noémie's eyes. "I didn't mean to. I had to make kids afraid so they wouldn't ask questions, but I also had to make them want to hang out with me. That day you caught me with Clare, I panicked. I'd used my perfume marvel, bewitching her, and making her sneak into the teacher's lounge to get student timetables. I had to track the kids Gia asked me to." She glanced up at the clock-lantern.

"If I don't meet my mother tonight, Gia will know something is wrong. She's watching everything. I have to get to the greenhouse." She held up a vial labeled ABINA ASAMOAH. "I have to give her this."

Ella gulped. She wanted to destroy whatever lay within that bottle.

"My mother says Gia's going to put on a show. She's going to make the whole Marvellian world sick like she did the kids."

"But how?" Brigit asked. "How could she do that?"

"On Election Night. She's going to use the decorations, the firework-balloons. They're supposed to be over every Marvellian city to celebrate," Noémie said. "I overheard her talking."

Dread pooled inside Ella. How could they get to them all? Celestian City floated over the Mediterranean Sea, Betelmore sailed over the Atlantic Ocean, and Astradam was over the South China Sea right now. The task felt impossible.

"What are we going to do?" Brigit asked, defeat slipping into her voice. "We can't get to each city in time."

Ella balled her fists.

"You'll need a flight marvel," Noémie said. "My mother and I are going to leave for Paris. Only Fewel cities will be safe."

Ella and Brigit looked at each other and smiled. "Izulu!" they said in unison.

The Marvellian Times

OFFICIAL ELECTION POLL

With two days left to cast votes, the polls for President of the United League of Marvellers are irregular and unpredictable. Find the latest below:

President Noor Al-Nahwi
INCUMBENT

Johan Fenris Knudsen I
CHALLENGER

Sir Walter Tull
CHALLENGER

Jefferson Lumen
CHALLENGER

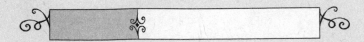

★—★—★— **STARPOST**—★—★—★

Dr. Silvera,

    Can we visit Izulu in the Arcanum menagerie?

Best,

Ella and Brigit

★—★—★— **STARPOST**—★—★—★

Ella & Brigit,

    She's been away with Jason watching over him.
You'll have to await her return.

Best,

Dr. Silvera

CHAPTER TWENTY-NINE
THE EUGENES

Y ou know what you're doing, right?" Brigit stared down at the travel coin in her hand. Ella looked to her left at Abina. "She told me a thousand times," Ella assured her.

"Like a million times." Abina smiled at Brigit, and Ella felt like it was the first time she'd ever seen them being nice to each other.

"What does it feel like?" Brigit fussed with the coin.

Ella didn't know why Brigit was such a scaredy-cat right now. She was usually the one who was ready for adventure. Last year she'd made her very own parachute and planned to leap off the edge of the Arcanum grounds and try to somehow swim her way back to New York City. This year, she seemed changed. Maybe it was because Gia had visited her. Maybe it was because she knew there was an evil villain out there trying to get to her . . . and that person was her actual mom.

But in this moment, Ella needed Brigit to be brave. They needed to get to Celestian City and check on Jason and get Izulu; otherwise, they'd never be able to carry those poisonous firework-balloons away, and everyone would get sick.

Abina patted Brigit on the back, explained how it worked again, and gave her some tips, but it didn't seem to help.

"Remember when we traveled from Mississippi to New Orleans last Christmas by conjure pin?" Ella reminded her of that sensation, even though it was a little different. "That's how it sort of feels. You did that."

Ella flashed the travel coin Abina had given her. "We need Jason."

Brigit nodded. "Fine. Okay!"

"I'll be here when you get back," Abina said, then whipped around and stared at Feste. "As long as *that* thing stays away from me."

Brigit rolled her eyes. "Feste, can you stay out of sight, please? *Someone* is afraid of you like a big baby."

"Living poppets can turn evil. I've seen the films." Abina pulled her legs into the chair until Feste sauntered into Brigit's closet.

"Ready?" Ella asked.

Brigit nodded and clutched the coin and reread the inscription: *Travel Well, Travel Blessed.*

"Irin Ajo," Abina reminded them, and they mimicked her.

Ella felt sucked down a drain. Her ears filled with the sounds of Brigit screaming. She plugged them until she felt the grass beneath her. The soft honks of stellaric cars along a busy Celestian City street echoed alongside Brigit's panting.

Ella rolled over, her cheek slick and wet. "Ugh, the dew."

The house sat just ahead with a tiny door and a porthole-shaped window. One wobbly porch wrapped around its face like the perfect smile.

"Help me find the coins." Ella brushed herself off and started digging through the wet grass.

"Couldn't we have landed in his bedroom?" Brigit asked.

"I wouldn't want anyone just landing in my room." Ella reached down. "Got them."

"Guess you're right. Does he know we're coming?" Brigit walked toward the door.

Ella winced. Well, she didn't exactly tell him this part of the plan. Most times she knew better than showing up unannounced and that Mama would be shaking her head and preparing a long speech about having good manners, but Ella had told herself this was an emergency and she'd sent Jason a starpost an hour ago. So technically, he'd been warned of their imminent arrival.

As they approached the porch, they passed an overflowing starpost box. Ella and Brigit played a silent game of Who Will Be Lifting That Heavy Door Knocker and Announcing Our Presence. Brigit won and gave Ella a little shove forward.

Ella lifted the iron knocker and let it fall. The door eased open, and a little brown face peered back. One of the twins, Priscilla.

"Hello," came the little voice.

"Hi," Ella squeaked back. "Is . . . is . . . Do you remember me?"

"PRISCILLA! What did I tell you about answering the door?" An exasperated Mrs. Eugene appeared, her hair a storm of coils and her chubby baby Cookie pressed to her hip. She gasped. "What are you doing here, girls?"

"We wanted to check on Jason. He didn't tell you we were coming?" Ella fibbed a little and hoped she didn't have a truth marvel or know any of the conjure techniques her mama used to root out a lie.

"You've certainly been keeping the stars busy and our starpost box full with your letters," Mrs. Eugene teased.

Priscilla wrapped her pudgy arms around Ella's legs. "Want to see my room, friend?"

Ella smiled down at the little kid. She reminded her of a smaller version of Winnie.

"Well, come on in, girls." Mrs. Eugene waved them forward. "Jason's been miserable holed up in his room, but I suspect that mostly has to do with him not getting to be in the Arcanum menagerie every day and seeing you two."

Mrs. Eugene moved Priscilla out of the way. "Also, shoes off, please."

They followed instructions, but before their boots hit the floor, they floated just above the ground.

A broom swatted them out of the foyer and into the living room, where the twins chased around a flying toy chest.

"Go on up. Hare will lead you." Mrs. Eugene whistled and her tortoise companion trundled out. "Jason's all the way in the back. You'll be a good boy and show them, right?"

Hare led them up the stairs. His tiny legs moved faster than Ella anticipated. He stopped before a door with the sign KEEP OUT OR KEEP QUIET! ANIMALS SLEEPING!

"Your turn to knock," Ella said.

"Jason!" Brigit shouted, which made Ella cringe. "Put some clothes on, we're coming in . . . Three, two—"

The door opened. Jason stood in his pajamas, mouth wide open. "What are you doing here? How did you get here?" He still looked sick, his eyes droopy, his burns still healing, and the remnants of a recent nosebleed sat on his upper lip.

Ella flashed the travel coin.

"Whoa! Where'd you get that?" He grinned. At least that seemed to be the same.

"Abina!" she said proudly.

Brigit rolled her eyes. "Can we come in?"

"Yeah." Jason stepped aside. "I guess . . . welcome to my lair."

His room was exactly how Ella had imagined: an animal or two tucked into every corner, a disheveled desk full of glue and paper and twine, and a hammock for a bed. Izulu on a perch beside the window. "She hasn't left my side," he said.

"Jason, we need her—and you!" Ella exclaimed.

He looked startled.

Brigit rattled off all that had happened since he left school, recounting everything about Noémie and her evil perfume, how they'd forced a confession out of her, and how they had to save everyone during Election Night.

"It's a rescue mission," he said. "We're pretty good at those!"

CHAPTER THIRTY

ELECTION NIGHT

The Arcanum sky-ferries lined the dock like majestic pods of whales. The sunlight turned their brass noses into molten gold, and the A.T.I. symbol on their sides twinkled. The stellacity engines washed them in a bright blue as Ella walked aboard with her dormitory group.

Headmarveller Rivera's voice trickled through the speakers: "Today you will witness history, my neophytes. You will see the peaceful democratic process—and the promise of our ancestors and their hard work to set up a community where all can exercise their voices."

Ella and Brigit made sure to sit as far away from Noémie as possible so no one could even suspect anything. Ella tried not to even look in her direction even though it was so hard. Her heart pounded. A nagging question whispered inside her: Maybe she should tell an adult about Gia and her plan. But another part of her couldn't bear not to be believed . . . or worse . . . for the things she needed to say, wanted to say, to get her thrown out of the Arcanum because they were contested information by the government.

Samaira slid into their booth, and Ella squirmed with surprise.

The speaker crackled again. Announcements began. "Good afternoon, Level Twos, this is your sky-ferry captain speaking. We are third in line and will be airborne soon. Our flight time is one hour and three minutes. Celestian City is above the Greek Isles and reporting pleasant weather, so we should have a smooth ride. Please secure your seat belts."

Brigit pressed herself back and prepared for takeoff. Ella peered out the window, spotting a black bird in the distance. Izulu and Jason were close by. The thought of it slowed her heart a bit as the sky-ferry rose into the air.

Ella played the plan in her head over and over again: They would need to find the firework-balloons and destroy them before Gia could release her toxic perfume and hurt everyone.

Neither Ella nor Brigit could enjoy the fizzlets and ginger stars the attendant handed out or get excited about all the other sweets available for purchase. Her classmates gorged themselves. Bex ate several Marveller-bars while Pierre shoved as many milk dragon eggs in his mouth as possible.

"I'm surprised you're coming with us and you're not with your family," Brigit said to Samaira. "Is this all weird?"

A faint blush colored Samaira's cheeks, and she shrugged. "My moms want this to feel normal for me. I don't really know what that is. But when we get there, I'll go backstage with them. They're waiting with my younger siblings." She fussed with her mantle and smoothed the gems on her hijab.

"Do you think she's going to win again?" Brigit blurted out, and Ella shot her a look. Embarrassment flooded Ella's stomach, mingling with the nerves already there, and she didn't think she could survive it. She hid her face in her hands.

Samaira pursed her lips. "I don't know. I hope so. But I saw a poll that showed her and Johan Knudsen even."

Ella didn't know how things would change if any of the candidates won the presidency and governed the United League of Marvellers, but she could feel Samaira's sadness, and she wanted her mom to win, even if it was just so Samaira would be happy. She remembered how kind Samaira's 'umi had been last year during her discipline hearing. President Al-Nahwi didn't have to come to the Arcanum to clear up the issue with the missing lantern, but she had made the time.

As Ella gazed at Izulu in the clouds, the sky-ferry journey went by faster than she wanted. Her pulse thrummed. They could do this, she told herself, trying to calm her heartbeat as the sky-ferry started its descent into Celestian City and the Cloud Nests parted.

Besides her brief visit to Jason's house, Ella had only seen heliograms of this Marvellian city, and in that moment, she realized that they didn't do it justice. The city spread out as long and wide as a great ocean, boasting white buildings with their perfect columns. Lamps laced every walkway, and bulbs outlined every building, creating the most beautiful feat of stellaric illumination.

They landed at the Assembly House Transit Hub and docked beside the black sky-ferries from the Arcanum Training Institute upper school.

"This way, my dears." Mrs. Francesca and the other Tower Advisers led them outside. They walked across the footbridge. Trollies entered the Assembly House, carting statesmen, celebrities, and Marvellers from all over. People dressed in what Gran called their Sunday bests: sharp suits with bowler hats, tailored dresses with ornate headpieces. Broad avenues and narrow paths twisted their way among a gorgeous lawn and beds of the most beautiful flowers, making the whole place resemble an enormously decadent maze.

"Look," Brigit whispered, pointing around. The firework-balloons created a beautiful canopy over their heads.

Ella spotted a streak of black, then a stretch of lightning, knowing Izulu was still close by. But if she was honest, she was still a bit afraid because if Mama knew what she and Brigit were up to, she would've never allowed her to attend this field trip. She could almost hear her voice in her head this far away: *You aren't to put yourself in harm's way for Marvellers.* She pushed away her mama's voice, tucked her conjure-cameo deeper into her shirt, and strode forward, passing the deep waters of a grand basin where the Celestian City Cardinal stretched high.

Her heart thudded, the crossing tug strong, and Ella couldn't parse out if it was just her nerves or really that. Her conjure still felt out of sorts after failing the stapler test and their tumultuous adventure at mind-walking Noémie. The shame of it made her almost afraid to use her gifts.

Brigit took her hand, then whispered in her ear, "I'm a little afraid."

"Me too," Ella admitted as they passed the security coppers at the Assembly House entrance.

"Please remember your decorum and manners. You are a representative of the great Arcanum Training Institute," Mrs. Francesca chirped.

The students stood in long lines to have their heliograms taken one by one before being led into a grand amphitheater. Chandeliers of stellacity lights shone bright, and Ella felt like she'd landed in a city within a city.

Ella scanned the ceiling of every space they entered, looking for more celebratory firework-balloons. They were everywhere. She'd already counted hundreds of them. With each step Ella took, she felt the task grow larger and larger, and feel even more impossible. She'd already saved the world once, but here she was again absolutely terrified of the plan, of what needed to be done. She clutched her chest, scared of what would happen next, of what she'd have to do.

"This way! This way!" The Tower Advisers herded them into a gargantuan amphitheater. The very center held a platform with four high-backed chairs, a dais with a floating microphone, and the Tricentennial exhibit.

A thick knot coiled up in Ella's stomach.

The blueprints. Their faint blue glow called to her.

Brigit elbowed Ella, letting her know that she'd seen them too. They had to get them out of harm's way, but how?

A sea of Marvellers filled the seats, from important diplomats of the United League of Marvellers to the entire Arcanum student body, both the upper and lower schools. The conversations hummed like a stellacity current.

As Ella surveyed the space, thinking Gia might be hidden among them in one of her various disguises, she felt Noémie's eyes on her. She slyly turned in her direction, pretending to try to get Mrs. Francesca's attention.

Noémie nodded and touched her nose. The signal that she'd spotted her own mother and that Gia would be backstage now. Ella nodded with acknowledgment, then thumped Brigit's knee. They locked eyes.

It was showtime.

THE OCULUS

While Ella and Brigit pretended to go to the bathroom and slipped out of sight, Gia did some of her very own skulking about. She walked around the most beautiful dressing room, much like the one she used to have at Trivelino Troupe's Circus & Imaginarium of Illusions.

The energy felt alive. The Marvellian world on the precipice of a new leader.

She ran her fingers over his suit jacket, the threads tailored expertly to ensure every person coveted it, the colors harmonious, and the scent . . . she picked it up, pressing the fabric to her nose, an elixir meant to draw every eye, intrigue every mind, and silence every question. But Gia would be the last person he'd want to deal with. The last person the whole Marvellian world would want to see.

Gia removed her trusty pocket watch from her trousers. Just in case. Her marvel hummed just beneath her skin. The new ones too. Ready. Eager to be used.

The door eased open. She heard the man tell someone he'd only be a minute.

"That'll be a lie," she muttered.

He froze, his icy blue eyes finding her leaning against his vanity. Johan Fenris Knudsen I was still one of the most handsome people she'd ever seen, and she had to remind herself that it wasn't really true. The scar she'd given him was still visible along his face and didn't seem to make him as hideous as she'd intended. If she worked hard enough to see him correctly, it'd push through his charisma marvel . . . or was he calling it an oratory marvel to clean it up for the masses.

"Are you here to ruin my night? To seek revenge and be a cliché villain from some child's nightmare?" He moved through the room unbothered, sitting in front of the mirror and reaching for a brush to slick his paper-white hair. Not a single strand sat out of place. Ever. "I've heard about your antics since breaking out of the Cards of Deadly Fate. Impressive."

His voice held a challenge.

She would rise to it. Exceed it. Hot anger pulsed through her veins. She picked up one of his campaign posters. "A Time for Marvellian Greatness is Here! You really think you are the answer?"

"If not me, then whom?"

Gia smiled. His ego always was the thing that got the best of him.

"Don't tell me you think you're the answer."

"No, I'm here to teach a lesson."

"You're a schoolteacher now?"

"People are like clockwork, Johan. You of all people know that; otherwise, you wouldn't have to work so hard with your monstrous marvel to make people do what you want them to." She found his eyes in the mirror. "All clockwork must be wound. Something has to start it up and get it moving once it slows . . .

and this world has come to a screeching halt. Some kind of force must act on it. How else will things change?"

"You have only ever wanted to make a mess."

Gia grimaced. "I helped you clean up yours. Erased any knowledge that you were once my husband, my right hand, my most important Ace. I let you forget me."

"And yet . . . *she's* still here. I saw her, you know."

The mention of Brigit, the last thing tying them together, wiped the smile from her face. "Well, that was my mother's deception. Like you, I'd thought she was dead." She held her palm out, tired of this trip down memory lane. "I've come for it."

He dug in the inner lining of his jacket. "What do you have planned?"

He produced a peculiar set of spectacles.

"Wouldn't you like to know. Enjoy your victory . . . and the show. I hear the fireworks will be the best part." She strode out of the room.

COPPER ALERT:

Three juveniles missing from Arcanum Training Institute Lower School group. See attached heliograms for their likeness. Stay on alert.

CHAPTER THIRTY-ONE
A TINY FLAME

Ella and Brigit tracked Izulu in the high ceilings of the Assembly House. Her dark wings were a smudge against the stark white walls and the animated frescoes flickering between constellation maps. Ella imagined Jason home in his bed, seeing everything they were experiencing through the lightning bird's eyes. She did wish he was right there beside them, though. Maybe that's why she felt more afraid.

As they raced down hallway after hallway, their footsteps echoed against the marble. Ella's pulse thundered so loud it almost drowned out her worries. What if they were too late? What if they couldn't stop Gia this time? She pushed those thoughts away and kept her eyes on Izulu. Jason would find those celebratory firework-balloons and carry them far, far away. They'd stop them from releasing whatever Gia planned to put in them.

Large windows let in the twilight as the sun set. Applause rumbled from the amphitheater.

"Coppers ahead," Jason warned. "Hide behind the statues."

Izulu perched on a ledge and froze.

Ella yanked Brigit behind the statue of Elizabeth Eulberg, the fifth Marvellian president. They huddled together as the coppers completed their rounds. Ella could feel Brigit's heartbeat through her skin. She wished she could whisper into her mind that everything would be okay, that they could do this, and remind her that they'd done it before. But even her thoughts felt unsure. Ella still didn't feel like a hero.

The coppers' footsteps grew quieter and quieter.

Izulu cawed, and the girls inched out of their hiding spots. The bird took off again. They reached the end of the hall.

"Wait here," Jason called out.

Ella and Brigit peered around the corner. The backstage doors had been roped off. Coppers and their wolves swarmed. Blimps sailed through the air, their banners full of warnings: RESTRICTED AREA. CANDIDATES AND STAFF ONLY.

"How will we get in there?" Brigit whispered.

"I don't know." Ella counted at least ten coppers. They'd never be able to get past them and through those doors. The impossibility of the task slammed into her. If they failed, what would happen to everyone? Would they all be sick . . . or worse? Last time she'd felt like an accidental hero. They'd set out to find Masterji Thakur and ended up stopping Gia from making more marvel-stealing elixir. This time she felt like the whole Marvellian world depended on them.

Her hands quivered, fear shaking every inch of her body. Ella felt Brigit slip her hand into hers as if she could hear Ella's thoughts.

"We can do this," Brigit whispered. "We have to."

Izulu reappeared overhead, then swooped down to the floor. "I can distract those coppers' wolves. Make them chase me while you get backstage."

Ella nodded. "Be safe."

"They'll never catch me." Izulu's wings stretched and covered with lightning.

Ella and Brigit watched as the bird took off and swooped at the coppers and their wolves. A ruckus exploded. The wolves broke their leashes and stampeded down the hall. Ella counted to three, then they ducked beyond the ropes and through the amphitheater's backstage doors.

People buzzed around, and Ella and Brigit went unnoticed as they hid in the thick border curtains. The itchy fabric swaddled them. Sweat slicked Ella's skin. Backstage filled with people arranging chairs, setting up celebration blimps and cameras.

"Make way for Lindsay Oliver from the *Star Weekly*," an attendant shouted. "Shoo, shoo. She needs her space."

An intimidating woman in a wide-brimmed hat stepped through the doors. A juju-trunk whizzed behind her. A tingle zipped up Ella's spine. Who was she? How would she have that? A flurry of assistants swarmed her, some powdering her white nose, others handing her note cards and mentioning procedures for the night.

"Bring the exhibit first, then the announcement of the election results," she ordered.

"But, ma'am, that's not the way it's . . ."

"THAT is what we are doing!" the woman barked.

Brigit clutched Ella's arm. "That voice . . . ," she whispered.

Ella listened closely. Gooseflesh covered her skin as she glared at the woman. She wore an expertly tailored suit. When she whipped around, Ella spotted her icy blue eyes and a tiny pin on her lapel—a sock and buskin. Ella's body went cold. "It's . . ."

"Gia." All the color seemed leached from Brigit's body.

"Bring the exhibit!" Gia demanded.

"Yes, Lindsay. Right away," an attendant replied.

A team wheeled out the large glass case. The crossing tug overwhelmed Ella's body. She saw the architect's blueprints and pressed a hand to her chest.

"You okay?" Brigit whispered.

Ella pointed at the glowing blueprints. "I can feel them. It's like . . . they need me . . . or something."

Gia crouched before the exhibit. "Someone give me a rag. There are fingerprints and smudges."

"We can clean it, miss," someone replied.

"NO! I'll do it," she barked, then softened. "Let me bask in the history and make sure it's befitting of this night."

They rushed around, handing her cleaning supplies. Gia grimaced, growing more and more irritated. "Leave me. I need a few moments of peace before the big night. There's too much noise! Everyone out!" She waved her hands in the air. "Do not return for fifteen minutes while I gather my thoughts."

The backstage emptied.

Ella and Brigit exchanged tense glances. It was just the three of them now. Ella's stomach knotted. Brigit held her hand. She wished Jason were on her other side.

Gia rubbed the glass exhibit case until it squeaked. "You must be the most beautiful object anyone has ever seen." She removed a pair of odd-looking spectacles from her pocket and put them on. She glanced into the display and held up the unrecognizable lump that Ella had first seen back at the Vellian Port. "Very interesting. Just what I thought." She tsked her tongue. "More Marvellian lies. Celeste will love this."

The name Celeste sent a shiver up Ella's spine. That name. Her long lost aunt's name. Her mama's twin.

"We should—" Ella started to whisper.

"Not yet." Brigit grabbed her, intently watching.

"You will survive this, though." She snapped at the juju-trunk and it zipped to her side, flipping open. With careful hands she lifted up a strange object. It looked like a blend between an hourglass and a lamp, with thick glass veins snaking through it. "What a gorgeous firework you will be." Gia opened the exhibit and replaced an object that looked identical to hers.

Ella gulped. Brigit shivered beside her.

"That's not a firework-balloon," she whispered, remembering what Noémie revealed about Gia's plan. Ella sniffed the air. The object smelled of saltpeter, sand, and heady perfume. Terror coiled in her stomach. That was an explosive. "We should stop her now—" Ella lunged forward, but Brigit yanked her back.

"Wait!" Brigit urged.

The backstage doors snapped open. Coppers and important-looking people flooded back in. "Make way for the candidates!"

Gia retrieved a tiny vial of little bugs from her pocket. "Such a tiny creature will change it all." She poured the wiggly bugs inside the lamp and closed the exhibit's lid before turning around to greet everyone.

Ella watched as the small bugs ignited.

"Fire ants," she whispered to Brigit. The lamp glowed purple, the sand swirling and the glass bulbs filling slowly with smoke. Her heart seized. It was going to destroy the blueprints, her only evidence. It was going to hurt everyone. Did Noémie lie to her about the firework-balloons? Did she know about this explosive?

The front curtains rose, and the candidates walked onstage to raucous applause.

They were too late.

CHAPTER THIRTY-TWO

TICK, TICK...BOOM!

G ood evening and welcome to the most important night in Marvellian history. Our Tricentennial celebration marking three hundred years of living in the skies together as well as our latest presidential election. Auspicious that they're both occurring at the same time," Gia, disguised as Lindsay Oliver, announced. "Tonight will be one that no one will ever forget!"

Cameras flashed and newspaper blimps circled through the big open space, their newsreels recording. The four presidential candidates sat in high-backed chairs. Their presidential banners fluttered behind them with projections of their slogans playing on repeat. President Al-Nahwi blew kisses at the crowd. Sir Walter Tull waved his bowler hat around. Jefferson Lumen saluted. Johan Fenris Knudsen I winked. Coppers flanked the stage entrances, and Johan's enforcer stood so close to the border curtains Ella thought he might spot them.

"We have to do something," Ella whispered to Brigit as the enforcer gazed around.

Brigit shook her head. "Not yet . . ."

"But . . ." Ella watched in agony, her eyes cutting between the glowing lamp inside the exhibit and the eager crowd. She could see the sand churning and the slow gathering of purple clouds inside the glass. She felt like a coward frozen in place. Not a hero. Not brave. Not able to save anyone or anything. A twist of fear turned her gut. How could she stop this? Her mind spun with conjure spells, but she'd never had to use conjure to snuff out a fire or stop an explosive.

Gia waved, and several attendants moved the exhibit forward. "But first let us admire all that we've accomplished and inhale our brilliance."

Brigit dropped Ella's hand and leaped forward. "STOP!"

The cruel line of Gia's mouth softened into a smile as she recognized Brigit. "Well, well, well."

Ella's feet finally unstuck, and she followed, heading for the exhibit, which now slowly filled with purple smoke. No one seemed to notice it. Their eyes fixated on the candidates.

Coppers scrambled across the stage in their direction. The crowd gasped.

An ear-piercing caw echoed through the amphitheater. People looked up and screamed, clutching their ears. The sizzle of lightning boomed. Izulu dove between Ella and Brigit and the coppers.

"She's not who you think she is!" Brigit screamed at the crowd. "She isn't Lindsay Oliver. She's Gia Trivelino!"

A few coppers released their red-eyed ravens after Izulu. Ella heard Jason's voice. "Let's go!"

Izulu barreled up to the glass ceiling, then turned left and right, sending the ravens in circles.

Gia laughed while slipping a pocket watch into her hands.

The lid flipped open, and the coppers and the crowd stiffened, transforming into an audience of dolls. "You found me."

Ella wrenched open the glass, grabbing for the blueprints.

"Don't you touch that!" Gia snapped, her voice hitting Ella like a punch to the chest.

Ella stumbled backward.

"Ella! Brigit!" Izulu plucked a stapier from the waist of one copper and another, dropping them into the girls' hands.

Gia turned a dial on her pocket watch again. Izulu froze mid-air, lightning stretched across her wingspan. Ella cupped a hand over her mouth as she watched Izulu crash to the stage "Jason! Izulu!" she screamed, diving forward.

"Don't you dare move," Gia said to her. "Or I'll kill that bird and your friend who's controlling it."

"What have you done to them?" Ella said.

"Don't worry, they can still see and hear everything happening, which is exactly what I want," Gia replied.

Ella stepped forward again.

"Now, what did I say?" Gia snapped her fingers. "And besides, you owe me a debt! I told your father this. I'm sick of you showing up and meddling in things you ought not to."

Her words felt like a slap. Her papa? She'd spoken to him. "Don't talk about my papa!"

"Your father has many secrets. People will know about them soon enough. But he was warned about what you owe me."

"You can't just hurt people!" Ella said.

Gia laughed, hardening the angry knot inside Ella. "When will you learn that you've picked the wrong side, little Conjuror? When will you believe me? I may be terrible, but I'm telling the truth. Conjure folk are the backbone of the Marvellian world. It was built on top of you." She motioned at the exhibit, now filled with smoke and rumbling. "You can feel what's in that glorious display of Marvellian pomp and circumstance. You know what's hidden there! I can see the tiny quivers racing across your skin . . . and it's not just because you're afraid of me. You feel the crossing tug. I know you do!"

Ella squirmed. She didn't want to agree with the worst person in the world. She didn't want this woman to be right.

"SAY IT!" Gia demanded, before turning to the audience and flashing the biggest grin. "Hear that?" She cupped her ear. "The cameras are still rolling. This is your stage. The entire world is watching. They aren't frozen in place. Tell them what's in that case before it explodes. Before it's too late."

The words felt like grit in her mouth now.

"NOW!"

"The architect of the Arcanum Training Institute for Marvelous and Uncanny Endeavors was a Conjuror. He was the sixth founder. The blueprints are made on conjure paper and show conjure technology at the school." Saying the words aloud made her feel sick. This wasn't how she wanted to tell the Marvellian world what she'd discovered. She didn't want this to be part of Gia's evil plan.

"But where is he, little Conjuror?" she taunted. "Will you dig him up in the Underworld to prove your case?"

"His body is missing. His memory-cask was stolen." Ella's body hummed with upset. She dropped the copper's stapier and crouched, feeling like she would throw up any minute.

"Doesn't that feel better?" Gia's voice held a mock-motherly tone.

Unexpected tears streamed down Ella's cheeks. "Why are you doing this? Why do you want to kill everyone?"

"Kill? Oh, no, there are some fates worse than death." Gia removed Lindsay Oliver's face, revealing her own. She threw the hat off and let her Joker smile out. "You have me all wrong, little Conjuror. I want to humble them. They deserve to be no better than Fewels. It's time to take away what makes them *marvelous*, what makes them think they can treat people like they're nothing. It's time to make them ordinary. Bring them down a peg."

"Leave her alone!" Brigit shouted.

When Ella turned around, Brigit's stapier glowed bright.

Gia cackled. "You plan to duel me? What is this, Marvel Combat?"

Brigit lunged at her.

Gia grabbed a stapier from a nearby copper's belt. "Is this mother-daughter bonding?"

"I have no mother," Brigit yelled back.

Their stapiers struck each other. Sparks flew.

"Oh, but you're much more like me than you think." Gia swung at Brigit. "I know you're wondering if you'll end up like me. The daughter of Gia Trivelino, the greatest criminal in the world."

Ella crawled forward, grabbing the stapier she'd dropped. Her eyes cut to Izulu. Her heart seized as she gazed into the bird's beady eyes and thought of Jason. Was he trapped in there, frozen back home in his bed too? Was it painful?

"I hate you!" Brigit screamed, striking Gia again.

Gia laughed. "Hate can turn to love if needed."

Ella clutched the copper's stapier with both hands. She closed her eyes and focused as hard as she could. She ignored Brigit's screams and Gia's taunts. She ignored the racing hum of her own pulse. She ignored the shaking sounds of the exhibit, ready to burst. She ignored the tiny whispering doubts that she wouldn't be able to get this stapler to work and help Brigit defeat Gia.

She pulled her conjure from deep down inside and the base of the stapler sparked. Her eyes opened, and the surprise of it made her jump. The indigo twilight climbed through the blade.

Ella charged ahead, joining Brigit. She'd never fought with a stapler before, but she'd played plenty of games with Winnie and Reagan using stick swords in their yard. She swung her stapler and crashed into Gia's. Violet embers rained down on them as Ella fell backward from the impact.

Gia laughed. "This should be interesting." She dueled with both Ella and Brigit, pushing them toward opposite sides of the stage.

"Come with me, Beatrice," Gia offered. "I can answer all of your questions. Like what happened all those nights ago and who your father is."

"My name is Brigit, and I don't care," Brigit shouted back.

"Oh, but you do!" Gia said.

"I'll never go anywhere with you."

"If you agree, I'll make this stop. I'll stop my firework." She pointed at the exhibit case. Lightning-shaped cracks appeared in the glass, and the purple smoke began to leak out. "Any minute now and everyone in this amphitheater will lose their marvels . . . including you both. You have the power to stop them." Gia removed a clear cloth from her pocket. It reminded Ella of the bell of a jelly-fish. She affixed it to her nose. "I can give you one too."

Ella gulped. Her heart flipped in her chest. "Brigit!" she called out, uncertain of what to do. She didn't want to lose her conjure. Her roots.

Brigit dove at Gia with her stapier again, hitting her jacket pocket and ripping a hole. Gia's pocket watch crashed to the ground.

"Ella, grab it!" Brigit screamed.

Ella got to it before Gia. She clicked it open. The coppers, candidates, and crowd reanimated.

Izulu stretched her wings and sent lightning shooting at Gia. She ducked.

The coppers swarmed. The candidates gawked at Gia with horror.

"What have you done?" Johan Fenris Knudsen I stepped forward.

Gia growled at him. "Here to save the day? Your first heroic act as president of the United League of Marvellers."

The crowd gasped as she revealed the election winner.

"Or just showing off for your daughter." Gia glared at Brigit. The color drained from her white cheeks. The stapier fell from Brigit's hand.

Ella's eyes volleyed between Johan Fenris Knudsen I and Brigit, the similarities now apparent. Pale blond hair. Intense blue eyes. He was Brigit's dad. The shock of it stunned her in place.

"Take her!" Sir Walter Tull shouted.

The coppers surrounded Gia, but the glass exhibit exploded into a million pieces. The amphitheater filled with noxious purple smoke.

CHAPTER THIRTY-THREE
THE ENFORCER

Ella coughed and coughed and coughed until her eyes watered. She waved her arms around but couldn't see anything or anyone. The cacophony of vomiting and hacking flooded her ears. Her eyes burned, and she called for Brigit but couldn't make real words. Thick purple fumes engulfed her. She buried her face in her shirt, but the heady perfume invaded her nose. The worst headache she'd ever experienced punched its way into her temples. Ella's eyelids grew heavy, and she fought against losing consciousness.

A hand lifted her from the ground. She looked up, finding Johan Fenris Knudsen I's enforcer. He placed a clear veil over her nose and mouth. "Breathe," came a muffled voice.

The veil felt like silken jelly, and the more she inhaled, the stronger she felt. She gathered her strength and stood.

The enforcer turned his back to the cameras and yanked off his helmet. Long twists cascaded over her shoulders.

Ella stepped back.

Her own mama's face looked back at her.

"What . . . ," she started to say.

"I'm your aunt Celeste," she replied. "I didn't intend for us to meet like this. I didn't intend for anyone to know who I am . . . at least not quite yet. Not until my work is done. I need you to keep this secret from anyone that is not *our* family."

Ella's mouth hung open with shock. "But where have you been all these years?"

"Near. I promise. I've been undercover in many ways." She put a gloved hand on Ella's shoulder. "There's no time to explain, but I promise, I will one day. We need to clear the poisonous perfume and purge their lungs. Has Gran taught you a cleansing spell yet?"

The way she said *Gran* showcased the slight New Orleans accent she had. Gran was her mother. The reality of it all sank into Ella.

Aunt Celeste shook her. "Did you hear me? Can you do it?"

"Yes, yes," Ella replied.

Aunt Celeste put her helmet back on and began to sing.

Ella joined in, her voice braiding with her aunt's, and it oddly reminded her of Sunday mornings when she'd sing with Mama and Gran and clean the house.

The perfume clouds thinned. Chaos filled the amphitheater. Ella looked around for Gia, but she was nowhere to be found. She started to run to Brigit, who was curled up in a ball, but Aunt Celeste put a hand on her shoulder.

"Now we cleanse. Repeat after me." She raised her arms. "*Clear skies, let us see the sun. Help us undo what has unjustly been done.*"

Ella parroted her. The whole room gasped for breath. Tendrils of purple smoke left their lungs. People started to gather their strength and stand.

"Open the dome," Aunt Celeste ordered the coppers.

They clustered around wall levers and pulled them in a circle. The glass ceiling cracked open like a giant egg. The purple clouds lifted out.

Johan stepped to the edge of the stage. "Do we have a Paragon of Spirit with a weather marvel?"

Several members in the crowd raised their hands or coughed out, "The heart beats true."

"Rid us of this poison," he ordered.

Three audience members darted into the aisles. They worked together to summon gale winds and then a deep, warm rain. Coppers carried the injured outside. Ella could hear the sound of sirens and stellaric cars arriving. Johan Fenris Knudsen I took charge of clearing out the stadium seats.

Ella wiped the drizzle from her eyes and looked around for Brigit. The wreckage of the Tricentennial exhibit sat between them. Glass shards and sand covered the stage. She scanned for the blueprints, then dropped to her knees. Only a pile of shredded paper remained.

Sadness and anger wrapped around her heart. She'd never be able to prove what she'd said. Now there was no proof. Exhaustion hit her and she couldn't hold back the tears. Failure drowned her insides.

Aunt Celeste knelt beside her and gathered what was left of the paper. "Chin up! You'll find a way to prove to the world what the truth is." She handed her the lump from the exhibit—the unrecognizable object, the only remaining thing from the blast. "Conjure can never truly be destroyed. Just like my love for you and our family. Thank you for keeping my secret. There's still work to be done." She tucked what was left of the blueprints into

Ella's pocket. "If they ask you who was singing, take credit. Cover for me—and ask your father to help cover my tracks."

Ella's eyebrow hitched with confusion. "I don't understand."

"He will."

She gazed into Aunt Celeste's mask, finding warmth in her eyes, and she nodded. Aunt Celeste touched the lump and whisper sang their revealing spell. The object shook, and layers of sediment began to molt.

"See you soon." She stood and raced to Johan Fenris Knudsen I's side.

As the object shed its final layer, its true identity began to reveal itself. Ella saw white stone, wrought-iron, and conjure-roses. The iron writhed and revealed the name, JEAN-MICHEL DURAND.

The architect's memory-cask.

CHAPTER THIRTY-FOUR
THE ARCHITECT'S SECRET

The sky-ferry ride from Celestian City back to the Arcanum felt endless. Newsreel projections filled the ceiling, and the speech of President-Elect Johan Fenris Knudsen I became an inescapable melody. Brigit curled up next to Ella with her fingers plugging her ears and her eyes jammed shut. She couldn't imagine how Brigit felt right now. Everyone whispered about all that had happened, and now Brigit's greatest fear had come true. The world knew she was the daughter of the most notorious criminal and the new president. Whispers about Brigit's mother became a storm, the words stringing together into needlelike sentences striking them both over and over again.

"It's going to be okay," Ella whispered, even though she didn't really know if it would.

She held the memory-cask in her lap as her pulse raced, drowning out President-Elect Knudsen I's words about peace and prosperity and his desires to make the Marvellian world be a home again for many feeling ostracized by the old policies. He promised a return to traditional Marvellian values and to usher in a golden age. She didn't know what any of it meant for Conjure folk and her, and she couldn't even process it if she wanted to. Her mind spun, and she gripped the architect's memory-cask tight to her chest, hoping it would help slow her heartbeat. Images flashed in her head like a newsreel whirling out of control: her aunt Celeste's face, the way Gia's lamp exploded, the screams and coughs, the chaos as people gasped for breath.

As the sky-ferry sliced through the clouds and she saw the tall towers of the Arcanum Training Institute, she wondered what her parents might say about it all and how much trouble she'd be in. Unluckily for Ella, she didn't have to wait very long to find out because the moment Ella stepped foot back in the school, her mama and her aunt Sera stood in the entryway with Headmarveller Rivera and Headmarveller MacDonald, lips pursed, arms crossed, and frown lines visible.

Brigit gulped. "Uh-oh!"

"Stay with me, okay?" Ella whispered as she took several tentative steps, clutching the memory-cask to her chest. She waited for them both to start fussing, but instead they pulled her into a hug, then grabbed Brigit too.

The scent of home softened her edges. All the anxiety and fear and confusion from the night washed away in that moment. She felt safe in the arms of two of the most powerful women she knew. Mama kissed her so much, she felt like her forehead was covered in red blisters from her lipstick. Brigit, too, couldn't escape it.

"We were so worried." Mama's voice was on the verge of tears. "We saw the reports and watched everything live on the newsreels. The explosion cut the feeds, but we heard all that you had to say . . . and learned that you saved the day. I came as fast as I could."

"I thought my heart was going to give out," Aunt Sera chimed in.

Headmarveller MacDonald put a hand on Aunt Sera's shoulder and flashed her a smile. "You both"—his eyes cut to Brigit—"stood up for the world tonight. You sacrificed yourselves for the greater good—and the whole world got to see it. That's what it means to be a good Marveller and a champion of fairness and justice."

"And a good Conjuror." Mama leaned in to kiss Ella once more before she could duck. "Your papa is on his way too. I got the last seat on the sky-ferry out of New Orleans, and he had to go to Mobile to grab one."

Ella gulped. She didn't know what Papa would say. If he would be equal parts proud and upset or just upset. She remembered his warnings. She remembered his requests. She also remembered what Gia had said about meeting with him and his secrets and what Aunt Celeste had said about him covering up her tracks? What had they both meant?

"I need to tell you something." Her eyes darted between her mama and godmother. She didn't even know how to say it aloud.

"Out with it," Mama urged, more worry knitting itself into her brow.

She pulled Mama and Aunt Sera to the side, away from Headmarveller MacDonald and Brigit.

"Aunt Celeste, your sister, was there," Ella said. "She helped save everyone."

Mama's eyes stretched wide, then she clutched her chest. "My what?"

"Your twin," Ella replied.

Mama grew unsteady, her legs giving out from under her. Aunt Sera caught her before she collapsed. "What did you say?"

"It was *her*. I swear."

"Can't be. Can't be." Aunt Sera's eyes found Mama's as tears filled them.

Mama gazed at Ella. "You're sure?"

"I thought it was you at first." Ella set the memory-cask on the ground, then reached into her pocket, where the heliogram Jason gave her was still tucked away. She'd kept it close ever since, afraid to lose it. She pressed the image and the projection sputtered before illuminating. She watched as Mama gazed at her twin.

Mama swallowed a gasp, and a tear skated down her cheek.

"The caption says it's someone named Camille Bell, but if that ain't Celeste, then I'm seeing things," Aunt Sera said.

"I just . . . can't believe it." Mama mopped her forehead with a handkerchief.

Crowds of students began to swarm. Headmarveller MacDonald approached. "Let's continue this in my office." He helped keep Mama upright and led Ella, Brigit, and Aunt Sera to the Headmarveller's Wing.

"This can't be real," Ella heard Mama say over and over again.

They settled on the office couches, and the whole story poured out of Ella. Everything she'd researched and they'd discovered. Aunt Sera and Mama sobbed. Headmarveller MacDonald served tea and handed Mama tissue after tissue.

"I can't believe it. I just can't believe it," Aunt Sera replied. "It's . . . a miracle. Wait until Gran hears."

"And there's this." Ella held up the precious memory-cask. "Look! It's Jean Michel Durand's memory-cask."

"We must examine it closer," Mama said.

Ella set it on the coffee table between them. After Aunt Sera and Mama thoroughly examined every inch to ensure it wasn't too damaged to work on, they turned to Ella.

"You up for this? As a family?" Mama asked her.

Ella said yes even though exhaustion tugged at her bones; she wanted to unravel this mystery alongside her mama and aunt Sera.

Mama turned to Headmarveller MacDonald and Brigit. "And you and Eoin will keep watch, yes?"

Brigit nodded and Headmarveller MacDonald smiled. "We would be honored to," he replied, reaching out his hand to hold Aunt Sera's.

Ella watched the way they looked at each other. Aunt Sera met her gaze and smiled, confirming Ella's suspicion. Headmarveller MacDonald and her godmother were secretly together.

Mama traced a finger across Ella's conjure mark. "It's headed down your back now, baby girl. Very proud of you. No doubt from your conjure work today."

Ella touched her neck, feeling the warm, raised lines. Her conjure roots were deepening. "You ready?"

"What's first?" Aunt Sera quizzed.

"Crossing powder."

Aunt Sera removed a bundle from her dress pocket, carefully opening it and spreading the sparkling powder over their palms. The three of them placed their hands on the memory-cask and sang the spell together.

Ella found Brigit smiling at her as her eyesight went dark, and she plunged forward into the memory-cask of her ancestor. She felt the strong grip of her mama's hand as her vision sharpened.

An architect's studio materialized around them. Long

worktables held iron-blue conjure paper. The walls contained shelves of miniature models of Conjure towns and cities. She noted tiny versions of Harlem; Washington, D.C.; Houston; Atlanta; Tulsa; and then of Cartagena; Havana; Isla Colón; Paramaribo; and more. Pencils and protractors and compasses sat lined up ready to be used.

Papers cluttered the desk. Mama gazed over them with Ella. "Here's plans for the Arcanum."

An owl hooted. Ella whipped around to find the bird on a perch.

"And here's the original charter that lists him as a founder." Aunt Sera pointed at another page.

"This changes everything." Mama's knees buckled like the weight of it all was too heavy for even her body. She sat at the desk.

"But what happened to him?" Ella asked, puzzled.

The owl hooted again.

"And who might you all be?" came a warm voice.

A tall, stately man stood in the doorway.

The architect.

Aunt Sera gasped. Mama scrambled from her chair and reached a hand out. "I am Aubrielle Baptiste-Durand, and I'm married to your great-grandson, Sebastien Durand, Grand High Walker of the Land of the Dead, and this is my cousin, Sera Baptiste, and your great-granddaughter, Ella Durand."

"I am Dr. Jean Michel Durand." His warm eyes scanned over her, and there was so much of him that reminded her of Papa. The rich brown of his skin and the thickness of his locs. And mostly, the deep baritone of his voice.

"I never thought anyone would find me . . . or my memory-cask.

I've been in here for so long, just me and Eve." He scratched his beard, then smiled at his owl companion.

Ella's questions overflowed and she couldn't keep them from pouring out of her mouth. "What happened to you? Your memory-cask was unrecognizable. Covered so badly it looked like a rock. They had it in an exhibit about the very first Marvellian civilization."

"Ella! Please slow down," Mama said.

The architect chuckled and his eyebrows lifted. "That was very clever of them. Hidden in plain sight."

A long silence stretched between them, charged with sadness and all the things he'd missed out on being trapped in here for over two hundred and fifty years. His soul never getting to rest in the Underworld, his altar never getting to be erected, his life never getting celebrated by his ancestors, his wife never getting to say a proper goodbye or find his spirit again.

"So, what happened?" Ella should've let the question ease out, but she was too overwhelmed.

He took a seat at his desk and put on his spectacles. He lifted up various blueprints and papers. "We'd finally made progress. All the gifted people of the world trying to figure out how to live together and away from the nonmagic Fewels who continued to make a mess of things. There'd been a council of folks from all over the world. We were supposed to lay out the plan for our ascent to the skies, our protected peace. I'd helped build successful safe havens for Conjure folk and they asked me to help do the same in the skies. I relished it. I loved a big project. I knew how to make things fly." He chuckled to himself. "It had already been part of our community for so long. Our twilight stardust."

She thought of the Arcanum Cardinal on his blueprints and how it had glowed with the special ingredient. Ella looked down, admiring the twinkling remnants of it on her hand as well from the crossing powder.

"But they changed their minds. One day I was delivering the blueprints to Olivia Hellbourne, and the next day I was here, in the prison of my own mind. Trapped and never at peace. I remember someone following me in the old Marvellian City of Dinium. I remember dying. But that's never been the end for us, so I didn't fear it."

Tears streamed down Mama's cheeks and Aunt Sera dabbed her eyes. Ella swallowed hard, trying her best not to cry.

"I waited to see the twilight. I waited to hear the music of my second line and listen to trumpets and voices singing me home. I waited to wake up in the Underworld and take my place with my father and grandfather. I waited to be able to see my wife again, my sons and daughters, when the veil turned thin. But nothing. I've heard nothing but silence until the three of you." He took a deep breath. "My family."

Without thinking, Ella rushed toward him, diving headfirst into a hug. He smelled of pipe tobacco and mint candies. He started to hum and pat her back.

"We'll find out who did this to you. We'll make it right," Ella whispered.

"More importantly," Aunt Sera chimed in, "we'll take you home. It's time to rest."

The Marvelous Inquiries

BY ANONYMOUS

The new president-elect, Johan Fenris Knudsen I, has many secrets . . . and it's not just a hidden love child with Gia Trivelino. (Don't worry . . . we're trying to break the story of that as well!)

He has other things he doesn't want anyone to know.

TWILIGHT STARS

Three days later, Gia leaned against a lamppost across from the great Marvellian Assembly House as the sun started to set. She pushed her dark shades up the bridge of her nose and adjusted her hat, though she ought not. There was no reason to be nervous today, for all eyes were on President Knudsen I as he took his first steps through those gigantic silver doors and his place as the new ruler of the Marvellian world. She had to admit that he'd been born for the role, his charisma marvel making him impossible not to love (even she'd succumbed at one point) and carrying him all the way to the top.

Cameras flashed, and the riotous applause almost gave her a headache, but she figured they'd all clear out soon; once he gave his little speech and did his little comforting wave and everyone got enough for their news-boxes and sense of safety. His smile would restore order. His voice would inspire faith. His confidence would erase fear. The newsies would fill their newsreels about her failed attempt to wipe out the entire governing body of the magical world alongside a heliogram of his perfect face. The savior. Just what she wanted. An easy distraction.

The sweet scent of the Underworld tickled her nose. An expected guest.

She glanced over her shoulder to find the Grand High Walker of the Underworld. The shadow of a tall top stretched across the pavement. "What is the great Sebastien Durand doing up here, so very far from home?"

"I'm here to cash in on a favor," he said, eyes fixated on the crowd.

"I wasn't under the impression that I owed you anything," she replied. "In fact, you owe me after your daughter messed up my plans now twice."

Gia saw his jaw clench and it amused her.

"I spent my time and resources trying to locate your daughter last year. Breaking many of my own rules for my Walkers. Risking—"

"I jest." She turned to him, smiling. "You forget that I enjoy a good game and a laugh above all."

He gritted his teeth.

"So, how can I help the most powerful person in the Conjure world?"

"I need to ensure that nothing happens to my family. Ever."

Gia handed him a bottle from her pocket. "Keep this close. I'll be in touch."

He tipped his hat and disappeared.

Gia lingered at that lamppost for hours, long after Sebastien left, long after the crowds thinned, and a great black quilt spread above her head. No one seemed to notice her. Or so she made it seem. Coppers patrolled with their curious wolves and red-eyed ravens. She leaned on that lamppost until the soles of her feet ached and the moon rose above her. Its silvery light found the centerpiece of the square: the Celestian Cardinal. Paragon symbols twinkled as the moonlight bathed each one. She read the tenet:

THE CELESTIAN CITY CARDINAL
THIS TOWER REPRESENTS THE TENET OF SOVEREIGNTY IN OUR GREAT MARVELLIAN WORLD.

Only by the many committing to a government created
and sustained by the people will all be able to
live in a protected peace together.

Laughter erupted inside her until her throat went raw. She retrieved a peculiar set of spectacles from her pocket, replacing her sunshades. The lenses fanned across her forehead like feather plumes and, as she clicked them into place, revealed the monument's hidden secrets. She'd made these herself, years of testing and perfecting them, and felt happy to have them back from Johan.

The tower glowed faintly. Pulverized twilight stardust snaked through it as though moving through hidden veins. Gia traced her fingers along the light. "You're a long way from home—all the way from the Underworld, here to let us fly, to power our dark delights."

Without it, the cities and the school would fall to their knees, to the ground with all the Fewels. Wouldn't that be something.

CHAPTER THIRTY-FIVE
MARVEL COMBAT

Ella waited in the competitor's room with other Level Two participants eager to try out for a Paragon team. She examined her stapier over and over again, trying to ignore everyone around her. A fireplace crackled in the center. Tables held energy fizzlets, and small blimps floated about with banners reminding trainees of the Marvel Combat rules. Jason sat in the far corner with his brother Allen going through techniques.

After all that had happened, Ella still felt out of sorts. She shouldn't technically be attending the tryout, but she'd gotten a starpost from Dr. Yohannes about meeting her here with her stapier. Uncertainty buzzed inside her.

"Ella."

She looked up to find Dr. Yohannes's warm smile alongside Masterji Thakur. Without hesitation, she jumped into Masterji Thakur's arms and hugged him.

"Missed you too," he said with a chuckle.

"You're okay. You're back." Ella leaned away to make sure it was actually him. His beard glittered, and his turban held beautiful mirrors that reflected the star-lantern light. His presence erased her unease and made her think some of her worries were disappearing. She might not get to be on a Marvel Combat team next year, but with him returning to the Arcanum, everything might be all right again.

He and Dr. Yohannes ushered her into a side room. "I've come to thank you. This seems to be a pattern of ours. You're my little hero."

Ella still didn't feel like one. She still couldn't believe that she and Brigit and Jason foiled Gia's terrible plan. She'd seen the newsreel footage of her and Brigit dueling with Gia and those toxic perfume clouds lifting into the sky and the destruction of all the firework-balloons. Part of it didn't feel real. Like she'd been watching a play. That she hadn't lived it.

"I'm not a hero. I didn't feel brave at all," she muttered.

"But you are," Dr. Yohannes added.

"I'm here because of you," Masterji Thakur reminded her. "We don't need to relive what happened last year. But *this* year, I've had the case against me dismissed. The world knows what we do now." He pulled down his collar, revealing his smooth brown skin, the *M* that was once branded there gone.

She gasped and hugged him again.

"We are heading in the right direction."

"The Marvellian government is scrambling," he added. "I've seen newsreel after newsreel full of excuses trying to explain away the evidence or discredit Gia's words and yours. We're going to need more evidence now that the blueprints have been destroyed."

"Aunt Sera is trying to fix them," Ella reported. "And now that we've spoken to the architect, we're looking for his body and who murdered him."

"The truth is coming to light," he replied. "But this is far from over."

"Speaking of light . . ." Dr. Yohannes motioned at Ella's stapier. "Ready to try again? I saw what you could do on the newsreels. I know you can wield it. Let's make it official for the records."

Ella smiled. Dr. Yohannes's words filled her with determination. She gripped her stapier and held it in front of her chest. Her veins rose and her heart drummed. Instead of pulling at her light and waiting for it to obey, she sang.

The stapier's base sparked with twilight, then it climbed through the blade until the entire room held a faint shade of purple.

Masterji Thakur and Dr. Yohannes clapped and smiled.

"You're ready!" he said. "You've always been."

The Arcanum Training Institute for Marvelous and Uncanny Endeavors

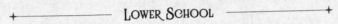

—————————— Lower School ——————————

Dear Ella,

Congratulations and welcome to the Paragon of Vision Marvel Combat team!

Over the summer, you'll receive a series of exercises to complete to be ready for practice at the start of Level Three. Dueling begins in October.

We look forward to many victories with you on our team.

Best,

Petra Alexopoulos

★—★—★— **STARPOST**—★—★—★

Ella,

I'm sorry about what happened. Thanks for saving
me . . . saving everyone. I'm sorry I was mean to you.

Noémie

★—★—★— **STARPOST**—★—★—★

Ella,

You cleared everyone's names. My grandmother
is grateful. I'll send you a gift this summer. Maybe we
can visit each other.

Luci

The Arcanum Training Institute for Marvelous and Uncanny Endeavors

—— Lower School ——

SECOND YEAR LEVEL TWO
FINAL MARKS
Name: Ella Durand

CORE REQUIREMENTS:

History of Marvels and Marvellers from the Eastern and Southeastern Hemisphere 5

Intermediate Marvel Light Channeling 4

Marvellian Theory—the Right Path 5

Conjure II 5

Global Incants: Form and Function 5

Marvellian-Adjacent Beings: Creature Study 4

Global Elementals—Fire and Earth 4

PARAGON REQUIREMENTS:

Future Forecasting II—Divining the Future Around the World 5

SCORING RUBRIC:

5 = Showing signs of mastery

4 = Showing signs of proficiency

3 = Satisfactory

2 = Needs Improvement

1 = Failing to Show Effort and Progress

NOTES: *Ella is doing a great job but needs to focus more for Level Three.*

Brother Sebastien Durand & Sister Aubrielle Baptiste-
Durand
c/o American Congregation
New Orleans Delegation
Orleans Parish

Dear Brother Sebastien and Sister Aubrielle,
    Our concerns remain the same despite the news
in the Marvellian press about the architect of the
Arcanum Training Institute. However, we will remove
the censure temporarily while we investigate the claims
and the harm done to the Conjure community by the
Marvellian government. We will be counting on your
support and cooperation as we form a response to their
crimes.

Sincerely,

Sister Adieux

Honorable President of the United

Conjure Congress

ACKNOWLEDGMENTS

I have so many people to thank in the making of this book. Sequels are hard—and this one took a village to get done. I am so grateful to be able to return to the adventures of Ella, Brigit, and Jason, and continue to expand the Marveller and Conjuror universe.

I'd like to thank my editor, Brian Geffen, for his patience, leadership, and fortitude in dealing with my messy creative processes. My imagination often consumes me, and you know how to be an anchor in that storm and help me find my way. Your insights are always so wonderful.

My backbone in these drafts, Margeaux Weston, for her editorial guidance, coaching, and expertise.

I'd like to thank my amazing agent, Molly Ker Hawn, who has an endless well of patience and helps me navigate all things. Thank you for being my champion.

Thanks to my team for all the magic and mischief behind the scenes: Mary Pender, Steve Younger, and Seth Michael.

Biggest thanks to my incredible copyeditor, Jackie Dever, who makes sure nothing is out of sorts and gives me such encouragement along the way. Thank you for making this part of the process so enjoyable.

All the love to Molly Ellis, the best publicist in the business. I am so grateful to get to work with you. Thank you for making sure the world finds my magic school and taking such great care of me.

I'd love to thank the entire Macmillan Publishing team: my

amazing friend, Ann Marie Wong, Carina Licon, Katie Quinn, Teresa Ferraiolo, Naheid Shahsamand, Samantha Sacks, Lelia Mander, Samira Iravani, and Jie Yang.

To my fabulous UK team: Ruth Bennett, Amber Ivatt, Isobel Taylor, and the entire Piccadilly Press team: thank you for taking a chance on this book and allowing UK readers to find a new magic school to attend.

Thanks to the following folks who let me pester them about all manner of things: Zoraida Córdova, Alys Arden, Marti Dumas, Rebecca Roanhorse, Olugbemisola Rhuday-Perkovich, Carlyn Greenwald, Ashley Woodfolk, Natalie C. Parker, Mark Oshiro, Samira Ahmed, Phyllis Wong, Julie C. Dao, Nigel Livingstone, Haneen Oriqat, Holly Black, and Kiersten White.

To my cover artist and illustrator, Khadijah Khatib, thank you for the love you pour into these covers.

To my Marvellian mapmaker, Virginia Allyn, you are amazing. Thank you for continuing to make magic real.

And to my readers, thank you for returning to the skies with me.

Springhill

Bayou D'Arbonne Lake

Bastrop

SHREVEPORT

MONROE

Ruston

Tallulah

ASHLAND

Winnsboro

Mansfield

Winnfield

Natchitoches

Tullos

POLLOCK

Ferriday

COLFAX

ALEXANDRIA

Leesville

Sabine River

Bunkie

St. Francisvill

De Ridder

Oakdale

LAKE CHARLES

LAFAYETTE

BATON ROUGE

Calcasieu
Lake

Grand
Lake

Abbeville

New
Iberia

Franklin

White Lake

Morgan

LOUISIANA

31901069656371